A Zero-Mile Journey

Absolute Author
Publishing House

Cover Illustration by Kate Lozovskaya

Book Design by HMDpublishing

Cataloging information is available from the Library of Congress

ISBN: 978-1-64953-824-6 (Paperback)

ISBN: 978-1-64953-878-9 (Hardback)

ISBN: 978-1-64953-825-3 (E-Book)

For information contact:

Samuelmaddae@gmail.com

Why was I born?
Why am I living?
What do I get?
What am I giving?
Why do I want a thing I daren't hope for?
What can I hope for?
I wish I knew

—*"Why was I Born" by Jerome Kern and Oscar Hammerstein II*

The Village

Life in Enkoho recalled the heavens and earth parting ways and the gallant Sahara trading its blood for salty sands. The village spoke for itself and kept to itself, alone. Yet, in some loud ways, Enkoho spoke for Ghana in whose womb it resided. Before 1964, not even a television had a presence; just one radio station rode the airwaves to bring music, news of the government and the world, and mouthfuls of cheap talk that shortened hope's lifespan.

The days preceding November 1961 saw a jolt in the village: Queen Elizabeth II was coming to Ghana!

She will bathe in our rivers and eat our foods—no, I am not mistaken, she will breathe our air too!

The villagers traded wild gossip as the queen's visit neared because no one in the reclusive village had a radio to hear the news firsthand. For days, this talk kept everyone awake as an exciting event.

To bring news of the event to the village, Professor Tetteh and an electrical-engineer friend entrusted batteries to students, which they were to bring to Enkoho before the weekend. The students had left campus early. Darkness drifted northward after they passed through the village of Aduman. They found themselves up against a forest that rose from the soil and obstructed their path. Finding their way to this unnamed village wasn't an exercise to test their endurance and navigational abilities, though they thought it was. Unbeknownst to them, no true outsider knew where Enkoho started or ended. One simply knew when one entered and left. They were told the general location of the village relative to Kwame Nkrumah University of Science and Technology. They were also told that their final destination was one of a few cement structures among a litter of mud huts in the village. A Dutch couple, botanists, lived there. Karikari, the name of the owner of the radio box that they would help install, was also provided. Professor Tetteh deliberately withheld the village's name and couched his instructions with a cavalier attitude to not alarm the students. Selected for their strong-mindedness, intellectual independence, and disbelief in matters of the paranormal and superstition, Professor Tetteh further detached them from such sentiments with the remark that they were to rely on their wits to locate their destination and complete the task. He wanted them to return to campus without knowing where they had gone.

The students unstrapped the batteries and sat on them.

"Which way do we go?" asked one of the students.

The question only elicited shrugs, so the students looked at their unsynchronized watches to figure out how much time they had to get to the village. Their watches diverged by several minutes, so they couldn't tell if they were behind or ahead of schedule.

The forest took shape as the rising sun peeled away the remaining morning darkness. Cashew, guava, mango, and almond trees were in the immediate purview. Between the exchange of ideas around the questionable motivation of why they had to get to the village on foot, not by car, it became obvious that the surrounding area of Aduman was awake. The morning saw adults en route to their farms, a scene replete with children.

The students got up and stretched. Strapping the batteries to their backs, one of them pointed out that the path lay where two people were approaching. Cutlasses and hoes were in the man's clutches; the woman they gathered was his sister, who carried a raffia basket.

"Good morning, my brothers. You look lost," said the man.

After returning his greeting, the students said they were searching for a path through the forest leading northward. They learned there was one main path that branched off in many places.

"Where are you heading, precisely?" the sister asked.

"It's north of here."

"There are many villages north of here. What's the name of the village?"

"We don't know. Our professors didn't tell us. They want us to find it—an exercise of sorts."

The strangers could be of no help. They had traps to check on, so they told the students to ask their father, who was following close behind.

The sound of footsteps was soon upon them. A man with an ashen face and deep-set eyes turned the corner of the meandering path, walking briskly.

They greeted him with waves.

"The bush is the worst place to be lost," he said.

They told him they weren't lost, just looking for the path.

"And where are you going?"

"To a village," they said, knowing this response was also senseless.

"You just walked through my village; are you sure that's not where you're going?"

"That's not it, sir."

"Which village do you want to get to?"

"It's north of here."

"You youngsters these days barely make sense. I gather you're college boys. Why go to college if common sense so easily evades you? You can walk to Burkina Faso if you keep going north, and you may even end up in Morocco and perhaps Spain if you can walk on water."

They knew he meant no insult. Indeed, they felt foolish for not knowing the name of the village. One of them intervened to curtail their embarrassment.

"It's a school exercise, sir, a test of our endurance and navigational abilities. They want to know if we can find our way to the village with minimal directions."

"I see. Geography students."

"Electrical engineering; that one there's reading physics."

The man grew suspicious. "I suspect you're taking those boxes to that village?"

"Yes, sir."

"Is it Kwamang?" He cleared his throat.

"No, sir."

"Ahenkro?"

"I'm afraid not, sir."

"Ahwiaa, Amoako, Domeabra, Tetrem?"

"I'm afraid not."

"How do you know it's none of the villages I've mentioned when you don't know its name?"

This was a question they couldn't answer. With no knowledge of the whereabouts of these villages from their reference point, nor their approximate distance from each other, they felt within themselves that the village wasn't among those mentioned.

"What am I doing? You don't even know the name of the place you're going to. And how did you suppose I could help?"

The man spat out crumbs of a chewing stick and trudged them underfoot, wiping his forehead of beaded sweat. Then he took his chewing stick out, for it had suddenly acquired a curious taste. He felt the dampness of the morning earth through his sandals, then saw the dew drain from the earth. The path was now concretized sand with sporadic placement of rocks. The shrubberies along the sides of the wooded path changed into immiscible hues of crimson, magenta, and lilac, drifting in and out of their distinctions into a bloody flare that blinded him temporarily. The sun was high when he looked up. The students watched as the blood in his face disappeared, turning him several shades darker as he staggered in confusion. All the greenery had dissipated, having morphed into the sun's own luminescence. The students began to see the forest for what it was; tranquil within, yet it fastened on them an intense feeling of lonesomeness.

"And how do you suppose I could help?" the man managed to say.

He beckoned before they could display their ignorance with another nonanswer. His knees grew weak; his eyes couldn't find their bearing. The earth felt strangely still when it should have been moving, though noisy with chirps of birds, whirring of trees, and whimpers of the lost students. In his haze, he saw the earth moving toward his face. The strength drained from his legs, and the students caught him before he collapsed. His shirt was dampened with sweat. He let out a sickly grunt when they lowered him to the ground. The students were anxious to know what they had just witnessed.

"Dehydrated?" they whispered.

The man's children, said one, couldn't be far off, so maybe they should go after them.

"Dizzy. Must be dehydrated," said another, while placing his hand on the man's forehead to check if he was feverish.

"Sunstroke," said another, who intended to dash after the man's children. The rest would stay with him.

"Don't go looking for my children," he said.

"Shouldn't we take you back to your village?"

The students looked down at the man's crinkled face, which exuded a sickness not present when they had first greeted him.

"I'm fine."

"You aren't fine, sir. You almost collapsed."

"I'm fine," he said, followed by a gusty snort.

"You're not, sir."

"Evidently, I'm not ready for work, recovering from the—" His chest rose and fell with heavy breathing. "Go about a mile— the road branches in two directions. Keep going east until you reach a place where it splits into four. Turn on the path to the farthest left. That path ends in the forest, not in any village... all I can say."

He got up slowly, propping his gait with a machete, then hobbled down the path without another word. The students looked at each other, unable to describe what they had just seen. They decided to continue down the paths he had directed them to take as the encounter hovered over their conversations. Whatever disease afflicted the man must have devastated him mentally.

They found the spot where the path branched off in several places. Theirs was a less-traveled path to the left, which cut through a densely forested terrain. The other paths were more traveled, clearly demarcated by their use. No sooner had they started out when one of the students saw a horned owl perched in a shea tree. He could see the movements of its head tracing their meandering path. Knowing what the sight portended to the superstitious, the student kept it to himself, thinking the others might ridicule him. Luckily, as their path branched away from the tree, they didn't go near enough to ascertain the truth and heighten the student's discomfort. Something about the look in the eyes of the old man had left this student with an uneasy feeling about where they were going.

The students' legs strained and ached as the forest grew dense. Sparse vegetation of wild orange, mango, and lime trees gave way to towering mahogany, oak, and other trees whose existence they hadn't known about. Trees with expansive girth and sprawling buttress root systems trailed them, and suddenly the path they had embarked on vanished. They couldn't have been more than three miles away from Aduman but felt they were in a virgin forest where humans had never been.

On the second day in the forest, the chirps of birds sounded unfamiliar, and the buzzing of insects seemed unlike any other. Growls, barks, grunts, roars, hisses, and brays were of a strange variety. There was a feeling that even hunters hadn't been there. It was the rarest of forests, which words wouldn't lend themselves to describe.

"The man said the path won't take us to where we're going," one of the students said, "so how do we know where to go from here?"

They were faced with a question they should have investigated beforehand.

"How could he direct us here if he didn't know where we were going?"

They lowered the batteries and sat on them, ensuring they were gathered closely. There was no sign of human presence near them, no clanging sounds of farming tools in the distance. Bird chirps and sporadic growls of animals, however, ran aplenty.

"We should leave," said another student. He tried not to convey the unease he felt for what seemed to be drifting toward them from the direction they had come. He wanted them to move in any direction, not just sit there for whatever might be approaching. At the urging of another student, they strapped on the batteries again and left.

One student thought they had been sitting on a burial ground. He kept quiet instead of mentioning that he had seen a skeletal hand and a foot protruding from the soil. He didn't seek corroboration from his friends. Because no one else might have seen what he saw, he wouldn't find an answer to the obvious: "Who would walk this far to bury their dead in the thick of the forest? We walked through it, too; why didn't we see it?"

A sudden scuffle up a tree sent leaves flying. Birds sputtered off in a panic. A guinea fowl was in the grip of a boa constrictor. The snake wound around the bird and the limb of the tree. They jumped back when the constrictor, in the throes of tightening its coils, inexplicably released the bird. They couldn't have been more than thirty feet away when the bird, in its variegated plumage, fell from the branch. It gave them an idea.

"Hey, Koranteng, how about whipping up one of your soups today? Fufu's on the menu when we get to the village."

They looked up the tree; the constrictor was still on the branch, staring at its prey below. They picked up sticks and went looking for the fowl. The sticks weren't for the prey, which would have had all its bones broken, but for the snake if it had changed its mind. They zoomed in on the area with sticks raised, edging toward where the bird should have fallen.

"Tomatoes, onions, cassava...where will we get all that?"

It was a foolish question. They were going to a village that likely had farms. They could get all they needed. They next argued about who would carry the bird in addition to their battery. *It should be determined by age! No, by grade! No, by height!* Sticks pointing to a small area, they parted a thicket, and there laid the bird, its feet and belly up. They jumped back and dropped the sticks without realizing it. They edged back and confirmed what they had seen: a guinea fowl wasn't lying there but a black, horned owl. Suddenly it was on its feet, turning its neck to look at them. It registered no fear. They left it alone. The two students who had seen things they had kept private felt vindicated for keeping what they saw to themselves. The others had an explanation for the appearance of a guinea fowl morphing into an owl—that the sun hit the forest at an angle, not uniformly on the terrain. What they had seen must have been the sun throwing shadows and creating illusive objects and colors. This explanation forced the two students to doubt what they believed they saw. The one student felt that what he saw were the remains of some animal, not a human's.

On their third day in the forest, the wind picked up intermittently. Ahead in the distance and off to the side, whirlwinds erupted as trees swayed. Clouds of dust hung thick in the air. The spectacle seemed bizarre and had an air of sinister mystery. Still, their anxiety didn't rise to fear. These phenomena would lend themselves to logic if exposed to science. Such a cavalier feeling kept them curious.

Descending a knoll, the dust particles didn't clear the air even when the wind died down. Then all was calm. It grew foggy all around. Without a compass, they risked going in the wrong direction. Luckily, the sun was visible to the right; aside from its color, which had now turned sluggish yellow, they could see enough of it to make their way northward. Their scientific minds were aroused: if the fog grew thicker and hid the sun completely, they planned to go in a straight line rather than walk side by side. One would go forward, with the rest lined up behind. By keeping the first person in a straight line, they would know they were going northward.

The terrain was flat after the knoll. Suddenly, the students saw goats grazing like human presence was normal there. A few left the herd and grazed near the students. The pasture was flat and unlike any other part of the forest. They couldn't see the grass or shrubs the goats were eating, for the fog was so thick they could barely see their own feet and the goats. With no herder and the risk of the goats being stolen or lost, it made sense that they were close to a village. Yet after walking another mile, they still didn't encounter a human or a village. Their prediction came true: the sun was now a faint yellow and on the verge of disappearing. The goats must have been an illusion; the movement of shadows around shrubs had given the appearance of goats. Yet the students couldn't explain the bleats they had heard.

The students kept to their path in a straight line. Their mouths were dry with thirst; their stomachs growled with hunger. A tangerine tree offered a respite when they came to another knoll. They untied their batteries and rested, standing up. The fog was still heavy. Unseen birds sang, chirped, shrieked, and hooted. They couldn't wait to be in the clear to brainstorm about what they hadn't been able to explain yet; they couldn't brush aside the unexplainable, which would be explainable with time. The fog wasn't alarming because it was November, and harmattan arrived and stayed through the end of the year. Its unevenness on the terrain should have been concerning. Over the next mile or so, they tried to rationalize the goats but were suddenly frozen in place with their hands plastered over their ears because of a deafening hoot.

The fog started dissipating when a bird with a wingspan of at least fifty feet flew overhead. Uncertain if this was an aberration or a bird they had never heard about, they looked at each other for confirmation that they had seen what they thought they saw. On impulse, they unstrapped their batteries and ran after the bird. The fog grew thicker again as it flew farther and farther until it was no more. By now, visibility was about a hundred yards, with trees faintly appearing beyond. The bird had flown northward. *No need to fear; there's no bird that large anywhere in the world. Something made the bird appear big, or the bird was bizarrely big, naturally. Whatever it was, it was an aberration of the fog. Even if there were a bird that big, unknown to the world, science could explain all this; no need to fear.* And so they rationalized, without incident, over the next six miles.

Coming to a clearing, all was different; they heard voices of chatting humans, men arguing, and a woman yelling at a child to return to the river and fetch something. A bald man with a prominent air about him looked on amid the yelling. He was an elder of the village. When the students came into view, he yelled at them to stop. A python had hidden under a brush a few steps away. They were a few steps from death, the man said with a toothless mouth, laughing. The students saw the snake and went around it. Expressing feelings of thankfulness, they arrived only to see no one, merely an outcropping of rock. In place of where the woman stood yelling at her boy, they saw a tree and an anthill. The students threw the tangerines away, agreeing that they contained a hallucinogen.

They had no memory of days after the third day. What they remembered was a fourth day could have been the tenth, twentieth, even the thirtieth day, or more. On the "fourth day" in the forest, they walked on and didn't attend to the true nature of the inexplicable. They continued northward in a straight line. The yellow sun had disappeared. They passed through an unnatural-looking thicket of neems; not even lichens clung to them. It reminded them of death. Exhausted, they kept walking, trying to leave their memories of the forest behind. When the fog lifted, they found themselves by a river. They unstrapped the batteries again and sat down to rest. They drank and talked, arguing more than discussing their distance from Aduman.

One said it couldn't be more than ten miles. "No," said another, "it's more like twelve." Others posited figures of seventeen and thirty-five miles. They could all have been right, and they could all have been wrong—the truth was a mystery. From where they sat, the river meandered away from them, taking a turn about twenty yards ahead and disappearing behind a new wall of fog, where the heavens descended to Earth.

Sitting by the river, they were frustrated that they had still not located any village after walking ten, seventeen, and perhaps even thirty-five miles or more. They were already late by several days. Like their differing perspectives of the distance they had traveled, their watches now diverged, not by minutes but by hours. They rationalized that the forest might have embedded electromagnetic fields. Their feet ached, and their bodies were exhausted. The undulating landscape and distance had taxed them. The nonsense of this exercise was apparent. One thing they would be sure to ask their professor once they got to the village, if they could find it, was the true reason for all this.

With the decision to cross the river, they immediately began to see nearby farms. Their hopes sprang up. They believed they could finally find someone who knew where they were going. They took one last look at the forest behind them on the other side of the river, and its fog seemed to wave them goodbye.

"The air feels thick," observed the only student who couldn't laugh off the strangeness they had observed. "I mean it." The others mocked in silence as if finding pleasure in denying what they had also observed. They came upon a woman who introduced herself as Adwoa Brago. Her husband, they could tell, wanted no conversation with them. He wore a disposition of unfriendliness. This couple was gathering firewood and herbs. Adwoa Brago didn't answer when the students asked where they were. Unable to feign nonchalance, they tried a different tactic, knowing they were likely north of Aduman.

"Mama, do you know Karikari? His wife is Agnes. Yaw and Gyambibi are his children."

Adwoa Brago looked at the huge batteries strapped to their backs. These boys looked worn and exhausted. She figured they had something to do with the rumor of bringing this *thing* to the village that could bring Queen Elizabeth to them. She told them where to connect with the path that led to where they were going, never mentioning the name Enkoho.

"What about the fog?" asked a student when he observed that the fog was still present before the river but clear after its banks.

"What fog?" asked Adwoa Brago.

"Can't you see it? Look over there."

They turned around to view the forest again, but there was no fog, and lush vegetation graced their line of view with the sun's rays reaching down. The students looked at each other in bewilderment, trying to keep their confusion over what they had seen to themselves, wanting to hide their embarrassment.

"It's the temperature inversion and wind direction, and it makes sense why it would clear," offered one student. Though, at this point, the two students who kept their visions to themselves had their confusion revived.

"It's the electromagnetic activity," said another, reminding the others that this was all explainable. There was no consensus over the visions, or absence thereof, of the past several days—whether real, imagined, or the creation of hallucinogens, which could be sourced to the wild fruits and tiger nuts they ate. The consensus was to take out their frustration later on with their professors by demanding the point and worth of this exercise. Unbeknownst to them, the villagers shared their confusion: the mystery was part of their daily lives. The students were about to enter Enkoho, a village where darkness paced in the heat of the day when the sun never failed to fall from the sky.

"The man you're looking for is that way. Keep on the path and go northward."

While the disagreements over the visions persisted on their walk to the village, they strongly agreed on where they were: they felt a malicious energy. Their educated brains prevented them from accepting what it was; it felt like entering an unknown dimension. Their thoughts were foggy, congested with perceptions that flowed from one into another, into another—all jumbled into unreasonable confusion.

Enkoho was a place like no other. As they neared the village, they saw sparse placements of thatched huts. They had no formal designs; they seemed haphazardly made, all about eight feet high, after which a thatched roof rose. The earth had an olive color with a hint of red. It was unlike any place they had ever seen. The mud huts were similar in complexion, though contrasted with the ground because they had more redness to them. Tree trunks had been fashioned into benches that leaned against various compounds of huts. No hut was fenced, yet the students could perceive their boundaries in walking past them. There were wooden platforms here and there on which lay dried cocoa beans. Cashews, tiger nuts, mangoes, pears, and other edibles grew in some compounds. There were neems too. Then something else drew their attention: all vegetation had leaves of this same olive-green-red color, which was different from the previous forest. The color was the same in the trees encircling the village. It appeared the leaves had seeped into the earth, endowing it with its strange color. The ground and the plants were somehow united by this sameness, which defied explanation.

The earth shifted beneath them as they walked on. They entered the forest and continued. Nothing seemed out of place until the same unfriendly man they had seen in the forest walked briskly by them, heading toward the village. Adwoa Brago again appeared and asked them if they'd found the man they were after.

"No, we're going to the village," one student said.

"You're heading back into the forest. The man doesn't live there."

Adwoa Brago walked them back to the village; she turned when they entered the village proper and pointed toward Karikari's house. They looked at each other, wondering how they had entered the village yet had somehow walked back into the forest.

"It must be the electromagnetic fields," one of them whispered. But there was no need to whisper if there was surety to that assumption. Their hidden fear betrayed the unspoken: it could be something else altogether.

A few stares darted from corners while some people greeted them from here and there. Nobody said anything close to acknowledging them as outsiders. The villagers shared a common air: the college boys couldn't gather why they seemed so happy. Dark thoughts roamed among them amid infrequent stretches of hollow happiness at their arrival.

They had reached the village immeasurably late. The weight of the batteries had caused them extended periods of rest, they told Professor Tetteh, who was just happy to see the batteries. Karikari offered them his house since they hadn't slept in days. After a few hours of sleep, they woke up. Perhaps it was the newness of the place or the strangeness of it; they felt as if they had slept for half a day. Upon waking up and being served food, they toured the village. They couldn't say how Professor Tetteh, who taught in the agriculture department, and Dr. Agyapong, from the engineering department, came to know Karikari and the village. They wouldn't have time to inquire because touring the village brought them into contact with two interesting boys who introduced themselves as Yaw and Preprah. This Yaw, they learned, was a son of Karikari, whose radio box they were there to install. Preprah, they easily figured, was lost and a mystery unto himself. He was left-handed but seemed nervous, perhaps afraid, to use his left hand. There was a strangeness about him.

Nevertheless, to them, Yaw and Preprah were like them, normal people one could see anywhere, unlike the rest of the villagers, who had an air of dark mystery about them. Being in the midst of this duo gave the students a sense of normalcy in an abnormal place. While their anger toward the professors hadn't yet abated, seeing Yaw and Preprah replaced their anger with excitement because accompanying this debonair duo were girls with seductive faces and inviting hips. The ratio of girls to these male villagers gripped them: it seemed two to seventeen or so. Their impulse to ask their professors how they had gotten to the village sooner than they had was replaced by a desire to get their job out of the way so they could mingle with Yaw and Preprah—to get to the girls.

The students' anger toward the professors started to melt away when they realized there was no road to the village; thus, one couldn't drive a car there. Also, the batteries were too heavy and too many to have been carried there by the two professors, hence why the task fell to them. In hindsight, the professors' direction was more than adequate when they considered it against their finding that there was no clear path to the village. Now they understood the cause of their visions not by critical analysis but by reasonable assumption conveniently attributed to what they felt were hallucinogenic fruits and nuts and electromagnetism. That might well have been the case— or not—but whatever the explanation, subconsciously, it made sense to resolve whatever was left of their confusion later. In the interim, they would attend to a worthwhile purpose. Thank goodness for the girls, who weren't ephemeral like the objects of their visions, but like girls on their campus, only without a trace of sophistication!

The students' faces confirmed Professor Tetteh's hunch: they felt the different energy of the village but assumed there was a logical explanation for it. If only he could have carried those huge batteries to the village, he would have spared them.

Karikari's house became a magnet for the villagers as the radio box's chosen location. They had to see the device that would "bring the queen to them." Word spread, and the crowd grew bigger and louder. Farmwork would have to wait, and housework and chores would, too. The quiet morning was suddenly populated with villagers milling around. Karikari's living room and adjoining hallways were filled with people.

After a brief rest, the students proceeded to the roof to mount a metal pole, a signal enhancer of sorts, for the radio's native antenna. Instructions came from Professor Agyapong on the ground. A raucous jubilation erupted from below when flickers of voices came through the radio. The students oriented and reoriented the metal pole for better reception. They kept up the work until late evening but couldn't produce more than a weak signal.

Professor Agyapong was at the head of the ladder, instructing them on the positioning of the metal pole. Two students separated themselves from their friends on the roof under the guise of heading into the forest to urinate. In the bush, they discussed whether their suspected "electromagnetic activity" was interfering with the radio signal. That could explain their difficulty or not. But to bring this to Professor Agyapong's attention for guidance to rework the signal properties would surely bring up what some claimed to have seen in the forest. The two students rejoined the group and shared their discussion after Professor Agyapong was off the ladder and out of sight. But one student noted that Professor Agyapong walked the same terrain as they did but might not have experienced those "visions" and "electromagnetic activity." Professor Tetteh, in particular, was responsible for their coming to the village. He wouldn't have them there if he had been privy to the circumstances and objects of the so-called visions. Moreover, this student observed in hindsight that there were no high-tension cables on the terrain to justify the suspicion of electromagnetic activity.

Not entirely discarding the possibility of electromagnetic-signal interference and recognizing the strain of reworking the metal pole and wires to produce a strong, crisp signal through the treacherous forest beyond, they thought they now understood their professor's intent to have them complete the hard task of signal enhancement in a remote terrain.

Slowly the villagers dissipated as unnoticeably as they had appeared. The next morning, they occupied the same spaces as if they had never left. The students' resolve persisted through the late evening again when the signal was finally strong enough to hear the program. The village erupted in shouts of joy. Radio programs lasted about ten hours at that time, so the villagers' celebration was short-lived when the program ended.

Everyone gathered at Karikari's house again the following morning; farming and other household work had to wait while everyone listened to programs about Queen Elizabeth's visit.

The students joined in the joy their work brought the villagers. But not everyone was there. Absent from the gathering was Preprah's father, Danfo, who hated that the gathering was about a woman: the queen. Also absent was Agya Kobi, the mean-looking man they had encountered twice while trying to enter the village.

The students were at last free to mingle. Girls in shifts and wrappers were in the company of Yaw and Preprah. Their hair wasn't permed or fashionably embellished, nor were they made up; they wore it in simple braids or Afros. Underneath their uncouth exterior was a quaint beauty that held the eye. At least a good third of them were of astonishing beauty. The students wisely ascertained that they needed Yaw and Preprah to get to them. The first day they saw the duo, they got acquainted with them in the absence of the girls so as not to arouse suspicion.

Now they were free to act out their plan; however, because they had overstayed their exeat, Professor Tetteh suddenly intervened, "You boys need to get back to school," he said without alarm that it had taken the boys much longer to get to the village than they had thought. It wasn't about four days; rather, it had taken several times that.

But the boys hadn't traveled this far, only to learn about the mechanics of signal enhancement. Koranteng said they should stay at least two more days to ensure the setup worked well. It was a remote place. Three days of uninterrupted transmission would ensure there wouldn't be problems with signals soon. Besides, they had no desire to trek that terrain again. Once they left, they wouldn't be coming back. Professor Tetteh promised to have their exeat extended, adding, "That's considerate of you. Stay two more days. Karikari will have no problem hosting you." He didn't disclose that he had an empty hut in the village because he didn't want them to know he was from the village. Enkoho was too mysterious to parade as the place of one's birth. He left the village without the students' knowledge. The students found out when they went to ask if he knew any shortcuts out of the village. The thought of going through that uncertain terrain to return to campus kept them on edge. One thing they were sure of was that they didn't want to leave the way they had come, even though they had no idea where that was. Yet they couldn't be too bothered by what they didn't know; for now, there were urgent matters to attend to.

While the village had its eyes and ears on the radio, the middle schoolers got the distraction they craved. Not only them but the college boys too, who were privy to Yaw and Preprah's plan to officiate a beauty contest. The participants, seventeen women and four girls, ranged from fifteen to thirty-eight years old. The wide variety of contestants brought the judges, Yaw and Preprah, to a dispute. Preprah sought to disqualify anyone over twenty-nine with more than one child. One woman was thirty-six with four children; she was the reason for Preprah's contention. Yaw objected because he anticipated a torrent of more disqualification criteria from Preprah if he agreed. Preprah had first sought to disqualify that woman, and when he didn't get his way, he came up with a criterion to remove her. The contest had started and ended many times because Preprah had gone to great lengths to change or propose more rules to ensure his choice, Efia, won. Having the college boys there ended the stalemate. The contestants welcomed their inclusion as honorary judges; for these were college boys who knew better. Their participation was timely, and it seemed the competition would finally come to an end.

The students were drawn away from the girls to the tree under which the contest was being held. With a girth of about thirty feet, this baobab was the biggest tree they had ever seen. The trunk resembled a complex of thirty trees bundled together. Its crown spread a hundred feet across. Professor Tetteh had once concluded it was about two thousand years old, having sprung from the soil when Jesus walked the earth. Before the students could be introduced as honorary judges, Preprah proposed another rule change: contestants not in footwear ought to be disqualified. Coincidentally, Efia was the only one in footwear. The college students didn't know what difference it made until Efia strutted in wearing boots. Originally, they had belonged to the Dutch botanist Dr. Maarten, who had given them to Preprah as a gift. They were fieldwork boots with raised toecaps and thick rugged soles. Because the boots were several sizes too big for her, Efia had stuffed the toe space with dry leaves, which made crunching sounds when she walked. As she moved about, the college students' teeth gnashed. They couldn't bear the noise.

"It's only fair to the others that she removes the boots," Yaw said.

"If a contestant had come naked because of lack of clothes, for the sake of uniformity, would you tell the others to undress? Of course not; you'd disqualify her or advise someone to give her clothes. Why can't they find their own shoes?" Preprah protested.

"We would if there were enough boots for all," Yaw replied.

"Why put Efia at a disadvantage if they can't find their own boots?" Preprah continued.

Efia enjoyed seeing Preprah fight for her. He also enjoyed impressing her. For the occasion, he wore gabardine pants rolled up to his knees with a T-shirt, which he wore inside out and backward. Were he not perfumed to give the impression that this was his serious attempt at fashion, they would have thought clothes were a new undertaking for him. The college boys noted he had dressed similarly the day before when they were all in the company of the girls. They couldn't tell if his odd dress was because he didn't know how the clothes were worn or because he didn't want them ruined. In any case, Efia wanted to win, and she was happy Preprah shared this interest.

The college boys gathered that Preprah was attracted to Efia and did all he could to steer the contest in her favor—a gesture Efia appeared to relish. However, judging by Efia's apparent disregard for Preprah, the students perceived the potential love interest as one-sided. The students felt that if their perception of Preprah was accurate, they might have a window into Efia's character. They would soon verify the truth of that thought.

The students could tell that the other contestants were admiring Efia's advantage without knowing that a woman's feet didn't belong in such grotesquely masculine boots, even if only to ward off snakes. In beauty contests, the college boys explained, contestants must also show how adept they are and how intelligently they can handle a hypothetical situation. They proposed hide-and-seek, and the contestants agreed. The proposal was foolish to Yaw, especially regarding how they could stratify who won and who lost. For this, the college boys successfully synchronized their watches. They explained that the judges would note when they found a participant and use the time for the placements of the contestants. Still, the idea was silly to Yaw, though not to Preprah, who knew Efia to be the most elusive, as evidenced by his constant and unsuccessful courtship of her. He further sidelined Yaw's objection because the honorary judges had as much right as they did. It was six to one, Preprah reminded Yaw.

"But why do it in the evening?" Yaw protested.

"Night would be worst, that's why," retorted an honorary judge.

"The forest is too vast a place for hide-and-seek," Yaw persisted.

"Okay, one shouldn't go more than a hundred meters out. The beginning of where the river turns should be fine," Preprah suggested, looking toward Yaw, who seemed irritated.

"It's not a bright idea," Yaw concluded.

Not wanting to participate, Yaw stayed behind. Suspicious, Preprah also stayed behind to keep an eye on Yaw so he wouldn't tamper with the results.

With that, the contestants bolted to the forest on a minute head start.

Preprah told Yaw that Efia would be the last to be found. He was right beyond his own prediction; the contest was aborted two hours later when Efia wasn't found.

"You have my permission to go crazy," Preprah poked at Yaw, thinking Efia was already declared the winner.

"What are you excited about? She must be found to be declared the winner."

"Get over it; she won!"

"She wasn't found in the area demarcated for the competition and probably went home to hide. In that case, she shunned the instructions. Disqualified!" Yaw yelled.

"You don't have to go crazy now," Preprah said.

Yaw quickly stated that he wouldn't go to Efia's hut in search of her. Preprah concurred. The animosity between his father and Efia's grandfather would naturally exclude his participation in any effort to see if she was home. Two of the college boys asked why they were afraid of her grandfather.

"Cross the man, and you'll end up in a cycle of cold, dark death at the unseen hands of cruelty," Preprah warned. Yaw nodded. The students laughed, only to meet Yaw and Preprah's nervous stares, which stripped them of their façade and exposed their own fears.

"You really believe such things?" the students questioned.

Listening to the nature of the person whose existence the village feared, the college boys reconsidered the mean-looking old man they had encountered days earlier.

"Cross him and find out," Yaw said.

The college boys didn't laugh.

"You don't believe in such things, so why don't you go to Efia's grandparents' hut to see if she's there?" Yaw suggested.

"We don't believe in such things, you're right, but—"

"All right, I'll show you the way," Preprah said.

"But I do believe in death," the college boy finished his thought.

Preprah sat back down.

"Yaw's right," said one of the college boys.

Another echoed, "If our mates don't find her, she's disqualified."

"Well, I permit you two to go crazy too," Preprah said.

It wasn't Preprah's words that changed the students' mood.
They were angry for a different reason: suddenly, they felt suf-
focated by the village. It was as if they were becoming aware
of its dark energy. When their friends joined them, they started
shouting about why their professors had sent them there. They
left the next morning, not staying the full two days they had
suggested to Professor Tetteh. In fact, they would have left after the hide-and-seek if their memory of the forest, real or not,
hadn't resurfaced.

Several months later, Efia's family dragged Preprah before
the elders about her pregnancy.

"Me...vanjema? No, I haven't seen one before. How can I be
the child's father? I have not seen vanjema before," Preprah
protested.

After Efia gave birth to Asamoah, Preprah stood before the
elders again. In the middle of a select group of elderly wom-
en, the soles of his feet and palms were compared with those
of the baby boy. The findings were suspiciously exculpatory:
Preprah's soles were chafed, cracked, warped, and the heels
and balls of his feet were effaced. Moreover, the creases of his
palms and soles, if they were visible, were in strange, haphaz-
ard orientations. These findings combined to make nonsense
of their investigation. It mattered not that his soles were so
because he walked bare feet like most of the villagers. And it
mattered not that Preprah's palms were covered in callouses
because he was agrarian like the rest of the villagers. The group
of elderly women forced a visit to the village healer, who put
Preprah's feet in a formula of herbal wrap. His hands were
treated similarly. When Preprah appeared before the council of
elderly women on the seventh day, his soles and feet were like
a newborn's.

The elderly women were secretly motivated to pit Preprah's father, Danfo, against Efia's grandfather, Agya Kobi. For each of the women had had clashes with Preprah's father—sometimes violently trading fists. That was usual for Danfo: every disagreement with a woman was an opportunity to tame the man within every woman. The women detested him and desired to see him destroyed; hence they were disappointed again when the paternity was negative for the second time. Had Preprah been found to be the father of Asamoah, the women would have celebrated the inescapable thrust of Danfo into the destructive orbit of Agya Kobi, who, rumored to be destroying everything in his way, would have added Danfo to those who didn't deserve to be walking among the living.

The issue was put to rest when the women accepted that Preprah wasn't the boy's father. No other man in Enkoho was investigated for the paternity of Asamoah. No one was surprised that the investigation of Efia's pregnancy started and ended with Preprah, despite his innocence. Preprah was a strange creature in Enkoho. He could be grouped with plants and wouldn't know enough to feel insulted. Preprah was the only resident of Enkoho to be romantically desperate to go near the household of Agya Kobi, despite his intense fear of him.

Chapter

Life Under the Red Clouds

*T*hirteen years younger than his brother, Yaw, Gyambibi was many things his older brother wasn't. Both got a coveted measure of handsomeness, and both were clever. Yet Gyambibi was more handsome; by age five, people knew he would be more intelligent. More restrained of the two, Gyambibi carried his mother's heart and his father's resolve, sprinkled with his paternal great-grandmother's daringness.

Gyambibi was up before the rest of Enkoho. From his window, he could see traces of huts standing in the early morning shadows. Beyond them, the farms and forest blended into blackness. His room was across from Uncle Salifu's, who was asleep. Yaw's bedroom was farther down the hallway to the left, while his parents' room was at the back of the house. Gyambibi tiptoed across the living room, and upon emerging from the porch, his feet soon touched the cool, moist earth. Limbs of trees flickered in the wind against lanterns, whose light billowed from huts along the path. The wind blew chills over him and reminded him that he was alone. He strolled in the shadows so no one would see him, and then a sound froze him. He waited before turning the corner, leaning against a familiar hut. Gyambibi disappeared before anyone saw him, reappearing in a neighbor's yard too close to a pen of goats. He left before their scuttle alerted anyone to his presence.

Gyambibi walked briskly over a hundred meters, then tiptoed once he neared Agya Kobi's compound four huts away. Rumors he had heard about the man terrified him, but he wanted to see what evil looked like close up. He peeked into the man's living room, sparingly lit by a lantern. Agya Kobi was bowed before an open Bible with eyes closed and mouth moving, having his morning devotion. Gyambibi wondered why the old man was so different, unlike his wife, who was a friend of his mother's. Gyambibi wasn't impressed with what he saw. Perhaps he had to be older to see what others feared. He decided to leave, intending to come back a few more times to find confirmation of what the villagers had said of him.

The morning had dawned, and the village was mostly awake. Skipping other huts, Gyambibi went to another house that haunted his curiosity. The house was situated with its back against the edge of the village. It constituted three buildings joined into one: a storehouse, the middle main house, and the third for farmhands. He looked through the biggest of three windows, located away from the villagers preparing to go to their farms. Its drapes were pried open to let in air. Two cane chairs with a table between them sat in the middle of the room. A third cane chair was set in a corner with all sorts of things stacked on top of it. He counted six corsets hanging on a clothesline that ran against the breadth of the wall. He wondered why one woman would need so many corsets. Beyond the door, seeing through to the adjoining room, the living room, he heard a brawny snore. A fight had separated the married couple into different rooms. It could also be one of the relatives living with them. Back to the bedroom, Gyambibi could make out several closed barrels. As his forehead pressed against the window bars, he was greeted by a malevolent odor from the stacked barrels in the corner, repelling him a few steps back. Here lived Danfo and Esi Eluwah, a couple that frequently fought, often physically, with one always threatening to kill the other. Gyambibi wondered when one of them would eventually carry out the threat. For the rest of the day, he would search for the couple, and the one he didn't find would possibly be in pieces in the barrels. Other than that, the barrels contained the items of Esi Eluwah's trade: cured meat she sold at the market.

Gyambibi was consumed by what he had seen, though he kept it to himself. He returned home before his family awoke or any villager came to the porch for a program beaming from the radio box.

The villagers now flocked sparingly to the radio box because, after two years, it wasn't special anymore. Moreover, some of the pronouncements made on the radio insulted their intelligence. For example, they would hear about rain falling and wrecking whole villages—rain they never saw. In their minds, the sun went up and came down at the same time everywhere. And so with the rain. Thus it was nonsense to speak of rain that they didn't see themselves.

What's more, their initial excitement about the radio box was fully satisfied in November of the previous year, during the first anniversary of Queen Elizabeth's visit, when the villagers got to hear events of her stay—events they'd missed because the students had been late in bringing the batteries. The villagers were surprised to hear the newscaster speak of the end of colonialism four years before the queen's visit, which was a farewell to a former colony, the newscaster added. This seemed a grand deception carried over the radio box. The villagers wondered how they could have missed the presence of the queen's people in the country for a hundred years and the knowledge of the presence of other Europeans in the country going back over four hundred years. In their collective memory, however, was a remote history of an interaction their ancestors had with some White missionaries who came to the village, in which the subject of the location of Satan on Earth was discussed—a discussion that surfaced when frustrations flared in searching for the cause of their struggles. Besides the Caucasian couple, Dr. Maarten and Xada, and a White American woman who visited now and then, it had been over a hundred years since a White man or woman had stepped foot in the village.

In any case, the villagers' fascination with the radio box was now lukewarm. When a program interested them, they learned when to be there and when to leave based on the device's workings. The radio box had no physical on-off switch, so it was always on; it was "off" when programming finished at night. Karikari kept it out on his front porch. Around 9:00 a.m., a few people were scattered about the porch. Gyambibi walked through them to join Dr. Maarten and his wife, Xada Von Nal-la, who were passing by. He intended to nag them into taking him on their field trip again.

"How are you, my boy?" Xada inquired.

"Fine, madam," Gyambibi replied and hugged her. He rolled the backpack off Xada's shoulder.

"That's nice of you." She smiled.

Dr. Maarten patted him on the head. "You're a great kid."

"And so are all the children here," Gyambibi said.

"I've never seen you sad...always happy. I wish I were like that growing up," Dr. Maarten observed.

"Maybe you were; you just don't remember it. All the children in this village are happy. I can't say that about old people. Old people worry too much," Gyambibi replied.

Xada looked at her husband coyly and laughed.

"Ah! The pangs of adulthood," Dr. Maarten said to Xada.

The conversation continued as they walked through vast acreages of cocoa orchards. Farmhands worked and sang in the distance. Gyambibi picked three ripe mangoes, which he wiped off on his shirt, and handed two to Xada to share with her husband. In her usual ornate and soft-spoken voice, she said, "What a darling you are," caressing his ear.

Their path meandered as it approached the shoulder of the river and intersected at its shallowest point. A vast array of plants and tall, thin grasses adorned its banks. Wild animals foraged nearby; some basked in the sun, and others crouched in the underbrush at a distance from the path. Below the river's clear surface were stepping stones. Gyambibi ran across them, splashing along and startling all the animals as they disappeared into the reeds. A lush blanket of vegetation flanked both sides of their path. Matured perennials pointed to the heavens.

Gyambibi ran after a yellow-headed picathartes that was pecking at a rabbit jowl.

"Ah! The sweet old world of childhood!" Dr. Maarten exclaimed.

Unsuccessful in catching the bird, Gyambibi climbed a tree.

"Dr. Maarten, Dr. Maarten, it's beautiful up here," he called, overlooking the silent meadows, a sea of variegated blossoms and exotic smells. "Climb up and see what I see. I'm coming down to help madam climb!"

Xada smiled and shook her head. Gyambibi descended with mangoes, which he again handed two to Xada.

"How many fruits do you want me to eat today?"

"Enough."

"How many fruits are enough?"

"Enough to make you want no more."

They arrived at the greenhouse; Gyambibi offloaded the backpack, opened it, and handed a logbook to Xada.

"Not yet, Gyambibi. I'll tell you when I need it."

Gyambibi again left their company. He was a few trees away from the greenhouse attending to his pet but still within whispering distance of Dr. Maarten and Xada. A day prior, he had made a clay mound with a room inside, into which he placed a grasshopper. In his hand were bites of mango for the grasshopper. He opened the makeshift door over the mouth of the mound, only to find the grasshopper dead in a pile of mango pieces. Dr. Maarten and Xada heard sobs and went to Gyambibi. Xada clutched him to her bosom. Dr. Maarten took hold of the grasshopper and remarked, "It isn't dead, Gyambibi; it just needs water. Did you give it water yesterday?"

"No," he sniffled. Dr. Maarten left and returned a short while later with a live grasshopper.

"So it just needed water," Gyambibi said, smiling and wiping away tears. He didn't know it was a different grasshopper. "You're good and learned, Dr. Maarten. How do you know so much about animals?"

Dr. Maarten smiled and asked Xada for herbarium sheets. Gyambibi lowered the grasshopper into the mound and ran to fetch the backpack. After handing it to Xada, he returned to the river for water, which meandered by the greenhouse.

"I've never seen such an energetic child in all my life," Dr. Maarten said.

"True," Xada said while making entries in the field log.

Dr. Maarten would later prepare two separate specimens of the herbarium: One he would give to Dr. Tetteh for an independent analysis; the other would accompany him back to his research laboratory in the Netherlands.

Gyambibi soon reappeared with pineapples, which he gave to Dr. Maarten as thanks for saving his pet.

"None for me, my dear?" Xada asked.

Gyambibi smiled and handed her a partially eaten slice.

"You can keep that. I've had enough for today."

"Dr. Maarten?" Gyambibi began.

"Yes, Gyambibi?"

"How do plants make food?"

"They take energy from the sun and use water, carbon dioxide, and nutrients from the earth."

"You forgot something," Gyambibi said.

"Forgot?"

"What you said last month. Do all old people forget? Agya Kobi forgets where he puts his glasses sometimes. Searching for a pair of glasses with eyes that can't see!" Gyambibi laughed.

"What's your question, little one?"

"How does a tomato plant know to make tomatoes and a cocoa tree cocoa?"

Xada looked at Dr. Maarten and smiled. She knew exactly what he was thinking.

"Think of it as every plant having a kitchen that tells it what type of food to make. We're done here today."

On their way back to the village, they met Karikari and his farmhands.

"Dr. Maarten and Madam, good morning. Why bother taking this brat with you on your important work?"

"What a gifted son you have, Mr. Karikari. He's a brilliant child. There isn't another like him in the village. I didn't ask what he asked when I was ten. His thoughts are weighty for his age."

"And you aren't helping by keeping his company," Karikari joked. "If you keep teaching him, it's just a matter of time before he sells the village out from under our feet."

The Maartens walked back to the village as Karikari and the farmhands continued on to the farm. Karikari later told Gyambibi that Efia had brought Asamoah to their house, for he needed a playmate.

Chapter

2

*G*yambibi kept to his ways. By the age of six, his curiosity was unrelenting, and his intelligence sharper. His eyes opened suddenly like a timed mechanical device, his inner clock alerting him it would be roughly an hour before the villagers awoke. He tiptoed the hallways to avoid detection; his parents had threatened punishment if he left the house unaccompanied by an older person, but Gyambibi didn't take their threats seriously—they had never carried them out. Uncle Salifu's threats, on the other hand, were as serious as the canes he had been soaking in a bucket to punish his nephew's infractions. While his parents had never caught him (they had heard rumors of his disobedience), Gyambibi suspected Uncle Salifu had actually seen him leave the house.

Gyambibi's sights were set on another early morning mission: the mystery of Agya Kobi still haunted him, in addition to unraveling the mystery of Danfo's house. His playmates, Moro and Asamoah, were disappointed when he failed to turn up evidence to substantiate his claim that human flesh was stored in Danfo's house. He had observed that many people came to the house and suspected the corsets he saw in the bedroom were used to strangle them. He would see these residents for a few months, and then they would disappear. He also told his friends of the strong odor through the open windows. It was better to prove this to his friends than be branded a liar. Gyambibi had a heightened sense of rightness, a boy who couldn't understand why someone would lie in the face of truth or why one would choose vice over virtue. Gyambibi was baffling and pesky.

A sound came from behind him; he turned and saw something creeping on the ground. It merged with the shadow in an attempt to hide. Gyambibi walked quickly to a hut that streamed light onto his path. He turned the corner and froze, watching in confusion and fear as the shadow of a creature on all fours was cast onto one of the structures. The shadow merged with another hut, where he could see its shape but couldn't tell if it was human or animal. Because Uncle Salifu was crippled and got around by dragging himself with his arms, Gyambibi felt it could be him. Then again, this was Enkoho, and what appeared to be trailing him could be what his fear told him. The creature pulled itself off the ground on the strength of its forelimbs. His urge to scream was swallowed up by the fear of Uncle Salifu and his parents discovering his absence. He couldn't run home. Suddenly, the creature's shadow retreated from the huts and disappeared, a sign that it had moved away from him. Gyambibi continued walking toward Agya Kobi's hut, which was lit. He sensed that he was being followed as he heard the sound of something dragging across the ground. He finally gave in to his fear and ran home, where he found Uncle Salifu, cane in hand, on the front porch. Gyambibi recoiled and ran. He was afraid to return because he knew what awaited him. Karikari wouldn't intervene, for he had warned Gyambibi many times.

When the villagers began to walk to their farms, Gyambibi decided it was safer to return home, for enough people were awake to come to his rescue. His mother would intervene too. When Gyambibi got to the porch, Salifu lunged at him, and Gyambibi jumped back and dodged a swing of the cane. Uncle Salifu's handicap stood in the way of chasing him.

Meanwhile, Gyambibi continued backward while shaking his head as Salifu insisted he should come for his punishment. Gyambibi bumped into someone; it was Agya Kobi. Salifu dropped the cane to signal he wouldn't punish him; he preferred Gyambibi come home than approach Agya Kobi. Gyambibi saw the fear and discomfort in Uncle Salifu's eyes. Defiantly, Gyambibi took hold of Agya Kobi's basket and cutlass in a gesture to help him.

"Uncle, I'm going to the farm with him. I'm learning obedience," Gyambibi said to the nervous Salifu. Salifu was helpless to pull Gyambibi away from the elder and had nothing more to say, for, though he had lived in the village for many years, not once had he exchanged words with Agya Kobi, as it was with all the villagers.

Gyambibi walked alongside Agya Kobi, who would look at him casually, not saying a word. His skin was like weathered leather, veiny and tired; his palms were covered in unsightly callouses and scarred enough to confuse an experienced palmist. His legs moved with the crepitation of dried sticks. With a hunched posture, it seemed life itself had worn him down. Gyambibi placed the cutlass inside the basket and carried it atop his head. He whistled and jumped about, happy to have escaped Uncle Salifu's fury. So close to Agya Kobi, Gyambibi didn't feel the fear that so easily captivated the villagers' perceptions. In the elder's right hand was a lantern. The old man seemed welcoming in a lukewarm way.

"Thank you," Gyambibi said to him for the timely rescue. Agya Kobi looked at him but said nothing. Gyambibi felt an air of comfort walking beside him. "They say you don't like people. Is that why you don't say much?"

Agya Kobi ignored the question and asked if Gyambibi had eaten breakfast. Hearing he hadn't, Agya Kobi asked him to return, assuring Gyambibi that Salifu's threat had passed. Agya Kobi took back the cutlass and basket.

"Are you going home?" Gyambibi asked.

"I'm taking you home."

"Why? I want to help you on the farm."

"I know you do, but you haven't eaten breakfast."

"I'm not hungry."

"You will be."

The two turned back. Salifu's threat still hovered over Gyambibi's conscience.

"I don't believe that you don't like people. You like me," Gyambibi said.

Agya Kobi looked at Gyambibi. "What made you say that?"

"I don't know."

As they walked back, the old man responded sparingly. About fifty yards from the village, Gyambibi heard his name. The two stopped, and Moro—Gyambibi's best friend— approached them. Agya Kobi left Gyambibi in Moro's company and urged the two to return to the village, reassuring Gyambibi that he should not be afraid to go home.

"I've been looking for you. Uncle Salifu told me you went to the farm with the old man," Moro said."Was that him?"

"Yes, that was him."

Gyambibi's mother and father were looking for him. Their worries about his whereabouts overtook Uncle Salifu's threat. Karikari was unaware that Gyambibi had run to the farm with Agya Kobi on a threat from Uncle Salifu. It appeared Uncle Salifu had kept it to himself because the anger that would have ensued toward him would have been greater than his anger toward Gyambibi. After ascertaining his whereabouts, not even his mother could keep him home. Gyambibi and Moro left the house.

Moro was excited to be back in Enkoho with Gyambibi. But he was also excited for another reason: the shouting and anger in his hut the previous night had ended up being to his and Gyambibi's benefit. "Being back from Bawku has its luck this time," he told Gyambibi. Moro showed him a Tissot watch, which he had found in a dustbin. It was a gift to his stepfather, who was so angered by the watch that he threw it away. It had been a parting gift from his Lebanese boss, who was leaving for Lebanon for good. This boss didn't think well of him to give him a used, broken watch after all his years of dedicated service!

"This was what all the shouting was about," said Moro as he showed the watch to Gyambibi.

Moro wanted to know if Yaw would buy it. Gyambibi said he might, but not if it was broken. Moro explained his intention to fix it. He had learned to fix many things from a multifaceted repairman who lived near his father in the Northern Region.

The next morning, Gyambibi found Moro, who had the watch disassembled. Moro asked why Gyambibi hadn't visited the greenhouse with Dr. Maarten and Xada. Gyambibi responded that he had gone to Danfo's house instead for evidence of a corpse, and Uncle Salifu had seen him again. Moro repeated that Uncle Salifu wouldn't punish him. Moro's reassurance didn't take away Gyambibi's fear of returning home this time. He felt Uncle Salifu needed time to calm down, so he and Moro followed Agya Kobi to the farm without his knowing. Moro told him not to bother the poor old man, and Gyambibi said he wanted to help him. Recognizing his voice, a man called to Gyambibi.

Startled, they turned around to see one of his father's farmhands, who leaped up and grabbed Gyambibi.

"What are you doing here?"

"I don't know!"

"You've walked a mile here, and you don't know why?" he said, still holding on to Gyambibi. He asked Gyambibi if his father was home. After he found a log for them to sit on, he offered them a gourd of water.

"He's hungry," Moro said.

"Are you?" the farmhand asked.

Gyambibi, still preoccupied with Uncle Salifu's threat, wasn't thinking about food, though he was hungry.

"Don't worry; we'll cook something."

The farmhand asked Moro to gather some wood for a fire. When Moro turned to leave, he looked behind to see if Gyambibi was following him. He heard nothing and went in search of wood. The farmhand, Mumuni, called out to Osei, another farmhand, who joined them. Osei spoke fondly of Gyambibi's father. Karikari had never spoken to them harshly.

"Where did you find it?" Osei inquired about a guinea fowl.

"There," said Mumuni and pointed to an area.

"What is it?" Gyambibi asked.

"Guinea fowl," Mumuni and Osei said in unison.

"How did you find it?"

"I saw it there, chased it with a stick, caught it, and wrung its neck."

"Did you not think it could belong to someone?" Gyambibi asked.

"It's a wild guinea fowl," Mumuni responded.

"A wild guinea fowl, here?" Gyambibi asked.

"Yes," Mumuni replied

"That's a domestic guinea fowl," Osei corrected.

"No, those types stay in the village, right?" Mumuni retorted nervously.

"How could you tell if it's wild or domesticated?" Gyambibi asked Osei.

"The domesticated ones are, well, domesticated...I mean, they're timid. Not timid but less fierce than their wild siblings. The wild ones are very aggressive. I'm surprised Mumuni could hunt down one in so short a time. That's why it couldn't be a wild fowl," Osei clarified.

"This one's dead. How could you tell if it's domesticated or not?" Gyambibi asked.

Mumuni had no answer. In its place, he offered that the fowl belonged to Yaa Adubia. He said that he and the other farm-hands had no desire to tell anyone.

"But you know it will get to the village somehow," Gyambibi said.

"How will it get there if none of us tells it?"

"You're asking a question whose answer was a mystery to our ancestors. Just keep quiet and don't ask again," Gyambibi said to the surprise of the farmhands. They knew the statement was about the mystery that inhabited the village.

Moro was uneasy. If the news got to the village, which it would, though none of them would tell it, he knew he was done for. His name would be tied to the lost fowl and a one-way ticket to Bawku. He had been a source of trouble for his mother and stepfather. Yaa Adubia and her guinea fowl would be the least of his worries; for she wanted out of the village as much as the peripatetic guinea fowl. Nevertheless, Gyambibi assured Moro not to worry.

"We won't tell lies; we'll tell them just enough to make them question what gets to them as truth," Gyambibi promised he would tell Moro what to say before the story got out.

Moro dropped the firewood beside a makeshift coal pot. Mumuni poked the fire and threw some onions and tomatoes into the pot. Roasted to his liking, he removed them and tossed them into a mortar, applying a pestle. As he cooked, Osei saturated Gyambibi with conversation. With Mumuni's help, Moro deplumed the guinea fowl and gutted it.

Gyambibi recognized Adwoa Brago's voice approaching. He signaled for Moro to come with him. Their appetite for the unfinished cooking was gone for different reasons. When they appeared on the main path leading to and from the village, Gyambibi and Moro saw that it was Adwoa Brago heading back to the village with her husband, Agya Kobi. Gyambibi was excited to join them. Moro didn't share the same view, for fear of Agya Kobi clung to him. In fact, Moro watched as Gyambibi ran and hugged Adwoa Brago, then Agya Kobi, who, like before, remained nonchalant; however, he looked quizically at Gyambibi.

"You didn't spend much time on the farm," Gyambibi observed and reached for the cassavas Adwoa Brago was holding. He also asked to carry Agya Kobi's cutlass. Agya Kobi hesitated, but realizing Gyambibi wouldn't leave him alone, he handed it to him. Moro went back for the guinea fowl, for his appetite had returned. If he was going to be sent back for having a part in stealing a guinea fowl, at least he owed himself a taste of it.

Gyambibi followed Agya Kobi and Adwoa Brago back home. Agya Kobi sat on a bench outside while Gyambibi followed Adwoa Brago inside the hut. Inside the hut reawakened his curiosity about where evil was rumored to hide in Enkoho. He didn't have to hide outside to investigate the evil within—now he could see if it existed. The walls of the hut were rough and aged, but the cracks that went through them to the out-side walls weren't wide enough for insects to exploit. Runs of veiny shapes covered the walls; a prominent one emerged from the ceiling, meandered mid-wall, and went behind a stack of portmanteaus. Newspapers and aged straw mats were folded against the wall. In a corner, wooden planks lay on the floor to protect a stack of notebooks from dampness. He opened one and saw handwritten years, months, and days. He would later learn they were calendars. Next, he saw the lantern that the villagers ridiculed as the Eternal Lamb, which he took care not to disturb.

Moro came to Agya Kobi's hut when he learned that Gyambi-bi wasn't home. Agnes wondered where Gyambibi was, for his cousins were visiting from Kodee. Moro didn't tell her where he suspected Gyambibi was but promised to find him.

Chapter

3

*P*ots of cocoyam, plantain, cassava, rice, and the best the village had boiled away. White coils of aroma billowed out of Chief's compound, yards away. The food, when ready, would fill the village square, where the villagers were celebrating Dr. Maarten and Xada. The elderly women had taken up cooking for the occasion, which Adwoa Brago oversaw. She took a break and joined Gyambibi, surrounded by his peers, and watched him lecture about the importance of Dr. Maarten and Xada's work. The children couldn't grasp the scientific thrust of the work as Gyambibi explained it but were attuned nonetheless.

Adwoa Brago had a tenuous understanding of what Gyambibi said but was convinced enough of his intellect not to doubt the accuracy of his claims. She nodded, smiling at his mannerisms and self-confidence.

Jeefa arrived with her father, Mawuli, who had returned from Kumasi with Uncle Salifu. They had been collecting payments from their buyers. Jeefa ran to Gyambibi and stood by him as he lectured as if she were his assistant. Adwoa Brago returned to her culinary duties. Mawuli sat next to Karikari and also watched Gyambibi. Mawuli was frustrated with some buyers who, predictably, had deferred payment for not having sold enough produce. Mawuli and Uncle Salifu had a disagreement:

Mawuli had told Salifu his desire to solicit new relationships with new customers, but Uncle Salifu had asked for patience. Karikari trusted them and didn't want to take sides, so he interrupted their disagreement by recounting his trip to Accra.

It was dark when Dr. Maarten and Xada joined the villagers in the company of Chief, his wife, and the linguist. Dr. Maarten and his wife arrived in Enkoho in 1949. Through the Cooperative—the name the villagers gave to the entity that bought their cocoa for the government—the couple learned the village would suit its research interest. Chief and the villagers had allocated a plot of land of the Maartens' choosing. With a hut of their own built by the villagers, they had immersed themselves well in the community, learning the language and traditions. They couldn't do without the local food they had developed a passion for. They often came home to various fruits at their doorstep, depending on who had gone to the farm. Before Xada learned to cook the local foods, village women took turns cooking for them so they wouldn't go without. To these elderly women, the couple was a son and a daughter from a distant land.

Dr. Maarten shared these memories in front of the entire village. He thanked the villagers for their generosity, which they had extended toward strangers, and this had been a pervasive attribute throughout the country. Everything had come to them freely. People genuinely cared about foreigners. The villagers not only gave them what they had but gave of themselves as well. He recounted the story when Xada decided to cook for him after months of Agnes's culinary tutelage. She had learned, among other things, to prepare porcupine—particularly the delicate art of dismembering it to avoid the release of bile into the meat, which would render it inedible. They had laughed when she took notes of recipes. Dr. Maarten thought them to be as detailed as her fieldwork notes, including times when ingredients were added and tasted and suggestions of what ingredients to use in place of others to prepare different types of soup. Looking at the margins of her notes, she sometimes squinted to make sense of what she had scribbled. She had walked her husband through the recipe for garden-egg soup with smoked tuna, pig feet, and cured beef. One day, confident and unaided, she tried her hand at it. After all the ingredients were deployed in a pot outside, she and her husband went indoors, intending to return in fifty-three minutes and thirty-nine seconds, the precise time it had taken Agnes to make a perfect soup. But in barely half the estimated time, the smell of smoke drew them outside. She had forgotten that coal pots had no thermostat and how fast or slow food was cooked depended on the number of fiery coals in the coal pot. She had put in far too many, so the soup had "walked off." In its place was a charred residue of inedible blackness.

"The soup had taken off running on some kind of culinary Rapture, and my stomach was on the cusp of developing a phobia of soup!" Dr. Maarten, inebriated, recounted. "Let me take this opportunity to correct the rumors that I ran from my wife's cooking...her cooking ran from me! I've never doubted, since then, the gods' love for me and their ability to avert dangers heading my way," he said to Xada and the group's loud laughter.

From then on, not only had Xada been impressed with the women's ability to cook without following a written recipe but also that they seemed to have an inner thermostat and timer to be anywhere, yet still knew when their food, sitting on fiery coals, would be done. Since Adwoa Brago had gotten hold of the incident by way of Dr. Maarten teasing his wife, days later, Xada redeemed herself by retrying her hand at the same recipe. This time she sat by the fire and sampled her soup multiple times, as Adwoa Brago did. However, she took a bathroom break before eating with her husband. As Dr. Maarten explained, she was so serious about avoiding another cooking embarrassment that she had neglected her body. At one point, she couldn't hear her husband's repeated calls. To another round of laughter, Dr. Maarten said that if the dead did cook, he knew what they looked like—referring to his wife's unresponsiveness to all else while she perfected her soup.

"Every now and then, I'm afraid to look up at night. The dark sky, like today's, reminds me of the day I came dangerously close to hating food forever."

The villagers burst into laughter.

"Stop picking on your wife, Dr. Maarten, or all the women will unite against you," Adwoa Brago retorted to more laughter. Dr. Maarten mimed forgiveness, humbly slapping the back of his right hand in the palm of the left hand while receding into his seat. The villagers laughed and fell out of their chairs. Xada had redeemed herself; Adwoa Brago spoke up to say how well her soup had turned out.

For this farewell occasion, Xada had prepared food for the children—a sign of her culinary confidence. Dr. Maarten thanked the villagers for awakening in his wife a talent she didn't know she had.

The ongoing celebration occasioned the introduction of Karikari's newest acquisition, a gramophone, which now supplied the music of Onyina Guitar Band. Dr. Maarten now beckoned Xada to her feet. They crossed the middle of the dance floor to the many dishes that had been prepared. All eyes trained on them, Adwoa Brago escorted them back to their seats. She asked what they wanted and brought jollof rice. There would be more food to follow because the couple didn't have just one favorite food, which had informed Adwoa Brago's choice of meals to prepare.

The stars were frugal, so lanterns were set out. A bonfire was started inside a circle, around which the villagers were seated. While some ate, others danced. Gyambibi was stretched out on a bench, his head on his mother's lap, asleep.

Though the sun had receded, its heat had stayed behind. Mawuli, who had entered the dance floor in a singlet, was sweaty, and his soaked singlet clung to him. That got his wide-eyed wife, Daavi, and daughter, Jeefa, on their feet, for they hadn't seen him dance in public since he had embarrassed them at a funeral. Generally, Mawuli wasn't predisposed to eccentricity, but disinhibited by alcohol, he danced as wildly as his drunken feet would let him. He didn't seem tired as he went around the bonfire. Dr. Maarten thought the dance was exciting and placed himself in Mawuli's path to more laughter. He moved before Mawuli could collide with him. Mawuli didn't stop, as if he hadn't noticed the botanist. Dr. Maarten followed his posture with his eyes, then assumed the same and started to move wildly. Mawuli stopped and gave him a quick lesson. Dr. Maarten followed him around the bonfire, dancing with such wild imprecision that one would think his feet were foreign to the ground. His feet were out of place, but, like an injured bird, alcohol kept his feet on the dance floor while he flapped his arms, looking to Mawuli.

All the laughter woke Gyambibi. After watching Mawuli and Dr. Maarten, he joined them around the bonfire, at which time Dr. Maarten's achy feet sent him back to his seat. All clapped for Gyambibi as he kept pace with Mawuli, then stopped intermittently and twirled. He fell with a thud. Minute objects floated around him, and he fell again when he attempted to stand. His mother helped him to his feet, took him off the dance floor, and sat him next to her.

Dr. Maarten was also seated and having his second round of food: fufu and palm-nut soup served with smoked catfish. He drank raffia wine. Xada had rice and chicken stew, opting for ntunkum to drink. The villagers continued to dance while music thundered into the night sky. A cold, howling breeze diluted the heat, encouraging dance around the bonfire. Finally, the linguist beckoned Yaw and Preprah to halt the music; Chief would address the departing couple.

"We've gathered here tonight to celebrate our sister and brother, our daughter and son. They've been with us for many years. It seems so short a time. I remember how nervous they were when they first appeared. Today they talk and laugh with me. And the marvel of it, they do it in Twi. They're as much a part of this village as we are. This is their home, though they've chosen to leave for the land of their birth. That's understandable, for home is where one has a psychic and emotional connection. Home is where the heart finds happiness. Home is where the homeless long to go. Home is what you don't forget, even when you've forgotten everything. Home is where you go when the entire world deserts you. Yes, this is their home, but so is Maastricht. I hope you'll pave the way for us to visit you. I speak for myself when I say that every eye should see the Netherlands before death. We've learned from Xada and, equally so, from Dr. Maarten. They've learned from us too. Who knew Xada could cook? Not me, not you—and not even her husband. She had the talent all this time, unknown to her. That talent was awakened here on our land. We have all enjoyed her cooking. We'll miss your presence and even more so the children, who have grown accustomed to your good cooking. Our message to you tonight, in the hearing of God and our ancestors, is don't forget us. We desire this one thing: that you come back from time to time, not as researchers, but as people visiting your distant relatives in the commonwealth of humanity. *Mo nnante yie, mo nnante yie ooo ooo,*" he concluded, words the villagers loudly echoed—safe journey.

Chief presented kente cloth to the couple. The women also presented beaded jewelry, carvings, fertility dolls, and traditional clothes made from dumas and tie-dyed prints. The queen presented Xada with a gold necklace, which the villagers recognized had been handed down from previous queens for hundreds of years. That the villagers approved of the gesture attested to how fond they were of the couple. Chief's wife had a separate gift for the couple.

Danfo was seated with Mawuli and Karikari. Being a cripple, Uncle Salifu had a bench to himself, next to Karikari. He chose to stretch out on it rather than sit. Gyambibi placed himself among them, interrupting their conversations. Karikari looked at his son and hoped he would leave them alone. Uncle Salifu beckoned him to sit beside him, and Gyambibi appeared as if he didn't hear.

Danfo watched his wife from the corner of his eye and saw Esi Eluwah laughing, slapping her thigh. Danfo shook his head. How did he end up with her as his wife? This was a question he had asked for two decades. Their marriage had produced one son, Preprah, who tore the parents apart rather than bring them together. And it was no fault of Preprah's. He was a disappointment to his father on many fronts—being born left-handed, his nonexistent intelligence, and even the way he looked. Danfo shook his head, looking at his son standing next to Yaw. Danfo muttered something when his gaze swung from his son back to his wife. He was living with a wife and a son—neither of whom he wanted to be associated with him. He shook his head for the third time and looked at his friends beside him. He had something to share and wouldn't want Gyambibi to hear it.

"All that dancing is sure to make you thirsty. Here." Danfo offered Gyambibi a drink. "Go sit with your mother. You're not old enough to place yourself in the orbit of conversing men." He pointed to the other side of the bonfire, where Agnes sat. His wife was seated there too. Gyambibi waddled off, drinking the beverage.

Everyone stared at the dancers. Between their feet stomps, a dust cloud formed a whirlwind around the bonfire. A flare of the bonfire blew shadows elsewhere, exposing what was in Gyambibi's line of view: his father and Danfo talking. The wind blew the flare in another direction. In the intervening light, Gyambibi saw Jeefa walking toward where he and his mother were seated. The dancing grew louder. Xada peeled away from Dr. Maarten, who struggled to convince her to return to the dance floor. The wind blew the flare elsewhere and held it still. The sway of the flare revealed a nonhuman presence over thirty feet tall. Its posture was human, but it wasn't human. Its many feet were fused together, merging with its trunk, above which were many limbs sashaying in the wind. The limbs branched out further and further. They seemed like braids but pointed outward and didn't drape loosely like human braids. Its skin, every part of it, was cracked like clay exposed to the desert sun. The wide-eyed Gyambibi, his heart palpitating with fear he had never known, wondered if this was all there was to see of this creature or whether the rest of it was secreted behind the darkness.

Gyambibi's vision cleared a little, and he made out Agya Kobi in front of the tree. No, he was *in* the tree. More likely, Agya Kobi was merging in and out of the tree. He was shape-shifting. The rumors were true. Agya Kobi zoomed in and out of the tree; his head had tentacles coming out of it. While the rest of him remained in place, his head elongated and stopped over the bonfire, causing Gyambibi to almost jump out of his seat. Another thought assured him: maybe this was just the ill effects of falling and hitting his head. But then, as he continued to watch, Agya Kobi's head retreated from the bonfire. His neck elongated toward where Karikari, Uncle Salifu, Mawuli, and Danfo were sitting. It stopped midstream because Preacher was in the way. The head tried to go over Preacher but ran into an invisible wall. Gyambibi almost screamed, promptly placing a hand over his mouth, when Agya Kobi's neck elongated upward, slithered in the wind while gaining height, slithering higher and higher as the festal ambiance thickened, then arched downward and descended sharply on the other side of Preacher, with Agya Kobi's head stopping just above where his father and friends were, listening in. Herein was confirmed for Gyambibi another rumor: Agya Kobi was within reach of every villager, whether behind mud walls, concrete walls, in the river, or on the farm. Even a mosquito buzzing in one's ear, a housefly buzzing over one's food could be him.

The dancing and excitement grew, stirring the bonfire and sending flakes of embers into the air. The embers didn't die out but glowed brighter and bigger as they gained height. Floods of embers hovered above the village to the farthest reaches of the starless horizon. Beyond that was a heavy, dark mist, darker than the night sky, its exterior waving in the wind. Gyambibi saw many shades of black that he had never seen before in this pitch-blackness. Goosebumps covered his skin as he wondered how this could be. The heavens held the impression of a feathery dirigible into which the embers collected. He shifted in his seat as he mulled the spectacle. He watched as the embers rose into the dark mist while new ones formed in a continuous, fiery display. The more intently he looked, the more transparent the bonfire became until he could see through it to the other side, where Yaw and Preprah sat in front of a tree. Gradually his eyes, conscripted by some dark power, made it up the tree. He couldn't look away when he tried. As he kept looking, in the moving shadows of dancers and swaying leaves, he saw the silhouette of a bird. Finally, he was able to break away. He looked at his mother to his right and Jeefa to his left, but the festal dance consumed their attention. The air was thick with heat, but suddenly, the air around him became icy. The peculiar cold rubbed against his skin.

Meanwhile, a horned owl landed on one of the bloated embers and rode it toward him, its beak open wide. Gyambibi, again, looked at his mother and Jeefa. In a panic, he thought the bird would swoop down and swallow him. Convinced no one was seeing what he was seeing, he moved closer to his mother, trembling, and watched as the bird flew over him. His mother asked if all was well. He was silent because if exposed to such spectacles, one must be cautious talking about it. So he kept to himself as the visions continued. His mother bent him toward her until his head was on her left thigh. She unfurled her cloth and spread the edge over him. Jeefa moved closer and put her arm on his legs.

Xada was on her second serving of ntunkum when a mob of women whisked her to the dance floor. Imitating the women, she attempted to swing her hips and shuffle her feet while mimicking their fluid hand gestures. Yet her movements were guarded, rigid—her hips swung blandly. Wobbling on drunken feet, Dr. Maarten waved two fingers over Xada to encourage her to loosen up. His mindless eyes peeled away from Xada's discomfort. A short, bulky man in Chief's circle, the linguist, managed to whisper a private message to Dr. Maarten. After that, Chief departed.

Gyambibi awoke from his false sleep to the loud sound of music. His mother was pressing a fifty-pesewa coin against the swelling on his forehead, which he sustained when he fell on the dance floor. He cringed with pain and pried her hand away.

Gyambibi looked at the bonfire. It was now a transparent glow, not anchored to anything. Observing this against the charred sky astonished him. A fog of confusion overtook him; his body started to shiver and perspire with a fear he didn't know he had. It wasn't just cool; a mysterious breeze had stolen into the night. Sensing his sporadic, jumpy movements, his mother again asked if he was all right. He didn't hear her, though he thought he heard something. He was asleep, yet he wasn't. Everything he was looking at was the content of a dream—or a nightmare—except it wasn't. It was intense darkness, the darkness one saw at night or felt in the day, a darkness that never went away. He had a glimpse of what an adult would dare not comment on in Enkoho, what the elderly could only whisper of in coded verbiage.

The dancing continued late into the night: girls in tie-dyed shifts and women in blouses and wrappers danced and inflamed the bonfire. Boys frolicked among girls.

Gyambibi had turned away from his mother, who still tried to press a coin against his forehead. Now his head was propped on Jeefa's lap. Though they were of the same age bracket, Jeefa placed her arms around him with a mother's caring embrace. Gyambibi's paternal grandfather had had a reputation with women. His mother would only look at her son and could imagine girls flocking to him. She shook her head while visions of dark shapes and faces courted Gyambibi.

Chapter

4

*G*yambibi squatted by the river, catching tadpoles and re-
leasing them. He was waiting for Moro at their meeting
place. Visions of the previous night weighed on him because
he couldn't make sense of them; he didn't know why they had
come. Neither did he have the desire to seek anyone's perspective except Moro's. He dipped his hand in the water and moved
it from side to side. The sound it made kept him company.
Then footsteps rose above the noise and alerted him to Moro's
approach, hauling a bicycle beside him.

"You took your stepfather's bicycle? How's he going to get
anywhere?"

"School starts next month for me, and he and my mother went
to the market to shop. I'll be leaving for the Northern Region
next month," Moro said.

"This is your surprise?" Gyambibi asked.

"We can ride it. You don't like it?"

"Have you ridden one before?"

"No."

"You don't think riding a bicycle for adults is dangerous?"

"I'll learn first, and you go after me. You can sit on the back platform while I ride."

"Where did you get these!?"

"I made them."

"I like them."

Moro leaned the bicycle against a tree, and Gyambibi dropped some stones into the basket mounted on the back platform. Moro reached into the basket and fetched a slingshot for his friend. The two, each with a slingshot in hand, walked about. Gyambibi wanted to see who could hurl a stone the farthest. Moro took up the challenge. Gyambibi strung the slingshot a few times and flung a stone first; Moro said his went farther. They walked around to recover the projectiles, which didn't have distinctive marks. They walked along the river and throughout the vicinity without finding their stones. Seeing ripe pawpaw, Moro flung a stone at its stalk. His next attempt tore off the flesh of the pawpaw. Gyambibi's next shot carved out the middle flesh and fell it off the stalk. Another pawpaw was ripe on the other side of the tree. Moro used a stick to pluck it. They washed the fruit in the river and tore it open. Moro took his half and scooped out the seeds. Gyambibi shot stone pebbles into the river.

Unable to bring up the previous night's visions, Gyambibi continued to shoot stones into the river. Instead, he shared that Jeefa said Kofi Nsenkyire had been to their house to share the news that an American girl her age would be coming to the village in a week. Jeefa was excited. The girl's mother was no stranger to the village, having been coming there for several years. Her daughter was Jeefa's pen pal. In her excitement, Jeefa had asked her parents for space in their meager hut for her American friend. Moro, however, wasn't interested in the subject, so Gyambibi stopped talking about it. The two continued walking about the bush. Moro was curious Gyambibi still hadn't explained why they were meeting. It couldn't be about the American girl visiting the village; he could have told him that elsewhere. He shot a pebble into the air, and Gyambibi did the same.

As they walked, they heard the grunts of someone working on a farm. They got closer and saw Agya Kobi; he stopped and looked at them too. Moro couldn't run, for Gyambibi had told him that he didn't want the old man to know they feared him. Gyambibi knew Moro was fearful of the old man because, although Moro came to the village only on school vacations, he had succumbed to rumors about the old man—rumors that had existed before he and Gyambibi were born. Gyambibi wanted to know if what was said about Agya Kobi carried any truth. Adwoa Brago appeared and inquired about their parents, after which she went about her work and left them with Agya Kobi. Seeing him close up, the fact that Gyambibi had seen the man shape-shift into a tree and back into a man the previous night didn't daunt him now. There was an unexplainable conundrum in his mind: the actuality of Agya Kobi's shape-shifting evil on the one hand and his innocuous presence on the other. In the daylight psyche of Gyambibi, the latter overrode the former. In fact, Gyambibi sported a renewed excitement in the chance encounter with the elder. He started a conversation. Moro hid his fear with a stick in hand, piddling around nervously. Adwoa Brago was nearby; this man wouldn't harm them, he assured himself. The old man, as some attested, could read minds, so Moro didn't want to ruin Gyambibi's plans. He dropped the stick. He would go and talk to Adwoa Brago a little but keep a close eye on his friend, ready to rescue him with the stick if it came to that.

Agya Kobi watched Gyambibi, who simply said, "Agya Kobi."

"You're here, I see."

"Am I still your friend?" Gyambibi asked.

"Was I ever your friend?" The man spoke without emotion; one could feel no difference in how he talked to a child or an adult—a serious man who spoke what he meant.

"Yes," Gyambibi replied.

The elder said nothing. Gyambibi engaged him nevertheless, even fetching him water. The old man thanked him, but his attitude didn't change. He always wore the same disposition.

Chapter

5

*T*he American girl's name was Helena. Happy to see a white person their age, the village boys and girls flanked her wanting to play. She was delighted to be in their midst; one would think she had grown up with them. With a stick in hand, she drew a circle in the sand and numbered the arcs according to the number of participants in the game. She placed five of the participants on the numbered arcs. She instructed them to focus on the middle of the circle. Clutching a cloth, she blurted out the signal.

"Antoakyire!"

"Yaaay, yay," the participants responded.

"Obiba!" she yelled.

"Yaaaay, yay."

"Wobesu!"

"Yaaaay, yay," the participants returned.

Helena circled the children while gauging them.

"Don't cheat!" she told Jeefa.

She told them to keep their focus on the middle of the circle. Another *"antoakyire,"* and she dropped the cloth behind Moro, who hadn't noticed. When Helena circled back to him, she gently slapped him on the head and upper back. The group joined in. Her mother and her friend, Kofi Nsenkyire, both smiled.

"Enkoho is what she needs," Mr. Nsenkyire said.

After complaining to her mother that the village didn't feel right, Helena adapted well. Enkoho was thick with something she couldn't see or touch, nothing like the drag of walking through water. Still, it was the closest thing she could come up with to explain the unexplainable. That was her mother's observation as well, who said it would go away with time. Elizabeth was right and couldn't believe the change she now saw in her daughter.

Moro took the cloth and circled the group while Helena took his place in the circle. Mr. Nsenkyire couldn't stop talking about the shy, withdrawn girl he saw yesteryear. Neither could her mother.

Two years ago, Elizabeth received notice to talk to Helena's school principal in Chicago. Helena had become withdrawn after the death of her father. She didn't respond to her teachers and ignored her friends. A psychologist's consult did no good. Helena skipped classes and was isolated in the school cafeteria. Moreover, she told her mother she didn't want to go to school anymore because she didn't belong there. Alternative schooling was suggested. Then, as an afterthought, her mother got her Jeefa as a pen pal. The suggestion came up during one of her visits to the country as a volunteer with the Christian Medical Mission when she had discussed Helena with Mr. Nsenkyire and his wife. Elizabeth started noticing subtle positive changes once Helena started corresponding with Jeefa. For the first time, Helena was interested in something: she asked questions about life in Ghana. When some of Elizabeth's answers lacked specifics, she thought a trip to see Jeefa might help. Their first visit proved right; this year cemented it. Helena hadn't been the same since.

It was July, the middle of the rainy season. The weather soon gave way to paroxysmal drizzle, so the youngsters dispersed. Jeefa left with Helena, holding hands and galloping about. Helena told Jeefa she wanted her hair braided like hers. Jeefa didn't know how to do it, but her mother did. Helena also wanted to know when they would sit by the fire and listen to more tales of *Kwaku Ananse*. Jeefa said Danfo had planned a session for that Friday.

At nine years old, Gyambibi was changing. His parents saw the change; sometimes he laughed when nothing was funny and was easily excitable. With Dr. Maarten and Xada gone and his father's constant warning that he stay away from Agya Kobi, Gyambibi found the mature company he craved in his brother. Problem: Yaw wanted him to stay with children his own age. But Gyambibi had a plan to be with his brother: the Tissot watch. He spoke to Moro and then got a little money from his mother for a new battery. They took the watch to his brother. Preprah was there, too, discussing Efia with Yaw. Though Efia had had an illegitimate child a tad younger than Gyambibi, Preprah hadn't given up pursuing her. In fact, he was still plotting and colluding with Yaw on other means to endear himself to Efia, who still avoided Preprah.

"Meet me there tonight," Yaw said, pointing to the baobab.

"You know everything about rheumatism," Preprah said.

"The word is *romanticism*. Meet me there tonight, and we'll take care of it."

"And where are you going?" Gyambibi asked and held on to Preprah, who was emerging from their porch. Yaw was following behind. He showed them the watch. Yaw took the bait and arrived at an idea: Preprah should buy it as part of their plans for that night. Gyambibi got their attention and, at least on that night, was part of their inner workings. Yaw and Preprah knew they could use Gyambibi to feed them information about the whereabouts of Efia under the guise of going to see her son, Asamoah.

Preprah returned in the evening, anxious to hear Yaw's plan for Efia. He found him brandishing some vegetation.

"What are these?" Preprah asked.

"Your ticket to Efia's heart," Yaw replied.

"Some strange idea you've got here. How do I get a girl who doesn't like me to cook for me in order to like me?" Preprah asked, baffled.

"These aren't for cooking; they're to help you win her heart."

"With...plants?"

"With these flowers, yes!" Yaw said.

"Where did you learn this?"

"Dr. Maarten. Didn't you ever see him giving flowers to Xada now and then?"

"I think so."

"Well, he did."

"Will Efia get it?" Preprah asked.

"Explain it to her."

"How will I win her heart by explaining this strange idea to her?"

"It will show her you're willing to do anything to win her heart."

"Hmmm."

"Start with a dandelion and finish off with a dandelion. If this doesn't work, nothing will."

Preprah was silent. Why did he have to go to such extremes to get a woman he liked? He had pursued Efia for many years, and her son reminded him of how long he had pursued her without success. He hurt inside; no girl approximated his romantic interests.

Preprah wasn't idle in his fight for romance: Days ago, he was chased out of a compound with a machete for making a pass at a man's thirteen-year-old daughter. Yaw explained to Preprah that the girl's father was right to be enraged because she was underage. Preprah never quite understood when he was chased out of the same compound this morning, this time with a hunting rifle, for suggesting that the man allow him to add his eight-year-old daughter to the mix because the combined age of his daughters would now be close to Preprah's. This time, Yaw couldn't explain the math well enough to make Preprah understand his own stupid logic. Preprah felt his friend was hiding the truth from him.

"Am I ugly?" he asked Yaw.

Yaw looked at him, wondering why he had conjured up such a ridiculous question. "Are you supposed to look good? Is any man supposed to look good?"

Preprah didn't know how to answer. Yaw rested an arm on his shoulder and assured him, "Looking good is natural for women. God created them beautifully. Men were created men; that is all."

"But girls flock to you. I get close to them when we're together; otherwise, they avoid me."

"That isn't it. You see, I have confidence, and girls like confidence."

"How do I gain confidence? Look, forget that. What is it about dandelion that made you select it?"

"It grows everywhere. You don't have to go deep into the forest to find one. If you want to get into a woman's good graces in the throes of a disagreement, you don't want to go wandering in the forest looking for a particular flower, right?"

"Are dandelions not weeds? Did Dr. Maarten ever give one to Xada?" Preprah asked.

"Not that I know of. Look, the man worked with plants. That's what he did for a living, so he'd know more about these things. That's beside the point. He had a preference for flowers. You have yours and don't have to do what he did. A flower is a flower."

Preprah thought long and hard but couldn't grasp the idea.

"If I give Efia a dandelion because it grows everywhere, doesn't that imply she holds no value to me?"

"Air hasn't lost value though it's everywhere. To begin with, is it not embarrassing enough that you have to give her something as meaningless as flowers anyway?"

"Right. So doesn't that defeat the purpose?"

"Not at all. The fact that you're willing to adopt such a meaningless custom would have the opposite effect. It tells her you'd go to great lengths to win her heart."

Preprah thought about it, not that he was bright enough to grasp the pitfalls of what his friend was suggesting. The idea seemed too silly not to make sense.

"Master of rheumatism! Indeed, you know what you're talking about! I like your idea of flowers, but it would be better to give her the whole plant," he said, finally embracing the idea.

"*Romanticism,*" Yaw reiterated.

Preprah's father, Danfo, had baked a poor self-image in him. Preprah's meager intelligence, unimpressive appearance, and the fact that he was left-handed were all disappointments to him. Danfo's hatred of left-handed people was only second to his problems with Agya Kobi and women. No famous person in history was left-handed, he would say to his son. Among the favorite subjects of this assertion, he would tell the villagers that Jesus was right-handed because, as evidenced in the Bible, Jesus would use his dominant right hand to send people to heaven; His left hand would direct His enemies to hell. Preprah's left-handedness conferred failure on his future—a point amply supported by the Bible. Danfo treated Preprah unlike any of Preprah's peers.

"If all goes well, I marry her and get to see my first vanjema," Preprah said.

When Yaw tried to correct his friend, nothing came out: the weight of the female's sacred anatomy was too heavy for his tongue.

Yaw wished someone would mistreat Danfo as he mistreated Preprah. Preprah's mother, Esi Eluwah, was gifted with her hands; however, Christianity and a desire to show herself as a woman of faith stood in her way of beating her husband at will. Her time came when her husband forgot and took his nonsense to her. She saw to it that none of the opportunities went to waste.

Friday crawled and dithered but eventually came around. The children were seated in a circle with Danfo at the head. Helena adjusted herself next to Jeefa, giggling. She was herself in the village, as she should have been in America. Most days in Enkoho, Helena went home late, having to be pried away from her friends. When she woke in the morning, her mother would find her with Jeefa. She went to the farms and bathed in the river with Jeefa. She ate on the farms; she brought food home from the farms. She had become so fond of the village that her mother arranged for her to sleep with Jeefa's family while she went about her medical-missionary duties in Bolgatanga. She carried no concerns because the village accepted her as one of its own and would care for Helena in her absence.

So far, it appeared that Elizabeth and Helena were free of the mystery inhabiting Enkoho. Perhaps this was because they hadn't stayed there for extended periods for the land to claim them. Or perhaps they were oblivious to the mystery because America and her distorted sense of metaphysical realities still clung to them.

At the storytelling session, Moro gave Gyambibi three cedis for the battery for the Tissot watch, as well as his equal share of the windfall. Preprah had bought the watch for nineteen cedis; a new battery was all it needed to function. Moro was excited sitting next to his friend. They were the least frightened of the stories, so they sat on the edge of darkness when the circle bulged. Sometimes the stories dragged late into the night and became scary, so sitting in the middle gave the listeners a feeling of protection from images conjured by flickering lanterns.

Danfo had promised an installment of Kwaku Ananse in creation. However, having just walked out of a fight with his wife, Esi Eluwah, he had a slight change of plans: the children needed to learn about the evils of women. He incorporated the biblical account of creation as a backdrop for his own version of humankind's beginning, veering from history to local tales, to Apocrypha, and back to history. It was no storytelling but a gleeful vent after losing a fistfight.

"What about the snake that spoke to Eve?" Asamoah asked.

"What snake?" Danfo retorted.

"The snake that told Eve to eat the forbidden fruit."

"Ahhhh!" He sighed. "It was no snake."

"There was no snake?" Asamoah asked.

"The sort of nonsense that perverts a child's ears! Stay away from tall tales like that so you don't grow up thinking God's a misguided hermaphrodite. No, there was no snake. God's ventures were all a success until he created the woman. You see, God never recovered from that because He knew He was a failure from that point forward."

"What was it then, the snake?" Asamoah persisted.

"Birds teach us to fly; snakes teach us about women. The snake was Adam's first wife, Lilith, who planned with Eve to cause Adam's downfall. Lilith rolls off the tongue like a snake's hiss. Snake! No other animal describes women better," Danfo lectured.

An abject disappointment for Helena. Jeefa could feel her friend's yearning for real Kwaku Ananse tales of the type she couldn't get enough of when she visited last year. Jeefa looked for signs that Danfo would revert to Ananse stories but was disappointed to see him still drumming into Asamoah that the snake in the creation story of the Bible represented a woman. Jeefa gave up, but not before an idea came to her. She whispered something to Gyambibi, who agreed to take up the task. The group broke in two. Part of the children left with Gyambibi, while the others stayed behind.

Helena was in the group that broke away with Gyambibi, who took the group to his front porch. When the storytelling began, with Gyambibi doing the narration, Helena had an extended peek into the person of Gyambibi. She was captivated by his presence, eloquence, confidence, skill with word usage, and intellect without a trace of arrogance. She couldn't tell who told better Ananse stories between this boy about her age and Danfo. Had Agnes not broken up the storytelling to have

Gyambibi inside to finish his dinner, Helena would have preferred it went on for much longer.

"I like him. Smart. Cute. Handsome. I like him," Helena kept whispering to Jeefa as they walked back to the other group, still listening to Danfo. Jeefa laughed at her remark.

"Snakes don't talk back; women do," Danfo said. "We know it was a woman because Adam was ruined after that."

Chapter

The Heart of Dandelion

The dandelions were supposed to get to Efia through Moro. That was the plan. But Efia wasn't home, so Moro gave the plants to her grandmother, Adwoa Brago, who had sent Efia to the farm to fetch spinach for their evening meal. Efia still hadn't returned after an hour. Waiting by her fiery coals burning away, Adwoa Brago read the note attached to the dandelions. Yaw, who had left for Accra with his father, had previously agreed on a plan with Preprah. To address the recipient of the dandelions, as Yaw had suggested, the initial flurry of words entering Preprah's mind—for, fore, and four—confused him in terms of spelling and linguistic application. At the same time, two other words came to him: to and from. Knowing only the spelling of these English words, he discarded for, fore, and four in case their incorrect presence on the note added another layer of confusion to the plants, whose esoteric love message, without his explanation, Efia might find confusing, even insulting. Preprah's left-handed brain addressed the flowers: *from Efia.* Adwoa Brago could only interpret it for what it was: that Efia had foolishly fetched these weeds instead of spinach because she was distracted. Worse, in a conspicuous flout of her authority, Efia had had it delivered by Moro with a message that they originated from her. Adwoa Brago felt Efia was preoccupied with someone, likely a love interest, and likely Preprah. Overcome by a spastic rage, she flew to Preprah's house, where she predictably met his absence. With him and Efia missing, she concluded they were together. Later that evening, Agya Kobi and Adwoa Brago brought it up with Danfo and Esi Eluwah, with Preprah present. Of course, Agya Kobi recognized that the writing wasn't his granddaughter's and felt the need to discuss this issue based on the subtext of the plants and note: an expression of love interest using a *coded* message.

After the confrontation, Preprah would be thrown into a meeting with his father's fists because his foolishness had invited the devil, Agya Kobi, to their house.

Weeks later, after Yaw returned from Accra and heard of Preprah's disaster, he devised a new plan, still trying to win Efia's heart for Preprah. Yaw invited Efia to his house under the pretext of helping her with schoolwork, as Karikari and Agnes were conveniently out of town. And so was Uncle Salifu, who was in Kumasi with Mawuli. Through Gyambibi and Moro, Efia received the signal to come to the house. Yaw had suggested that Preprah prove his love for her through music. Efia would naturally be excited to see the gramophone close up. Yaw would watch through an inside window in a corridor between Uncle Salifu's bedroom and the living room. Under Yaw's direction, Preprah had rehearsed for weeks using Jeefa as a stand-in for Efia. Now the day was here to act out what he had learned.

Preprah sat confidently with a flair for the debonair afforded him by his outfit: a pair of corduroy shorts and a long-sleeve crimplene shirt with the left sleeve rolled up to his elbow to show off his Tissot watch. He didn't bother rolling up the other sleeve because he wanted Efia's eyes drawn to the watch. In line with his thinking, he had objected to closing the window curtains because he wanted more light shining on his appearance, from his chemically treated hair to his mauve socks and fieldwork boots. With the confidence to dress as he liked, he yielded to Yaw's advice not to wear his brand-name shirt inside out, as he normally did. The long-sleeved shirt stood in for his usual T-shirt. Beads of sweat mingled with pimples on his shea-butter-painted forehead. Growing confidence was on his face. He avoided Karikari's fragrance that Yaw had offered because it hadn't made sense to him. He needed a female fragrance to attract a female, as a male fragrance would only appeal to males. So he was drenched in the aroma of Agnes's perfume, emptying part of the bottle into the bucket of water he bathed with and dabbed the remaining all over himself. The occasion was special; he had to impress Efia.

The sight of the gramophone disarmed Efia's disdain for Preprah. She was as impressed with the machine. Preprah turned it on, walked a few feet away, and leafed through the stacked LPs, blowing on the one they had preselected, as Yaw had instructed. He heard Yaw's admonition: "Do not improvise! Do not. If you forget anything, say you have to go to the bathroom. Do not improvise!"

He placed side two of the LP on the gramophone and moved the stylus over the grooves. However, in his nervousness, he dropped it, making a loud, scratching thud. Quickly, he replaced it and stepped back, now afraid of having broken the gramophone, forgetting the script, and looking the fool in front of Efia. He forgot everything they had planned but approached the gramophone carefully as Efia watched excitedly.

"Are you all right?" she asked, as his nervousness broke through.

"Of course, my dear. You're here with me."

Nonetheless, a spontaneous flood of sweat poured from Preprah; he was drowning in anxiety. The sofa and loveseat seemed to have traded places. A dense fog stood where the curtains used to be, and the paneled walls were missing their warmth. Which window was Yaw standing behind again? The room slowly spun. He stood firm, digging his toe into the boots he had gotten back from Efia, trying to secure his feet to the ground.

"Are you all right?" she repeated.

"I am. Wait patiently for what I have in store for you. Only for you would I do this."

The world would soon hear a song weeks in the making. It was written from scratch and rewritten—all words scrapped and revised many times until it became the perfection he and Yaw aimed for. It would be sung over the solemn instrumental of "Air in G." While the room spun, Preprah searched for the window behind which Yaw stood. He couldn't see his hand behind the parted curtain; he had no way of seeing Yaw's signals. He gave up and simply lifted the stylus by barely touching it. As Efia's excitement piqued, he paused to recall Yaw's direction. As he slowly began the song, he was to engage Efia with an apology and other romantic pleasantries. Luck led him a few steps but soon left him alone: his discordant voice and nervousness made the song unrecognizable. Yaw became uneasy when he saw his friend abandon his predetermined place on the arm of the chair Efia sat in and erupted in emotional hand choreography and epileptic leg movements. His hand gestures were dominated by his left hand, but he must have heard his father's voice in his head, for they stopped abruptly. His right hand took over. He reminded himself that he was born left-handed but couldn't live under his father's roof the way he was born. He clutched his belly many times with grimaces that only he must have thought resembled affectionate gestures. Watching from the other end, it looked like Preprah was gesturing that something was pulling his intestines out.

Yaw broke out in a nervous itch, scratching himself sore, watching his friend improvise what they had carefully planned. He felt the discomfort of watching his friend commit romantic suicide. Preprah's handling of the first verse wasn't hopeful, but Yaw held out hope. His ears couldn't turn away from the rendering of the song. The itching of his soles sent him on a trotting tirade with the concrete floor. There were still moments in the song, he thought, for Preprah to redeem his love message.

When he was finished singing, Efia had an awkward feeling that Preprah wanted nothing to do with her. Yaw was frustrated with Preprah's mishandling of the refrain because he had rehearsed it more than the other parts. More puzzling, Preprah's version was missing the three "love" words. Later, Yaw admitted to his friend that all hope was lost. Preprah arranged to have Efia come back so he could sing for her again. However, reports of an attempted coup in Accra brought the villagers to the house during the evening news at the very time he had arranged a do-over. Efia left the house degraded and insulted, her disdain for Preprah's romantic advances forever obituarized in her memory.

Danfo was embarrassed by his son's lack of intelligence. He had denied paternity of him on that ground when he was about four years old. Nonetheless, what Preprah lacked in intelligence, he made up in perseverance. That removed him from the bottom of his class, but not by much. Yaw felt sorry for his friend, who craved his father's acceptance but struggled against life in all directions.

When it came to Efia, Preprah persisted. Weeks went by, then months. At about the seventh month, Preprah had gone over why Efia didn't like him. He had been nice, kind, and generous—which had gotten him nowhere near her. An idea came to him, a risky one that would be rewarding if his instincts were right. He stayed up all night, dusting it off and polishing it. This was it. He stayed in his room for two good days, entertaining only food and insomnia. He turned the idea in his mind a few more times and told Yaw about it on the fourth day.

"You said women were created beautifully, and men were created men," Preprah began.

"Right."

"So if I have confidence like you, as I now have, there's no reason a woman should pick you over me."

"In essence."

"So there's no reason Efia shouldn't like me except for how I've approached this romantic thing."

"Yeah."

Preprah was excited about the way the conversation was going.

"Nice, generous, kind, pleasant—I've been everything but a monster, and it took me nowhere. After all these years, we still don't know who Asamoah's father is. I think Efia harbors an attraction for ruthless monsters. It's an enticing theory I'm going to explore."

Yaw scratched his temple. Preprah explained what had given rise to his logic: women like fighters, rebels. Women like men who would fight for them, men who would remove obstacles impeding their happiness. Agya Kobi stood in Efia's way. Preprah's plan: he would destroy the old man's farm. The shock would send the man to his grave. And then he would win Efia over.

"Where would you get a crazy idea like that?" Yaw asked.

"You," Preprah replied.

"Me?" Yaw's heart caught in his throat.

"You know more about America than anyone here, even though no one here has stepped foot there. Were you not the one who told me some American women are attracted to criminals, serial killers, prisoners?"

Yaw quavered.

"If women are the same everywhere, as my dad says, then some of our women may share the same diseased attraction for ruthless monsters. I've given it serious thought. Efia might be one such woman."

This wasn't the usual false bravado of Preprah. It was pure, though dark confidence, something Yaw had never seen in Preprah until today. The details of his plan: since the entire village hated Agya Kobi, Preprah would have more to gain than to lose by precipitating his death. Heck! He could even come out a hero with Efia in his arms. Yet there were apparent downfalls. For one, Preprah's father, Danfo, openly hated Agya Kobi, so destroying Agya Kobi's farm would undoubtedly bring the men into a face-to-face confrontation. Yes, Preprah acknowledged, but thought of it another way. While his father hated Agya Kobi, a close second was Preprah himself. Thus, if all went well, Preprah claimed he would finally win his father's acceptance, bask in the liberation of the villagers, and celebrate a chance at romance. Efia would get the signal and accept him. This was for the liberation of the entire village, he emphasized.

"That's some crazy idea," Yaw acknowledged.

"An idea is only crazy if it doesn't succeed," Preprah replied.

"What do you do if the elders slap you with the cost of his farm?"

"I don't see the dead coming back to settle a debt, do you?"

Yaw cautioned, "He has relatives. By the way, how can you be certain he will die?"

"The man is old enough to drop dead before we finish talking. Look, after what he went through in Libya, he only survived because he was young. This is different. Destroying his farm will nudge him into the grave. Besides, the elders can't tell me to pay back what I don't have, especially after he's dead. This is for everyone: you, me, everybody. We need liberation!"

"When do you plan to do this? How do you intend to do this?"

"To be determined... Burn down his farm."

Yaw's heart beat faster. "You haven't given much thought to what could go wrong."

"Such as?"

"Well, for one, it rains almost every day. How do you burn soggy plants? Two, if you succeed in burning his farm, you'll probably succeed in burning all the farms, ours included. You realize the man's farm isn't on a moat, right?"

Preprah admitted these potential problems, but they didn't derail him. He tweaked it.

"Fine, I'll take a cutlass to his crops."

"We're talking about fifty acres, at least. That would take weeks, if not months."

"Not if I have determination, my friend."

"How will Efia, Asamoah, and Adwoa Brago survive if you destroy everything?"

Preprah was lost in thought for minutes.

"I won't destroy everything. You think my plan is stupid. Just forget about Efia! Hasn't everyone here, haven't we all, in one way or another, suffered from the man's existence? The village, you, me, everyone stands to benefit from his death."

Preprah couldn't be deterred; confidence led the way. He would hide in Aduman after his scheme and wait for Yaw's word before proceeding.

To his credit, Preprah did much thinking contrary to his perceived intellectual shortcomings. Though he had explicitly said this was for Efia, he had corrected himself by saying that it wasn't so. He made it appear that *all* would benefit from his impending ruthlessness, which would be true in a way, but the thought that went into his scheme hadn't involved much of anyone but himself. Getting Efia to accept him alone wouldn't justify Agya Kobi's death. There was more. What he told Yaw only hinted at his overarching intent to want Agya Kobi dead. Like Yaw, his mother had also assured him that he should have no difficulty finding a woman in the village. That wasn't wholly satisfactory to him. He also wanted his father's assurance but stopped short of involving him because he kept hearing echoes from the past: "If the afterbirth had shown signs of life, I would have brought it home as my son instead of you." Preprah heard these words from his father when he was old enough to understand him. The imagery was revolting and, the point of it, crushing. It had stayed with him through young adulthood, even now, when he sought to indirectly confront the man responsible for him not getting what easily came to others.

When he was old enough to understand the source of everyone's problems in the village, Preprah also learned to place his at the doorstep of Agya Kobi. For several months, mulling why Efia rejected his advances, it came to him that Agya Kobi might be superimposing a revolting image on his person, such as the imagery conjured by his father's words, via the occult. In other words, girls saw a misshapen horror instead of him when they looked at him. The blame for his own father hating him fell at the feet of Agya Kobi. Agya Kobi's death would solve many, if not all, of *his* problems. He had hidden these thoughts from Yaw, for he didn't want his coming act attributed to selfishness. Rather, he wanted his carnage to be seen as the case of The People of Enkoho versus Agya Kobi. Because things said in secret in Enkoho had ways of getting out, it was prudent to keep his real intent to himself in case the old man survived the assault on his farm.

Yaw had a reason to be concerned about this scheme because a silly one had preceded it years prior. Preprah went to anyone he felt was sick and said the village healer had trained him. Because of the secrecy of herbal formulas and training, none doubted him. In fact, the sick saw proof of the curative powers of Preprah's brews, which he said were the same recipes as Healer's, at a fraction of the cost. But relatives and friends of the sick complained that the sick sometimes stared far into space, laughed, and giggled for no reason. Preprah explained that this was evidence of the soul of the sick being happy for the purging of the body of diseases. One day a patient woke up crying for not knowing all these years that goats spoke Koine Greek. The next minute, the patient couldn't find his legs and hands. When one hard slap brought his missing hands and legs into view, the patient asked, "Where did you find them?" Then a violent coughing fit and clutching of his throat followed. When the patient collapsed, Preprah rushed to Healer for cough syrup. Healer uncovered the marijuana scheme in no time. The soiling of his name cost Danfo seven guinea fowls and two goats. Money Preprah earned from the scheme went to Efia while he alone absorbed the head-on collision with his father's fists. Now he risked a repeat.

Hiding behind a tree on Yaa Adubia's farm, Gyambibi mischievously aimed his slingshot at Agya Kobi's lantern. Moro had shot a projectile first but missed, skimming past Adwoa Brago, who flinched and jumped. They laughed.

"Why do you want to do this?" Moro whispered to Gyambibi since the lamp went everywhere with Agya Kobi, day or night. The rumor was that the village was dark because of him; he needed light to see his way. Gyambibi wanted to know what would become of the old man if the Eternal Lamp was extinguished since it was always burning. Gyambibi's shot missed. Adwoa Brago jumped again. She told her husband she suspected a grasscutter burrow nearby. Moro's next shot knocked the lantern onto its side. The old man ran and stood it up before it went out. He topped off the kerosene and held on to it. Gyambibi and Moro slipped away before the elder saw them.

~ ❖ ~

Esi Eluwah and Preacher held an hour-long thanksgiving for an answered prayer. Scraping against the rough edges of aging, Esi Eluwah had given up all hope until Healer confirmed what she had felt for months. This might be her last egg on the verge of bringing a new life into the world, and menopause might be next if this failed.

At home she warmed her soup, which she'd prepared the previous day and hidden from Danfo. Nyamenkum the Gossip helped her prepare fufu to go with the soup. Esi Eluwah sampled the food and was delighted with the outcome. Nyamenkum the Gossip told Esi Eluwah where to find her husband before leaving for home.

Times had changed. In the good old days, Esi Eluwah would feed Danfo his food to endear the news to him. For once upon a time, Danfo held that a man shouldn't feed himself because the role was already assigned to women by Nature. As a child, he understood that a man falls out of the womb onto a woman's breasts. Thus the roles of the sexes concerning feeding were demarcated at birth and shouldn't be lost to time whether a male is teething at a young age or toothless in old age. Being one of fourteen children, and with each child separated from the next by a year, Danfo thanked his stars for being the first-born. As long as his mother kept cranking out children, there was always breast milk. No one knew when his hatred for his mother began. However, he hated his left-handed father because he always sided with his mother on matters involving him. So the seeds of hatred for women and left-handed people might have been sown when his mother cut him off breast milk at eleven.

In the early part of their marriage, to save her own ears, Esi Eluwah's fingers had fed him to atone for the crime of neglect that Danfo kept lobbing at his dead parents. After their first hand-to-hand combat as a married couple, when Danfo had tasted the raw powers of his wife's hands, he asked Esi Elu-wah in a rather unusually calm voice if she had been born a man. She had a son with him, so she disregarded his comment. However, she knew her husband was serious when he returned to the subject, explaining that she might have had a male twin who merged with her in the womb. Danfo didn't say it, but this male twin was evident in her punches. She was just too big and strong to be one person. She was two-in-one—two people merged into one—a discovery Danfo started to spread in En-koho, possibly to explain the one-sided outcome of their fist-fights, though he'd never admitted to losing one. One day, with Esi Eluwah's enraged fingers reaching deep down his throat while feeding him, Danfo choked. He was near death when the villagers' screams brought Healer to the house. Danfo told the elders that Esi Eluwah intended to kill him. Her defense was that her hand was in his throat, but she was saving him by attempting to retrieve stuck food. "Since when did tea stick to men's throats?" Danfo had asked. Nothing came of the charges because he was also known to chew his water, a point his wife raised to make nonsense of his rebuttal. Convinced his wife wanted to kill him for uncovering the truth about her real sex, Danfo had learned to feed himself since. Today, Esi Eluwah was left with no tricks to endear her news to her husband but to do what appealed to him: set the table and leave him alone. She had done the former, but the day would be pointless by obeying the latter.

Esi Eluwah pulled her husband home from the midst of his friends to share the news with him. Danfo's nose took a few turns and landed on the dining table. The soup's temperature and the fufu's texture felt right. He could see parts of the deer he brought home the other day smoked to taste, along with pig feet, tilapia, snails, and uncut okra. The only thing missing was palm wine. By the time he was finished sniffing the aroma, a third of the food was gone. Esi Eluwah thought to start talking before the food was gone and her husband vanished from the house again.

"We are expecting, my husband," she said.

"When did you and I come to expect the same thing?" Danfo asked.

"This time, yes."

"You've come to your senses and decided to leave my house?"

"I'm pregnant, have been pregnant for months. Healer tells me it's a girl," she said before Danfo could ask her for a loan to buy gallons of palm wine to celebrate. A trip to Healer was just about to replace his plans.

"I didn't pray for this. You did. Ask for your God's return address and send this thing back. Woman, have you ever looked at *your* son? Are you sure you want to bring another one of those things into the world and, worst of all, a girl?"

"Send back? Ask God to take back His blessing? What I should rather do is castrate you. Should I?" She grabbed him by the collar, lifted him off the chair, and pushed him against the wall.

"I have seen *your* son, and he's not an anomaly, for you have also had miscarriages and stillbirths in the past, and we got to see what grows inside you. It isn't my womb that's cranking out these Medusas," Danfo said.

Esi Eluwah let go of his throat, clutched her belly, and broke down. Her tears dried up soon enough to see Danfo's brow furrowing with disgust at her or his unborn daughter—or both. Esi Eluwah laid her Bible down and pretended to leave. Then she landed a hard backhand across her husband's head with enough force to shut off both his ears and leave him seeing double. Danfo regained his appetite and hearing days later on the same day Esi Eluwah had a movement of her wrist. Unfortunately, Healer had to discharge both to make room for new patients, with Danfo in a herbal neck wrap and Esi Eluwah in a hand wrap. At home, she cracked his skull again when her wrap came off. Danfo was found on the floor, twitching. Not that they cared for Danfo, but the elders investigated Esi Eluwah for attempted murder. However, they found her hand in the same herbal wrap she was discharged home in, still in pain. They concluded Danfo must have slipped and fallen on his head. The investigation faulted Healer for discharging patients who were not well enough to go home.

Preprah used the commotion to flee the house. The farm was silent when he arrived and waited patiently for Agya Kobi and Adwoa Brago to leave. Convinced the farm was devoid of people, Preprah leaped off a tree, clutching a machete in each hand. Again, he scanned the surroundings to ensure he wouldn't be seen.

Preprah wasted no time cutting down their crops. It felt right to him as he beamed with malignant excitement. His disappointment with life and his father's mistreatment of him found an outlet in the machetes, exacting vengeance. It was *for* Efia or, more importantly, *because* of Efia! Her repeated rejections served as a reminder of all that was wrong with him, for which he held her grandfather responsible. Agya Kobi had to suffer as the cause of Preprah's meager and shameful existence. Agya Kobi needed to be punished because he stood in the way of everyone's happiness. He had to go. His farm had to go.

Preprah's anger flared with each swing of the machetes. Before the blade had dulled, he'd gone through about an acre of the farm, cutting down corn, cocoa, and every crop in his path. His palms ached, and his elbow joint felt like it might dislocate. Holding each machete, he swiped the blades against each other. He smiled at the sparks. He stopped and walked about two hundred yards to Karikari's farm. He helped himself to some of his freshly tapped palm wine, but the last swig didn't go down smoothly because of the consequences if Agya Kobi didn't die. The villagers would be happy about his destruction, but most were too poor to help him pay the price if necessary. It was too late to stop what he had started, and the potential reward was too enticing. He cut his enjoyment short and returned to Agya Kobi's farm, boiling with rage. His right palm teemed with bullae and pain. No one saw him, but he knew *other* eyes were watching—those of faceless darkness. He felt a presence with each swing of the machetes. His carnage would get to the village before he did. He was suddenly overcome by Yaw's observation that perhaps Agya Kobi wouldn't die, and Preprah would be slapped with the cost of his destruction. He was re-thinking his revised plan to cut down so many acres. Paying for a few acres of devastation would be much easier than a third of the farm. With this thought, he buried the machetes in the dirt and ran to Aduman.

Preprah's focus on destroying only crops proved a mistake. He didn't cut down a single dandelion in the acres that saw his destruction. It wasn't tricky for Agya Kobi and Adwoa Brago to connect him to the crime because of his newfound apprecia-tion for dandelions. The devastation kept Agya Kobi in bed for weeks. After that, he petitioned the elders for justice: Preprah was hiding in his parents' house and should be brought out to face them. No, he isn't there, responded Danfo, adding, "You can search my house if you want." The elders disliked Danfo enough to want to use the occasion to exact vengeance. They took the reference to "you" searching the house literally and a direct challenge to Agya Kobi, who they then ordered to go into Danfo's house. After that, it took three days of cleansing by Preacher for Danfo to have any surety that his residence was habitable, although that still wasn't enough. At his hefty expense, the fetish priest-cum-healer was also called to cleanse it for another four days. Even after that, he was afraid to go to his house, though he encouraged his wife to do so.

Even though Aduman was several miles away from Enkoho, when the news got to him, Preprah knew he was close to death at the hands of his father. He left Aduman with no plans to return to Enkoho.

Chapter

7

*B*lank stares, unprovoked laughter, sweating, headaches, and anxiety were all becoming commonplace for Gyambibi. Visions—or hallucinations, in the arrogant perspective of medicine—were an added seriousness. Agnes and Karikari were alarmed; Gyambibi was changing in ways they couldn't grasp. A trip to rural clinics yielded diagnoses as different as the heavens are from the earth. This time, it was an infection of the central nervous system—perhaps *monilial* in origin. They didn't have to know what that was because a regimen of three prescriptions would treat it in two weeks after receiving a one-week course at the clinic. Indeed, his symptoms improved somewhat when he was discharged from the clinic. However, his flesh became sensitive to mosquito bites; throughout the night and in the heat of the day, he felt the stings. He saw no mosquitoes but slapped himself where he felt the stings. It took days to figure out he was allergic to some medicine he was taking. The symptoms reappeared weeks later. Perhaps it was toxic psychosis, another clinic posited. Then the symptoms would disappear for months.

Danfo took the lead role when it came to where Gyambibi sought treatment. Karikari went outside the village but only for business. The village healer handled his medical needs and his family's, so he knew nothing of clinics and hospitals. For Gyambibi's problems, he deferred to Danfo, who was once a taxi driver and knew the surrounding villages well. He took Gyambibi to clinics there but not in clinics and hospitals in the metropolitan cities that could have adequately handled Gyambibi's problems. Medical practitioners in these rural villages where Gyambibi was sent had a mindset that was no different from their auto mechanics. These mechanics could fix any vehicle. One could say repairing a dysfunctional nuclear submarine wasn't outside the purview of their skills. If only one could find a way to haul one to their workshop. One could hear the sales pitch: they're vehicles, too, but with a preference for water. That was the mindset of the clinics where Gyambibi was sent. They wouldn't lose money by referring a patient to a more capable and better-equipped facility, no matter how complex one's medical problems were. And in the event of a patient's death, the explanation was that death was a matter decided by God and not man. Gyambibi's problems persisted, waxing and waning with no discernible cause.

At eleven years old, Gyambibi was still pesky with a sharp mind for independence. He and his gang of Moro, Asiedu, and Asamoah hunted and ate what they liked. He might have eaten something that affected him but not his friends. His parents were almost certain it was something he was eating. They were almost right, except for what they didn't know. Convinced of what they felt was the source of Gyambibi's affliction, they allowed him to be a child again but told him to stop hunting his own food.

Gyambibi woke Sunday morning and dressed. He was going to see Adwoa Brago, he told his mother. His less obvious motive was to get to know Agya Kobi. Adwoa Brago was surprised to see him at their hut. He said he was there to accompany them to church. Adwoa Brago laughed. What made him want to go to church with them? Because they kept to the ways of the Bible, he told her, and he wanted to go with them so he could adequately learn. She reminded him that his parents went to church, too. His father had stopped going, Gyambibi reminded her. Anyway, his parents were good, kind people to emulate, but he had learned everything he could from them, he told Adwoa Brago. So he wanted to learn from others. She went into the inner room to finish dressing. He sat between the couple during worship rather than with his mother.

After church, Agya Kobi was on his way to the farm when he saw Gyambibi trailing after him. Agya Kobi said little as they went to the farm, though Gyambibi talked throughout. He asked many questions about every aspect of the worship as if that had been his first attendance. How can God be everywhere and still have a home in heaven?

"You don't act like a Kojo," the quiet old man said, referencing Gyambibi's day name.

"I'm Kwabena, Tuesday born. I can't be Kojo, for I wasn't born on Monday."

"I know when you were born, and it wasn't a Tuesday. I should check my book," Agya Kobi replied. He got some plantains and headed home. Gyambibi walked beside him, pelting the elder with questions, talking of the mysterious illness that had befallen him and which he no longer had. The elder had no change in countenance, nothing to say in response to his questions or anything else. Gyambibi kept talking, hoping to stumble on a subject that would provoke a conversation.

Agya Kobi arrived home. Gyambibi followed to see Asamoah, he said. Because Asamoah wasn't there, he went to Adwoa Brago. He wasn't finished with Agya Kobi yet. He asked for a calendar to check his day of birth. Neither Agya Kobi nor Adwoa Brago was in the inner room when he reviewed the calendars. His date of birth didn't coincide with a Tuesday day name, as the old man had said. Either his date of birth was wrong, or his day name was. Both couldn't be correct. He was excited to share the discovery with his parents, but his father was angry because he had told no one where he was.

"Where were you?" Karikari demanded.

"Adwoa Brago's. To see Asamoah."

"You think you're smarter than I, you little brat? Did you not go to see Agya Kobi?"

"Dad, that isn't totally correct. Adwoa Brago, Agya Kobi, Efia, and Asamoah live in the same hut. I'm not saying I wasn't at their hut because I was. But how could you say I visited one and not the other?"

"Did I not warn you to stay away from Agya Kobi?"

"Dad, you taught me to treat all men alike. Would I not be going against your word to visit Asamoah and mistreat Agya Kobi, even if I intended to keep away from him?"

"Stay away from the man. Do you hear me? Where's your mother?"

"She's at Adwoa Brago's, getting her hair done."

After eating lunch, Gyambibi sought permission to play outside. Instead, he went to Danfo's house, ate there again, and asked Danfo about the creation story of the Bible. He took over where Asamoah had left off and held his own against Danfo. Between the exchanges, he wanted to know if his father would be coming there for a visit. Karikari never began or finalized a decision without Danfo, so Gyambibi figured he would likely be here to discuss his trip to Accra. Danfo confirmed his hunch. Later, Moro and Asamoah dropped by with a soccer ball, saying they would play by the baobab tree. In any case, Gyambibi's cover story was complete should his father wonder about him, for he planned to revisit Agya Kobi.

Adwoa Brago knelt before a grindstone on which she ground ginger root, adding more and more until the quantity was to her liking. She scraped it off and formed it into a ball. Efia had embarrassed them enough. She had cost them enough.

Losing her virginity and the resulting pregnancy, in which she couldn't identify the man responsible, had tarnished their parenting reputation. To disregard their admonition to stay away from Preprah was an added affront. She was the reason that rascal had cut down acres of their crops. Upon learning what Preprah had done and the potential connection to her, Efia fled to Kodee but couldn't stay. Adwoa Brago would teach her a lasting lesson. Efia had to be severely punished. Adwoa Brago muscled past the pleading Agnes into Efia's room to burn into her memory a warning against her carnal excursions. A struggle ensued as they bumped into walls, and belongings were thrown about. After the sounds of battle had died down, screams of Efia's pain broke through as Adwoa Brago got to work with the ground ginger. The village didn't intervene; taming Efia's promiscuity was long overdue.

Adwoa Brago, satisfied, reemerged to join her friend, Agnes, who pulled a strand of cotton thread from a roll and severed it between her teeth. She passed it over her shoulder into the expecting palm of Adwoa Brago, who, in turn, began to wind it around a clump of Agnes's hair. She had plaited the hair on Agnes's right temple and was working her way to the back of Agnes's head when they saw two boys approaching.

"Isn't that your Gyambibi?" Adwoa Brago said.

"That's him," Agnes replied.

"His handsomeness is easy to spot. Hungry, maybe? Looking for you to cook him something." Adwoa Brago added that Agnes was overdue for another child.

"Maybe if God wills it."

"Tell that husband of yours I need another grandchild," Adwoa Brago said. This time Agnes's laughter dimmed. Adwoa Brago read her discomfort. Apparently, Agnes and Karikari had been unsuccessfully trying for years.

Gyambibi clutched a soccer ball under his arm.

"*Abrantie—Gentleman,*" Agnes addressed her son, who didn't seem too interested to stop and chat.

Gyambibi greeted the two, then felt his mother's row of plaited hair.

"That's nice," he said.

"Thank you. Have you been looking for me?"

"No." The word barely passed through his sealed lips.

Gyambibi had a muted excitement for seeing that his mother's hair wasn't finished. She would be his added cover story if his father found out he was at Agya Kobi's.

Adwoa Brago said, "You're looking for Agya Kobi, right?"

Gyambibi's silence answered the question.

"We both know he isn't here for us," Adwoa Brago told Agnes.

"He wants to talk to Agya Kobi," Asamoah chimed in and walked his friend into the hut.

Adwoa Brago alerted her husband, yelling over her shoulder.

"Agya Kobi, your friend is here."

The elder had no friend, so Asamoah needed no other qualifier for the elder to guess who this might be.

"You don't like the company of your peers much, do you? You left this behind," Agya Kobi said in his deep but unintimidating patriarchal voice as he beckoned Gyambibi into the hut. The elder was slowly welcoming him, Gyambibi assured himself. The fact that he had held onto the flute and hadn't sent it back to him via Asamoah also assured him that the elder wanted his friendship.

"You left it here," Agya Kobi repeated.

"It's for you. I got it for you," Gyambibi said.

With Efia in the adjoining room, the two were alone after Asamoah left. Gyambibi felt the elder would open up because their interaction wasn't public for those who thought him evil.

The elder gathered that the flute was why Gyambibi had returned, to see if he liked his gift.

"For me? Thank you. Where did you find the money for this?"

"Moro and I sold a watch and shared the money," Gyambibi replied.

"Where did you two get the watch?"

In these few minutes, the old man had exchanged more words with Gyambibi than he could remember.

The old man held Gyambibi in his heart in a way Gyambibi never knew. Gyambibi owed his name to the old man and his wife. Decades ago, when Adwoa Brago started pestering Karikari about marriage and children, Karikari had sought a list of names from the elderly couple to ease the pressure from Adwoa Brago. Anytime she brought up marriage and children, Karikari threw out a name and said, "There you have it, your grandson—[or granddaughter, if he hurled out a girl's name]," to which Adwoa Brago would respond, "I want faces attached to the names, my son." Pertinent to the relationship, the elderly couple was all Karikari had because he was orphaned at a young age and relied on the couple to learn about his own family history. This underscored the depth of the paternal-maternal relationship that preceded Karikari's hatred for the elderly couple. Danfo's *discoveries* about the old man changed everything for Karikari. Certain occurrences would deepen his suspicions about Agya Kobi.

Gyambibi couldn't contain his surprise at the old man's openness. He needed to get to the point before the old man recoiled into his shell.

"Can I be your friend?" Gyambibi asked.

"You can't buy friendship."

"Can I be your friend, anyway?"

"Yes, but on one condition: you must promise to do as your father says."

"I can do that!" Gyambibi grinned, exposing a missing front tooth.

"When did you lose it?"

"My tooth? Days ago." Gyambibi said, trying to contain his excitement.

"How does it feel?"

"Fine. It will grow back."

"What if it doesn't?" Agya Kobi asked.

"I didn't lose all of them," Gyambibi said, eliciting silence.

Gyambibi felt accepted by the elder. Changing the subject, he blurted out, "You said I didn't act like a Kojo." This was his pretext to go and scour the elder's calendars, which he had found in an alcove next to some clothing. When he had asked his father, his birth date wasn't a subject Karikari wanted to pursue. He was born at night, was all that Gyambibi was told. Karikari didn't mention the circumstances surrounding Gyambibi's birth: that Agnes had carried him for fifteen months and that it had taken the intervention of some twin midwives to bring about his birth. Karikari was uneasy about this memory, so he said very little and dismissed him. Since his birth was at night, Gyambibi felt the unschooled, elderly midwives, whose knowledge of the denominations of time didn't go past day and night, might have been calling him "Kwabena" before he was christened; when the night of one day and the darkness of the next day's early morning were conflated.

Something else caught his attention in the elder's hut—a book atop another pile of calendars. At the inside corner, he saw the letters ABC. The next page spelled out what it stood for: Adam's Black Child. He saw entries of birth dates. Other pages of the journal had notes he didn't understand. Hearing approaching footsteps, he replaced the book and walked right into Efia, coming out of her room. Tears ran down her face; her eyes were red. She staggered about and held her belly and groin, aching with pain.

His curiosity didn't tempt him to look into the room she had emerged from, but Asamoah had taken him there many times. It was an add-on. The configuration seemed odd initially, but it made sense somehow: it ran the length of the original hut with its own living room and bedroom, though it had no separate entrance. One had to go in through the original structure with an adjoining door linking the two structures. Added on when Asamoah was born, the lack of a separate entrance was perhaps because Adwoa Brago wanted the benefit of helping the new mother, even in the middle of the night, without having to go outside to get in.

Another reason, albeit surreptitious, was to monitor Efia's movements. There was no window at the back of the hut, only to the right and front. If Efia went out through the side window, she would land on Nyamenkum's gossiping tongue. Another detached hut sat on the compound belonging to Adwoa Brago and Agya Kobi's deceased son—Efia's father. It had been Efia's hut before her pregnancy and before the need to keep a close eye on her. The location of this hut to the left, which now functioned as a storehouse, forced the addition to the right.

Gyambibi's food sat beside the elder's when Agya Kobi emerged from the hut. Adwoa Brago had covered them to shield them from hungry insects.

"How old was my great-grandmother when she died?" Gyambibi asked.

Agya Kobi was uncomfortable and wouldn't talk about it. He watched Gyambibi prepare to eat his food, but before he could take a bite, Gyambibi shuddered. He fell out of the chair and convulsed on the ground. Agya Kobi thrust his hand into his foaming mouth before it clamped shut. He was having his first seizure. Agnes screamed and jumped out of her chair. Agya Kobi yelled to Adwoa Brago to grind charcoal for him. Agnes was suspended between halting whatever the old man had in mind and her once veneration of him. She did nothing, shaking and shocked. Without a word to Adwoa Brago, Agnes threw Gyambibi on her back and ran home with the back of her head partially plaited.

Karikari was enraged. It was Agnes's fault their son had a disease unheard of in the entire village. From where the disease had raged, it was clear Agya Kobi was the source, a charge Agnes had dreaded even before she carried her son home.

"You went to Adwoa Brago. How many times have I protested that? How many times, Aggie? Tell me."

Agnes was too guilty to speak up.

Karikari lashed out, "Gyambibi wasn't afraid of Agya Kobi. Why? Because you go to his hut. Not once has Gyambibi heeded my warning about the old man. Why would he, when you go there as if the man hasn't killed many people? Who knows what this will turn out to be? My son, our son, epileptic?" Karikari threw up his hands.

Agnes understood her husband's anger. Until now, she had remained close to Adwoa Brago but kept a cautious distance from Agya Kobi. She never drank nor ate at their hut. For decades, and right up to Gyambibi's birth, Agya Kobi and Adwoa Brago had been like parents to Agnes and her husband, Karikari. Then the deaths began, and later, the rumors erupted. Karikari cut his ties right away. The entire village abandoned the couple to varying degrees. Agnes was uncomfortable doing so, though she understood everyone's fear of Agya Kobi.

As Karikari seethed, Agnes became quiet as she always did on the rare occasions when he was angry with her. He toned down when he noticed her shaking. He regretted his outbursts but was too agitated to stop. Looking at her awoke a nostalgia for the girl he had married. Gyambibi, Yaw, and Karikari meant the world to Agnes. They were the only family she knew, the only family that mattered. Born in Cape Coast, her parents had sent her off to serve another family at a young age. And she had grown up thinking that the woman of the family she served was her mother until she learned otherwise. The clothes she wore while in servitude were clothes for which the other female members of the family had no use. Her life didn't change much when she returned to her own family. She was the one to get up early in the morning and walk distances to fetch water. Enkoho heard parts of her story now and then. Karikari would assure her that that was in the past, that they were blessed with a family of their own, and that they were the wealthiest in Enkoho. Still, the pain of her childhood was too much to forget. Karikari was the medicated poultice that numbed her painful past. Just days ago, she had told Karikari why she appreciated him so much: that they had been married for many years, but not once had he laid hands on her.

Agnes had brothers and sisters but was treated differently by her own family ever since she could remember. The villagers had initially struggled with her story—not that they didn't believe her. Some felt she might have been adopted and not an extended or a first-degree relative of those she claimed were her family. They weren't doubtful for long when they saw her family visit from Cape Coast. It was then that they learned that

Karikari's pet name for her, Kak, was short for Kakra: she was the younger of a fraternal twin. She had one other sister and two brothers. With her family, the villagers saw one blood unit but recognized why Agnes felt different within the bunch. Karikari remembered that her story was his, that they both shared an upbringing smeared with pain and abandonment. Karikari understood the whys of his abandonment, but no one understood Agnes's. She had no family besides him. Something about her solemn calmness poured cold water over his outbursts. He remembered that she had no one to turn to but him. With that realization, he walked out of the room.

Karikari suspected that Agya Kobi was responsible for Gyambibi's visions. With Gyambibi contracting a seizure in the man's presence for the first time, his suspicion was now carved in stone. Karikari had avoided seeking treatment for Gyambibi from the village healer because Agya Kobi frequented his services. So Karikari and Agnes returned to the medical paths of seeking help for Gyambibi. From meningitis to psychosis, from idiopathic epilepsy to metabolic encephalopathy to cerebritis to encephalitis to medicine-doesn't-know-everything, no practitioner in the rural clinics could definitively say what was wrong with Gyambibi. His was a disease of the central nervous system, but month after month, drug after drug, Gyambibi waxed and waned. The journey took them to rural Tetrem to see a practitioner who combined Western medicine and naturopathy with a knack for the occult. Just from shaking Karikari's hand, she knew what Karikari had withheld, that they had come from a village he would rather not talk about. She gave him two scripts for what ailed Gyambibi. Karikari was about to ask when to administer the medications when he noticed they weren't what he thought. On one of the scripts was the location of a church, and on the other was the name of a fetish priest. Medical science has its limit, she said.

The evening of their return from Tetrem, Agya Kobi visited. Karikari would have killed Yaw if he weren't his son for allowing the man into their house.

"Get out!" Karikari yelled at Agya Kobi.

Before he turned to leave, Agya Kobi asked to allow him to say one thing. If Karikari had had the nerve to touch him, he would have dragged him out, but he feared his hands might shrivel. Agya Kobi stood there, wondering how such hostility came to be. He said in the calmest, nonetheless alarming, voice, "Don't let Gyambibi eat anything brought to you by anybody from this village. Not just him, but all of you should do like-wise. Only eat what you buy at the market. Do not eat what is brought to you. My son Karikari, my daughter Agnes, may the Lord be with you."

Karikari slammed the screen door behind him with such force that the top hinge tore off. Anxiety blinked at him. He couldn't believe Agya Kobi's shameless temerity. That evening he found his Bible, dusted it off, and began badgering God for forgive-ness for having kept away from church services. He went from room to room, reading aloud and saying prayers. What non-sense did he just hear? Did he see Evil speak—in his house? A mild-mannered man who rarely subjected his family to out-bursts, Karikari had just had several layers of skin peeled off by Agya Kobi's unexpected visit. His raw nerves felt racked. He stopped the prayers, suddenly awash in the uncanny illusion that Agya Kobi hadn't been to his house. His mind couldn't hold such a reality. What he had seen and heard were halluci-nations. Gyambibi's disease was contagious; he was infected, and so were the others in his household. But when Agnes and Yaw came to him, their faces showing regret for their actions, he had to accept that he hadn't hallucinated. Indeed, Agya Kobi had been to his house, and therefore every inch of it, even that which his feet didn't touch, was contaminated with evil. The preacher of the only church in Enkoho was called to join the family in purging the evil that Agya Kobi had deposited.

"His removal and banishment from church gatherings have been proposed. I'll make sure you won't have to see him when you come to church," Preacher assured Karikari.

Gyambibi was a unique child. His guidance spirit was potent, Preacher had told them. While Preacher didn't have the benefit of esoteric visions, his observations were procured from Gyambibi's knowledge of the Bible. Gyambibi read it seriously and casually—a part of his routine that let his parents overlook some of his disobedience. Preacher had been at the receiving end of his questions. God's spirit was with the boy, so he was fearless of Agya Kobi. Preacher assured Agnes and Karikari that the old man's evil couldn't surmount the boy's spirit.

The evil subtext of Agya Kobi's caution didn't evade Karikari; he thought all night, remaining sleepless through the morning. Gyambibi had been across from Evil, eating with him when he became sick. For Agya Kobi to say he shouldn't eat anything from the village carried the double meaning that he would chase the child and plague him with whatever he saw fit for as long as they were all confined to Enkoho. Karikari could do nothing about it. Agya Kobi was taunting them as payback for Karikari withdrawing his friendship. Thus Karikari stretched the man's words, and this rendering stared him down whichever way he looked at it.

For Preacher to have a hand in Agya Kobi's banishment from church wouldn't be entirely surprising. At times Preacher sided with the village's collective impression of the elder. Preacher hadn't put his displeasure with the elder from years ago behind him. Because the village had pulled away from Agya Kobi at the time of the death of his son, Papayeasa, Preacher was the only consolation Agya Kobi had. Only Yaa Adubia and Preacher went to his son's funeral.

"I don't fully understand God, but this I know: God is always right. My friend, death isn't the end but graduation from this life to the next. If we understood this, there would be no tears and no pain when we meet to say goodbye to our departed. Graduation is a time for celebration, not a time for tears." These were Preacher's consoling words, which helped Agya Kobi to accept his loss. The words were ordinary and the meaning basic, but

Agya Kobi's faith saw profound truth in them. There was no need to cry; there was no need to suffer the pain of the loss.

Sometime later, Preacher's son died. Agya Kobi repeated the same words to his friend, hoping they would help him heal as they did him.

"How insensitive of you! I now understand why no one likes you. Why would you say that?" Preacher asked furiously.

At a loss for a response, Agya Kobi replied, "Your words... they helped me heal and accept my loss."

Preacher couldn't believe the blatant insult. "But this is different. Your son died as an adult. Mine was a child, just beginning life."

From then on, Preacher joined the villagers in keeping away from Agya Kobi. No one knew exactly when they became friends again. Likely, their respect for God and His Word must have brought them together, their friendship dating back decades when they evangelized the village to bring many into their Christian faith. The two men started the church in the village. But given Gyambibi's condition and Preacher's take, he seemed eager to unite with the village against Agya Kobi again.

Gyambibi's problems wrinkled Karikari's face, sunk his eyes, frustrated his mind, and narrowed his conversations. The ceiling stood in his way of seeing through to the heavens, to the very throne of God, where he could shoot his anger. He turned on his bed, assumed a kneeling posture, and prayed for his sinful rage. He prayed for conceiving the thought of blaming God for Gyambibi's problems. He knew better than to blame God for any reason. He laid down again, facing the ceiling, trying to suppress his fury.

Agnes pleaded with him to come for lunch, but he didn't acknowledge her. She could sense her husband was unwell, ailed by a disease she couldn't pinpoint. Because of his anger, she couldn't even convince him to go to Healer.

Karikari went to the porch, where his food was set.

"How're you feeling?" Agnes tried to engage him after exchanging the soapy water for fresh water for washing his hands. Karikari didn't respond. Instead, he took the Pyrex bowls of boiled cocoyam and sauce to the living room to get away from her. Agnes followed.

"My dear, how's the salt?"

Karikari ignored her.

"How's the taste?"

"Can't I eat in silence?"

She flinched, smelling anger on him. "If I could do it over again, my dear—"

"The world knows how evil the man is. You know it; you had a chance to never go near him. But you placed yourself in his orbit, and your son followed your lead."

"I'm sorry. I'm so sorry. I would if I could die to make things better for you and our son. Please don't ignore me. You and the children are all I have."

Karikari licked his fingers, grabbed his food, and went to the bedroom. Alone, Agnes stared out onto the porch, brooding. She felt there must be something wrong with her to place herself on the compound of Agya Kobi when everybody else avoided him. She couldn't conceive a way to undo her sins, so she left for the playground to watch Gyambibi play with his friends— doing anything to keep her mind away from her husband's cold distance.

Gyambibi was his old self, barking instructions here and there to members of his boyhood gang with whom he played soccer.

Agnes strolled the breadth of the playground, stopping at the other end where Yaw and his friends and some girls mingled. Agnes felt her presence made her son uneasy, so she stood against the baobab tree and instead watched some girls play. From the other side of the tree, a whisper broke through. She went around the tree, turned every which way but couldn't locate the source of the grandmotherly voice. She turned again; there was nothing around to explain her anxiety.

It could easily have been fifteen minutes since she came to the playground. Only it wasn't. Hours had passed, but she couldn't account for them. Had she left? Where did she go? Who did she visit? And for how long? She couldn't think of any name, just Agya Kobi's. Did she go to Agya Kobi and have no memory of it? Did anyone see her go to his hut? If this got to her husband, the damage would be irreparable. Her anxiety erupted. She was angry about leaving the house. She had to return. Now she feared Agya Kobi wanted to destroy her, her marriage, and her family.

A feeling of sadness, of dense uneasiness, swept over her. She couldn't discern why. The front door opened as she approached her house like the wind was leading the way in. She saw the shape of a woman behind the door, walking in as if she lived there. Maybe she didn't shut the door securely on her way out. Having had a cursory look at her, Agnes had a vague impression of a woman she had only seen in pictures. But Kari-kari's grandmother had been dead for decades. Then again, Agnes feared this could also be a villager itching to gossip about her visit to Agya Kobi—a visit that resided in her mind and might not have happened. The woman turned the corner and headed for the primary bedroom. All the kerosene lanterns were mysteriously on when Agnes yelled, "Who are you?" and ran after her.

Agnes searched the primary bedroom, rummaged through the wardrobe, and looked under the bed, above the bed. The woman wasn't there, so Agnes ran out searching for her, dashing from room to room. Agnes was perplexed when she didn't see the woman in the entire house. It must have been the strain of Gyambibi's problems on her mind. She caught her breath on the porch, where she saw bloodstains in the shape of her feet leading from the house. She traced them to every room she'd entered and the source of her bleeding soles to the primary bedroom, where Agnes saw the broken Pyrex bowls on the floor, their contents spilled out. She had cut her soles on the broken bowls and was unaware of doing so while chasing the mysterious woman.

She noticed that Karikari was on the bed, still. Agnes felt his cheek and forehead. She screamed.

"Karikari!"

No answer.

"My husband."

No answer.

"Can you hear me?"

Karikari didn't respond. The severity of his illness so gripped Agnes that she couldn't think right. She laid on top of him, got up, and turned him while screaming his name.

She felt a soft wail of the grandmotherly voice that had whispered to her earlier. Agnes felt responsible. Gyambibi's problems had affected her husband in many ways, and now this.

"God, help me. How do I alone care for the children if you take him away? God, don't. God, please!"

Agnes was trembling. She rushed to the kitchen, not knowing why she was there. She dropped a couple of items in her hands and ran for Healer. On her way, it came to her that Healer was outside the village that day. Adwoa Brago could help, but her proximity to Agya Kobi killed the idea.

Agnes ran back to the bedroom and knelt beside her husband, held his hand, released his hand and turned his face toward hers.

"Speak to me, dear. Speak. What is it? What's the problem?"

No response, only incoherent grunts.

"God, God, my husband, my husband. Karikari!" She lifted him off the bed and sat him straight. Karikari draped to one side, his eyes going in and out of his head, his mouth mumbling rubbish. He looked at his wife with fear in his blank eyes. Jeefa came to the house in search of Gyambibi; Agnes yelled to her to fetch her mother. Mawuli rushed to the house with Daavi. When help arrived, the energy Agnes had felt, the sudden anxiety, the unsettling feeling—all vanished.

Chapter

8

*K*arikari recovered from his illness with more questions about how, than why, he recovered. Right before he fell unconscious, a woman from the village entered his bedroom. She told him she was going for help. The next person he saw was his grandmother, who, in turn, promised to find help. She had fetched Agnes. It turned out Karikari saw his grandmother as Agnes did. There were unanswered questions about how this woman from the village had ended up in Karikari's bedroom to help him. Agnes had her concerns too. She didn't doubt her husband's dedication to her. She wanted to know if this woman harbored a romantic interest to the extent that she would come to the house in Agnes's absence. Karikari wanted to thank this woman. She wasn't home when the couple visited. Asking the villagers took Karikari and Agnes to Healer, who told them the woman they were after had died hours before she showed up at Karikari's house. Karikari and Agnes were now sufficiently clearheaded to know that this woman must have died to locate Karikari's grandmother to help him. Now there were two dead people and one live person to whom Karikari owed his life. He didn't know how to thank the dead. He forgot about Agnes's indiscretion like it never happened.

"My father, I should have heeded your advice when I came before you about Gyambibi's problem, which I instead blamed on my wife. When I came into consciousness, the terror that had filled Agnes, her panic, her fear of losing me, all converged on me. She would have died if she knew I was dead. My Agnes would give up her life to save mine if it came to it. She saved me," Karikari confessed to Mr. Osei, an elder whose farm bordered Karikari's. He taught Karikari the ins and outs of cocoa farming.

"I'm happy my words have been confirmed. If you didn't forgive Agnes, who else could you learn to forgive?"

"You were right, my father. Take this—." Karikari handed him an envelope.

"You called me here to give me money, my son? I've thanked you so often that it has lost meaning."

"Then don't say it," Karikari replied.

"I don't know what to say or do to express how thankful I feel."

"Don't say anything, don't do anything. I don't expect any gesture in return."

"I don't understand your heart. If I were many times richer than you, I still couldn't do what you do for the poor."

Karikari was silent.

"How you do it says a lot about you. You've helped me for many years, always in the absence of your family. More than that, you save me embarrassment by ensuring that neither my wife nor children know I must rely on your generosity to care for them now and then."

Karikari remained silent.

"You don't want anybody knowing what you do for others."

"There's one thing I would ask in return," Karikari said.

"Name it, my son."

"Stop drinking."

"My son, you're just a child. I don't drink because I like the taste of alcohol."

Karikari listened intently.

"No, that isn't it. I'm poor not because I'm lazy; you know that, and so does God. I'm poor regardless of what I do. Who spends more time on the farm than I do? No one, but look at me. I remain poor, no matter how hard I try. Alcohol isn't a beverage for me; it's medicine. If you're as poor as I am, the problem isn't that I drink alcohol around the clock; the problem is that it—"

"My father, please, just cut down on your drinking."

"You're only a child, my son. Learn from Danfo. I agree with him that alcohol must have been the last thing God created to help man cope with His imperfect world. God knew that man would have pain and heartache. The problem isn't that I drink; it's that I didn't start sooner to help numb my mind to the severity of suffering that was coming my way. It was late by the time I started drinking because my problems had already hardened into hopelessness by then. I now have to drink more and stronger alcohol to cope. I can't bear seeing my children being sent home from school because I can't pay their fees. I can't stand the sight of my children in clothes they have grown out of. They don't eat nutritious meals because my wife can only cook with what I give her. Can anybody believe this? We live in a village of farms, yet food is hard to come by. Can you believe it? Enkoho!"

"My father, I understand...but—"

"No, you don't understand, my son. Killing myself isn't a solution; neither is watching the hardship my family goes through. Neither can I leave this village and start over elsewhere."

"My father, you're right. I have to be in your shoes to understand."

"I can't leave if I want to," Mr. Osei nearly shouted.

Karikari was uneasy. Mr. Osei couldn't leave if he wanted to, but by saying so, he was on the verge of broaching an anathema. He stopped short of finishing his thoughts when he read Karikari's discomfort.

"It's true what our elders say: people like you are on Earth because of people like me. I pray to God that people like you will always be rich because of people like me."

He started to get on his knees, but Karikari pulled him up before his knees touched the ground.

"There's no need to kneel to thank me. My greetings to Nyamenkum and the children."

"Forgive me, my son. I can do no such thing. I can't send Nyamenkum your greetings. The whole village will hear I came here to panhandle."

"Never mind, my father. I'll come to visit you and greet her myself."

"That would be better."

Before Karikari closed the door behind him, he signaled to his visitor that there was something he wanted to talk about. Karikari needed electricity tapped from Aduman to Enkoho. The difficulty lay in the number of trees to cut for overhead power lines. The second problem was the awkwardness of explaining to anyone about electricity going from Aduman through the forest to a village no one knew about.

"We'll need a lot of poles," Mr. Osei said.

"True. I asked Yaw and Gyambibi to come up with some numbers. They came up with comparable numbers, depending on how far removed we are from Aduman, which, from our ancestors to us, no one knows. Gyambibi pointed out that the terrain won't be flat all the way from Aduman; there may be rivers or lakes. I don't know how that boy thinks these things. Assuming he's right, the numbers may change a bit."

"That boy!" Mr. Osei shook his head in admiration.

"Don't get me started about him, my father. He came to me later, stood before me, and stared at me as if something was wrong. You've heard of his problems, so I thought it was one of his visions. He asked me why I'd asked him to calculate the number of poles. Then he told me his previous estimations were wrong. We probably only need five poles or fewer. He thinks the terrain isn't open but filled with so many trees and vegetation that we'd have to clear the forest to plant the poles—a futile undertaking in his estimation. So he suggested we hoist the cables onto trees along our chosen path and route them from tree to tree to this village. He said we'd need tree climbers and only enough poles to route the cables into the village proper, probably less than five. Amazing. We should ask Professor Tetteh to talk to his friend, Professor Agyapong."

Mr. Osei laughed at Gyambibi's suggestion. This undertaking would have been much easier if the precise distance from Enkoho to Aduman had been open knowledge. It was enshrined in the mystery that is Enkoho.

"I forget Gyambibi's much younger than his brother. Imagine him any older. Where does Yaw stand between the University of Ghana and Kwame Nkrumah University of Science and Technology?" Osei inquired.

"Yaw has no interest in going to the university. His interest lies in going to America," Karikari said, frustrated.

"What's wrong with children nowadays? All they talk about is going to America, going to Europe. Where did we go wrong?"

"I don't know what the fascination is. I'm grooming him to take over the family farms and businesses if he has no desire for college. I'm not sending him to America. He can harvest happiness here as much as anywhere else," Karikari said.

In any case, they would have to cut down the palm tree against the house to get the electric cables over the parapet. Karikari objected for the fourth time. He gave the same reason: the tree symbolized much in his life; he had a sentimental attachment to it. It was one of two palm trees he planted forty years ago when his grandmother was alive. It was so close to the walls that its roots had formed a union with them. It had put cracks in the walls and unsightly warps in the eaves. That hadn't bothered Karikari, for the tree was as much a part of his life as his imperfect children. So they would have to hoist the cables over the tree. The discussion turned to why Karikari had to go to these lengths to bring electricity to the village. Many years, lots of manpower, and lots of money would certainly go into the project, and for what? Television. Karikari had heard about it on his last trip to Accra.

"What is this television? Why do you think you need it?" Mr. Osei asked.

"You like the radio box and the gramophone, right?"

"Very much! I'm here every other day and on weekends," Mr. Osei affirmed.

"Right. But television is better. You don't only hear people speak, but you can see them as well."

"It shrinks people to make you see them?"

"In a way, yes; in a way, no. You'll see." Karikari smiled.

"I believe you, my son, but this one... How do you shrink people into a box without killing them?"

Karikari laughed. "No, no, it doesn't physically shrink the people. You'll see when it's here."

Four long years later, Enkoho had its first television.

Karikari heard whispers and clanging sounds. He listened closely and determined the source of the sounds: the kitchen. He walked in and saw two dead pigeons lying on the floor. Gyambibi and Moro were standing there.

At twelve, Gyambibi and Moro craved independence, more so now because Moro had become a permanent resident of Enkoho. His mother and stepfather had decided to have him in the village rather than have him rotate between Bawku and En-koho. All thanks to Gyambibi! One could also say the village had claimed Moro.

"What are you boys doing?" Karikari asked.

"Nothing," Moro responded while standing beside the two birds, a cooking pot, and a bottle of palm kernel oil, all sitting next to a coal pot filled with charcoal.

"Do you think I can't see the birds on the floor? What's wrong with you, Gyambibi? You know what, you know what, I don't have to say anything. Your mother will be home soon and can deal with this."

Not long after this warning, Asamoah joined them with a tuber of yam. They now had something to go with the pigeon stew.

"I can't have you boys in the house; I have a meeting with Mawuli here," Karikari said, leaving.

"What's with all these meetings he has with people?" Moro mumbled to Gyambibi.

"The odd thing is that it's always with one person," Gyambibi replied.

"Why do you think it's with Mawuli today?"

"Jeefa was sent home from school the other day; Mawuli still hasn't paid her fees. I think Father wants to give him the money for it."

"That's understandable," Moro said.

Karikari had no knowledge that Gyambibi and Moro had overheard most of his meetings where he had offered help to people.

The village well was situated in the northwest corner against the bush, covered by the shade of the baobab tree. Nearby was cleared land, which doubled as a playground. Though communal bathrooms were littered throughout the village, bathing and laundry were routinely done at the river. For a village with a river, a well would seem out of place, but not if one knew the dynamics of Enkoho. The well was reserved for days when it was too dangerous to go into the forest or the farms. In essence, the shady vicinity of the well belonged to the village's children as a playground until such a time when using the well was unavoidable.

Today, naturally, this area was devoid of adults. Gyambibi had brought the coal pot with the birds. His father's "meetings" were long so as not to give the impression that he was giving alms to others. Gyambibi and his boyhood crew took advantage of this. Moro oversaw the cooking while the rest of them played soccer. Being two years younger, Asamoah was outside the core of the gang. When Asiedu was prohibited from associating with Gyambibi because of rumors associating him with Agya Kobi and thereby contracting a strange disease, Asamoah slowly edged into the group. Today, Asiedu had stolen away from home to be with them again and began overlooking the cooking. Moro went off and played. Then it was Gyambibi's turn at cooking. When the food was ready, they ate, argued, and ate again. They played until Gyambibi knew his father's meeting was over. Asiedu sustained a gash on the shin at the pointed edge of the coal pot when he ran into it while chasing after a soccer ball Gyambibi had lobbed his way. Gyambibi went into the house for a bottle of TCP antiseptic, which he used to irrigate the wound.

Chapter

9

*W*ith no structural damage to his brain confirmed by radiological exams, the unknowns of what plagued Gyambibi persisted, Jeefa wrote to her American friend Helena. The village kids added messages for Helena. They had all gathered across from Gyambibi's house to see the pictures Helena had taken and processed upon returning to America, sending copies back to the village through Mr. Nsenkyire. He was at the village for the cocoa harvest. Gyambibi wasn't among the throng, though his parents thought he was. He had orchestrated this cover to join Agya Kobi at his farm. Uncle Salifu's threats didn't deter him. He felt if nobody saw him with the elder, he was safe from Uncle Salifu. The elder didn't want Gyambibi there; however, making a fuss would alert people that he was with him again.

Agya Kobi went about his work as Gyambibi sought to deepen their friendship. He asked the elder to play the flute he had given him. Agya Kobi didn't protest, but after belting out a few tunes, he dropped the flute into a basket. Gyambibi moved about carefreely, took out the flute, and asked the old man to play again. Agya Kobi did as before, but Gyambibi didn't comment.

"Tell me what's on your mind," Agya Kobi said.

"Let's go to the river," Gyambibi replied.

They negotiated a few minutes of a meandering path to get there. On impulse, both looked out to ensure nobody saw them.

"I've sworn not to ever lie to you. But that will work if you also swear to me,"

Gyambibi began.

Were these the words of a child? Agya Kobi shook himself out of wondering. "What do you want me to swear to?"

"The same thing that I swore to you: that you don't ever lie to me," Gyambibi stated.

"All right. But why couldn't you tell me this on the farm? Adwoa Brago isn't with me today."

"Because I want to perform the rite of *di nse*," Gyambibi said.

"*Di nse*? Where did you hear that!?"

"I don't know; I think I've always known it."

The old man looked away, shaken. He scooped water from the river and washed his face. A phrase that belonged in the mouths of elders from previous generations had somehow found its way into the child's mouth. He couldn't remember the last time he had heard the phrase. It was certain that the boy's father wouldn't even know what it meant. He looked at Gyambibi. He was staring at a child much older than his own eighty-four years. Unease crept through his feet as he stood up.

"Mr. Gyambibi."

"Gyambibi," the boy corrected, then left Agya Kobi standing there, bound by an oath to die if he lied to the child.

Agnes barely left the house following Gyambibi's accident at Agya Kobi's. Adwoa Brago came to visit her instead. After she left Agnes's house, Agnes went to Esi Eluwah's. She kept an eye on Gyambibi and allowed him to be himself, doing what children did. Karikari grew closer to him; he traveled less, putting business plans on hold. He, too, allowed Gyambibi to be himself within the boundaries they had set. Karikari looked to bond with him in new ways. Several times Gyambibi had asked about his grandparents, and though Karikari met his precocious interest with suspicion, he finally had little choice but to oblige. He needed this change as much as Gyambibi. He and Agnes had brooded over the boy's behavior. What stood out was that he was undeterred in going to Agya Kobi because he needed to know about his grandparents and, to a worrying extent, his great-grandparents. Gyambibi was so clever a child that even though they were his parents, Karikari and Agnes harbored a deep fear of his curiosities. Karikari would oblige his curious impulses but only as far as his grandparents; he avoided the topic of great-grandparents because of a dangerous secret resting there. They wrestled with the possibility that Gyambibi might already possess a hint of this secret, hence his scouring for information about his forbearers. Karikari decided to take the lead and do it cleverly so as not to make the boy suspicious of his sudden desire to talk about his grandparents. Gyambibi's fondness of music traced its lineage to his grandfather, Yaw Donyinah, who was Karikari's father. This would be a good place to start.

Karikari shared his father's love of music, particularly his music routine. Pachelbel's *Canon in D*, Elgar's *Enigma Variations: Nimrod*, and Faure's *Pavane* drifted through his early mornings. By the time Warlock's entire *Capriol Suite* had finished its turn, followed by Bach's Sheep May Safely Graze, Vivaldi's Largo, and Satie's Gymnopédies, among other nostalgic compositions, Karikari's problems were asleep. He would sit upon his mat, consternated by a piece of music whose language he didn't speak yet somehow understood well through the emotions it evoked. The songs were pure, alluring, and imbued with emotionalism. His youthful mind considered the compositions "music of the soul," awakening emotions in him that reached past his mortal body into his immortal soul. Yet for Karikari's father, music was also in step with the women in his life.

Sitting one nostalgic evening with Gyambibi, Karikari relived the times when his foundling heart, on lonely mornings, conversed with a piece of music whose language he didn't know. Overwhelmed by a sudden need to dredge up his family history, he also told Gyambibi about his grandfather's womanizing ways. Besides Yaw being named after his grandfather, Gyambibi knew nothing else of him. Karikari's father and mother fought all the time because of the many women he kept. He finally left Karikari and his mother after one altercation and didn't return, except to send for Karikari and Tabuah, occasionally, to stay with him in Tetrem. Even when Karikari was with him, there were still fights about other women. Karikari witnessed many women invoke curses on his father. Some wished him a painful death. Every variety of woman known to humanity that found her way into Ghana, it seemed, somehow found her way into his arms. Women flocked to him at the same rate as they egressed.

Opinions about him were so sordid that one day, upon seeing him coming to Enkoho, a boy ran to the village yelling what was essentially gibberish. When calm, he told the villagers that a goddess was bringing Yaw Donyinah to the village to kill him. The boy was delirious and not without cause, as the goddess he had seen was a yet-to-be-identified species of humanity. When the couple emerged on the path, presumably from Aduman, the villagers were confronted with the sight of Yaw Donyinah sashaying toward them. Behind him was a woman of Chinese and Australian aboriginal lineage, with blond hair and light skin of melanic sheen. She was proportionally built and curvy.

Moreover, her mannerisms complemented her sacred beauty so well that it was said among the villagers that she was one of God's creatures that man couldn't improve upon in any way. Even the enamel of her teeth bore such an unblemished, pearlescent complexion that one would think it had never encountered food. Her hair was so thick and lustrous that the wind obeyed its wish to remain undisturbed. Truly, she was an exotic human goddess! Karikari recounted that his father had come to the village to pick him up to spend the weekend with him. However, his mother was so incensed at the other woman's presence that she followed him everywhere with insults and ultimately forced him out of the village. That was the last time Karikari saw his father. Others maintained he had been buried somewhere by a jilted woman. Karikari felt that his father died before his mother. News of his mother's death had spread wildly, and even extended relations from Tetrem, where Yaw Donyinah lived then, attended the funeral. Despite his living-on-the-edge lifestyle and freethinking ways, Karikari held strongly that his father would have come for him and Tabuah after their mother's death if he were still alive. Though Yaw Donyinah's presence in their lives was scanty, and Karikari stayed with him only a few times, he had ensured Karikari had all the comforts of life. At the age of sixteen or so, when Karikari returned to Enkoho after running away to Accra, his grandmother showed him what his father had left for him: his records. Doing all he could to erase painful memories of his father, High Life and Western pop music had supplanted his early exposure to classical music. He tucked away his father's music collection.

Gyambibi, who wasn't fond of music at a young age, took to it once he chanced upon his grandfather's classical music collection in the wardrobe, which he then played with the same fervor as his grandfather. Gyambibi's love of the music awoke Karikari's fond memories of his father and memories he had wished to stay buried. Adding to Karikari's discomfort, he would look at Gyambibi and foresee his father's tall handsomeness, natural charm, and wits that magnetized women. The thought of Gyambibi's distinctive good looks, in light of girls' natural fondness for his company, had Karikari's stomach turning acidic, thinking that the future might be on a collision with the past.

Then Gyambibi's questions began.

"I may have aunties besides Aunty Tabuah. I may have uncles too. I may have cousins besides Atobrah, Abrafi, Kofi and Obeng," he said.

Karikari looked away from Agnes. They must tread cleverly.

"What made you think that?" Karikari asked, feigning nonchalance.

"Grandpa had many wives. He must have other children," Gyambibi stated.

"The other women weren't his wives," Karikari corrected.

"Men have children with women who aren't their wives, right?"

"Sometimes."

"Okay, I may have other uncles and aunties and many cousins then," Gyambibi said, edging toward exasperation.

"Perhaps," Karikari consented.

One last thing Gyambibi left with his parents was that they needed to go to Tetrem and search for their relatives. His grandfather had lived there and brought women there. He must have left his DNA imprint. The discussion wasn't going in their direction, so Karikari and Agnes had to improvise to curtail this dangerous curiosity. Their strategy involved disclosing a secret they had kept from everyone for fear it might get to Agya Kobi, who could destroy a child before birth.

Agnes was pregnant with her third child. Gyambibi received the news well. Agnes hadn't seen him so happy since his problems started. Gyambibi suspended all questions he had lined up about his speculated cousins and aunties in Tetrem. Instead, he asked questions about the baby.

Maybe they should all go to Healer right now to tell them the sex of the baby. His father said it was time for bed. Before bed, Gyambibi told his parents that his hunch told him the baby was a boy. He couldn't wait to be a big brother. His baby brother would join his gang, Gyambibi told his parents. Wanting to keep his interest in the matter, Agnes asked how he could be so confident that his baby brother—if indeed the baby was a boy—would like to join his gang.

"I've never met anyone who doesn't like my company, except maybe Yaw."

His parents laughed. Their plan was working.

"Yaw doesn't want you in his gang. How could you be sure your baby brother would want to be in your gang?" Karikari asked.

"I'll talk to him every day. I'll persuade him before he's born. Mama, can I ask him now?"

"I think he's sleeping. Let's wait until tomorrow."

Agnes and Karikari celebrated their success with yet another round of laughter. However, their anxiety about their son's waning intellect arose on the other side of the laughter. Though still a child, the questions Gyambibi had asked about the baby were beneath his intellect and intelligence. In the coming months, Agnes and Karikari would have more anxiety whenever he talked about the baby. They held out hope that God would provide a solution.

Karikari and Agnes went to bed bewildered, though not disappointed, for they had found a new activity to engage their dangerously clever and curious son away from Agya Kobi. Gyambibi, meanwhile, relocated his grandfather's records to his room. He began a routine following in his grandfather's footsteps: listening to the same songs in the same sequence that his father had recalled right after the BBC signature tune blasted from the radio box outside, signaling that morning was here.

Chapter

Rain of Crow Feathers

*A*siedu's wound didn't heal. He started to spike a fever, sweat uncontrollably, and sometimes felt his heart beating out of his chest. Then he developed a stiff neck and jaw. His parents hadn't seen other wounds devolve into these many symptoms and asked if he had had an encounter with Agya Kobi. Asiedu answered, no. Perhaps he had had interactions with Gyambibi? Again, no. How did he get the wound? Cut by a coal pot while playing. Playing with whom? He played alone, he said, for implicating anyone would surely implicate Gyambibi. He feared his death would come at the hands of his parents if he told the truth, so he kept to his story. When he progressed to swallowing difficulties and choking on his food, a trip to Healer followed. He died weeks later.

News of Asiedu's death devastated Gyambibi. As days went by, he associated less with his friends and stayed indoors. Karikari and Agnes were no longer worried about him sneaking out to associate with Agya Kobi. The only people he responded to were Moro and Jeefa. Agnes encouraged them to come to the house. Gradually, he found comfort outdoors again but slipped into reclusiveness once in a while. Agnes chanced upon him sobbing in his room.

"Son, what's bothering you?" she asked.

"I killed my friend!" he wailed.

"You didn't kill your friend. You don't have the heart to hurt anyone."

"Asiedu died because of me. If I ate what you cooked, I wouldn't have cooked for myself, which caused him to die."

"Son, accidents happen. Cheer up. You didn't kill him."

"I have to tell Mr. and Mrs. Nkatia what happened," Gyambibi persisted.

"Your father and I will do that if it'll make you feel better," Agnes said.

His parents knew he was a boy of firm mind, disturbed by impropriety. The onus was on them to tell Asiedu's parents. If they didn't, he would—they were sure of that. They didn't want to hide anything; the boy's death had been an accident. But if they talked to Asiedu's parents, they, in turn, would want to speak to Gyambibi, and gossip would spread, making the story linger. Karikari and Agnes thought this would only worsen Gyambibi's condition, so they hesitated. The evening they were to tell Asiedu's parents, Gyambibi told them Asiedu had said they should not and that Gyambibi had seen Asiedu, who talked to him and ran into the forest. He wasn't dead! The next morning, Gyambibi's parents took him to a rural medical practitioner, who deemed that Gyambibi wasn't afflicted psychiatrically. Days passed before taking him to another psychiatrist, who again confirmed that he had no psychiatric issues. They did learn, however, that he hadn't been sleeping.

Gyambibi told his parents about visions of rains flooding some towns and devastating others—Agnes and Karikari connected news from the radio box to Gyambibi's statement. Because the rains and flooding were ongoing, the news reportage was constant. Gyambibi's mind, under the strain of guilt for his friend's death, in addition to sleeplessness and a constant backdrop of stories about his friend, must have derived his "visions" from the radio and village gossip brewing outside his room.

"Can't you have him today?" Gyambibi asked his pregnant mother.

"It doesn't work like that," Agnes said, laughing.

"Why, you can have him today if you want to."

"No, he has to grow in there until he's ready to come out."

"I'll share my food with him to get him to grow."

"Babies can't eat foods like that."

"He eats the same foods you eat, which I also eat."

"Yes, but it isn't solid food."

"I can take a pestle and mortar to mine and feed it to him. I'll feed him porridge."

"Why these questions?"

"I want to play with him. Yaw doesn't want to play with me. He doesn't want me with his friends."

"You should play with children your age. You have Moro, Asamoah, and other kids."

"No, Mama. When it rains or when evening comes, you make me come inside. I need someone I can play with all the time. Can't you have him today?"

"I said it doesn't work that way. He decides when to be born."

"I thought parents decided for their children. You decide when I should be outside."

"And do you listen? Don't you come home whenever you feel like it?"

"It's different, Mama. I'm a man; he's a baby, not even born yet."

"How do you know it's a boy, anyway?"

"How do you know it's not?"

Adwoa Brago dropped by for a visit. "Stop disturbing your mother," she said to Gyambibi.

"He tells me he's a man, and I should have this baby today."

"This boy!" Adwoa Brago exhaled. She helped lower Agnes into the sofa.

"I suppose you've picked a name for the baby since you haven't stopped bothering your mother for several months now."

"Donyinah," Gyambibi said.

"Let's see what your father has to say about that," Adwoa Brago said to Gyambibi, shaking a finger at him.

"He's already told his father about the name, Donyinah. He wants his brother to be named after his grandfather."

"And how does he know it's a boy?"

"Ask him for me."

But Gyambibi was long gone.

Months went by. Gyambibi kept to his ways, pestering his mother about his unborn brother. One hot afternoon, Agnes finally said his brother would be born—if God willed it—by the week's end.

Then mysterious gusts of wind began their slow creep through the village. Harvest was two weeks away, and these intense gusts renewed the villagers' anxiety. Cause for concern came when they saw whirlwinds in midair, moving about and eventually resting on the ground, uprooting weeds and shrubs. They saw this once, twice, then five times, at which point their anxiety about the faceless forces of the village arose.

The villagers, used to weather cycles running their normal course, unpunctuated by strange meteorological anomalies, began to grow concerned. Crops were cultivated in March through May and harvested in September and October, with the rainy season sandwiched in between. It was uncommon to have constant rainfalls close to harvest, particularly in October, even though it rained sporadically before and after the rainy season. Lately, however, things had been different: rainfall was sudden and poured with enough ferocity to ruin the crop harvest, not to mention the sporadic whirlwinds.

The weather forecasts that came through the radio box meant nothing to the villagers. Were the meteorologists or newscasters insensitive to others' existence? How could the meteorologists not know that it rained and stopped at the same time everywhere? News of devastation caused by rainfall in a suburb of Kumasi was discarded as a fabrication because the same rain didn't appear in Enkoho. If nothing else, this belief system told how reclusive the village was. Even those who managed to "escape" couldn't tell how different the outside world was from their village because of their heavy preoccupation with what inhabited the village, which never left their mind wherever they settled. And it was never the case that weather conditions outside the village were much different from that of the village the day one returned. They eventually ended up back in the village without a different perspective from the villagers. So it was foreseeable when the villagers ignored the voices from the radio box forecasting a cataclysmic rainfall.

However prepared the villagers might have been, they couldn't have been ready for what did happen. Just like any other weekend, in the morning, the children of Enkoho converged on the communal playground after chores. Eager to start playing, some of them skipped breakfast, undeterred by the gusts of wind. Danfo had promised to referee their soccer game that morning, so he was there too. He brought breakfast for Gyambibi because Agnes said he had left the house without eating. Karikari went to the playground and returned with Yaw. Because Gyambibi had recovered from what ailed him, Karikari resumed his occasional trips to Accra. Before leaving again, Karikari paid a courtesy visit to Mawuli, asking him, as usual, to take care of his family in his absence. In the meantime, the kids played. Karikari hugged Gyambibi and left.

It was 7:47 a.m. when Karikari waved to Danfo. By 8:00 a.m., he and Yaw were out of the village. At 9:49 a.m., Agnes and Daavi came to the playground. Daavi was now with Agnes all the time because she was far along in pregnancy, and Karikari was out of town. They left at 10:00 a.m. when the soccer game resumed after halftime.

At 10:36 a.m., the sky began pulsing with sunlight, which cut through the ensuing darkness. Gyambibi was fixated on the sky, his curious mind wondering what was to come, while his play-mates carried on as if nothing out of the ordinary was unfold-ing. Sensing the impending devastation, he felt like screaming to alert everyone but didn't. For years, he had seen what others didn't see. So now he would be silent and not divulge what he felt was happening. From another angle, he saw Agya Kobi, the only adult on the playground besides Danfo. With Danfo there, Agya Kobi didn't stay long and left with his great-grand-son, Asamoah.

Thunder reverberated across the sky, sending sinuous light-ning through the quickening darkness. Though nervous, Gyam-bibi waited patiently. Thunder continued to peal louder. It was dawning on many that *something* was happening. Many flocked outside to investigate. Every man cast a suspicious eye on his neighbor. Could someone be behind this strange event?

The wind picked up, whipping everything in sight. Sparks of electricity stuttered across the top of Karikari's house when the palm fronds brushed against the electric cable passing overhead. The sight would have reminded Karikari of the danger Mr. Osei foresaw, against which he had suggested the palm tree be cut down to route the electric cable properly. This fiery spark between the palm fronds and the live cable had occurred twice before but not on the scale that was occurring now. As the wind died down, a brilliant iridescence of blue, red, and yellow hues flashed against the backdrop of darkness. Streams of pulsating colors, like clusters of giant chromatophores dancing in synchrony and silhouetted between the horns of the wind, were a sight to behold. Gyambibi looked about, wondering if others saw what he saw. Seeing this strange thing confused and frightened him. Be it a disturbance of the "electromagnetic activity" encircling the village, a novel dispersion pattern of plasma interfacing with atmospheric debris, a yet-to-be-discovered astronomical phenomenon, a chance confluence of all these, or simply that the gods were airing out their polychromatic kilts in the heavens—Gyambibi couldn't process what was unfolding only to him. The violent wind and potential devastation, however, were seen by all. Now all were awake to the preamble of their destruction.

The villagers were afraid to share what they thought of it, for affairs of this nature deemed to originate from the gods weren't to be discussed. Nevertheless, the perception that the heavens had unleashed bursts of exotic meteorological and cosmic energy to relay a message to them lay buried somewhere in their collective psyche. What was being communicated, however, couldn't be deciphered.

Explosions of thunder continued, and winds sent debris everywhere. Dust filled the air. Both children and the fainthearted sheltered behind closed doors. Before long, everyone was convinced that destruction was indeed lurking behind the vaulted sky.

A covey of crows flying overhead foreshadowed a disaster. Soon afterward, lumps of ice began falling from the sky, hurtled by high winds. Only some elders knew about hail or had heard of it through oral history. Droplets of rain followed. The sky began to clear unexpectedly, enabling hope. That faded quickly, though, when the gentle drops of rain suddenly turned brutish, descending on the village with unreserved venom. Loud crashes of violent winds stripped away leaves and uprooted trees. Thatched roofs were stripped off. Wooden structures were stripped naked and whisked off. Huts disintegrated and were carried away by rivers of water. Whole buildings dissolved into nothingness. Families saw their meager belongings taken by the rain. It would have been suicidal to go after them. The cataclysmically imposing scene appeared imagined, surreal. Those whose huts were destroyed left their fate in the hands of unmerciful floods and powerful winds.

Chief saw his village in utter chaos. Having one of a handful of cement-constructed structures in Enkoho, the homeless scrummed for space in his multiunit palace. At one point, his two nephews, doubling as sentries, had to turn away some of the villagers because the only rooms left were off-limits to the uninitiated—and for good reasons. Tradition had it that the uninitiated who had forayed into these restricted areas didn't come out whole. Some died instantly after making a wrong turn into the room for ritual sacrifice.

Chief was apprised of the damage the village had sustained. He authorized the custodian of the palace to send out an attendant, also the master drummer, to summon the elders to consolidate ideas on how best to thwart further destruction. The attendant and the noisemaker wasted no time fetching a pair of Atumpan drums and heading into the torrential rain. They turned the drums upside down to keep their surfaces dry. The drummer and noisemaker ran, impeded by the soggy ground and forceful winds. Once the drums were near the village square, the noisemaker held an umbrella over them to keep them dry. The elders heard the message through the deafening rain.

With most of his living quarters occupied, Chief went into one of the off-limit rooms, recited some formulas, and joined the elders in the courtyard. From Chief's livestock pen, his half-brother brought two sheep and all full-grown bulls, un-blemished and uncastrated, to the palace and tied them down. Later, a roan bull was added at the urging of Healer. Cartons of Schnapps and calabashes were amply supplied. The goal was to exceed the items used in the last ritual ceremony, for perhaps the will of the implacable gods would succumb to greater enticements. Healer took a final stock of the ritual panoply, after which he left to consult with the oracle.

All formalities, such as prostrating before Chief, were abandoned. Everyone seated around Chief avoided the formal communication protocol of going through the linguist. Hurriedly, he demanded to know what each elder thought about what was happening and its remedy.

"Why didn't they reveal this to us? Could they be angry with us, and could these rains be our *nkrabea*? Did we not offer them enough blood days ago during the *Awukudae* festival?" wondered one elder.

"Perhaps a child of Enkoho had done something to offend them, or we may have angered them in a manner that's not apparent? Either way, we have to appease them," another added.

Everyone agreed. "They" and "them" were understood to be the *forces* that inhabited the village.

The pouring of libations began amidst the recitation of formulas by Healer. Standing to the left of Chief, the priest-cum-healer placed three white eggs into Chief's right palm, one at a time, which he, in turn, tossed to an area of the ground that was freshly stained by libation, breaking each one of them, while pleading with *them* to free the village from destruction. After the Schnapps had dulled their senses, Healer took a knife and, one after the other, slashed the throats of the sheep and bull while reciting secret formulas. Blood gushed from the animals and squirted everywhere as they gyrated. The elders looked on without cringing. Bright-red blood flowed out of the compound and merged into a rivulet of the village's destruction through the somber village. It faded in intensity as it journeyed—seeping into subterranean culverts, draining into the dry cups of "them."

The darkest day in the history of Enkoho had finally arrived, uninvited, and would forever be seared in its memory.

The rain hadn't lost an ounce of lust for savagery. Mawuli left his hut with his wife, children, and a bag of vital family items, seeking Karikari's house for refuge. Nearby, he heard the loud wail of a woman cutting through the noise of destruction. The cries were in the direction he was heading. It was Agnes. Gyambibi wasn't home. Mawuli handed the bag to Jeefa and beckoned them inside. Karikari's house had many rooms. Mawuli found it odd that no one besides his family had sought refuge there, instead choosing to go to Chief's. Yet rumors of Agya Kobi's presence lurking in Karikari's house were rife with the villagers; a refuge there was too risky. The storm served as a reminder of the limitations of what Preacher did to cleanse the house after that.

Agnes had followed Mawuli out onto the porch and down the stairs. Mawuli instructed her to go inside before disappearing into the torrential rain. A river of water had swallowed the first four steps; the water rose to the knee on the ground. Agnes cringed at the thought of what might have happened to her son when the baby moved. As clever as Gyambibi was to be safe, he was nonetheless vulnerable to hurt or death. The destruction was fierce. Agnes held her belly and soon took steps one and two. A peal of thunder upset her balance when attempting to scale the third and fourth steps simultaneously to get indoors quickly. The palm fronds caught fire as they brushed against the parapet and overhead cable, with lightning adding the spark. Agnes fell backward.

Mawuli was frantic: the safety of Karikari's family had been entrusted to him. The playground was recognizable only from its location and the baobab tree. The wooden benches had fallen prey to the raging waters. He covered every inch of the expansive field but came up empty, so he scoured the trees—no sign of Gyambibi. With the playground about a hundred twenty meters from Karikari's compound, he asked Jeefa where she had last seen Gyambibi. While there, he was confronted by another alarm: Agnes was missing. They had heard the thunder, which had shaken the building, and they were filled with many disturbing thoughts they couldn't suppress. Had Agnes fallen? They were alarmed but reassured by the possibility that maybe she had changed her mind and went after Mawuli to find Gyambibi. Now they were all nervous wrecks. She couldn't survive this. Daavi and Jeefa had gone searching for her but returned, thinking she was with Mawuli. All blood drained from Mawuli's face, for he knew Agnes couldn't survive the floods and destruction. He cursed the heavens.

The storm continued its unrelenting brutality. Mawuli walked back to the playground, this time even more impeded because of the drag of rising water. As he approached the northern flank of the park, his right foot touched what he felt was the bony promontory of a human nose. Could the boy be dead? How was he going to break the news to his mother? He kept his mouth closed and his abdominal muscles tight to avoid throwing up. He clutched his stomach and prayed under his breath. He was frozen in time for a slow minute, overwhelmed by unexplainable emotions. He reminded himself why he was there and submerged himself to retrieve the boy's lifeless body. It turned out to be the corpse of a different boy trapped under a tree trunk. He stood there speechless as he contemplated what to tell the boy's parents, whom he worked with on Karikari's farm. He couldn't help but be relieved that the boy wasn't Gyambibi. While that was good enough for him, pain clung everywhere around him.

Grief overcame him, for he couldn't fathom what was happening. He held the corpse and stared at the gushing water, unable to suppress a sob. Then it thundered again so loudly that he fell backward, immersing himself fully in the floodwaters, heavy with the weight of the corpse, which then slipped out of his hands. He stumbled up, only to trip on the edge of a cement embankment and fall forward. He spread his arms to protect his face. Strangely, his hands never touched the ground. He realized he had fallen into the village well. He wasn't alone: he felt another corpse there, against a tangled mass that also threatened to capture him. Fighting to free himself, he swam to the surface, his eyes red and panic-stricken. His body was shaking and covered with sweat, mud, and floodwater. The stress of not finding Gyambibi alive terrified him, and the thought that he and Agnes could both be dead right now brought tears to his eyes. He cursed the heavens! He shook his head in total disbelief. Would there be one person left in the village after the cataclysm? He hung his head, gasping for breath.

Why would God watch unconcerned? How could "they" and the guidance spirits of the ancestors watch while the entire village was destroyed? Mawuli's frustration spiked each minute he connected "them" to the devastation. Maybe "they" simply were acting out their occult penchant for sadism. Or, because Christians were suffering the same fate, God was permitting "them" to do this for reasons best left to Him?

A battered corpse floated past him and terminated his thoughts. The dead woman used to peddle porridge and doughnuts in the village every morning. The few times he and Daavi had had disagreements, she was always there to tell them what she thought, always taking the side of Daavi. Mawuli dropped his head in disbelief over her death. His chin found a resting spot on his clenched fist. He looked up and cursed the heavens in Ewe, Twi, and Ewe again. He lowered his head and let out a yell, sobbing loudly now. The prospects of returning home and finding his family whole preoccupied him. He came to himself and stared about as if wondering how he'd ended up in the middle of the playground, waist-deep in a pool of rising flood. Although he hadn't found Gyambibi, he would be much more comfortable telling that to his mother than handing her his lifeless body. Not forgetting that she could be dead also. He was shocked by the destruction around him. Only then did it come to him that a heavy fog had descended on the forest. If the destruction he could see about him had also happened in the forest, the crops stood no chance. He could see trees tottering against the wind. The devastation was too sudden and horrific not to be a nightmarish dream, but he could smell his own terrified sweat. And sweat wasn't falling from the sky.

Mawuli's weary legs succumbed to the drag of the rising flood. He could swim faster than walk. It was 12:16 p.m. when he contemplated abandoning the search and going home to protect his own children and wife. However, another thought quickly offset that: how could he look Karikari or Agnes in the eye again, knowing he hadn't done all he could to save their son? Adding to that stress, Karikari's family had been left in his care, and they had always been kind to his family. Karikari had taken up his children's school fees when they were sent home. In many respects, they were more of a family than close friends. Ultimately, no matter how Mawuli turned his options, his spirit of loyalty prevailed.

As he completed that thought, in front of his field of view was the body of a boy floating facedown about an arm's length from him. The sight was excruciating and nauseating. He'd found what appeared to be Gyambibi, but suddenly his mouth was agape, vomiting from pain and shock. The water current began to move the body away. Collecting himself, he swam after it and wrapped his arms around him from behind—without the strength to see his face. Memories flooded his mind of the interactions he had had with Gyambibi. Just two days prior, he had sent his daughter and him to buy roasted plantain and groundnuts. His daughter reported how Gyambibi objected to the burnt plantain the seller had initially sold them. He had made it clear to the seller that he wouldn't, under any circumstances, accept such plantains, even if discounted, for Jeefa's father. Since these were the only ones the seller had then, she had to roast fresh ones. Gyambibi had convinced Jeefa that they should wait for fresh ones. Mawuli questioned why they had been late that day: it was because of the love that Gyambibi had for him. The memories were painful.

Just then, he heard voices that jolted him, and the corpse fell out of his hands. The rain blurred the voices, making it difficult for him to discern. He had heard stories of the dead talking or appearing to the living before departing for the afterlife. He didn't know what to make of the voices. Putting the experience behind him, his attention returned to the corpse that continued to drift away.

Securing the corpse once again, he heard a clash of two voices! This time, however, it appeared they were yelling his name. The voices seemed to emanate from the baobab tree in front of him. Looking intently at the tree, for a moment, he couldn't believe who was staring down at him. He wiped his face and focused his tear-dimmed eyes on the tree. Yes, his vision was perfectly fine! He dropped the corpse and dashed for the baobab tree!

Sparse vegetation allowed the moonlight to sneak onto the forest floor. Tree branches and leaves swayed to gentle winds. Birds and other arboreal animals, usually visible in large numbers during the day, were now out of sight, away from the open view of nocturnal predators. In the meantime, a pair of preying eyes lurked in the dark, scanning the forest for the right trophy to take home.

Danfo took ten silent steps. As if pacing himself, he repeated this into his fourth hour of hunting. There was a built-in mechanism somewhere in him. Despite the distances that hunters covered and the mental and physical exhaustion that hunting entailed, Danfo managed to stay obese, probably the only known obese hunter in history. Perhaps this was because he relied more on faunal ethology than the physicality of hunting. He refused to believe that nocturnal hunting didn't require great skill. In an intense argument, his wife would ask him what skill was needed to shoot a sleeping deer. His answer was that it took a man to march into the forest at night in Enkoho, knowing his chances of not returning alive were greater than returning home with game. Hunting the forest at night carried dangerous risks: some saw things that couldn't be repeated.

Four hours into hunting, he hadn't seen so much as a mosquito. Luck continued to evade him. He wondered why. The name Esi Eluwah kept coming up the more he thought about it. That witch of a wife must be at it again. She had no greater wish other than to see his destruction. Of all the women in the world, how did he end up with Esi Eluwah? Merciless witch! Her nocturnal consorts with the Devil were meant to make him live a hard life. She would foil his chances tonight and meet his empty hands in the morning with a sorrowful tear, always ensuring he was present to witness her weeping prayers. If God exists, He should have seen through her duplicity long ago and struck her down.

A troop of startled monkeys leaped from tree to tree as they sensed subtle movements in the forest. Danfo's feet stepped on a cluster of fecal pellets. He sampled it between his fingers and realized it was moist and freshly deposited. He paced his steps and looked around. A deer must be nearby. A few strides later, there it was, lying down and staring straight at him as his headlamp focused on it. Leaning uncomfortably against a tree, he aimed between the deer's eyes and fired. The lifeless forest exploded with the din of startled animals, bringing into view the forest's faunal diversity. Danfo ignored the commotion, unwilling to return home empty-handed.

He walked through the brush to retrieve his trophy. The thought of going back, smoking and skinning it, lightened his mood. Karikari would buy it in a heartbeat. As such mundane thoughts were going through his mind, a pointed stone pricked him, redirecting his winding thoughts back to the fact that he had shot and incapacitated a stag. He stopped walking and looked around.

There was nothing.

And no bloody trail.

He knew he had shot a deer and had heard a death rattle. Somehow he had also seen clumps of skin come off between the deer's horns, where he had hit. Maybe he wasn't alone. If anyone or anything had dragged off his kill, at least there should be a bloody trail. Yet not even paw prints. He circled the area in bewilderment. Nothing. This was Enkoho, after all. He had a strong feeling of a presence around him but quickly killed the temptation to dwell on it. Entertaining such thoughts could stifle his reason for nocturnal hunting. If an evil presence manifested, he wouldn't have enough legs to outrun it.

The *feeling* he perceived now came into focus. The sounds of wind and rain, barely audible before, were now intense. He touched the headlamp and rubbed his skin. But there was no water on him, though he was sure it was raining. Neither did leaves or the forest sway with the wind; moreover, there were worrying human voices, which agreed with him that a cataclysmic rainfall was ripping through the forest and village.

With an overpowering sense of a rainfall he didn't see, his nostrils confronted a strong smell of sulfur. As he walked back to his hunting equipment, his attention was drawn to a sheep bleating yards away, in the same spot he'd shot the deer. He was startled. Hunting for about three decades had never exposed him to a sheep covered in pure white wool with red streaks, like a creature from a fairytale. The forest was lit as if it was daytime. It was somewhat serene, as if torrential rain wasn't descending. Thinking back, Danfo hadn't slept well the night before. Revolving thoughts entered and fled. Minute objects floated in his peripheral vision. This sheep may well be an ectomorph of a god. He tried to make sense of this otherworldly creature. If the gods wanted to say anything to him, the forest wouldn't be an ideal place for that. Then again, maybe it was.

The stench of sulfur grew denser. A couple of minutes had transpired since the sheep appeared. It had crouched on a patch of grass, perhaps waiting for this valiant hunter to take it home. Without further hesitation, Danfo fired his loaded rifle and hit the target. Its white fur became drenched in bright-red blood. It was dead. He couldn't have shot a god, for gods don't die. The sheep hadn't moved an inch. The musket ball had liberated a chunk of wool upon impact, so he watched in astonishment as the blood slowly faded from the sheep's coat, soon returning to its original snow-white-red color. Then everything around him began to move slowly, which stoked fears in him he didn't know he had. Drool streamed down the left corner of his mouth. He reached into his sack for a powder horn, opened it, and emptied its content into the barrel of his rifle while keeping an unblinking eye on the sheep. As fast as he could, he shoved a musket ball down the throat of the barrel. And then, while his foggy brain slowly processed his next course of action, he made a throwing gesture with the ramrod. The sheep didn't flinch. With his tongue pressed against his lower lip and sweeping the corners of his mouth, he disengaged the flintlock and aimed. This would be the third time he would be firing the rifle tonight. Suddenly he realized he didn't have the strength to squeeze the trigger. His right hand felt heavy. He couldn't lift it when he tried. He and the sheep were locked in a stare-down. Danfo wanted to get out of the forest, but he couldn't find the courage. Worse, his legs had become weak, unable to support his disproportionately large upper body. The smell of sulfur stood boldly, overpowering his senses.

He heard himself bleating like a sheep, unable to stop. It didn't take long before he realized what was happening: the sheep had psychokinetically taken control of his faculties. Before long, he was a sheep roaming the meadows. Then he fell into a trance-like state, unable to move, having been transformed back into a human, now back to the same place he was before, with the sheep still staring at him. When he tried to bolt away, he was unable, for his legs were weak. Even if he could run, a part of him feared he might slip and fall because of rainfall he didn't see. His arms had regained their strength, though. He found the trigger and quickly squeezed it, barely aiming. The force of impact lifted the sheep and dropped it on the limbs of the *tree without a name*. His legs regained strength. Even with that, he was torn between running away and taking home this mysterious creature. The former would probably ensure his safety since the sheep would be out of sight and out of his mind. The latter would endow him with fame in Enkoho, as he would be the only one to achieve such a feat. Well, if he had to tell his story to the villagers, which he intended to do, he might as well collect the supporting evidence.

But again, when he went to retrieve his kill, there was nothing. A cold breeze swept through, and everything became suspiciously calm. He could sense movements nearby. He had seen a lot in the past forty minutes or so, but he was still alive. He would die someday, but not today, he assured himself. He brushed his fears aside, and instead of going home, he decided to search his traps to see if they'd caught anything. Wandering through the forest, he thought his time would have been better spent in bed. His fears began to dissipate, and with them, his will to continue hunting. It was dark again, and moonlight flashed here and there. The sensation of violent rainfall and wind hadn't left him, just like the worrying human voices about the rainfall. He looked about him: there was no water pooling on the ground. The rain was falling upward, from the earth to the heavens.

Returning home, his headlamp cast a wolfish, beastly shadow in the distance. In his decades of hunting, he couldn't remember if this had ever happened. Then his head began moving up and down in synchrony with more shadowy objects he began imagining. He couldn't stop it; it was as if a force had possessed him. He had a vague, remote apprehension that he would see something on his path. As he continued, a strange vision emerged: a female in a grass skirt hemmed at the waist with what appeared to be a sheepskin of the same strange hue he'd encountered earlier. Several bony artifacts were suspended from it. Danfo's eyes were drawn to her unusually long breasts that were scaly, drooped just above her waist, and completely tattooed with the rest of her bare torso in numinous glyphs. Her jaw moved subtly. Her tongue rolled into a ball something she was chewing, which she lodged in one cheek, then released and lodged in the other cheek. This was repeated with precision. Danfo watched closely as the ominous figure faded into thin air like a hatchling of the Devil.

Danfo recalled youthful competitions with his siblings to simulate terrifying monsters by placing whatever they could find between the flickering flames of a lantern and the walls of their room. The images didn't terrify him then; they surely didn't now. The obvious difference was that this shadowy figure had acted independently of his manipulations. He blocked the invasion of terror from his mind, purely focusing on getting home.

Before he knew it, the apparition reappeared and spewed something toward his face. He felt the impulse to avoid it but couldn't. When it hit him, he was pulled into a vortex. He leaned back to avoid being swept up, but instead, he fell on the ground, his face covered in a slimy mass that reeked of masticated kola nuts. Aware of snapping twigs and crunching dead leaves, he knew the force was running toward him again. Danfo scraped off the kola from his face, struggled to his feet, and ran.

Several minutes went by before he reached the village. It was still dusky, with an overwhelming sense of a cataclysmic flood he couldn't see. He could hear voices talking about the flood but couldn't see anyone around.

He was returning home empty-handed. He staggered as he walked toward a chicken coop. He put down his hunting accessories and watched the hencoop mysteriously open. So he reached into the coop for some eggs. One of the eggs vanished in his hands and changed into the apparition that had chased him out of the woods. He threw the other eggs away, gripped with fear. Strangely, none of the hens cackled or scuttled. A cold sensation enveloped him as he bolted, feeling the apparition's cold breath over his shoulder. He took a sharp turn to get to his house. He stumbled and fell. Disoriented, Danfo got up and continued on. He felt blood leaking out of his body, slowing him down. Feeling an intense pain crawl up his thigh, he stopped. He realized he'd been running for several minutes, yet his house was nowhere in sight. Trees, the ground, huts, the sky, stars...everything seemed to have been moving with him, giving him the impression that he hadn't moved at all. Perhaps he was dreaming or imagining things. No, that couldn't be. He had been running for sure; he knew that. Nevertheless, he should have reached home several times over.

Something was eerily out of place.

Danfo was short of breath. He stopped and waited for the apparition to overtake him. He sat in the dirt, slumped forward, and started scribbling in the sand, not knowing what he was doing. He raised his head and saw a boy standing before an elderly man; the apparition chasing him was forgotten. The boy and the elderly man were people Danfo knew very well in Enkoho. The boy's bodily constituents began separating from his body and suspended in midair while his feet touched the ground. He could feel the boy crying as an unknown force pulled his arms and legs apart. Danfo fed the boy a floating body part. Each time the boy ate a piece of his own flesh, Danfo saw pain crawl throughout the body of the elderly man. Danfo, now possessed by the apparition chasing him, took joy in seeing the hurt it caused both of them. Then Danfo realized that even though the boy was eating his own flesh, he was somehow eating the old man too. Whenever the old man pursed his lips to utter anything, the boy would stop; when he turned away, the boy would ingest another body part. The nauseating sight continued till the boy's heart was the only anatomy left, hanging in midair. Danfo knew its consumption would signal the boy's demise.

Danfo watched with a satisfied smirk. The boy realized that Danfo was interested in his destruction and turned to the old man who had been warning him to look away from Danfo. The boy seemed to run toward him, smiling, with arms outstretched. Through this image, somehow, Danfo felt the boy running toward him as well. Danfo opened his arms to embrace him when a flare of lightning flashed, flooding the crowded room, nudging him out of sleep and this nightmarish dream. Thunder didn't follow the lightning.

Danfo was now fully awake, and the crowd at his house had him to contend with! Danfo looked at people's faces as if seeing them for the first time.

A man cracked open the louvers of a window by which he sat and looked outside. He then closed them tightly and folded himself into a corner, shaking. No one else dared look outside to see what couldn't be unseen. What had he witnessed? The man was speechless, bobbing his head up and down. The farms were destroyed. The horde was alarmed, but their alarm soon gave way to doubt. That couldn't be true, for the farms started at least a hundred meters from here. How could the man see that far? The villagers breathed a sigh of relief. The man ventured into the storm, but some men wrestled him to the ground and pulled him back in.

"It's raining feathers...black feathers, like those of a crow," the man said through a catatonic face. He must have lost his mind, for how could he make out feathers in this storm? Those gathered agreed though they couldn't say how a mentally competent man could become crazy in a flash. In the meantime, tumbles of wind and the rush of flowing water grew more intense. Loud crashes could be heard outside. The occasional howling of dying monkeys, squeals of animals they'd never heard of, and tumbling sounds of destruction instilled fear. The damage was severe enough to make them believe that what they were perceiving was happening well beyond the village and surrounding forest. The crash of a tree against the building sent nervous jitters through the villagers.

Danfo was relieved to be awake from that terrible nightmare. At first, the gawking faces seemed an unwelcome continuation until he heard a familiar insult.

"You're a disgrace."

Esi Eluwah had been unable to wake Danfo since he had come home from the playground drinking. The rush of villagers followed, and she was embarrassed by his appearance. Confronted by his wife's insult and unaware of what was happening outside, Danfo's first order was to demand everyone get out of his house. Men, women, and children might have met their death if Esi Eluwah's insult didn't force him to consider what was happening.

"Yea, impressing the world with a Bible under your armpit on your way to church every day the church building opens its doors. Some good women go to church. Your motive is questionable at best, and there's the other question of whether you are even a woman. Birds of a feather cavort together; that makes you a disgrace, too," he replied, rolling over.

Alcohol didn't impact Danfo the way it did before they got married. It loosened his tongue now, but it no longer left his thoughts in disarray. His thoughts were now more focused and forceful when he was drunk.

"No, you are the disgrace. Do you see yourself as a man?"

"I was man enough for you to marry." He shrugged.

"Stupid drunk! How could a man allow himself to be destroyed to this extent by alcohol?"

"Don't be mad because I love alcohol more than I love you. By the way, who did you think found you a husband: alcohol or God? Had my brain not been crippled by alcohol, do you think I would have married you?"

"I'm jealous of other married women in this village. They have hardworking husbands who think clearly. What did I do to deserve this?" Esi Eluwah felt sorry for herself but continued to berate him. "Drinking this early in the morning when our village is on the brink of annihilation...you just can't seem to sink any lower."

"I sank the lowest when I married you."

A man intervened. "Don't treat your wife this way, Danfo. You know better. You had a mother at one point; please mind your words."

Danfo found the words for him in a convoluted rant: "The witch you call my mother better be quiet in the grave. If you can communicate with the dead, tell her to stop showing up in my dreams. She can't just show up on this side of life to make up for her crime of weaning a boy who wasn't ready. May her tormented soul roast in hell! Now you: At the crossroads of feminism and male relevance, you're the lone, smug one who doesn't belong on the battlefield. Feminism, that polluted dust blowing through the Western world, I will not allow to settle on our land. The battle is already lost in the West. Some of the men there are cross-dressers, Yaw tells me. May God grant that fine young man an extended lifespan to learn and share with me what goes on in the West. He tells me that in America...some of the men...some of them...let me stop before my drink changes direction and heads for my lungs. British monarchy with a woman at the helm? Such nonsense explains the downfall of the British Empire. Our brothers in the East are holding the line, thanks to God! I'm determined to defend men everywhere until I draw my last breath. We own women; they can't be equal to us. Do you think women want equality? If they have equality in mind, why can't I talk to one like I talk to you? You know why? They crave men's subservience, not equality. They seek our reverence, our unrequited servitude. If they want equality, then what I was doing was exactly that. That's the essence of equality. They're not to be treated any differently than men. That still means you could wag your tongue at a woman as you would a man, you idiot! I'm beside myself lecturing a grown man who allows his wife to slap and punch him at leisure. Fool, if a woman throws punches at a man, she's not supposed to get a discount on the number of punches he throws back. That's the essence of equality. And I need not remind you or any man that women often need a surplus number of punches to calm down. That's the fight for equality. I'm just doing my part. Men and women are simply that: *men* and *women*. Women can dream up any similarities to make themselves equal to us because that's their Satan-given right, but don't tell me we must be subservient to them!"

"I...I...," Esi Eluwah lost her thought.

"Let me help you, woman. You're not good for me; I don't have to be smug about me meaning a lot to your family," Danfo said, responding to a point he thought she was going to make.

"A useless man like you can mean nothing to my family."

"Don't judge me useless because I drink, for you're no better than I. Let me be honest: you were better at picking me than I was picking you. And to be clear, I didn't pick you; I woke up married to you. You've left my house..." he counted his fingers, having lost track of how many times she'd left, "Each time you've returned because you know you have a good man."

The squabble seethed across the room, with women holding onto and comforting Esi Eluwah. No man restrained Danfo. He restrained himself because he knew better than to escalate into hand-to-hand combat with his wife in the presence of all these people.

"You've got it all wrong. It's my parents who told me to come back," Esi Eluwah said.

"Your parents know better than you, and even they know you can't find a husband better than me."

"That's not why my parents encourage me to come back, and you know it. They don't believe in divorce. You? A man of no use for anything. Had I known you were everything a married man wasn't, I wouldn't have bowed to their marriage pressures!"

"Woman, my marriage to you is a divine punishment for my childhood indiscretions. If I'd known you would be the punishment God would reserve for me, I would have married myself and carried on an extramarital affair with alcohol!"

Fear of being thrown outside into the rainstorm restrained both men and women. Esi Eluwah needed help from no one. She was capable of fighting her husband fist for fist. Her hidden respect for her uninvited guests restrained her. Any other day would have been different.

Screams of people from other rooms broke the arguments when loud gusts of wind crashed by, stripping part of the roof off with its attached trusses. With the medley of thunder, rushing floodwaters, the forest blowing through the village, and the concrete floors shaking beneath them, both young and old slipped over the edge of fear; they were terrified to death, not knowing if there would be a tomorrow. The anxiety over impending death was overwhelming. Covered in sweat, their hearts sunk with each clap of thunder. Instant annihilation was preferable to this slow, torturous tease of death. For the man who perceived his farms being destroyed, every tumble of the wind, every crash of lightning tore a piece out of him. This was death in slow motion.

One man suddenly jumped up, broke from the horde, and tore the door open to surrender to the storm. Preacher, who had taken refuge there, yelled out that the signs didn't signify it was the end of the world.

Preacher wrapped himself up in a corner, tormented by what he had just said. The end of the world! Would there ever be an end, as he had always held? The source of this mental torment would be none other than Gyambibi. The concept of the end of the world would come before Preacher after the storm when an argument broke out between Gyambibi and Asamoah. In all his years of studying the Bible, when Gyambibi's idea came before Agya Kobi, he could neither accept nor reject it. The debate came before Preacher, who was already familiar with Gyambibi's thoughts on the matter. He would wrestle with it for years to come.

Chapter

11

*O*ne couldn't take a step without being reminded of death. Seventeen days had passed since the cataclysm, and the destruction was everywhere. There were forty-six deaths: thirty-five confirmed and eleven missing, who were later confirmed dead when they never turned up due to the unspoken bond between the citizens and the village; that is, no child of Enkoho could leave and not return. There were many funerals to plan and attend, many broken memories to suppress, and too much pain to forget.

A stranger walked by, unperturbed by a scene of four corpses. The man slowed down as eyes settled on him. He nodded to the unfamiliar faces—a greeting that carried a deep understanding of the pain they were going through. He was stoic; the sight of dead bodies didn't trouble him. The dead were a man, his wife, and two children. Their hut had collapsed on them, and they were found in different places, carried by the flood. These deceased villagers didn't have much, but the vacancy their death created would be felt for years. The man was a farmhand; his dead wife was a porridge and doughnut peddler, whose presence the village recognized every morning. She had sold food with grace, chatted heartily with her customers, and didn't mind sharing her opinion, no matter how unwelcomed it might have been. She was blunt, and people sometimes felt uncomfortable around her, but she was liked nonetheless; the villagers equally loved her children. Now the ambiance was one of sorrow and pain. As attention returned to the deceased, the stranger slipped away, trailed by a cacophony of funeral dirges and wails.

Walking through the village wasn't a pleasant experience: garbage and mud were everywhere. There was a cleanup attempt, but it was limited to areas where funerals were taking place. The waysides still had patches of standing water with recrudescent reeds standing in them. Next to the road, mud was piled up, and the landscape was swathed where running water had carved a path. Antennae poles with their connecting wires lay on the edges as he walked by. A few steps ahead, an electric pole lay on the ground. The stranger didn't know that electricity had made it to this secluded and strangest of places. The stranger paced his steps to take in the full scope of the devastation.

More telling were storm-battered huts that had withstood the storm's devastation: concrete-slab foundations with their tenants of mud walls evacuated. There were also remains of many foundations where huts had once stood and housed families whose existence might be no more, having been washed away together like the mud walls that once shielded them from the elements. A whiff of deathly decay blew by. He caught sight of a mud hut with windows painted orange in the distance. He looked at his watch: it was 1:47 p.m. He would be thirty minutes late if he arrived at his destination by 2:00 p.m. While he walked, he saw black specks in the mud pile running along the side of the path. He scooped up some dirt and examined it. They were black feathers. Where had they come from, and how could there be so many? He fought a sudden urge to turn back. Besides, Mawuli had brought him to the village, pointed to Karikari's house, and then joined the funeral he had just witnessed. The stranger couldn't find his way back on his own. He told himself he would do his job, get out, and never step foot here again. If only he had known that the sole person to have seen the rain of crow feathers was also the only one among the dead to die while sheltered at Danfo's—the fact could have intensified his fear and forced him out of the village.

A few strides later, he found himself walking beside a man clad in black who must have been returning home from the funeral service.

"Good afternoon, my son," the stranger said in greeting.

"Good afternoon."

"I'm looking for Mr. Karikari, who lives in this area."

"Mr. Oteng, I'm Karikari."

"My condolences to the entire village. I've never seen anything like this," Mr. Oteng said. He withheld his impulse to speak of devastation in neighboring Kodee and Aduman, for the destruction in those villages was ordinary by comparison.

"All share that sentiment."

"How did this happen?"

"That's a question for God, Mr. Oteng. My brain is burned out. It's best not to think about it."

Oteng didn't even know the name of the village, but his curiosity was replaced by an intense fear of what he felt he couldn't see.

Tears began to stream down Karikari's face. A cold silence hung over the two men as they walked, continuing until they reached Karikari's house. Tabuah stood when Karikari fell within her field of view. She ran to him and latched on, crying and hugging him, muttering gibberish, overwhelmed by emotions. He held her as Oteng looked on without a word and began searching for something to occupy him. With Tabuah and Karikari in a tight embrace, Oteng lifted his feet one after the other and stared at them. Plaques of clay adhered to his sandals and weighed down his feet. He went to scrape them against the bark of a tree. He looked up and saw Karikari's eyes still fixed on his sister, one consoling the other.

"Why, why, why?" was all that escaped Tabuah's lips as Karikari maintained his silence because he choked up when he tried to speak.

As an aged mortician from Kodee, Oteng saw a side of death that most people never did.

Inquisitive minds refrained from asking why he would take up such a profession. In fact, he looked like death. If his remains were to be exhumed in five hundred years, one would still not know if he was dead. Five days a week, he worked as a butcher. About twice a month, he worked as a mortician. One skill enhanced the other. He wouldn't have come here if it weren't for the disruption in his work as a butcher. He had said that much to Mawuli, who had come to seek Oteng's services on behalf of Karikari. There had been a virulent outbreak in the North and in neighboring Burkina Faso, which had ravaged the cattle population. Karikari had heard about it from Danfo because Esi Eluwah had complained about an interruption in beef supply. Experts came from Kenya to look into it because veterinary medicine wasn't prominent in the country after the colonial era. Outbreaks of animal diseases were largely handled by the nontechnical staff of the regional outpost of the Veterinary Services Department, who had thought the source of the outbreak a form of rinderpest. It took experts from Kenya to trace the cattle deaths to babesiosis and heartwater.

After being taken into a tent where he was to perform his trade, Oteng flung a burlap sack across a table, emitting the sound of clinking metals. The sight of a corpse to prepare for burial took his mind off his own fear of dying in Enkoho. He walked around a table on which a pregnant corpse rested, sizing it up. He sat on the edge of the bench, his mind preoccupied with the task ahead, scheming how he would approach it. He popped open a partial bottle of rum and took a long swig, then poured some on his hands, rubbed them together, and wiped them on his smock. He turned to the sack and retrieved knives of different sizes, which he placed on the table. These were more of a culinary variety than actual surgical scalpels.

He turned the supine corpse so that her right side faced him. Placing the heel of his left hand in the middle of her chest, his thumb pointing toward him, the rest pointing away, he pinned down the corpse as if she would flinch once he started. Then, with the combined pious skill of a medieval surgeon and the culinary proficiency of a charcutier, his fingers slowly traced her bulging belly. At the same time, his right hand made a long, crude incision between them, moving the knife back and forth as one would do in cutting into a pig. The incision spanned below the chest, through the navel, and stopped short of her groin. He must have put too much weight on the blade and penetrated the amniotic sac, allowing seepage to the surface of a malodorous fluid. Nothing could have hidden his disgust: his face contorted to the likeness of his tongue having taken a dip in porcupine bile. He spat away from the corpse, dragging his left forearm across his chapped lips. Putrid air engulfed the tent and made breathing torturous. He went outside. Several minutes later, he made it back into the tent with swollen cheeks of fresh air, which he inhaled slowly as his hands quickly evacuated the amniotic sac from the corpse's abdominal cavity. This he held in one hand, and with the other, he severed a network of vessels and tissues adhering to it. This he put in a miniature pine box.

The depressed abdominal cavity was inflated with herbs to conform to the corpse's stature. She was cleansed with a new sponge and wiped with a new towel to mark the regeneration of life, as tradition dictated. She was adorned with ornaments that Karikari had supplied. The body was laid in a casket with gold-plated motifs; the bier was equally adorned. Colorful wreaths added a touch of opulence to the deceased.

All of Enkoho was gathered in the village square, talking about Agnes. Much like her surviving husband in character and upbringing, Agnes's life had been filled with hardship and abandonment. As a child, she had been sent off to work as a servant for a family friend. Agnes never got answers from her parents about why she had been sent off while her siblings weren't. As fate would dictate, she and Karikari crossed paths in Accra: she was in the market to shop, and Karikari was a porter. Her death threw Karikari back to repressed memories of family abandonment. Now Agnes had left him to carry the weight of life alone without her reassuring company and comfort. Family and friends surrounded him. He was in the place of his birth, enveloped in an encomium of well-wishers, yet he felt dislocated and lost. His wife was dead, as was his brother and loyal friend Salifu. Karikari's farm had been the most severely devastated. Certainly, God had decreed these senseless misfortunes for his own good. In due course, their justification would lay bare. "God knows best; only He does," he had comforted himself. Still, he was unsettled by the abounding theocratic despotism of God to decree suffering upon unsuspecting man at will, who had no say-so about such events.

The funeral would start at sunrise, and Karikari still hadn't slept. It was predictable that Agnes's death would impact him, but his pain and emptiness were more than losing a spouse. He felt deserted. He and Agnes were bonded by the pain of life that only they understood. Others said they understood, but in reality, they didn't. Agnes was dead; life should go on, especially with two children to care for. But life wouldn't go on—not for Karikari, who couldn't imagine living without a helpmate with whom the ups and downs of life made much sense. From now on, life wouldn't only be at a standstill but could move in the direction of the pain of his childhood that only Agnes could have helped him cope with.

Karikari forced himself to sleep, his eyes shut against memories of his wife foisted upon him by the sight of her belongings. His efforts were interrupted by crickets. The dark and somber night thus remained awake for a few more hours before being swallowed in the tranquility of dawn.

There was no electricity for the gramophone or radio box providing news of the outside world. So the village returned to the days of old. There were no mechanical means to amplify the low, tearful tone of Karikari's eulogy, so it was carried to the attendees farther away by word of mouth. One commentary after another followed the eulogy, all telling of the impact the deceased had had on their lives. Danfo showed himself a true friend, delivering a memorable commentary about a woman he called his sister, not just the wife of a friend. Agnes's niece erupted in an uncontrollable wail, interrupting Danfo. She interposed her wails with a dirge, her palms lifted toward the sky, pouring her heart out. A chorus of siblings sitting close by, with conspicuous daubs of clay on their foreheads and upper arms, joined her. The attendants joined in and sustained the requiem until all eyes were wet. They recalled Agnes's kindness—her tragic death cutting short her generosity upon which the needy depended, including orphans. Some of them she'd nurtured and supported through hardships. These were emotionally unpretentious soliloquies, spilling their pain for losing someone so helpful whom God had sent to be a caretaker of the unfortunate, an aid to the downtrodden, and a light that shone on their dark and hard existence. Sorrow and pain were now gaping on her storied face as she lay there on a bier of love for those in whose memory she would forever be enshrined.

There was no break in tears streaming down Gyambibi's face. He didn't respond to anyone, just sat stone-faced with tears running. Mawuli couldn't quantify his pain; neither could Daavi, who cradled him like a child. They could tell he felt guilty for his mother's death as if he alone bore the responsibility. Mawuli, Daavi, and Karikari, who knew the circumstances of his mother's death, hadn't shared it with Gyambibi; nevertheless, he seemed to know. He hadn't said so, but his tears did. Uncle Salifu might have died for the same reason, looking for him when the storm broke out. It was heart-wrenching to watch. Karikari stood behind and patted him on the shoulder, but Gyambibi didn't register his father's presence.

Yaw, on the other hand, held up well. Perhaps he thought tears were a feminine emotion; maybe he didn't want anyone to see him cry. Whatever the reason, he was more determined to go to America than ever. His father, Danfo, Mawuli, Daavi, and others thought it a means to escape from the pain of his mother's death. They didn't know that his friend Preprah, the unlikeliest of all, was even closer to going to America.

Chapter

12

*M*oro Abubakar protested the assignment of goalposts. Each of the four players had one, and anyone could score against the other. The advantage lay in the positioning of the goalposts: indentations of the land after the cataclysm had positioned some vantage points better than others. He hadn't agreed to the formula for assignments: a coin toss had the goalposts assigned by day of birth. The area assigned Moro had a small washout newly carved into it; once a ball fell into the depression, it would follow that trajectory through the goalpost. Moro wanted the goalpost moved to the right, close to Asamoah's. The other players objected because Asamoah, being left-footed, would have an unfair scoring advantage.

Gyambibi watched from the sideline, sitting on a bench beneath the baobab. Since he hadn't left the house much after his mother's death, Daavi sought to keep him around his friends when they played. Yet the battered field stirred memories of his mother and his unborn brother. If only! He cried in his sleep, talked in his sleep, and seemed to be sleeping when awake. Why would God allow a mother and her unborn child to perish in such a manner? Gyambibi was tearing up and pulled his T-shirt over his face to hide his emotions from his friends battling it out on the field. His tears soon gave way to sobs; he slipped away, placing himself on the path to the farm.

His friends wouldn't have stopped him if they had seen him; they treated him as an adult because of his independence and intelligence. Here was a boy who knew things adults didn't even know, understanding something would happen before it occurred. He always seemed to have the answers to pluck his friends out of trouble. Years earlier, Moro was being shuffled between his divorced parents and was due to return to his father. Gyambibi had advised him to talk to his parents, preferably interrupting them when they were asleep. This, he explained, would create the impression that he was as bothered by his problems as they were. And then, in a subdued tone, Moro should apologize for his ways and how they had affected his parents. That alone would probably not be enough, Gyambibi said, when Moro got up to leave. He told him to add the following guilt trip: "This place is the only hope I have to change. If I'm sent back, I may be caught in the skirmishes in the North (alluding to the ethnic clashes between the Kussasis and Mamprusis in Bawku, where his father lived). I might never return to you again." Days passed, and Gyambibi hadn't heard from Moro. However, Moro was still in the village after his expected return to his father. He told Gyambibi that his parents hadn't said a word to him, good or bad, about his apology. Gyambibi explained that that was the way adults sometimes responded to children when they didn't want them to grasp their parental vulnerabilities. Gyambibi assured him that his parents had likely rescinded their threat. That was years ago, and Moro had been living there ever since. When Moro asked Gyambibi how he'd come up with that advice, Gyambibi told Moro that his mother, at forty-three years of age, had been married to his stepfather for six years already. And in a culture where childlessness was stigmatized, it was plausible to assume that his parents weren't childless by choice. The realization that Moro might be their only heir may have occurred to them, as well as the idea that "a stubborn child is better than no child."

An argument suddenly broke out between the players. Moro ranked third, with six goals. Fifty minutes into playing, however, Asamoah passed him, sending him to the back of the pack. Twumasi, one of the other players, overshot the ball into the woods on Moro's side. Naturally, Moro would have to retrieve it; he returned with a deflated soccer ball. The others faulted him for doing this deliberately. Moro disagreed. Karikari had to run over and pull Moro off Asamoah, whom he had hurled down and whose neck he was squeezing. After separating the two, Karikari asked where Gyambibi was. They searched until they found him at the farm, seated by his father's lone palm tree, where his mother and unborn brother were buried. He returned home with the others, where Aunty Tabuah served him a late lunch with his friends.

Eventide slowly pushed away the amber sun and tucked it into the cloak of blackness. With its descent, sadness again settled on Gyambibi. He was deep in thought when his father motioned to him to join his friends, mostly females, but his attention was elsewhere. That he was a handsome chap whose company girls his age craved was common knowledge.

Those around him noticed changes in Gyambibi. First, he went out less often. Second, as his aunt Tabuah learned, he had a sudden aversion to poultry. He didn't touch the foods she cooked with chicken. He never said why, but this was related to his guilt in the death of Asiedu. His sudden proclivity for reclusiveness inspired in them the haunting feeling that he knew he held a role in his mother's death. If he had kept indoors, his mother would be alive.

Those close to the family devised activities to lure him away from the changes. For this reason, Jeefa now walked stealthily behind him and covered his eyes with her palms. Gyambibi pried them off and turned around, startled. She leaned in and whispered something to him, to which he answered, "I think I might." The two held hands and left with Moro, convening in Danfo's compound. Danfo had the village children gather at his house for storytelling. It would go on for days, incorporating participation exercises like riddles. Danfo was now seated on a makeshift throne, with his linguist to his right, sandwiched between two other children acting as guards. He was robed in makeshift royal regalia with ornamented headgear. He held a scepter in his right hand for theatrical effect.

"All of you want to succeed me as chief of Enkoho," Danfo said. Glancing at Gyambibi's choice of clothing, he continued, "I've never seen a chief wearing shorts to an important function. I won't listen to anyone who's not appropriately attired" to the laughter of the spectators. Before he had finished, Gyambibi had already disappeared from the gathering and was running back home with Jeefa in hand.

Ten days prior, Danfo had announced the following challenge: "I, the chief of Enkoho, am about to join our ancestors. I'll pick one of you to succeed me: the one who makes the most compelling argument as to why you would make the best chief."

The children had had a week to present their arguments, many of which were advanced. One now argued that he would use all the financial resources he would inherit to memorialize Chief Danfo daily. Another argued that he would continue with the excellent work Chief Danfo had started and complete his projects in memory of him. Still, a third argued that he would rule the people based on Chief Danfo's unsurpassed wisdom. After these presentations, there was no clear winner. Therefore, the top-five finalists were confronted with a riddle.

"Soon, I'll join my ancestors," Danfo said. "I have one wish. At my funeral, I want my successor to sacrifice a specific animal to the gods: a bovine that's neither male nor female. I want to see this beast before I die. Whoever brings me this rare beast will be my successor."

The deadline for answers had arrived, and the contestants, attired correctly and seated, were eager to present their responses to the riddle. Also present was Kofi Nsenkyire, who had attended Agnes's funeral and was staying through the weekend;

he was an honorary judge. The first contestant argued for a sheep because it was neither a male nor a female bovine.

Danfo retorted, "It's ovine, not a bovine."

The second contestant seemed excited because she thought her response was superior to what she had just heard. She was confident enough not to wait her turn, blurting out, "My lord, I went to the market and interviewed bull and goat herders. And I think I have your answer: castrated cattle. It's bovine, neither male nor female."

The other contestants said she should be disqualified for impatience. Danfo disqualified her, though, for a different reason. "A girl can't be a chief. I won't have a girl or a woman succeeding me."

Meanwhile, back at home, Gyambibi hurriedly put on a cloth. "It's inside out, Gyambibi. Besides, it's crumpled!" Jeefa cried. She put some hot coals into the pressing iron and got to work.

"Here, try it on," she said, handing it back to him. After Gyambibi did so, she fussed, "It still doesn't look right. It looks different from how the other kids are wearing theirs. Shouldn't it drape around your ankles? It's barely over your knees!" Gyambibi had outgrown his cloth. He was too tall for his age.

"I'm not contending for the world's-most-handsome-teenager trophy. This will do, don't you think?" he asked, flashing a boyish grin. Jeefa shrugged and smiled, holding on to his hand as they ran out of the room before he was disqualified for lateness. Nearing Danfo's house, they heard claps and applause. This was after the other two contestants had provided their responses. Gyambibi and Jeefa stopped and looked at each other.

"They've declared a winner. Did we do all this for naught?" Jeefa asked, pointing to his cloth.

"Maybe," he replied.

"This is what you missed: contestant number one proposed a goat, which is wrong. Contestant number two proposed castrated cattle. That's wrong because, as an example, a castrated bull still urinates from the same part as a male bovine; that is, a castrated bull doesn't lose its sexual identity because it's been stripped of its virility. A castrated bull is still a male bovine. The other answers included that there was no such animal, and a chicken, respectively. We want the best answer of all. Let us hear from you!"

Gyambibi processed the dismissed responses. Both Kofi Nsenkyire and Danfo scribbled something on their scorecards. All eyes were on Gyambibi.

"Linguist, please let it reach my lord's ears that he's a great chief known here and afar. If he wishes to have a specific animal sacrificed at his funeral, that request must be met. Because of this, I traveled to Bawku to find this unique kind of bovine. Cattle rearing is prominent in the North, so it makes sense that it's the only place to find this animal if it exists. Yes, I was able to purchase one, but I couldn't bring it to Enkoho because of its size. I have one request to make of my lord, Linguist, and will ask it on the condition that he promises to grant it since I'm the only contestant to find this unique animal."

"I promise to grant your request. What is it?" Danfo answered before the linguist spoke.

"Linguist, please let the chief send his servants to pick up the bovine in Bawku on the condition that they go when the sun is neither up nor down," he said to laughter.

Danfo, together with Kofi Nsenkyire, shook their heads and clapped. Even they hadn't thought of such an answer. Everybody joined them in applauding Gyambibi.

The praise sunk him into depression: it reminded him of his mother, who celebrated his intelligence every time he brought home his report card. Gyambibi was quiet. His answer to the riddle would be his last words spoken the entire night. He would be returning home and crying himself to sleep.

Mr. Nsenkyire accompanied Gyambibi home. Mr. Nsenkyire appreciated the boy's mind. He couldn't help but be frustrated with the problem of nurturing such a fertile mind in the village, whose only school building had just been razed. The school had only been one building, a rectangular thatched structure with no partitions. Attendance was demarcated by grade. At a scheduled time, one class of students went into the building. The middle schoolers occupied the last block, going from 3:00 to 6:00 p.m., because they would either be helping their parents on the farm or working on their own before school. That building was no more.

Mr. Nsenkyire didn't hide his fascination with Gyambibi. He returned months later to see Karikari privately. Gyambibi was on his mind. The boy was too gifted to let his potential rot in a village without a school. Mr. Nsenkyire was aware of Karikari's loss in the rainstorm: all the money expended to bring electricity and television to the village, the utter destruction of his farm. The man was financially devastated. Mr. Nsenkyire proposed to take Gyambibi to Accra to live with him if Karikari would allow it. Gyambibi could attend some of the most excellent schools, all expenses paid. Aunty Tabuah revisited the proposal with her brother and suggested that Karikari accept it. But Karikari wouldn't listen; he could already see and hear the vicious rumors: the show-off is too broke to care for his own.

Days of lamenting his mother and unborn brother's deaths drove Gyambibi further into reclusion. Keeping to himself, he did nothing but think about his life, the village, and everything in between. Agya Kobi occupied the bulk of his thoughts. As an afterthought, the elder's journal repeatedly came up: Adam's Black Child. Moro had to know about it. But Moro showed no interest in the journal. Instead, he wanted them to search for the elusive hermaphrodite who no one in the village had seen. The rumor was that he came out when the village was asleep at night. To help his friend reclaim his happy, carefree life before his mother's death, Moro proposed going into the forest at night to catch a glimpse of this man. Gyambibi's interest was elsewhere, however—on Adam's Black Child.

"I wasn't born here, so why would my birth date appear in the journal?" Moro said.

"You don't know until we look in the book," Gyambibi answered.

"How could Agya Kobi have known my birth date?" Moro asked.

"Maybe he asked your mother. If he didn't but somehow knows it, it proves what everybody has been saying."

"If you need proof of the man being a devil, the village has already established that. We don't need his journal to prove anything."

Moro's words aroused another curiosity: the writings in the journal itself. What were they? Random thoughts that came to Agya Kobi? A record of happenings in the village? An assessment of the character of people Agya Kobi was interested in? An account of Agya Kobi's life? A confession of his evils?

A confession of his evils! This possibility was particularly interesting to Gyambibi as it may somehow explain his mother's death. Ever since Agnes's death, a part of Gyambibi had been searching for ways to explain the death that wouldn't involve him. He had been haunted by the thought of his mother dying because she was outside looking for him. No need to carry that heavy burden now if there was proof of the elder's confession of having caused it. For one, it made no sense to Gyambibi that the rain-drenched palm fronds caught fire. The cascade of events that led to his mother's death was suspicious. Maybe Agya Kobi was behind it. The thought was liberating. Now he needed proof to liberate his conscience fully. If he had stayed indoors, his mother wouldn't have died. Maybe it was Agya Kobi's occultist plan: that Gyambibi should be outside to lure his mother into the storm to cause her death.

"Can't we just ask Asamoah to verify if my birth date is in the journal?" Moro asked.

"There are writings in the book." Gyambibi was divulging another reason for his interest in the journal.

"About?"

"I don't know. It may be the man's confession of his evils."

"You're interested in the writings and not my birth date."

"Both."

"I share no such interest. Ask Asamoah to do that for you."

"If Agya Kobi catches him, he won't lie to him."

"Neither will you. You're as honest as Asamoah."

Gyambibi stated his intention: he wanted them to *start* reading the journal. Their disagreement went on, but Gyambibi eventually won Moro over. This exercise fit their rambunctious adventurisms before death landed and scattered everything. Perhaps Gyambibi needed this to reclaim what he once was. Their obstacle was how to access the journal from time to time and read it bit by bit until they'd read it in its entirety. Assuming that was at all possible with a family living there.

Chapter

13

She piddled around the lobby of the Posts and Telecommunications (P & T) office in Accra, away from the humid outdoors. Her outfit piqued onlookers' interest, not only because of its sartorial flair but because they thought it betrayed her poor sense of geography, particularly in terms of the country's position relative to the equator. She wore a beige turtleneck sweater inside a jacket made of shimmering fabric, possibly a silk blend or polyester, which was exquisitely tailored to exploit her body's contours. It had a slim-fit quality that augmented her frame. Its lapels were large, peaking behind the frill of the turtleneck sweater with off-white purl stitches. Her beltless, pin-striped denim pants were fitted at her abstemious waist, tapered toward her knees and flared around her ankles, further exaggerating her hips. A burgundy leather handbag and matching platform heels completed the outfit. Her sensuous face peeked through her hair, cropped shoulder-length.

A sensuous beauty, she didn't carry herself as a God-given treasure. She had a down-to-earth, uncondescending air about her. Her ease conveyed a sense of belonging to the land. Yet she was a foreigner, so everybody wanted to help her. During these pleasantries and exchanges, she told someone she was waiting for Mr. Nsenkyire. When she had freed herself from the onslaught of people desiring to help, an onlooker approached.

He was waiting for the same person she was and told her that he wouldn't be long.

"Thank you, sir."

"Tell me, is this your first time in Ghana?"

"Fourth. My first was when I was seven years old."

"I see. Those clothes must be uncomfortable," Mawuli said.

She had arrived the previous day, but there had been a delay in retrieving her luggage at the airport.

"It's winter now in the United States. It's been so long since I was here that I forgot the weather."

"It's okay. How do you know Mr. Nsenkyire, if you don't mind me asking?"

"A friend of my mother's," Helena replied.

While respectful in speech and mannerisms, she was also shy but at ease talking with him. Mawuli spoke about how he had gotten to know Mr. Nsenkyire, who worked for the cooperative that bought cocoa beans for the government. Helena talked about her mother, the last time she had come to the country, and a small village they had stayed in. They spoke at length about the Ashanti Region, for the village her mother stayed in was there, though they had never known its name. About forty minutes into their conversation, Mawuli had a hunch he might know her.

"Don't call me crazy, and forgive me if I'm mistaking you for someone else, but is your name Helen?"

"Close—it's Helena," she said, amazed. "How did you know?"

"I'm Jeefa's father, Mawuli."

"Oh, my goodness! What a surprise!..." She paused, not knowing whether to hug him or not. She was too shy for that.

Helena bordered on seventeen years of age; she had changed so much that she was nearly unrecognizable, though her childhood beauty still shone through. Jeefa could match her for shape and looks, except that hardship had dimmed her a bit.

"My secret's out! I was going to surprise her!" Helena exclaimed.

"I won't tell her."

All heads turned toward them. When Helena's excitement calmed, Mawuli told her about the development of the village and its recent destruction. Through Mr. Nsenkyire's brother, who knew someone at the Electricity Corporation, it was known that Karikari had exhausted a fortune to bring electricity to the village. Every able-bodied man and woman had been availed for the project. It took years to complete—weeks before the Christmas of 1973. There was one television. It was a wise investment for Karikari, who had brought the outside world in since no one could leave the village for good. Then the deluge ravaged the village, apparently defying the change the villagers had imposed, sending them back to the Middle Ages. Helena had heard about all this; Jeefa had written to her. She turned quiet. Mawuli knew she was fighting back tears. She couldn't help it when recalling the names of some of her playmates who had died in the storm. Life was hard in the village; most of the farms were severely damaged. The village was struggling. There was no school building. She gave him a heartfelt hug as onlookers continued gawking.

They took a stroll while Mawuli talked about the village to avoid eyes and ears prying into their conversation. He was in Accra for money from Mr. Nsenkyire, who had asked to meet him here. Helena was also there to meet him; she was to go with him to retrieve her luggage at the airport. She told Mawuli she would go with him to the village as soon as he was ready. The village hadn't left her mind since the last time she had been there, about five years ago.

The streets were noisy; merchandise peddlers haggled with customers. People came and went in every direction. Helena was drowned in a sea of noise as she paced her walk to take in the work of artisans. Of interest was a variety of carvings, one of a mother carrying a baby on her back. A porter, carrying what appeared to be a bag of maize, nudged through the throng of passersby and unintentionally knocked a few people to the ground, including Helena, who fell into a gutter. The front of her jacket was splashed with gelatinous crusts of algae. A crowd jumped on the porter and started beating him; women threw insults at him. He ran away and left the load behind; its owner followed. Mawuli nudged them away and helped Helena to her feet. He gave her a handkerchief to wipe off the dirt and algae. Next, she entered a kiosk, inquiring about necklaces and bracelets made from cowrie shells and mollusk whorls.

They were hungry when they returned to the P & T. Helena had an appetite for nothing but "that goat meat on sticks." Mr. Nsenkyire took them to a kebab seller. While the seller barbecued, Mr. Nsenkyire returned to the P & T, promising to return and take them to his house in an hour. Night dawned while they waited for the kebab. The seller lit a lamp. The wind blew the flame toward the seller, and Helena was drawn to his face. The seller felt uneasy, noting the White girl staring at him.

Why was she so fascinated? The seller's mind churned out different possibilities. The wick was almost down to the stub before the seller had lit it, so the flame went out quickly. The seller used the opportunity to excuse himself and took longer than usual to replace it, surreptitiously stealing glances at Helena. Again, he wondered why she had stared at him so intensely. The first reason he thought of soon evaporated, for it would take more than a miracle for a woman of such ravishing beauty to be romantically interested in him. Mosquitoes buzzed around his face, one settling on his cheek. It stung him; he slapped himself in an attempt to kill it. His hands, already covered in oily soot, made stripes on his face. Helena looked away. The man lit the lamp, illuminating his face and giving Helena a better look. She was particularly interested in his appearance—a young man, possibly in his late twenties. Three lines rose from either side of his jaw to beneath his ears, converging at the corners of his mouth. From both sides of his face, another scar split off the line closest to his ear and rose through his cheekbones. Where the two lines converged on the bridge of his nose, another scar emerged and ran to his forehead, where it had cicatrized into a bird with its wings spread out. It was more of tribal scarification than identification. From the look of it, the young man was from the Northern Region. Helena was captivated by the unusual facial marks. They looked uniform and had an artistic precision to them.

The kebab seller felt like a prisoner in Helena's eyes. He felt the urgency to get out of her head—or at least away from her curious eyes.

"Do I make you uncomfortable?" he asked her. He felt sorry, ashamed even, to consider this possibility.

"No...no. I like the artwork—your tattoo. It's unique," Helena replied.

"Madam, kebab is six cedis," he said while avoiding her gaze.

Helena reached into her purse but realized she only had dollar bills. Mawuli was about to pay when Mr. Nsenkyire arrived, paid, and asked, "Salifu didn't give you a hard time, did he?"

"Me? No, sir," Helena said and laughed.

Helena was relieved that Mr. Nsenkyire knew the seller. She felt she knew him too, for his name was familiar. Had he come from their village? No, Mawuli told her; that Salifu was an older cripple who had died in the storm.

Chapter

14

*D*anfo and his new wife, Oforiwaah, walked side by side, a rare spectacle. There was nothing romantic about it because they were silent and walked briskly. They got to Karikari's house, who was expecting them, though he didn't know what matter the couple wanted to discuss. They barely sat down when Oforiwaah stated, "My husband tells me you have something to tell me."

"No, woman, *you* have something to tell Mr. Karikari!" Danfo interjected.

Oforiwaah felt trapped.

"What!?" she retorted.

"What you said yesterday. I want you to repeat it in front of him because it was about him." Danfo instructed.

"What?" she demanded again.

"You know what you said; say it in his presence."

"I don't...I don't know what you mean."

"Let me help. Karikari, this woman wants me to stop associating with you. She wants to break up our friendship," Danfo said.

Karikari rubbed his mouth, not knowing what to say. He waited for Oforiwaah to respond.

"Oh, that! My brother, I didn't mean it," Oforiwaah said.

"How could you not mean something you repeated four times?" Danfo said.

"I don't deny saying it!" she said, rising and kneeling before Karikari, one palm in another, begging. "It was in the heat of confusion and sorrow. Our son, our Gyambibi, associating with Agya Kobi and contracting that mysterious illness caused panic everywhere. Moreover, Agya Kobi visiting this house, which prefaced Agnes's death...the connection the man has to your family, and what we've seen happen is a lot to deal with. I've cried, not understanding. I was confused when I said it."

"I understand," Karikari said.

He helped Oforiwaah onto her feet. She begged to leave, and Danfo reminded her to quickly return to her cooking so she wouldn't burn his house down.

Also, Danfo was here because Karikari couldn't see the way out of his financial ruin. He turned uncomfortably in his sleep, mulling the poverty in which he found himself as days turned into weeks and weeks became months. Before the rainstorm, he had thought days of living without were behind him. So in spending his resources to bring electricity and other conveniences to the village, sinking back into poverty wasn't even an afterthought. Not even the bottoming out of cocoa prices in the '60s halted his drive. Even the "path" that Gyambibi had drawn through the forest for the cables, Karikari had planned to pave into a road, stopping a few miles short of Aduman, in the forest. This effort would have helped the village truck its harvests to Aduman for pickup by the cooperative rather than have farmhands haul them there on foot. He got as far as clearing the path of trees and shrubs and leveling it with laterite. No bitumen made it there. Now life had taken a turn he couldn't have foreseen.

Danfo had a solution that wouldn't only reverse Karikari's misfortune but also enrich the village. Seated across from him, Karikari offered palm wine. This was the first time Danfo saw his friend drink, but it was just the beginning. Danfo couldn't have asked for such an opportune time, mediated by alcohol, to propose something so dangerous. Karikari slumped on the sofa and asked for the other purpose of his visit. Danfo's preamble was this:

"There's a rumor of Gyambibi and Moro wanting to enter military service. I'm unsure if this has anything to do with the news of Preprah joining the military. Anyway, let us focus on Gyambibi for now. We don't have to go into why he wants to join the military. The storm took everything away: the school building, your fortune, the luster of the village, and so on. There's nothing here for the boy or his peers. Gyambibi has the intelligence to be in any of the top high schools in the country. No school would refuse him, but here he is—misfortune keeps him stagnant. He's a child of the village, don't forget. We all have a voice in his future. He has the intelligence to be a doctor, a lawyer, or our president. Don't let him rot here."

"I don't have the money," Karikari said, nursing his temples.

"Dig up the treasure."

Karikari's mouth trembled, for fear had gripped him. He was afraid to talk about what Danfo had just proposed, for it conjured up memories of death. He wouldn't be the first to attempt to retrieve the buried treasure: some had, and death had followed. The treasure stayed buried. One difference between Karikari and those who had died trying to retrieve the treasure, as Danfo noted, was that Karikari was in the bloodline of the original owner, while the others weren't. The treasure was spiritually fortified, with occult denseness causing deaths on both sides of two warring factions. Karikari's uncles and aunts had died mysterious, unnatural deaths due to this.

"We can reverse the curse," Danfo said, eager to go into detail. Karikari made some fluttering signs with his hands. Danfo understood: Karikari was too shaken to speak.

As poverty deepened in Enkoho, helplessness ran amok. Adwoa Brago paid a courtesy visit to Karikari. She had helpful information: news from the government about awarding scholarships to students entering high school. This news, made before the cataclysm, had come through the radio box on his own porch, made it to Adwoa Brago, and back to his house. Karikari thought the impetus for Adwoa Brago's visit was none other than Agya Kobi, but that didn't matter. Karikari inquired about it and found it to be true. The scholarship awards would depend on O-level exam aggregate scores plus the score on the exam administered by the Scholarship Secretariat. The problem was that no national standardized test was held in Enkoho because the village didn't exist. After middle school, those who wanted advanced education studied on their own, since they couldn't advance in the village; then they took the O-level exam elsewhere. Because the official exam was administered at schools in June, students from Enkoho took the exam in November at test centers, when remedial exams were offered. Gyambibi did the preparatory work on his own using local as well as SAT materials that Helena had her mother send over. The village waited to see if he would do better than his older brother, who performed well enough to have gotten into any of the top schools in the country but had instead decided to stay close to his father, following him on business errands in the hopes that, eventually, his father would be satisfied with him enough to pay his way to America. Gyambibi took the O' level exam first, then the Scholarship Secretariat exam. Karikari and Danfo were part of the process, reviewing the application forms and taking him to the test centers. The villagers held their breath for his scores but in vain, for, in the end, he never received any test results. They went to the Exam Council and the

Scholarship Secretariat for an explanation. These institutions pored over documents and brought out rosters of applicants and the signatures each applicant had appended next to their name on the day of the exam. Gyambibi had done both, which Karikari and Danfo had seen. Nonetheless, there was no record of him taking either exam or even signing his name on the rosters.

Fear of the evil inhabiting Enkoho entered Gyambibi's mind. For the first time, he, who had no fear to speak of, started to fear what tomorrow might bring. So he, Asamoah, and Moro did preparatory work to join the military, hoping that this would break the village's spiritual hold on them, so they would never have to return. They noted that Preprah hadn't returned since leaving the village and joining the military.

Meanwhile, Chief and his wife were enchanted with Helena. They entertained her company more than they had with Dr. Maarten and Xada. Helena had a childish curiosity about her, wanting to know certain village beliefs, traditional mores, and ways of life. In the evening, or occasionally during the day, Chief and his wife would invite her over to explain things, sometimes bordering on tall tales and folklore that were palatable to her ears. Sometimes they took her outside the village and let her explore her fascinations—in Braha, an insular sister village more mysterious than Enkoho itself. Now entrenched in Enkoho's way of life, she wanted to be close to everyone. She had graduated from high school early but had placed college on hold to explore life in Enkoho. Not wanting to stand in her way because of how far she'd come and what Enkoho meant to her, her mother thought Helena's decision to stay beyond the summer was a temporary phase. Her mother expected her to return the following year to start college. But Enkoho had other ideas.

Helena craved acceptance by the villagers. She wanted to know Barbara Oforiwaah and, by approximation, Danfo. She read Danfo's intelligence, however skewed, through his drunken outbursts. Something was interesting about him and his thoughts that seemed worth becoming acquainted with.

Danfo gave her a narrative about the village: Over one thousand years ago, Enkoho was about two and a half square miles big. Now the village was smaller and enveloped by farms and forested glades. The land was seeded with evil, Danfo had cautiously whispered. He gave a winding, torturous oral history: circa the nineteenth century, when Ghana was a British protectorate, amid the lingering hostility between the colonialists and the Ashantis, some colonialists had penetrated deeper inland, having no interest other than to proselytize the villagers. One Mr. Dansla had come to Enkoho in the heart of the Ashanti Region. Mr. Dansla's father had been a flintlock-rifle merchant who died and left him everything. Mr. Dansla was a missionary before he took over his father's business, so when he arrived with his team of missionaries, it was about God. It was also about guns. They talked to the villagers about God and Satan. Already aware of the God of Heaven (whom the villagers knew by the name Tweredeampong—long before any colonialist set foot on the land), nothing piqued their interest more than the name Satan and a summary of his work on Earth. Did the Bible give any specifics about the coordinates of Satan's location here on Earth? The elders had wondered. Although the answer was no, the villagers were still interested in this Satan character. He may have staked a home on their land before their ancestors called it home. In him, they found an explanation for their many plights not found in any of the neighboring villages and beyond. Their hunters were turning up dead for unexplainable reasons. Satan, the devil, was no doubt occupying their land. The missionaries, who gleaned the implication of the villagers' concerns, politely denounced them as superstition. When the elders insisted, the missionaries gave them guns to ward off what they thought was a predator.

The second phase of the narrated history involved the barn-looking structure in the forest. About how it came to be, Danfo continued: this Dansla returned to Enkoho later, this time with women and a priest. Some of the women had been trained in midwifery. In the course of their stay, a young villager and expectant mother, whom they had educated about maternity, was in the throes of childbirth. This wasn't a stranger, nor was she plagued with health problems to augur the strangeness they saw next. They knew her before she was pregnant when her belly was as flat as a concrete slab until it attained the apotheosis of a viable pregnancy. In childbirth, she became unconscious, necessitating a prompt Cesarean section to save the child. When a knife had excavated every compartment of her abdomen and passed through the pile of leaves on which she laid, they knew there was no child to save. The incident got their attention and informed them of the danger of where they were. There was more to come.

After that, in the heat of the day, when the priest reclined under the baobab tree, he felt a sharp pain over his thigh. A spider had bitten him. Where he sustained the bite was a reddish, purplish discoloration, tender to the touch, which disappeared before he could show anyone. This he kept a secret within his frightened mind. Then the spider appeared in his dreams and spoke with him. In the dreams, he would walk backward on the same path he had first entered the village. Other times, he dreamt about playing the board game *oware* with the spider. Only once did he win; that was when his right thigh felt another bite. This time, he woke up and saw blistery wheals. It wasn't long before he fell sick. He knew he would die, so he asked that a mausoleum be built in the forest for his burial. It was done, but he changed his mind before his death. He asked to be buried in the village cemetery. To not use the mausoleum for the purpose for which it was built was senseless. Still, they had to honor the priest's request because this was the last sensible thing he said before they realized he had gone crazy.

The structure was there, still standing. Danfo stopped the narration, deep in thought, and restrained himself from saying more.

The elders later revised their understanding of Satan: he couldn't have fallen from heaven onto their land because the missionaries came from a faraway place and knew of him long before they stepped foot in Enkoho. They concluded that Satan must have landed where the missionaries came from. This potent representation of evil must have inspired terror in their land for them to go from place to place, warning others. It explained why they had guns and weapons to fight this Satan and the forces they deemed his representatives. The villagers started worrying about the missionaries and people of the land from which they came. For as bad as they had it, the missionaries had it worse because their existence was intertwined with Satan. Still, the villagers wanted to gather as much information as possible about Satan in case what they were experiencing wasn't him but other spirits aligned with him.

Danfo's narrative seemed one long, fractured, tall tale. Even his mention of some twin midwives almost made Helena laugh. She had first heard about them during her visits years ago in the context of their helping to deliver Gyambibi after fifteen months in the womb. Of investigative value to her was the fact that the twin midwives overlapped Agya Kobi's life. She wanted to know more about them but from Agya Kobi himself. She would need to befriend the old man to learn more. The narrative seemed too farfetched to be true. She was mistaken. In fact, Danfo ended the narrative without divulging what had become of the mausoleum. Its history and existence were a guarded secret among the elders. They called it a "barn," though it served no such purpose. No one spoke of it because it held a secret: inside was a buried treasure shrouded in death and pain.

Helena knew this wasn't all a tale, for Danfo's hunting rifle was a relic of this history. She didn't know it then, but for a lonely village that held onto its own, her presence did more than awaken the villagers' yearning for outsiders; it awoke memories of the village's past handed down through oral history.

Chapter

15

*K*arikari opened the door to Danfo, who nudged past him with two gallons of kerosene. Three gallons had preceded him days earlier when he saw his wife kill a goat to sell its meat on the market.

"You should have room for those in your house," Karikari said.

"That would betray my purpose, don't you think?" Danfo replied.

"What purpose?"

"Have I not told you? Oforiwaah wants to kill me. She'll cut me up like a goat."

Karikari hesitated to tell him that he sounded crazy.

"I watched her gut the goat. And then she started appearing in my dreams, repeating the task of dismembering the animal. I've told you about the dreams, the nightmares. Oforiwaah appears to me in a vision as a prelude to what she intends to do to me!"

Karikari looked at his friend, who appeared not to have slept in days. "What are the gallons of kerosene for?"

"If I don't survive this illness, promise to do one thing for me."

Danfo's disheveled appearance revealed a common cold mixed with fear of Oforiwaah slowly killing him.

"What is it?" Karikari asked.

"Burn the witch if I don't survive this."

Danfo added that kerosene wasn't volatile enough to burn the bones of a witch. That's why he had brought gasoline. He wanted to accumulate thirteen gallons.

"I'm not burning your wife; I'm not burning down your house... you're not dying."

Danfo took a sip of water from Tabuah. Just one sip was enough; he didn't want to dilute the alcohol in him. Karikari looked at his friend and then at his sister, who seemed lost in thought over what Danfo was wearing. He had on an aged paisley shirt. Danfo had been wearing the same shirt since he got married decades ago. Because he refused to spend money on clothes, when his weight overburdened them, which happened every other year, Oforiwaah would open his garments at the seams and fill them with cloth, mostly from his own garments. Anyone looking would see fabric as thin as a stained cobweb. In this way, his clothes decreased in number but increased in size. His pants and shirts were filled with gussets of every known fabric. Karikari could only concede that Danfo's appearance wouldn't help his cause today but hesitated to say anything because his sister was with them.

"What kind of friend are you?" Danfo asked when they started out for Kumasi, away from the prowling ears of Tabuah.

"One who's bound by morality," Karikari responded.

"If you can't exact vengeance, at least don't invite her to my funeral. Anyway, what's more moral than exacting vengeance on a witch who kills your friend?"

"You're not dead, and Oforiwaah isn't killing you."

"You won't even try to bring to fruition the words of a dying friend whose help you want?"

"Can we be serious and talk about the terms of the loan the bank has proposed?"

The trip to Kumasi was frustrating because Danfo talked throughout about everything but the terms of the loans for which Karikari needed him. Danfo was drunk before he showed up at Karikari's house; it was the first thing he did to start his day. And being drunk meant his tongue was loose and sharp. So, naturally, he would take issue with anything that flouted normalcy. The bank manager's name, Franklin Maximilian Wood, depressed him. Danfo asked him why he had three English names with an appearance to match. Their appointment didn't proceed beyond the ensuing altercation. Other personnel came in and escorted the two men out. Karikari told Danfo to stay outside while he returned to overcome the great encumbrance his friend had erected.

Danfo piddled around. He was stopped when he tried to get back inside the bank. He turned and strolled along the street, looking over its many street-lined shops. A penetrating aroma turned him around a corner into a restaurant. The owner, a buxom woman who smiled at everything she looked at, took an interest in her portly customer. Danfo walked about confidently, with a stride of effusive personality compatible with his obesity. His pendulous belly hid beneath a shirt that couldn't obscure all of him, as it was suffocating at the seams. If nothing else, his appearance conveyed to the owner that he spent more on food than clothing. Unusually tall and hunched to prevent scraping against the ceiling, the owner looked down at him with girlish excitement as that mammoth belly came her way. She swept away some chickens running underfoot and had forgotten all about the other customers.

Danfo's eyes danced around a medley of toothsome delicacies. There was a vast array of dishes, from rice balls and jollof rice to fried plantain and beans to fufu, as well as a vast selection of soups, including palm nut, groundnut, garden egg, and spinach. He savored the aroma as he walked past a bucolic male hunched over a mortar, pestle in hand, pounding away. At the same time, a woman performed skillful maneuvers to expose the fufu's lumpy areas to the pestle's thrusts. Danfo sat at the back of the restaurant and did a quick ergonomic assessment. He felt the hen and its chicks under the table, and his belly pinched by the table's edge. He sought to crush a beak pecking at his feet, but his shin found the table's legs instead. A cloud of feathers filled the air when the owner arrived to apologize. He ate his pain and followed the owner to another seat. Overstepping shards of broken utensils, he found a chair that ensured no part of him would be restricted—important to his near-empty belly that he would fill to its limit. This seat also put him in full view of the bank, where he could see Karikari once he emerged. Through smiles, the owner brandished her dimpled cheeks and gap between her upper front teeth. She shooshed away the hen and her chicks again, then pulled up a chair and sat across from Danfo.

While the woman was talking, Danfo's mind was elsewhere. He wasn't ready to eat yet, mulling happenings in the village. His anger shifted from the bank manager to Karikari. The loan would only help one person rebuild, Karikari, when what was needed was the means to rebuild the entire village. The village was devastated, from the farms to buildings to their well-being. The answer to restoring the whole village was in the buried treasure, not in a bank—a fact Danfo felt Karikari should know. The buried treasure wasn't folklore. Since the dawn of March 6, 1914, the circumstances of the treasure's burial and the warring parties were known to those who had the treasure on their mind. Only a few knew the path of blood and death that led to the buried treasure because the elders kept the circumstances of the deaths from the villagers. The treasure's value could rebuild the village and more. However, retrieving it was a challenge—possibly insurmountable. Danfo wasn't afraid. He believed it was retrievable, and the way to that was through Karikari and his sons because they were related by blood to its owner.

Thinking about Enkoho urged Danfo to save his money rather than spend it at this restaurant. He had a light breakfast, which should sustain him until they returned. He asked for water to avoid the impression that he was there to use the space and not their services. The smiling woman returned with iced water. Still, that would cost more money, so he asked for tap water. The woman returned, still smiling. Danfo was close to asking if she knew him, only to stop so a conversation wouldn't lead to a food order.

Why would the bank manager have a name like that and dress the way he did? To Danfo, it seemed a clever scheme to get loan applicants to say something awful so he would refuse them. He sought to minimize the role that his actions could worsen the odds for Karikari. Getting approval for a loan was more than difficult for Karikari; he had collateral, but a house and farm in a village that didn't exist were beyond a challenge. In the end, Mr. Nsenkyire intervened, cosigning for the loan because he could vouch for Karikari's properties. Now Danfo had dimmed his hope. Danfo's thoughts wandered from the loan to the village when the restaurant owner, who had left to attend to another customer, returned.

Willing to start a good relationship with this customer, she offered to have him sample any dish of his choosing. Danfo reclined in his seat at the urging of the owner as he entertained food samples making short voyages to and from his table. She left and returned with Danfo's order, a task that should have been performed by one of her servers: a large bowl of fufu and soup with an assortment of smoked catfish, beef, and snails. It was hot and vapory. Danfo seemed to have taken a rare interest in the owner's conversation. They talked at length. After thirty minutes, she excused herself. Before she left, Danfo asked for an itemized cost. The owner was pleasantly surprised because she didn't always have customers who ensured they could pay for what they bought before they ate.

Danfo noted that the owner was looking at him. She whispered about his healthy appetite to one of the workers. No one saw Danfo chew his beverage, which would have told them much about their customer. There was a conversation about his knowledge. When he heard a discussion about him being a man of means in unremarkable clothing, he leaned on his right back pocket to feel his wallet. It seemed light. He thought it was probably due to the thick texture of the pants he was wearing. When the owner attended to another customer, he washed his hand and wiped it with a napkin. He reached into his pocket, and rage appeared on his face. One cedi remained in his wallet; Oforiwaah had taken everything else. She had told him to increase her budget for the pantry. He had refused. She had taken it, and he could do nothing about it. The thought of him being unable to subdue his wife undid his appetite. He nursed the calabash of warm palm wine between his fingers. His tongue sucked the soup off his fingers as his stomach protested the near collapse of his appetite. He would suffer embarrassment at not being able to pay for his food. Now he coveted the dark powers Agya Kobi wielded to make this embarrassing situation disappear. He had a scheme cooking in no time, concentrated on paying only the amount he had on him or not paying at all. To blame for the scheme was the owner's aggressive habit of trying to sell as much of her merchandise as she could to her customers. Danfo had initially declined the palm wine, but the owner had insisted, convincing him that the wine was from the best tapper in the region. Enkoho had excellent palm-wine tappers, but this one was the best to hit his tongue. So Danfo was drunk—again! His mentation and tongue were oddly sharper.

When he looked up, the owner was taking a bottle of Guinness to another customer across but behind him. Danfo attacked his food voraciously as the owner threw him a smile while bringing a drink to another customer. On her return, her wayward hip brushed against the edge of Danfo's table, which had mysteriously moved half a step onto her path, sending Danfo's table and everything atop it crashing to the floor.

How could that table have been so misaligned? Chasing away those evil chickens must have caused that, she thought. The owner, surprised, apologized and entreated Danfo to a refill. Danfo told her not to worry, for he had lost his appetite. The owner was confused when Danfo opened his wallet and handed her one cedi. It became clear to her that he had planned to walk away and not pay for the rest. An altercation broke out. She said she was going to the police.

The presence of two female workers on either side of Danfo was all it took to keep him in his seat until the owner returned. When the police came, Danfo fired off his arguments.

"The food was cold," was the first charge he dropped.

"So why didn't you tell her to warm it?"

He explained it was to avoid embarrassing her about her terrible cooking and service. What's more, it was inhospitable for her to stare at him the entire time he was eating.

"Who does that? Could it have been a tactic to distract me from *what* I was actually eating?" Danfo asked, adding that he couldn't discount the possibility that the owner tumbled the food off his table purposely, for she could tell he was struggling to finish it.

His ridiculous answer didn't throw off the officer, who asked, "How could the fufu alone be at the temperature you liked and everything else cold?"

"Perhaps the starch content of the fufu enhanced its heat-carrying capacity."

"What?"

"You should ask her for an explanation if you don't appreciate my input. She said it was all hot when she brought it. I'm afraid I have to disagree. Either all the meat and fish weren't warmed before being served, or they were cold-blooded."

The owner was incensed at the tangential line of questioning, skirting the issue of him paying for what he had eaten.

"Keep those flabby hands out of my face, woman," Danfo lashed out at the owner, who was wagging a finger in his face. She retreated a few steps, creating enough space for the officer to place himself between them.

"Well, I didn't eat everything you served," Danfo continued. "You did my taste buds a favor by knocking over the table. Why pay for stringy beef that moved in my mouth like some kind of possessed leather? I spat out the meat. Why would I pay for food I didn't swallow? This woman was more interested in finding a husband in me than in her culinary presentation. I've never eaten anything so terrible."

"I was trying to make you feel welcome as a customer!" the owner said, being steered off course again.

"Keep your sexual fantasies far from me, woman. Those who walk in here are more interested in food than being made to feel welcome."

The police officer was struggling with a thought: Why would the man continue to eat if he didn't like the food?

"Officer, I assume you're well aware that to get food from that bowl into the pit of my stomach would require my fingers traveling in and out of my mouth."

"What are you implying?" the officer asked.

"Everything—fufu, beef, fish, soup, snails, water, palm wine, everything, water, everything—came in contact with viscid secretions in my mouth. Perhaps I shouldn't say this, but no doctor who's examined me has walked away not shocked to see one man walking about with half of the world's diseases—because of my genetics. But the gracious hand of God has found ways to correct its creative shortcomings by blessing me materially. To answer your question, once I dug my fingers in, I knew I couldn't leave anything behind for this greedy woman to sell to her next customer. I did NOT want to start a global pandemic."

The officer bit his tongue. His impression of Danfo was one of confusion. Either Danfo was the touchiest, craziest man he had ever met, or he was a genuinely wronged man with a knack for squabbles. The officer couldn't tell he was drunk.

"Why not pay for what you ate, then?"

"I tried to, but this promiscuous Gorgon with an eye for the vulnerable of society wouldn't accept my money. Instead, she left to look for you, instructing her minions to crack my skull open if I attempted to leave. Just look at her!"

"So you intend to walk away after eating almost everything put in front of you?"

That question pointed to the likelihood that the impression Danfo felt he had created with the officer was slipping away. He looked at the officer and sighed, dropped his cuffed hands on the officer's shoulder to assure him, took a step back, and said, "You couldn't be any older than my son, whom I'll be sending to America to study engineering! Your questions so far tell me that you're as intelligent and insightful as he is, so let logic and what your own eyes see guide you and not what this witch wants you to believe."

The mention of *America* and *engineering* didn't escape anyone's attention. The look on their faces: Could it be?

"You're telling me the chicken ate the bones attached to beef, whole mudfish, and so on?"

"That's wise to assume if you don't see any on the floor. I've never seen such ferocious birds in my life."

"Chickens ate the stringy meat?" the officer pressed.

"I never used to think chickens could eat that. Look, Officer, you don't need to see the chickens to believe me. Look at my shin; the same birds did that. They tore at my flesh; what can't they eat? I swear those birds have a carnivorous mien!"

"You're serious," the officer said after examining Danfo's scraped, swollen shin.

"Some hostile birds they are. They pecked through my pants and sock, then through my flesh to get to my bone. Besides, chickens aren't known to be strict herbivores, and definitely not these ones. This witch doesn't deny spilling my barely eaten food."

"Pay us!" said one of the on-looking employees. "You probably don't know me, but I know you. I live next door to Tabuah in Kodee. You and her brother visit our village all the time. Pay us!"

After swatting Danfo's hand away, the woman retreated a few steps and tumbled over a table. Danfo realized she was the same smiling woman who had served him water.

"So it is you. I thought you were wearing a mask. Your slave driver doesn't pay you enough to help you buy a mirror so you can see what she's done to you," Danfo lashed out, adding that she was marred by poverty beyond the likeness of a woman. The words penetrated the woman's bones and left her smeared with anger and humiliation.

Amid the parties talking over each other, Karikari entered and interrupted the altercation, demanding to know why his friend was in handcuffs. After paying the debt, Karikari stepped aside with the police officer and exchanged a few words.

Danfo had words of his own for Karikari: "Who permitted you to pay her without my say-so? It gives the impression that she's right when the facts of what happened favor my side. This doesn't concern you. WAIT FOR ME OUTSIDE!"

Something in Danfo's eyes pushed Karikari outside. Karikari wondered whether the spirits of Enkoho, and not alcohol, might be behind his friend's behavior as well as his own failed attempt at a loan. Surely, Enkoho had followed.

Karikari was in a sleek navy-blue, copper-buttoned, double-breasted blazer worn with an off-white shirt with cufflinks. His Oxford shoes exuded prominence and wealth. However, his appearing docile to the no-nonsense Danfo left the impression that he was Danfo's assistant, elevating Danfo in the eyes of the crowd. With that, Danfo had disarmed everyone arguing with him. Even the owner was subdued by what she saw.

The officer's countenance turned apologetic for handcuffing an innocent, apparently wealthy man.

Danfo sniffed the soupy air, "I'm late for my meeting with Mr. Maximilian. Did you compile all the documents without leaving anything out this time?" Danfo appeared to be asking Karikari, who he knew wasn't there. That question, nevertheless, got the officer turning something over in his mind. When Danfo turned to leave, the officer went ahead of him.

Danfo said, "You're an intelligent man of the law, but I fear your salary doesn't match your hard work. The thieves in our government think the national pie is baked in their kitchens, so they alone are entitled to sit at the table, eating what should be ours. They're driven around in Mercedes Benzes, Rolls Royces, BMWs, Aston Martins, fleets of Toyota Land Cruisers, and Bentleys. And they live in mansions with enough rooms to house entire villages. These crooks believe only *they* are worthy of the national pie, while hardworking folks like you are underpaid. That makes me angry. What's your name? Where's your precinct? I'll send my boy to you in a few days."

The officer put his hands behind him, walking alongside Danfo. It had come to the officer that he was in the presence of his superior. After a handshake, Danfo exited the door, which the officer held open for him.

Danfo met Karikari across the street and disappeared from the area. At the taxi rank, far removed from the scene, Karikari accosted him and disclosed that the bank manager wanted nothing to do with him because of Danfo's behavior.

"Forget him! Did you see the way he was dressed? Was that for some type of cotillion for slave drivers? His chemically roasted hair piled into a pompadour nearly drove all my blood into my eyes. It was that painful to watch. The man's confused, and keeping my mouth shut would have been a crime."

Karikari ignored him.

"That handle-bar mustache and bolo tie were too much," Danfo continued.

Karikari didn't blink.

"Did you see the neck scarf tucked behind the bolo tie? In this festering, equatorial heat? Did he dress like that for you? He's forgotten that those who dress like that no longer rule us. And who elevated that left-handed buffoon to such a high position? I guarantee that the bank owners are a clique of greedy, mischievous lefthanders. They're mustachioed devils and crooks! I saved you from a loan disaster. God works in mysterious ways."

Seeking to draw Karikari into a conversation, Danfo tried to update him on his travel for Twumasi's funeral. The deceased, like Karikari, had a wife from the coastal area of Cape Coast. Twumasi was the only one of Enkoho's dead from the rainstorm to be funeralized and buried outside the village. His surviving wife had the hidden idea that burying her husband outside the boundaries of Enkoho would help break the esoteric hold of the village on her and help her to escape. Karikari had been close to the deceased but couldn't attend the funeral. Danfo felt he would be interested in the details, a gesture to help Karikari overcome his anger toward him.

"Perhaps this is the time to talk about Twumasi's funeral, my brother. I haven't had the chance to tell you yet. Consider it your reward for saving me from bloodshed. You came to their rescue—you did. Did you see that neighbor of your sister's from Kodee? She had her talons out, ready to strike. I was going to backhand her into a corpse when you burst in. You saved her life. About my trip to Cape Coast, our deceased friend... Twumasi."

Danfo took a deep breath.

"Why our deceased friend traveled so far south for a wife, I'll never know. I've always believed that it had something to do with his death. The storm didn't kill him; he was dying long before that. The storm finished what that woman had started. Anyway, I was welcomed and treated hospitably when I went there for his funeral. No surprises! To their credit, they'd spent the previous night and day of my arrival cooking all types of dishes. I was treated most hospitably because I was the only one from his village to attend—besides his wife. The memory of the braised turkey tails they served still titillates my palate. And for the first time in my life—the only time in my life—I had the unique experience of being served shrimp doughnuts. Ever seen or heard of them? A recipe from the food fairies, my friend; it was nothing short of a culinary marvel. My taste buds haven't been that entertained since. After I'd gone through all my stomach could handle, they expected donations from all attendees to offset the funeral cost. For reasons I still don't know, they expected more from me than any of the attendees and weren't satisfied with my donation. You know, I felt if I had had extra money, it would have been better spent on loaves of bread and tossing them into the sea for the fish. This way, when my generosity fattened the fish, I could return there and catch them for nourishment. Karikari, those coastal brothers didn't like what I said. If I'd stayed that night, they would have pulled my intestines out and strained what I'd eaten."

Karikari showed no interest. In fact, he hadn't heard a word his friend had said. Having paid off Danfo's food and the police officer and being continually dragged into Danfo's theater of psychotic drivel, he debated the worth of going anywhere with him ever again. Karikari found his behavior disturbing but not surprising. Danfo had always been talkative with a dry, jovial bent. Yet, like everyone in Enkoho, the village had impacted him. To think him crazy was to think of the entire village as one big asylum, for, in strange ways, the villagers alternated between sanity and insanity. One called others "insane" when one was on the "sane" side. Hardships determined when the order was reversed. Danfo's transformation began after the birth of Preprah, whose paternity he rejected. When the elders wouldn't accept his reasoning, he settled for the guardianship of Preprah but not as his biological father. He said if Preprah showed a tenth of his intelligence, he would claim him, but Preprah hadn't lived up to that. In many ways, Danfo was worsening before the storm. Now he was at his worst. He couldn't discern when the thrusts of his outbursts were comical, nonsensical, rude, or plain crazy. They seemed to him intelligently worded retorts brought forth with all the seriousness he could muster. Intermittently, his mind was intact for extended periods, which told the villagers that something else besides alcohol motivated his behavior. Many thought him too clever to be crazy. In fact, Karikari relied on Danfo's company to help him avoid bad business transactions because Danfo had an instinctual adeptness at understanding financial contracts. Lately, however, every indication was that whatever remained of his friend's sanity might have been claimed by the storm's devastation—with his current behavior demolishing what would have been a hopeful day for Karikari.

"That restaurant's food was delicious, but I don't think they'll allow me back. Perhaps you could buy some to take home when we're in the area next time."

Karikari looked at him from the corner of his eye.

"You know what, Karikari, you're kind to everyone but me, your friend. You were kinder to the witch. I followed you here with nothing but your best interest at heart. You paid that woman for everything she claimed to have put into my bowl. I didn't eat everything. To be fair to me, you should have asked her to bear the cost of what she spilled. Better still, you could have told her to replace what she spilled, which she was going to do anyway."

He paused and mulled over what he had just said. "That tells me something, actually. You know what, I have some uneaten food there that's already paid for. Give me my portion of the taxi fare, if you don't mind. I'll see you at home. That witch hasn't seen the last of me."

Going back for his "leftovers" wasn't enough. Another motivation to want to return to the restaurant was access to the woman's cooking without having to commute there and back again.

"And if it's a husband she wants...good heavens, her height and girth! Did you see how big she was? Lot of woman for my money! Oforiwaah has been a disappointment, and I want her out of my life like Esi Eluwah. If the restaurant owner wants me, I'm all hers if she can cook that well. Those hips!"

Danfo was silent, mentally reconstructing the contours of the restaurateur's frame. She had suddenly gone from a foe to a potential love interest. Danfo was quiet, mumbling to himself here and there and gesturing absentmindedly. Karikari was relieved that he could wait for a taxi in peace.

"I need your input on something, Karikari. Give me your honest answer: Did you perceive that the restaurant owner was the type to beat up men?"

Karikari disgustedly ignored him. Danfo didn't understand, "Look, if this is about the bank manager, the eye saw what it saw, so the mouth had little recourse but to say what had to be said. It was either yours or mine. Who would have resisted the temptation to comment on how he looked? I fell on the sword for you. How was that wrong?"

Chapter

Knuckle Game

*B*arbara Akosua Oforiwaah was over six feet tall. She was built like Esi Eluwah with a raw, brute physique. She sold meat at the market, had a knack for gossip, and had an affinity for the company of rumormonger Nyamenkum the Gossip—just like Esi Eluwah did. In every way the eye could tell, she was Esi Eluwah number two.

Oforiwaah trundled by like a pontoon across the living room. Danfo was aroused by a sudden desire to beat her for secretly emptying his wallet, which had caused him all the embarrassment at the restaurant. However, he considered that if she gained the upper hand, he wouldn't survive her fists this time. He sank into his chair, thinking he could subdue her with his rifle. That thought quickly dissipated because the first time he had tried that, he had had to appear before the elders. His defense was that they were having a dialogue, to which the elders admonished, "Don't call it a dialogue when one party is armed."

A fight was brewing that had begun the previous day. The stew Oforiwaah had prepared for lunch was watery; Danfo had first mistaken it for soup. Oforiwaah wouldn't explain it as an accident, just that Danfo would be drinking with his food anyway, so it made no difference. Danfo thought it was the cleverest thing his wife had ever done until he sat down to eat.

He couldn't separate the taste of his palm wine from the stew; it was one strange, confusing taste. How could she empty his gourdful of palm wine into the stew? Danfo demanded. Ofori-waah said that she had already explained it. Likely, she had reached for what she thought was a gourd of water to thin her stew and had accidentally emptied her husband's palm wine into the stew. Maybe it was her revenge for him calling her a "man with a womb" the other day.

Insults were his weapon against her. He had had many successes that way. Not today, though; his voice was shut. The past several days, when Oforiwaah's cooking hadn't been exciting, reminded his gluttonous brain that he hadn't finished everything at the restaurant. He yelled at the whitewashed walls, adding to the strain on his throat from confronting the restaurant owner. He would revisit how to punish Oforiwaah when his voice returned. It would be daunting for Mother Earth to find her another husband when he finally divorced her. Her presence in the house was annoying and reminded him of the restaurant with good food, which he wouldn't be allowed into anymore. He had the urge to insult her, his hoarse voice notwithstanding. Mother Nature excluded her from things that described beauty. He was strong; that's all that is needed of a man, he believed. Oforiwaah, who could never be completely immune to Danfo's venomous condemnations, retorted that the world was yet to find a woman stupid enough to marry a man who shouldn't be walking but instead carried about in a wheelbarrow since he couldn't take a few steps without panting. She married Danfo, she said, because she didn't realize what would become of him. He was like a castrated dugong in the Sahara, she said, before erupting into one of her lacrimal downpours. Her penchant for tears was worrisome to some, for she could beat any man in Enkoho with her fists—a fact that she had to remind her husband of now and then. In any case, Danfo thought her remark rather stupid. Why would one castrate a dugong?

"No one has a reason to; it already looks castrated. Doesn't that remind you of you?" she said, and her weeping inched up many decibels. She had more to add. "Every woman who's been in your presence has had an itching desire to castrate you. I've cultivated such thoughts for a long time, but where do I begin when you don't even have the body parts for it?"

She had never used such words against her husband because her fists did a better job. This was new, and Danfo realized the insult wasn't conceived today. She had thought it through, a one-sentence punch to end his insults for good. Both of her feet were now in Danfo's arena of verbal combat.

Danfo sat down. He swallowed the last crumbs of guava to free his mouth. He shook his head to clear his mind. He got up, moved back from her, and maintained that distance in preparation for World War III. "Great observation, woman, that my loins go limp after looking at you, so much so that I even look castrated. How appropriate of you to insult yourself before you even think of insulting me. But then again, common sense doesn't come in your size. While at it, let me also confess that I have harbored the idea for a long time of cutting off your leg and counting the rings, like how Professor Tetteh dates a tree, to see how old you are. Methuselah must be turning in his grave for having such a wretched mess of a relative walking the earth today."

Danfo was hoarse and barely audible, but he had to ensure his wife understood him. He found his missing voice and aimed his tongue at her entire existence:

"There's no river anywhere called My Biggest Mistake. You are. It takes a special person to look at the sun directly; I'm not special. You, like the sun, are not good for my eyes. I've looked at you occasionally, but only to help me decide between suicide and natural death, like trying to find out if the dangers of living with you outweigh the pain of waiting for the inevitable. Your cooking frustrates my palate; your cooking hasn't gotten along with my stomach in years. Your cooking almost took me out of the graces of Healer. He went out of his way to make a concoction to help my appetite. It seemed worthless, and I came close to telling him that. Then I realized how close I came to making a fool of myself. It wasn't the concoction at all. Your cooking went down and flushed out everything with vomit, so I never saw it work. And while at it, let me tell you that burnt food isn't a new recipe. Woman, my back's broken in many places for carrying you to Healer in medical emergencies. Heck, I've spent more time at Healer's place myself for carrying you there than your illnesses have sent you there." He paused and racked his brain for more material. "And I haven't seen much of the corset you brought home last week. You're a hundred thirty-five kilograms of aggressive stomach hoisted on a suffocating pair of miserable legs. So I can rightly assume the corset has met its predictable destruction like the ones before it. That was number seventeen, or was it twenty-seven? I've lost count! The greatest philosophical dilemma in this marriage isn't why I ended up with you; rather, it's why you keep thinking corsets could take on a hopeless challenge like you. Or are the corsets to blame for thinking they could change a hopeless situation?"

Opening the lids of barrels to inspect her curing beef, Barbara Oforiwaah pretended she was untouched by her husband's insults. But she had turned several shades darker since Danfo started; all her tears had suddenly dried up. Perhaps she was overheating, and that had caused her tears to evaporate. Danfo wouldn't lose a fight of words to a woman. He had said much but wasn't sure his target was emotionally incapacitated yet. He wanted to keep their fights to words only; she wanted to keep their fights to fists only. Without disappointment, most of their issues were settled with both. Danfo wanted to avoid a fistfight, but he could not tell how effective he had been without his wife charging at him. His mouth following her around the room at a measured distance, Danfo began to see the effect of his words, moved back two steps to put more distance between them, and offered his closing argument: "As disappointed as I've been with the birth of Preprah, I've been secretly consoled by your miscarriage of a girl you were carrying, who would have taken after you. To have two of you in my house would have been the right number of nails to seal my coffin. A man only has to look at you once to be convinced that God doesn't answer every prayer. But as a non-Christian, I'm proud to say that He answered a prayer I hadn't even said by ensuring that the monstrosity growing inside you didn't see the light of day. If you had given birth to that girl, I'd have had to panhandle to raise money for a groom-price, the first of its kind, to get any man to accept and remove her from my house. My mind belongs in the mental asylum for always wondering how I ended up with you. Woman, we agree that no part of you is good for any member of my body. The sum of you, every inch of you, is offensive to my senses, even the ones I've lost, like my sense of taste in women, which is to blame for me ending up with you."

Oforiwaah stopped in her tracks, placed a finger to her lips, and turned her head sideways as if rethinking something. She started to inch backward toward her husband under the pretext of refastening the lids of barrels she had already inspected. Danfo was too focused on his insults to pay attention to what his wife was actually doing. Meanwhile, Oforiwaah gripped the rim of a barrel tightly, waiting for Danfo to fall within range.

"Hear me, woman: When I first laid eyes on you, I didn't like what I saw. I had already bought into that inner-beauty nonsense, not realizing that, when it comes to you, what's on the inside is even uglier than what's on the outside. I have more looks than you have brains, woman! It's a shame your mother even looks better than you, and poor old genetics would fault your father for the mess I see. But I refuse to soil the man's name, for he was too demented to dislike anyone, even me. May his kind soul rest—"

Danfo crashed into the bottom of the barrel, which sent him flying through a door. He woke up in the bedroom, not knowing how he had gotten there. The world had changed: a straw mat with pillows atop it was dangling from the ceiling; the room, stacks of portmanteau, cane chairs with folded clothes all faded in and out of view. The concrete walls now had shapes for colors, and the wooden clock was no longer in the living room but dangling from a clothesline running overhead. A surge of blood from bleeding chilblains made its way through cracks in the concrete floor, forcing him onto his feet. Danfo wondered why his mentation was suddenly distorted, blood leaking from his nose. He realized what was happening when Oforiwaah sat the barrel down and charged at him.

"This mouth of yours, this mouth...Keep your mouth shut and fight me like a man!"

She inched closer, throwing her hands in his face. She balled them into fists, which started landing everywhere. Danfo inched backward to avoid the blows but tripped and fell. He held onto her hands, which she had offered, and got up, only for her to push him down again. He slithered across the floor on his back, flailing his hands and feet to ward off her raining fists. Between the crash of his weight and her raging fists, the neighbors heard the prayerful grunts of a man who wouldn't survive the assault without their intervention. They rushed in. The women restrained Barbara Oforiwaah in one corner. With Danfo angered and breathing heavily, the men were nervous about getting near him. When he was almost up, he supported himself with his hands holding onto the barrels. He lost focus and exerted too much weight on the barrel edges, pulling the tops toward him and the bottoms away. He crashed to the floor with the barrels. The lids flung open, and beef poured out. Barbara freed herself and landed her entire weight on him. Her hands were free for assault. After a little while, and with great effort, the women succeeded in pulling her away.

"Barbara, Barbara! Your parents chose the easiest way to spell *barbaric*! Just like you ended up the same age as your mother because your demented father wanted your birthdate to be something he could remember," Danfo continued breathlessly.

"I'm not as old as my mother. How can that be, you useless man? Nobody knows when I was born."

"Correct, which can only mean, for all I know, that you may be in your eighties. No wonder you got along with my grandmother better than my grandfather did. I would be better off today had I asked my grandmother to set me up with one of her friends."

"Some say I've married a man with multiple personalities wrapped up in a shell of congenital bipolarism. It's not that at all, just simply the devil in you." She narrowed the gap between them with her fists raised. She struck his face in blistering succession—an attempt at shutting that venomous mouth or leaving him toothless. She left him with swollen and bleeding lips.

Danfo separated himself from the entanglement after the men intervened.

"Get out of my house!" he lashed out at Oforiwaah. "And get out of my life!" He spat blood at her.

Oforiwaah lunged at him, landing a couple of punches before being interrupted.

"Why wouldn't you fight me one-on-one if you're as tough as your weak mind tells you?" Danfo challenged.

He believed there was no way a man could lose a fistfight to a woman, under any circumstances, unless he were a corpse, in which case it wouldn't be a fair fight. It would appear Oforiwaah won decisively today as she had their previous fights. But things aren't always as they seem—definitely not how Danfo saw it! He had observed that Oforiwaah's fists were too efficient to have been hers alone whenever they fought. She threw them so fast, with no rest in between, that they violated the tenets of biomechanics. Some might attribute it to dizziness, disorientation, or even hallucination on his part, but he swore he saw more than two hands on her when they fought.

He claimed to have been able to immobilize her *actual* hands but still had seen and felt the brunt of blows. At first, he had thought other fists not belonging to either of them intruded in their fights. That explanation no longer satisfied him. In hindsight, Oforiwaah didn't get help just from those extra hands; she also got support from the bodies attached to them. So now Danfo's grand suspicion was that Oforiwaah's malicious gang of witches joined in and assisted her in their fights. In each of their fights, for example, he had consistently seen an extra pair of hands that he was certain belonged to Nyamenkum the Gossip. Some of the *other* intruding hands were uncommonly long, others grotesquely short and uneven. The strangest ones he had seen, which rarely showed up in their fights but fierce when they did, were malleable hands that were ticklish after each punch. Admittedly, he couldn't throw a punch during most clashes because the witches shrieked and took away his focus. The punching skills of some of these *extra* hands, however, he couldn't trace to any woman in Enkoho. These must be some vicious witches from other villages, he claimed. He would settle for the eight women from Enkoho, whom he had identified based on the appearances of their hands and about whom he could do much in the way of retaliation. They had to be dealt with. One of these witches wouldn't come to the aid of the other as they did Oforiwaah because she was their leader and needed their protection.

No need to refight Oforiwaah today; their scuffle had been decidedly a draw if he subtracted the intruding fists. Still, his fists had to visit those eight women—women he couldn't counterpunch because they had invisible faces and bodies. It would be fair to visit them all today, fighting all of them, one onerous witch at a time. Nyamenkum the Gossip was first!

Chapter

17

*T*wo months had passed since Gyambibi and Moro left for the military training camp. Asamoah didn't make it past the "body selection" phase. Jeefa went to the Armed Forces Regimental Training Center in Kumasi with a basketful of food. Helena had helped her with the cooking but stayed behind in the village.

"Come to A Company, #158 Platoon. You'll find me there," Jeefa told her in case she changed her mind. Helena didn't say why she wouldn't go with her. It was wise of Helena to keep her decision to befriend the face of evil in Enkoho to herself. Jeefa would have alerted her parents, Preacher, and the entire village to ensure that didn't happen.

For several days, and for close to an hour today, Helena had watched Agya Kobi and Adwoa Brago on the farm. Part of the time, they worked; other times, they took breaks to have a meal or drink water. Adwoa Brago returned from the river with a gourd of water and poured some over Agya Kobi's hands to wash them. He drank from the gourd and offered her the rest. When they took their cutlasses to the weeds, the sound of Helena's footsteps approaching got louder until she was with them.

"How are you, my dear? Looking for your way back to the village?" Adwoa Brago asked.

"I want to help you on the farm," Helena replied.

Agya Kobi was still working, not interested in their talk.

"And how do I pay you, my dear?" Adwoa Brago guffawed.

"No pay. I want to help you and Agya."

"No, my dear. Your hands don't belong in tilling the soil. They belong in the city. Besides, Mr. Nsenkyire wants to set you up with a job in Kumasi. He knows some of the local doctors who volunteer with your mother."

Helena was surprised that Adwoa Brago knew this.

"It's a small village, my dear. News travels fast."

"I want to learn to farm," Helena insisted.

"You youngsters...Hold out your hands; let me see them."

Helena obliged. Agya Kobi, tugging at some weeds, looked at his wife and Helena. There was discomfort in Helena's eyes when she saw the elder lean against a tree, breathing heavily. He struggled to take a hoe to a shrub.

"Look how soft and unscathed your palms are. I don't want you to ruin them, my dear."

Helena's eyes were focused on Agya Kobi; she must not have heard what Adwoa Brago had said.

"Stop and join us, Agya. We have a visitor, don't you see?"

The elder brushed the dirt off his hands and slowly approached to extend a handshake. Helena felt she was shaking hands with tree bark, scathed and cold as if blood didn't run through him.

"How can we help you?" His words seemed guarded and distant.

"I want to learn the ways of the village," Helena said.

Adwoa Brago waited for Agya Kobi to say more, but it didn't take long for her to be disappointed.

"She answered your question," Adwoa Brago tried, prompting her husband.

He nodded but wished not to say more. His wife pressured him until he finally asked another question.

"Why us?"

Adwoa Brago didn't like the question. She regretted pushing her husband.

"She had to pick somebody, and she picked us," Adwoa Brago answered for Helena.

Helena felt the elder's discomfort yet saw that Adwoa Brago was friendly.

"Come with me, dear. What do you want to learn?"

Adwoa Brago gleaned that her interest lay in befriending them, accompanying them to the farm if they would allow. She said she understood and was willing to take Helena under her tutelage on the condition that Helena also accepted the job Mr. Nsenkyire found her in the city.

"You can learn farmwork on the weekend," she concluded.

"I understand," Helena said, genuflecting. Agya Kobi paid no attention to them but turned to the weeds his weak hands could barely tame.

"We won't come to the farm tomorrow. We'll go to church. You can come to the farm on Monday."

Chapter

18

*K*arikari sat on the edge of his bed, wrangling with the disastrous misfortunes that destiny had allotted him and from which he hadn't had any relief. This kept him up. It was common for nightmares to disrupt his sleep nowadays. He would wake up in the middle of the night—or sometimes during the day when napping—perspiring heavily, fighting off the urge to curse God for his struggles. The only thing that kept him from breaking down was that he perceived himself as a hard man who didn't need to express emotions outwardly.

His eyes still heavy with sleep, he staggered onto the porch, spilling a calabash of raffia wine. After yawning, he picked up the calabash and filled it with water, which he splashed on his face. To erase any traces of sleep left, he strolled about with his fingers interlocked behind him, occasionally spitting saliva and smothering it underfoot while chewing a stick. His mind, congested with thoughts of the bleak prospects of his life, left him casting a wide gaze at the early morning sky, wondering which of the stars, his guardian star, would disengage if he were to die. Had he done anything to offend God? How could his punishment extend to the entire village, affecting even the poor if he had? Then again, everybody spoke well of him, so if God wasn't pleased with the rest of the villagers and wanted to punish them, why should he suffer a worse fate?

Mawuli had suggested they restart and expand their subsistence-crops business; he could find more customers for them. Yet these weren't as financially rewarding as cocoa, so the suggestion didn't advance. Laying uncultivated for years, the farmland was now uneven and overgrown with weeds. Trees felled by the storm required money to clear. It would take more money to level the land. Even if he could grow cocoa, it would take years to yield. The fear of being unable to return to the life of comfort he once knew was terrifying. Adding to his pain, all his farmhands, who had once been in and out of his house daily, now kept away, trying to survive.

But Karikari wasn't finished. Neither was his penchant for generosity. His kindness stood tall; if anybody believed he would one day regain what he lost, it was he. So today, he would provide for the village, dipping his hands in the little he had.

Atobrah and Abrafi awoke to Karikari's footsteps. Tabuah helped them bring firewood and kerosene to start the earthen stove. A wrought-iron pot filled with water was lifted onto it. Tabuah took the lid off a cask, scooped some millet dough, put it in another utensil, and added water. Abrafi slowly added the mixture to the boiling water while Tabuah stirred. Water was added as it thickened until it maintained a thin consistency of porridge, free of lumps.

Karikari observed his sister's mannerisms from the porch, mainly how she interacted with Atobrah and Abrafi. She had a gentle spirit and spoke kindly to them, the same way she talked to the old. Her medium frame wrapped in tie-dyed cloth and short hair plaited sufficiently reminded him of their mother. Tabuah went to the kiln to check on the cornbread. When she returned, sweat trickled down her face as steam rose from the porridge.

Around 9:00 a.m., Gyambibi showed up in military fatigues. Karikari embraced him and patted him on the head. The two went indoors and talked at length, after which Gyambibi went door to door, greeting the villagers. Mawuli got word of his arrival and joined him.

"How are you doing, my son?"

"I'm well," Gyambibi said, flashing a grin. "How's Mama Daavi?"

"Daavi's well," Mawuli said, with something on his mind. "You've grown handsomely, my son. Well, you've always been handsome. Not surprisingly, your mental growth has kept pace with your physical growth. Not surprising, not surprising. Like I say, if a man's physical growth outpaces his mental growth, he waxes stupid."

"Hahaha. You said that to me when I was twelve," Gyambibi said.

"Come home and see your mother before you leave."

"I will."

"She'll have a bone to pick with you if you don't."

"I will, I promise. My bus leaves tomorrow evening. Expect me forenoon."

Gyambibi beckoned to his cousin, Atobrah, to be patient.

"I remember when you were little...both you and Jeefa." Mawuli paused, searching for the right words. "You were like twins. You went everywhere together. You're children to me, still. You know she listens to you more than to her mother and me...Are you okay?"

Gyambibi seemed distracted.

"Yes. Please tell Daavi I'll be there tomorrow morning," he said, turning to go.

"I will," Mawuli responded, wondering why Gyambibi had cut short their conversation.

The village soon converged on Karikari's property to suckle on his benevolence. People were everywhere, with a calabash of porridge in one hand and cornbread in the other. Mawuli's hungry eyes lost track of Gyambibi.

The air crackled with sadness and despondency. Danfo was last to join the villagers, arriving close to noon with a sack of venison to sell.

"My people, my people, my people," he said, drawing their attention. "If Satan was cast down from heaven, we have a good idea where he landed. And if he had family members, they were also sent to Enkoho. The cataclysm marked their arrival, which we all haven't recovered from. By the sour look on your faces and loss of hope, they must feel right at home here. In all seriousness, Satan may have taken a vacation here and decided not to leave," he said to laughter, while others questioned the appropriateness of the joke. Danfo never ran out of alcohol-fueled rants.

"I don't know the current exchange rate for poverty, so poverty isn't a currency I accept. If you have no money, talk to me if you have something to barter." Danfo reached into his sack and started bringing up wraps of meat.

As usual, he had a separate package of meat that he discounted for Karikari, his biggest customer and close friend. While the villagers haggled over the meat, Danfo helped himself to a bowl of porridge and added sugar cubes to taste. Suddenly waxing serious, he continued to offer his advice between bites of cornbread and slurps of porridge:

"Look at your faces smeared with disappointment. Don't I hear from you religious folks daily that God works in mysterious ways? What's the mystery behind these deaths and ruining of the farms, huts, faiths, and dreams? There's no mystery here, folks. It's to make you sad and poor. Or is the mystery what's really behind your sadness and newfound poverty? I'd have thought you were amenable to common sense. Not so. Excuse me if I'm inappropriate; I'd rather tell you. You all pray to God above. What happened to praying to the gods below, gods of the earth? How do you read the Bible? You live here on Earth; whether happy or miserable, your life is tied to being here, so why pray to someone who doesn't live on Earth to help with your problems here? What does God the Father, who lives above, know about life on Earth? And Jesus! Like God, time doesn't define Jesus. As the son of God, He must have been running around heaven for trillions of years. Jesus relied on his Father for survival here, yet he barely made it past thirty. Here's an experiment designed by God Himself with a terrible outcome no one should ignore. Life on Earth isn't easy.

"What we are eating today should be familiar to Christians here. The only thing worse is Jesus's last meal: bread and juice— with a side dish of betrayal and abandonment. Any Christian here who doesn't feel betrayed and abandoned by God?"

Preacher wasn't there to correct his rant. Neither was Agya Kobi there to contextualize the biblical references and discredit him. Among the crowd were Asamoah and Efia, and the un-sanctimonious biblical references were for them. Danfo knew his words would reach Agya Kobi that way, who was rumored to cry for being deprived of the opportunity to correct, in re-al-time, Danfo's subtle desecration and distortion of Bible content because the villagers excluded him from gatherings.

Gyambibi followed his cousin, Atobrah, to the baobab tree. Atobrah then delved into secret whispers of a buried treasure. Gyambibi had objected when Atobrah first proposed digging it up months earlier. Atobrah downplayed the potential risk of death, saying the treasure belonged to their family line.

As Atobrah heard it, the secret whisper was this: Karikari and Tabuah's paternal grandfather owned the treasure. When he died, his wife Maame Dufie refused to let his nephew inherit it, as was customary. She had been married to her husband for decades, and they had endured hardships. She didn't share the spirit of the tradition to relinquish the product of their toil into the hands of a nephew at the expense of her own children. She vowed to die with the treasure if it came to that. In short, a dispute broke out between Maame Dufie and her deceased husband's nephew. Both parties dabbled in the occult to restrain the other. Maame Dufie died with few people knowing where she kept the treasure. Some of her children died mysterious deaths traced to the dispute.

A curse of barrenness was placed on her surviving children to prevent grandchildren from inheriting the treasure. Nonetheless, Karikari's mother and brother survived the curse. Before his uncle's death, Karikari learned of the location of the treasure. Karikari was privy to the details of the treasure and kept them to himself, but the strain of hardship had loosened his tongue. He told his sister, Tabuah, about it. As it turned out, Atobrah had eavesdropped on his uncle's conversation, but he didn't know the location of the so-called barn. But somebody in the village had shown him where it was. Gyambibi insisted Atobrah tell him who had done this, but Atobrah never revealed who it was.

Some villagers had tried to retrieve the treasure, and the outcome was insanity before death, always. Atobrah was aware of this but didn't care. To him, it bordered on idiocy for the village to wither away when a treasure could be sold to rebuild it.

"Look, if these rumors of death aren't true, don't you think others would have gotten to it before the idea came to you?" Gyambibi stated, but Atobrah was unwavering in his stance, his hand clutching a soaked rag pressed against his right temple. His eyes were strained almost to the point of squinting. Gyambibi inquired what the problem was but got no answer. Whatever plagued him was intolerable—and so was his feeling toward Gyambibi's hesitancy.

Atobrah had yet another reason to worry: Karikari's money problems had reached their doorstep. His mother now gave Karikari money to help him stay afloat. Atobrah had his own plans to go to America, so anything that affected his parents' financial situation affected that goal. Gyambibi softened his objection as Atobrah pressured him further: those who died had probably been wrongly linked to the treasure. Life is full of risks, so what if Atobrah was right and Gyambibi's fears were unfounded? Did the death of thirteen people outweigh the potential benefit of saving the whole village? It soon seemed worthwhile to pursue this treasure, so the two set out for the farm. Atobrah stopped to dip the rag in the river and drape it over his head. At the same time, Gyambibi remembered he had a team of children waiting to be taught in the village under the baobab tree. That was a task he had assumed now that there was no school building and parents were preoccupied with surviving more than schooling their children. He taught them every Saturday. How this had almost escaped him and Atobrah was a moment of laughter for both.

Atobrah helped Gyambibi maintain order when he taught the children. He repositioned his slipping rag on his right temple and told Gyambibi to skip today's lessons and resume the following weekend. Indeed, the lure of wealth could unmask the true nature of a pauper's altruism. Gyambibi decided to follow through with his lessons but would shorten them and join him shortly as a lookout. Atobrah told him of the structure with the buried treasure. Gyambibi's suspicion was confirmed. He knew the structure well; he and Moro had ventured into the surrounding woods several times. They thought of it as the burial place of a certain priest but had also speculated it could be the burial site of the treasure.

The plan was for Atobrah to wait outside the compound by a cashew tree until Gyambibi was there before entering the barn. But patience wasn't a virtue Atobrah possessed. The curse inhabiting the barn didn't withhold its deadly venom based on the number of people who entered. At least, that was the justification for his impatience.

Chapter

19

*A*tobrah strayed off the dirt path to the farm. Walking through the unruly terrain, he used a machete to pare down the nettles, thorns, and brambles. The weeds began to recede, leaving him with buzzing insects to worry about. He sustained multiple bites, wishing his exposed forearms could recoil into his sleeves. He raised his collar to shield his nape.

It seemed the compound of the barn hadn't been visited in decades, and thorny plants had sprung up everywhere as if by design. Atobrah was in front of a decrepit gate, which met the enclosing walls at a wooden crossbar latched onto metallic clasps on the other side. The cashew tree he was supposed to wait by was to his left, on the other side of the enclosure. It came to him that it was pointless to wait for Gyambibi when the potent force residing in the barn could kill, whether one or a million people entered. Rather than force the gate open, Atobrah opted to climb over the wall to keep the integrity of the overgrown vegetation intact in order not to arouse suspicion should somebody walk by. While sitting atop the wall, he overlooked a wild bloom of rhododendron shrubs, reassuring him that his feet would be safe landing there. Without hesitation, he jumped but overshot his landing to avoid an exposed boulder. His left foot, bearing the bulk of his weight, slid into a burrow, spraining his ankle. His foot showed no broken skin;

that was good because he didn't want to leave a bloody trail. On the other hand, he could barely walk.

Could this portend a bad omen, a sign that he should leave the treasure alone? He convinced himself he didn't come this far to be defeated by superstition. He refused to return empty-handed. He walked with a limp toward the barn.

Meanwhile, the children were excited about Gyambibi's arrival. Saturday was their favorite day, carrying their tables and chairs to school under the baobab tree and listening to hoary tales of Kwaku Ananse, the most intelligent of all God's creations, which had been told for centuries. Often, Gyambibi would embellish and retell them to make the stories more interesting for the children. At the beginning of his weekly lessons, he would complete a story he'd started a week prior. Then, after finishing the story, he would start another to be completed the following week—purportedly to whet the kids' interest. The caveat was that only those who scored at least 70 percent on their quizzes would be part of the listening audience. Because they wanted to hear the stories from Gyambibi and none other, the children would study hard.

On this day, all the pupils celebrated for passing their quizzes. Gyambibi stood in front of them, his back against the blackboard—a plank of wood nailed to the baobab tree. It was so quiet that one could hear the wind caressing the tree. He began: A long time ago, Ananse set out to grow the most succulent and delicious pawpaw the world had ever known. He went to his farm daily, fertilizing the seedlings, watering them, and pulling weeds. He grew them in three batches and under different conditions so that he would know which ones yielded the best fruits. Sometime later, the first fruit appeared. Back then, hyena and lion were identical twins: they were of the same size, weight, and fur thickness. They lived in the same village as Ananse. Their mother told them they both stood to inherit the kingship once their uncle died. With this information, hyena started being rowdy. Lion knew that if he were destined to be king, it would indeed happen, so there was no need to act it out before it actualized.

The village woke up one morning to find Ananse's plump, golden pawpaw fruits gone. Ananse voiced his frustration to the village, and no one claimed responsibility. When the next batch of pawpaw ripened, he woke up to find them gone as well. He was angry and again complained, but no one claimed responsibility. Before the last batch ripened, Ananse devised a plan: He plucked them himself, split them open, removed the meat, and filled them with a surprise.

The children interrupted the storytelling with laughs. Sitting nearby, Helena broke out in laughs, too, as Jeefa interpreted the story for her. The child in her never outgrew that arcane yearning for a life among the ancestors in the old world—a feeling she had had the first time she participated in storytelling in Enkoho. She was still fascinated and looked forward to storytelling as much as the children.

Gyambibi continued: When the village woke up the next day, Ananse's golden pawpaw fruits were gone. Ananse implored the king to summon the village. Once gathered, Ananse asked that hyena and lion come forward. He'd seen paw prints on the farm and knew they belonged to one of them. Since he didn't want to accuse either wrongly, he had devised a clever way to sort it out. When lion and hyena stepped forward, he asked that they open their mouth. He thrust his fist down lion's throat to induce vomit. Lion vomited a bit and was set aside. When hyena opened his mouth, pawpaw skin came out first, then the "surprise."

The children were up on their feet, applauding Ananse's ingenuity.

Gyambibi finished: Hyena vomited for several days. He lost weight, and because of that, he didn't exude the charisma and respect befitting a king. Lion thus inherited the kingship when their uncle died. Hyena, however, was banished from the kingdom, and the shame clung to him forever.

The children were on their feet again, clapping. While they discussed the story, Gyambibi slipped away to meet Atobrah.

Atobrah shouldered the barn door open and entered. He scanned the four corners of the empty room, save for ghostly weeds and thorns—dense networks of spider webs connected between brush and shrubs. Small animals scuttled about, some disappearing into a burrow. Areas of the ground were stained black, recalling the site of a ritual sacrifice. The stains became larger when he moved to his right, which led him to an area where three pots sat. He hoped these contained the mysterious treasure that would end his monotonous and laborious life in Kodee and help pay his way to America. He felt dizzy after looking into the pots. In his estimation, they contained shriveled specimens, though their very nature eluded him. He shook his head, and his dizziness dissipated. Then he looked closely at the pots and noticed, radially etched onto each side, the words "*Akwaaba, Niwura*" or "Welcome, Owner." Also of visual interest were crevice-like impressions emanating from the base of each pot and converging at a point in the ground. This area was black and fissured. He paused and processed these clues. Then, with a single thrust of his machete, he broke the soil at the intersection of the crevices and scooped the loose soil with his hand. He continued until the machete hit a leathery patch, drawing soot into his eyes. He groped the space toward cracks of light, which clouded his assessment of where the door was. Then the walls of the barn began to close in, turning the spacious barn into a claustrophobic lair—a deathtrap. He heard echoes of his screams for help, hoping that if Gyambibi were nearby, he would come to his aid.

Gyambibi returned to the palm tree on their farm that Karikari's hand had planted: the resting place of his mother and unborn brother. When he visited Agnes's burial site, he did so alone to tell his mother of his decisions. It was profoundly meaningful to Gyambibi. Occasionally, when the weight of life became too heavy and lonely, he would visit Agnes. He would sit silently; sometimes, his lips would move with no words pouring out; other times, tears forced their way out. Agnes would never have thought her son was capable of crying. Gyambibi never made a decision without telling his buried mother. From joining the military to planning to dig up the treasure today with Atobrah, Agnes knew of her son's undertakings. In death, she heard more from her son than when she was alive. From here, he left for the barn.

Gyambibi hid behind a tree. Atobrah had taken longer than he had anticipated. For about an hour or so, he piddled around the forest until his eyes were lured by a colony of ants that traveled in an unbroken, sinuous file. He followed them, lifting shrubberies under which they passed. This colony carried pieces of dirt to build their home or possibly food they were transporting to their storehouse in anticipation of inclement weather. The sight of dung beetles cleaning up after man left Gyambibi with the thought that lower animals could be united in a common goal to attain what humans, created in God's image, sometimes fail to achieve. The longer Gyambibi watched, the more convinced he became that man was devolving into wildlife, and wildlife might someday assume the place of God's prized creation. Gyambibi followed the ants for over ten yards and watched them file into an anthill.

Gyambibi returned to investigate what had taken Atobrah so long. As he got to the gate of the barn wall, he found it still latched. No signs of human presence were visible as he circled the perimeter. Furthermore, there were no movements beyond the gate—nothing!—except whispers of the wind. He called for Atobrah many times. No response! He wondered if Atobrah had had a change of mind. How could this be? He'd been so serious and undeterred. Or maybe, he thought, Atobrah had concocted a ruse to get him into the barn first to see if anything would happen to him. That was unlike his cousin. Unable to make sense of the situation, he went to the river to drink.

Walking by his father's palm trees, he found his palm-wine gourd empty of the virgin drink they both liked. Karikari wanted none nowadays—only the fermented, alcohol-heavy variant would do, which dulled his pain. In any event, it had been evident to his family that someone was stealing their palm wine, though they hadn't figured out whom. Hardship was sweeping through the village, so these petty thefts were getting on people's nerves, especially palm-wine tappers. In due course, they would take matters into their impoverished hands.

Chapter

The Second Casualty of the Palm Tree

*I*t was evening. Having nostalgia for the good old days, Kari-kari dusted off the gramophone. It dawned on him that he had allowed problems to take charge of his life, especially since his sister had drawn his attention to wild streaks of gray that had invaded his thick, bushy hair. Prying through his stacked records, which bore mild smears of dusty cobwebs, he picked up a record of the Ramblers International Band. It darkened his mood for reasons that didn't come to him right away. He placed it at the bottom of the pile, away from view. He stood there, troubled and lost. He flicked past EK's, Black Beats, Stargazers, and Broadway Dance Band. None of them interested him.

Then a smile crept across his face when he saw Kofi Sammy's *Agyanka Due*—Orphan, My Condolence. He slumped in a recliner and took a big gulp of palm wine conveniently placed in front of the sofa. *Agyanka* was a song he had played many times before. This day, however, he connected with it more profoundly, as its lyrics evoked painful memories of his difficult childhood: growing up without a mother to nurse and nurture his well-being and having an absent father whose sparing presence left him alone to navigate the darksome wilderness of an unpredictably cruel, unforgiving life. The first time music evoked such emotion from him was forty-five years ago when his father, with his fondness for a womanizing life, would inadvertently awaken him with enchanting adagios by the classical maestros. But sitting across from his gramophone, the high-life music blaring at him connected him to his position in life more than his father's classical music did. It came to Karikari that he had a vague recollection of using the words "Mom" and "Dad," which now represented sad memories of his painful past. Between the song's melancholic emotionalism and rhythmic stupor, Karikari was lost in a world of blissful sorrow.

Outside, the noise of children playing grew louder. The wind blew gently into the curtain that overlooked the front porch, sending in intense white light. The nightfall had faded into a bright day, like mid-noon. The air was neither cool nor hot nor lukewarm. It felt right on the skin and was visually perceptible. Livestock, mostly in pens or coops minutes before, roamed the village and possessed the same radiant whiteness as the children. Unlike the usual village chickens, however, there were fowls with incandescent plumage that fell out as they moved, exposing the skin beneath. The deplumed feathers then found their way back into their follicles. The feathers pulsated with light too piercing and spectacular for words. The feathers rose and fell, starting from the head and ending at the tail, giving the effect of waves. A sight to behold. The birds looked like a hybrid of the hoopoe and picathartes, but much bigger.

The goats now roaming the village were also not the type Karikari knew. These were like the aardvark but much taller and larger, with scaly skin of dappled sheen. Some bizarre-looking creatures they were, three- and five-footed types, some too brilliant to look at—creatures from a bygone era. Karikari, now drawn to the porch, couldn't tell whose huts were which because they were now simply mounds of tactile colors. The atmosphere was a glittery dust of topaz. The sun had fled the sky, settling in the topaz dust that glowed brighter than anything he had ever seen.

The flood of light was overwhelming, not to his eyes, but to the sadness inside him, the helplessness that described his life. The villagers looked at him as he drank. They couldn't say why he looked happy when his life condition drew sadness. The glitteriness had melted away his worries. As strange as the village had transformed, it also seemed as it had always been to him. The children frolicking about were discernibly recognizable, though each a blob of angelic whiteness. These were children, all right, with the flesh of pure strands of light, almost like an assemblage of white rays that filtered through his eyes. He looked up at the sky; although the sun was absent, the sky was so piercingly white that it hurt his eyes. Then he saw other humans emanating light of a grayer quality. He knew these were mostly adults. Looking at the children, something told him these were angels. While he didn't know what angels would be doing in the village, upon further reflection, the village was full of angelic beings. What he was seeing couldn't be ghostly apparitions, for something inside him told him they were as human as he was. This was when he looked at himself: he was flesh and bones, unlike the people he was looking at.

He returned indoors. The wind blew behind him into the room, melting away the curtain. Now the whiteness that enveloped the world outside was seeping into the house. He lifted the gourd above his slanted face and poured wine into his mouth. Several minutes later, he returned to the front door and opened it. Outside, on the porch, was Agnes. She was as humanly flesh and bones as he was. He reached out and pulled her indoors. Agnes looked at him with a repressed smile that gave way to peals of laughter after watching him dance out of sync with the music. How glad they were to see each other again! Though she had been away for years, Karikari felt she had never left. Again, nothing seemed out of place. He gestured to her to join him in dance. She floated off her seat toward him. With his belly brushing softly against her pregnant belly, he cupped her hands and swung her around. Her face was aglow as she navigated her feet in step with his. She put her hand on her belly and signaled she was tired, even as Karikari patted her on her bottom. Shortly, she got up and headed for the door. Karikari held her hand, walked her outside, and lowered her into a chair. His sight was renewed. The whiteness of which everyone else had been made was no more. A ruddy sky met him. Now each person was a motion of colors too peaceful to describe. His heart began to race when he saw his father, Yaw Donyinah, talking with Agnes on the porch. Across from them was a woman he had last seen over four decades prior, his mother, clutching Gyambibi to her bosom as his brother Yaw tried to beat him. In that instance, Karikari saw a continuum of his past and present. His face spoke of an upwelling of joy, a celebration of blissful contentment and euphoria. This lingered on despite the terrible sensation of another human walking toward him, who, unlike the others, was black light.

Karikari was overcome by sadness for Gyambibi, a gifted child who wouldn't realize his full potential. Gyambibi had skipped part of childhood. "Agyanka" replayed and replayed amid thoughts about Gyambibi. Then came a rush of bitterness and hopelessness, thoughts of poverty having plunged its toxic tentacles into the bowels of Gyambibi.

Agnes's voice brought Karikari to the door. However, she was no longer on the porch. As he wondered where he had heard her voice, he was startled by the sound and sight of a horned owl sitting atop the roof of a hut across from his porch. Its ominous eye movements broke through the whiteness that once again emanated from everything. He shuddered and lost control of his sphincter, soiling himself. The owl stared at him as he stared at it. The sky glowed red. None of the humans who were there seemed to have taken notice. The bird fluffed its feathers, and Karikari noticed it was sitting on something. As he looked to see what it was, a shriek came out of its beak. After that, it stood with a human being between its claws. Karikari screamed and ran toward the bird, which flew higher, clutching Agnes, until they were out of sight. He started to cry. As he walked back to the house, he saw that it was getting dark again: the second nightfall of the day.

When he reached home, he had forgotten about the owl and Agnes and sat down to listen to music that wasn't from the album he had been playing before. Now it was Saint-Saëns' *The Carnival of the Animals*. He had a feeling his father was nearby. In fact, Yaw Donyinah, after emerging from the porch, had replaced the record. Karikari's choice of music perturbed him. Before Karikari could argue, he realized his father had disappeared. He searched the house. There was no sign of Yaw Donyinah. Karikari peeked behind the curtain of the window overlooking the front porch. A ball of light with no distinguishing features, as all the humans appeared, laughed. By his emotional connection to this light, he knew it was one of his sons. By the quality of his energy, he knew it was Gyambibi. He played with other balls of light. He knew one was Moro, the other Asamoah. The happiness in their faces seemed misplaced, for they hadn't been this joyful since the rainstorm. He gathered that the ambiance was one of a celebration between the three close friends.

Karikari left the curtain and raised another gourdful of wine to his lips. A loud flash of light, followed by a shriek, sent him outside again. The horned owl had returned, stationary in the air, Agnes dangling between its claws. At the corner of his kitchen and porch was a pillar of brown essence that shot into the sky. He didn't react to it because he processed it as part of his compound. It teetered in the wind and then leaned toward the owl. Everybody went about their lives as if this was an ordinary occurrence because they didn't see this dense, brown thing heading for destruction. Trembling, Karikari rushed into the open to position himself below Agnes when the owl released her onto the now-falling pillar, which changed direction and landed away from Karikari but fell on Agnes. A loud shatter erupted as the pillar crushed her. The villagers, who didn't see this coming, gathered around the deceased. Karikari spread himself over his dead wife, bleeding and broken in a thousand places.

Women screamed. Children screamed. The man, whose light was black, dissolved in the air and enveloped Karikari, who turned around to see Danfo pry off the women and pull him away. Karikari kept screaming, "My wife is dead! My wife has been crushed to death!"

"Hold yourself together like a man," Danfo barked. "What's wrong with you lucky men whose wives are dead? Why cry? Would you rather be the one who's dead?" After pulling Karikari off and sending him back to the house, Danfo reminded him that Agnes had been dead for years. Danfo went on to lash out at him for having a death wish to be heading for the falling palm tree. It wasn't his time to die because, lucky for him, the tree had instead killed a member of the household of the evil ruining lives in Enkoho. Noting that Karikari was drunk, Danfo splashed water on his face and told him a sad incident had befallen the village. His palm tree had collapsed on Asamoah and crushed him to death, claiming another villager.

The palm tree was supposed to go after the rainstorm. Because of its size, height, proximity to the house, and infiltration of its root underneath, Karikari had decided to kill it rather than pull it down. The fronds were to be cut off, and longitudinal cuts were to be made in the trunk and infiltrated with kerosene, as Healer had instructed. At least that was the intent related to Yaw, a task to be completed before his father returned from another loan appointment with Danfo. However, he assigned it to Gyambibi and Moro, like most of his chores. Gyambibi refused; Yaw threatened to tell their father of his trip to Agya Kobi's hut again. With the task thus assigned to Gyambibi, the fearless Moro assumed the task of cutting the fronds. However, days after one of his hallucinatory spells, Gyambibi thought it was best to kill the tree from the root. Moro seconded the plan. And that they did, applying kerosene to the base of the tree.

The tree, rotten at the base, tumbled over that fateful night, killing their friend and Agya Kobi's great-grandson, Asamoah.

Asamoah's sudden death held no mystery. It wasn't the tree that killed him so much as the one who wanted him dead. His disappointment with not getting into the military with his friends was behind him. He'd been finally accepted, hence the celebration with his friends. It appeared someone didn't want him to take that step.

The reason for his twice rejection from joining the military hadn't made sense to his friends. In fact, Asamoah had passed the written test but failed the physical exam twice, although he had no physical shortfalls. Gyambibi and Moro, not wanting to leave their childhood friend behind, found the military doctor responsible for body selection—part of the physical exam for recruits. After locating the doctor, they saw a certain laziness in how he spoke, moving his lips like a snail nibbling on concretized flesh. He was composed like a sinecured retiree. Beneath this façade, though, were traces of dedication and honesty. While Gyambibi and Moro lacked the rank to look at an applicant's medical record, Preprah, already in the military, told them about officers who could arrange this for them. The report showed that Asamoah had many varicose veins. Curiously, there was a scribbled note saying Asamoah had too many veins. They wondered if one person could have more veins than another. Did the doctor think of varicose veins as new veins? Rejection of the flat-footed and prominently bowlegged made sense. If Asamoah had varicose veins, his rejection was in order. But having firsthand knowledge that Asamoah didn't possess such blemish, Moro exclaimed, "This is what we've come to as a nation: a blind man determines who's physically capable of protecting our country!" The military doctor missed what he said and asked for a repeat. "And he's lost his hearing too," Moro said, at which point Gyambibi placed a hand over Moro's mouth.

What they didn't understand was how the orderlies, on two separate occasions, had found the same blemish on Asamoah. It was a mistake. The office couldn't explain how, but Moro and Gyambibi thought it must have been a simple way to disqualify applicants to make room for others who had proffered a bribe. They offered to pay the officer for his time. He declined. Instead, he asked to have their friend come to see him. Upon reexamination for the third time, the doctor cleared him. Asamoah had been accepted just days prior and hadn't even finished celebrating.

Agya Kobi was home when Nyamenkum the Gossip arrived to break the news of Asamoah's death. She found the old man already crying, and something about his tears troubled her. They were genuine tears but seemed detached from emotional pain. They were the tears of one numb to the ache of life. Nyamenkum the Gossip was overcome by the realization that the elder already knew his great-grandson was dead. But how? Out of fear, she turned around and went home.

Chapter

21

*A*dwoa Brago returned Agya Kobi's Bible to the top of a portmanteau in their hut. He was finished with his devotion when a knock came. Helena entered the living room when the elder asked her to come in. She said her greetings and stood there, nervous at the sight of Agya Kobi. He didn't say more after returning her greeting. Helena offered him a newspaper. He thanked her and went silent. He stared at the newspaper and dropped it to his side. His words were unfriendly; his demeanor bore a hint of hostility toward the world, though unrelated to Asamoah's death. The old man had a flat, somber mood that changed little, if at all, with circumstances. This didn't put off Helena because she perceived something else: He wanted to be left alone. It didn't matter if strangers or relatives were around; he wanted isolation.

Adwoa Brago rejoined them to see Helena standing idly and nervous. She and the elder didn't seem to mix.

"Have you two talked?" she asked Helena. "My granddaughter, forgive us. Sometimes he doesn't even talk to me. He's quiet, minding his business all the time. Sometimes I think living with a dog would be better because a dog would at least bark now and then."

Adwoa Brago took notice of Helena's appearance. She was barefoot with a hoe and cutlass in hand.

"Not what I meant when I told you to dress comfortably. Why are you barefoot?"

No trinkets accompanied Helena's meager appearance. She was uncomfortable in footwear when Adwoa Brago wore none. She explained that all the elderly women and men were barefoot on the farm and in the village. Adwoa Brago laughed, and she sat Helena down to persuade her otherwise.

But a sudden commotion sprung up outside. It was announced that everyone was to appear in the village square. A bracelet of solid gold nuggets was missing from the annual inventory of Chief and the queen's ornaments. The inventory was unique to Enkoho. The ornaments were the property of the village because they had been acquired with village resources. Every year, on April 7, they were displayed in the public square for all to see. They hearkened memories of their past and celebrated their pride and bond.

Rumors began circulating that the missing Atobrah had stolen the bracelet and run away. This was a serious matter because all the ornaments were very valuable, made from pure, solid gold. The fetish priest was consulted to fish out the culprit. When everyone was gathered under the baobab tree, he rubbed two leaves together, blew them in the air, and pronounced a three-day ultimatum: return the jewelry or disappear. The village understood the latter meant death.

Chapter

22

*R*umors of Atobrah running off with the missing gold bracelet didn't mitigate Gyambibi's fear that something had happened to his cousin. He had left the farm when he didn't see Atobrah and returned days later when thoughts of the barn having swallowed his cousin overwhelmed him. He had explaining to do if he should tell someone, so he kept it to himself. He couldn't eat, sleep, or think. His fears were realized when, in an effort to investigate what had happened, he entered the compound of the barn again, walked around, and saw the barn door slightly open. From a safe distance, he could see a human hand and torso inside, with the hand close to the threshold. He screamed and jumped back. He looked about and walked outside the perimeter. He wasn't clearheaded after that.

In these times of hardship, a villager would be tempted to dig up the treasure. That meant it was just a matter of time before someone saw Atobrah. His cousin's death would be linked to him. Not thinking clearly, he had gone near the barn and held Atobrah's hand. Atobrah was heavy to drag out. Gyambibi would need the other hand to pull him out but risked looking into the barn and suffering the same fate. It was pointless; Atobrah was limp and had been that way for days. Gyambibi found a hoe on a nearby farm, reentered the compound, and started digging. He stopped when he became aware of what he was doing.

Gyambibi was withdrawn and depressed again, just like the days after the cataclysm. After his mother's death, he thought he would never see the world the same way again. Yet he recovered and somewhat returned to the world he had known. Then Asamoah's death, and now Atobrah's death, seemed to slowly imbue in him something he had seen only in Agya Kobi. Gyambibi wondered if it wasn't realistic to always be somber, gloomy, sad, and withdrawn so that anything untoward in life would be deprived of its shock value. The deaths around him, and life circumstances, began to mutilate his soul.

Gyambibi hadn't reported to the barracks in days but had an excuse ready for his platoon sergeant. Moro was already serving a seven-day IHL (imprisonment with hard labor) for the infraction of accusing his superiors of ethnic prejudice without proof. Moro's harsh sentence gave Gyambibi a reason to be concerned in light of current happenings. Moro had observed that the mysterious illness that had plagued Gyambibi had all but disappeared once they joined the military. Away from the village, not eating or drinking anything from there could partly, if not wholly, explain why there had been no recurrence. Whether it was a sign of his waning intellect wrought by his former episodic seizures or not, Gyambibi wondered how he hadn't made that observation himself. He knew Moro was right. Was someone doctoring the food supply in the village? But because the easy target of this theory had always been Agya Kobi, it was equally reasonable to assume that Gyambibi not having suffered any of his problems while in the military could be Agya Kobi's psychological maneuvering in the occult to prove himself right. After all, Agya Kobi was the one to state the source of Gyambibi's problems and propose a solution, which annoyed Karikari enough to throw him out of his house. Lately, Gyambibi had been questioning the sense in believing he was right about Agya Kobi not being evil and everyone else wrong. Considering all aspects, Gyambibi wondered how someone could target his food without affecting the rest of his family since they ate from the same source. Adding to his confusion, in his absence, he had heard accounts of his father exhibiting symptoms similar to his. However, it was known that Karikari had been drinking heavily, so it was difficult to say.

Mawuli didn't hide his suspicion that Gyambibi might know Atobrah's whereabouts and shared his suspicions with Karikari and Danfo. However, Gyambibi told them about Atobrah before they asked. Karikari took the disclosure hardest. He had lost his wife and unborn child. His sister, Tabuah, had been coming with her eldest son, Atobrah, to help Yaw with housework now that Gyambibi was a good 250 kilometers away in the Teshie barracks. And now Atobrah was dead! The cycle of death in his family numbed his mind. Karikari didn't want to believe it, but Gyambibi wasn't known to be a liar.

Atobrah's disappearance wasn't news that the village would treat kindly. Disgrace and scorn would be fierce. Karikari and his two friends decided to go and see for themselves before deciding the next course of action. When the barn came into view, it dawned on Gyambibi that he had forgotten to cover the hole he had dug. If they saw this, there would be no confusion about his motive. Gyambibi was sweating. If his anxiety got any worse, it would precipitate a heart attack. He tried to keep calm. The gate to the compound was open when they got there because Gyambibi had forgotten to close it. They entered facing the south side of the barn. Gyambibi put himself at the back of the pack, thinking of a response in case they asked about the hole. Danfo was first to reach the barn door, with the others close behind; all were careful not to step inside. They didn't act in a way that conveyed that they saw anything unusual. Gyambibi soon found out why: the hole had been filled in. The ground didn't even look disturbed. Gyambibi was shaking, and his eyes were red with fear. Mawuli pulled him aside and assured him all would be well.

The hole was gone, and Atobrah's body had also disappeared. Gyambibi was covered in sweat and nervous itch. He stamped his feet, took his boots off, and turned them sideways as if to evict pebbles that had taken residence in them. He felt lightheaded and leaned against a tree. He tried to look normal.

The door to the barn was hinged to the right with raised ground keeping it slightly open. Danfo kept his gaze in the other direction so as not to see inside and used a stick to push the door shut.

Danfo implored Gyambibi to go home and sleep off any lingering hallucinatory spells. What Gyambibi had seen and done must have been a figment of his imagination or bad conscience. Atobrah had detested village life. He'd run away—simple.

"He could be hiding somewhere, acting out his plans to go to Europe or America. He stole the missing gold to fund his way there. You, Gyambibi, are as trustworthy as any man, so Atobrah knew we would have to believe you. Your cousin would have fooled us if it weren't for the timing of the missing gold bracelet. All this business about his dead body in the barn was a cover," Danfo presumed.

Quiet and confused, Gyambibi bit his lower lip. His face flushed with more despair. Perhaps Atobrah wasn't dead. Yet neither was Gyambibi merely asleep and dreaming. He had dug a hole and seen and touched a dead body.

He would visit his mother's gravesite. Perhaps she would help him make sense of it.

23

S hielded from view, Preprah laid on the ground amid dandelions and rhododendron shrubs. He'd uprooted any flower-
ing plant he'd seen, totaling nine, one for each month since he
had last seen Efia. Resisting the temptation to wipe his hands
on his military uniform, he got up to drink from his canteen,
which he found empty. He walked over to an adjoining farm,
pulled a gourd from under a newly felled palm tree, and filled
the canteen, noting its first batch of palm wine. He took a long
swig. The wine's rancid aftertaste made him swirl the container
for a homogenous mix. The taste was strange, so he swirled it
again and took another swig. He must not have cleaned the
canteen well before filling it. After several rinses from the river,
he again took the gourd from the felled palm tree. He emptied
the rest of the wine into it, which he intended to share with his
paramour.

He returned to Agya Kobi's farm, sat by the flowers, and
waited for Efia, but not before ensuring his uniform was wrin-
kle-free. The full canteen was too heavy for his web belt, so he
took it off and laid it by the flowers. His uniform was starched
and pressed. He leaned against a tree trunk, stiff like frozen
bread. It was routine for him to come to Kodee the day before
he met Efia, press his uniforms, then walk in them to the farm
for their rendezvous. This way, his uniform was impeccable, as

ing one from another. Why pay more for a better brand and then hide the label? In his own way, he corrected this nonsense. When he ordered St. Michael underwear from Marks & Spencer, he would wear it inside out, back to front, to display the label tag. He followed the same fashion protocol with brand-name outer garments. When he received clothes with missing, blemished, or torn tags, he would return them. They were useless. The military dressing protocol didn't make room for that; else, he would be wearing his uniform inside out if it had a tag worth showcasing.

The military did Preprah good. Respect for the uniform got girls to accept him. From the Armed Forces Training Center in Kumasi to his transfer to Takoradi, his difficulty with women dissipated. Though his accessibility to women was healthy from then on, Efia was the one girl he didn't forget. His joining the military wasn't what changed her mind, though; it was his plan to go to America. Upon learning of this, Efia entertained their rendezvous without protest. She tried to convince him to return to the village because her grandfather had forgiven him. Preprah couldn't count on the forgiveness of the devil, though. His best friend, Yaw, wanted his return too, but Preprah would only meet him in Kodee. What Yaw knew, to his consternation, was that Preprah was also now on good terms with his father, Danfo, who recently described his son as a "recovering retard." Even though Yaw knew that Preprah craved his father's acceptance, something about their newfound closeness unsettled him.

When it came to Efia, Preprah only wanted to meet her on her grandfather's farm, which his own hand had tried to destroy. No longer stationed in Accra, he hadn't seen Efia in months. His reassignment had come about for inadvertently discharging a round of bullets at a drill sergeant he didn't like. After months in IHL, he was demoted to the rank of petty officer. He expressed a desire to be a military truck driver, but a brick wall of exams stood in his way. With three failed exams behind him, a fourth attempt opened up. These opportunities were possible because one Air Vice-Marshal George Yaw Boakye, born and raised in Aduman, became aware of Preprah, who had used the man's village as his residential address due to the problem of Enkoho's nonexistence. The remedial written exam for Preprah was scrapped because it was clear he couldn't read.

The oral exam began: What would it signify if a driver came to a road sign with a picture of a deer? Preprah's answer: a restaurant must be nearby. Trying to appease the Air Vice-Marshal, the officer had to find another way to pass Preprah. He was taken for a road test because it was thought that he learned by doing. He showed promise until he drove a military truck into the Kpeshie lagoon at the sight of an oncoming truck carrying a load of timber. His superiors couldn't understand how he passed the written and physical exams to enter the military. For days, Preprah cried for not amounting to anything despite his perseverance. He felt hopeless about a life with no direction. He felt life was outside his control and that his meager intelligence wouldn't show him the way. He couldn't determine which course to chart going forward, so rather than face discharge, he begged for transfer. Out of pity and with Air Vice-Marshall George Yaw Boakye's help, Preprah was sent to the second battalion in Takoradi. He sought to leave his disgraces behind and start afresh where no one knew him. Danfo brought these unflattering accounts of Preprah's military life to the village, if for no other reason than to prove himself right, that is, his son was a moron.

Efia met Preprah on her grandparents' farm when they performed devotion at home because Agya Kobi wasn't allowed
in the church gathering. Efia didn't participate because she had
severe menstrual cramps. In times like these, she went to the
river to bathe with Helena and Jeefa. Agya Kobi doubted her
story now and then because no matter when her cycle started,
her flare-ups always coincided with the weekend when they
were to have family devotions. Even though Adwoa Brago's
feminine instincts could ascertain that her cycle hadn't started,
Efia found it convenient to invoke her premenstrual headaches
and cramps to avoid devotion. Agya Kobi said there was little
they could do since she was set in her ways of carnal promiscuity. They could bolt her to her bedroom floor, and she would
still find ways to do what she wanted. She was well into adulthood, with multiple failed relationships behind her. One almost
led to marriage but dissolved before her grandparents could
intervene. Rumors were also rife about the death of Asamoah
finally pushing her further down the dark waters of whoredom.

Yaw proved a loyal friend, still the one to arrange their meetings. He would tell Efia of the date and time to meet in Kodee,
unaware that the meeting actually took place on her grandfather's farm. Occasionally, Yaw hinted to others of Preprah
coming to the area to tamp down the rumors that he was dead
elsewhere, in defiance of the reality that no child of the village
could leave for good or die outside its boundaries. Some of
those interested in Preprah's whereabouts were palm-wine tappers who couldn't ignore the coincidence of the appearance of
this oaf and the disappearance of their wine. In any case, Yaw
had a reason to be loyal: he and Preprah had a pact. Whichever of them made it to America first would help bring over the
other. Karikari had been uncooperative with Yaw's goal. With
Karikari's resources dwindling, Yaw felt that his chances of fulfilling his dream were better with Preprah. Yaw was hopeful,
knowing how far his friend had gotten.

Efia's head appeared through the flowers, to the fright of
the daydreaming Preprah. He peeled away the dandelions and

embraced her. She told him they had two hours more than the time she had given him before. She had overheard Nyamenkum the Gossip and Obra Noara say that Chief planned to convene the village after church services because of the missing jewelry. Her grandparents, like all others, would be engaged.

Efia was quiet, almost melancholic. She told him about the death of Asamoah and other happenings in the village. Preprah consoled her. She told him that poverty was consuming the village and that farmers now relied on subsistence crops to get by. There was no money to go around because there was no cocoa to harvest, and it would take years to see another one. That wasn't even the worst. There was a severe insect infestation of mirids also threatening the farms.

Palm wine would help with her pain, he assured her. He took several gulps, finishing off a third of the canteen. The taste was still perverted. He handed the canteen to Efia. She had a gulp and agreed that the taste wasn't right. She took the canteen into the sun, gave it a swirl, took another gulp, and saw a yellowish-brownish, slushy mass bubble to the surface. Her nose was close enough to get a sniff of scatology. Their mouths rang out with choking and vomiting as they ran to the river. There they heaved, rinsed their mouths, scrubbed their tongues, and retched some more. Their eyes were strained, the veins on their necks sticking out. Their stomachs cramped and churned. Their eyes were red and watery; their throats were sore and hoarse. Water isn't pure enough to wash off the thought of what they had swallowed. They returned to Agya Kobi's farm exchanging no words, only Efia's glances of anger and irritation.

Vengeance had found its rightful target: a palm-wine tapper was angry with Preprah for stealing his wine in times of hardship to exact vengeance this way. Preprah thought quickly before Efia's impression of him changed once more, perhaps this time for good. He dropped the suspense and broke the news that he had secured a visa to the United States. With that, Efia forgot she had just ingested human feces.

Chapter

24

"**C**alm down. Please, Tabuah, please!"

Tabuah was beside herself after waiting months for Atobrah's return.

"Tabuah, hear me out. Please, just, just hear me out."

She crumbled to the floor, and Karikari helped her into a chair.

"Atobrah isn't dead," he assured her.

"How can you be so certain?"

"Sister, calm down and listen: children leave home all the time."

"Yes, they do, but without telling their mothers of their where-abouts? He went *missing* here, in this village! In Enkoho!"

Karikari beckoned her to stop for fear of what she might say next.

"The village has killed my son!"

Karikari stomped his feet and punched the wall in frustration. Tabuah was on the verge of delving into what was anathema.

She saw the fear of the village's faceless forces in Karikari's eyes and kept quiet.

"Nothing I say is certain; nothing you say is certain. Let's think about it: how do you know Atobrah hasn't just left?" Karikari resumed.

"For what reason?"

"To plan his way to America, Europe...who knows?"

"Where would he get such an idea?"

"Don't be silly. I told you about Yaw and all his peers. You've heard him talk about Preprah's dream—going into the military and using it as a springboard to America. That's all they talk about: America and Europe. They haven't learned that there's no place called Paradise on this diseased Earth. Perhaps we've failed to instill in them that paradise is everywhere and in everyone if one can find it. We can't take all the blame, for our leaders also see paradise elsewhere rather than in the country over which they preside, which their own hands have ruined after wresting our resources and future from the hands of colonialism. Can our leaders look at our children and answer the embarrassing question of whether they would be better off under the tyranny of colonialism or under their misguided oversight of our resources? But I digress; Atobrah's dream was to go to America or Europe!"

"How could I have missed such a thing?" Tabuah shook her head.

"Would you have agreed if he had told you of his plan?"

"At the time, maybe not! I needed him. I *need* him!"

"Our timelines don't align with children's aggressive goals nowadays. You and I both know that the children of my village and yours only aim to go to Europe, America, anywhere but stay in the land of their birth!"

As incredible as Karikari's assessment was, it was possible. Tabuah could see it.

"But that would be uncharacteristic of him," she hedged.

"What?" Karikari returned.

"To do something that daring and complicated...without telling his parents."

"Daringness may have skipped our genes but not our children's. I'd be right to say that associating with Agya Kobi is the most dangerous thing one could do in this village. Yet Gyambibi started going to him when he was four or five, without his mother or me seeing him. It was early in the morning when the village was asleep. I'd never dare it knowing what I know, but that boy did...knowing what we know!"

Tabuah was reassured. She held out hope to hear from her son one day when he was settled overseas. Calmed, she asked Karikari about his portion of the drums of pesticides that Dr. Maarten and Xada had shipped from Holland. Chief claimed they had been sent to him alone. He furnished a letter to all who could read to prove his point. Out of kindness, he would keep eleven drums and give two to the rest of the village, which he advised they dilute with water and share.

In the meantime, the mirid infestation was devastating the farms.

Chapter

25

*K*ofi Nsenkyire's family house had one main structure and two adjoining buildings. There were multiple outbuildings for residential and farm-produce storage purposes. The multi-structure residence was centrally located in Enkoho. An ancestor had selected the location for its convenience, as farms surrounded the village. The ancestor bought the harvests of the farmers, which he, in turn, sold to sellers in the markets of other villages. Kofi Nsenkyire carried on this tradition, except he worked for the cooperative, buying cocoa for the government. The location was secure. Helena's mother found it so because she stayed in one of the outbuildings assigned to her by Nsenkyire whenever she came to the village. She had no worries when Nsenkyire suggested the same outbuilding for the young Helena when she packed her bags for Enkoho after high school. Nsenkyire never stayed in the village for more than a few days, so Helena lived alone across from the main building that housed the remnants of his family. The location was several hundred meters removed from Adwoa Brago and Agya Kobi's hut. So when Adwoa Brago sent her home again to put on footwear, she knew it would be some time before she returned.

Adwoa Brago had drawn closer to Helena since they had started working together; Helena's meekness drew them together. Agya Kobi wouldn't pass comment on Helena, even today, when she was to meet them on the farm. Adwoa Brago was in a monologue as she worked on one part of the farm, and Agya Kobi worked on another. When Helena joined them, she entered through the mouth of the farm where Agya Kobi worked. She rallied her courage and genuflected in greeting. The elder responded with a nod but didn't point her to where Adwoa Brago was as she thought he would. She stood sheepishly until her instincts informed her to look for her herself.

"Helena, over here!" Adwoa Brago found her first. Helena genuflected and repeated her greetings.

"You're not mad at me for sending you home again today?"

Helena said she couldn't think of being mad at her for any reason.

Adwoa Brago said, "I like your spirit. But there's nothing magical about coming to the farm barefoot. The Romans and Greeks were barefoot at times. People of different cultures have done this at one point or another. It isn't uniquely Enkohoan. I suppose you Americans are so mighty to bother with history outside your own. For me, it's just that I didn't grow up wearing shoes or boots; I can do with or without them. When I was in Libya, I wore shoes everywhere. It would have been weird to them if I didn't. Same outside Enkoho: I wear footwear. It's when I'm here that I lose those ways. It's like the comfort of being in my hut."

Helena said that she understood and noted to Adwoa Brago that she wasn't alone in that tradition since other elderly folks also weren't in footwear. Helena reiterated that her reason for showing up barefoot occasionally was to partake in the rustic ways of the ancestors.

"Don't be silly," Adwoa Brago said with a guffaw. "If there had been nothing wrong with the first, nothing would have been sought to replace it. You remember that, don't you?"

Helena explained in her soft voice that she didn't understand what Adwoa Brago was referencing.

"You do."

Helena insisted she didn't.

"I saw you with a Bible this morning."

"Yes, that's true," Helena said, still puzzled.

"It's in there," Adwoa Brago said.

Helena might as well have never heard of the Bible, despite taking one with her to Adwoa Brago's hut that morning. Adwoa Brago relented and clarified her analogy. As the superior New Testament replaced the Old Testament, so were the old ways of the ancestors walking about barefoot inferior to the new ways of putting on footwear. Helena repeated that her preference to be barefoot on the farm and in the village was to taste that unique experience of the ancestral ways. Adwoa Brago objected to this because she couldn't bear the thought of Helena's feet becoming cut, chafed, and scarred. Her feet were hardened into a toughness that did not need shoes, but Helena's feet were fragile. Even though Helena wouldn't go against her word because that would be disrespectful, she begged Adwoa Brago to allow her the practice now and then to have a feel of it. She had that unquenchable urge to dabble in that moribund tradition. She wanted to know what the ancestors did before such things disappeared from the traditional psyche. It wasn't a tradition per se, Adwoa Brago corrected, explaining that the hot climate was an impetus to wear as little as possible. The ancestors were familiar with footwear but weren't rigid practitioners. In any case, Helena felt out of place in boots while Adwoa Brago walked about barefoot.

Living in Enkoho for a few years now, Helena had seen how Adwoa Brago went about life, how she comported her interactions. She wanted to be like her, barefoot and all. Adwoa

Brago appreciated Helena's friendship as much as Helena appreciated hers. Helena's time was disproportionately spent with her more than with her peers. Not only did they work on the farm together, but Helena also had an interest in learning the culinary tradition of the village. Besides helping Jeefa cook now and then, she couldn't manage on her own.

The intermittent drizzle turned into full-on rain late morning. Adwoa Brago and Helena returned to the village. The unproductive morning gave Helena another opportunity to seek access to Agya Kobi when they returned to the village. The old man's distance from Helena remained unabridged, despite Helena's friendship with Adwoa Brago. When Asamoah died, Helena had been there daily to condole with the couple. One would have thought the elder would be softened by such a benevolent gesture and reward Helena with his friendship. But no, the elder clung to his Bible and ignored the world. Helena wouldn't give up, for the old man responded to her without malice or hint of animosity.

After going home to change, Helena returned to their hut. Agya Kobi was seated in the living room when Adwoa Brago ushered her there and left the room. The two had agreed on what Helena planned to do. She said her greetings and tried to engage the old man in a conversation. She had learned that he knew her mother. He returned a few sentences, saying he did, but not as well as his wife. She kept the conversation on her mother, thinking that at least she was making inroads. Before she came to Enkoho, Agya Kobi had heard rumors of the daughter of their American visitor coming to the village. On her arrival, he had seen her here and there but didn't know if she was the one. He was silent after sharing what he knew and then returned to the Bible on his lap.

"I brought you this." Helena handed him a package. He was going to put it aside when he saw her looking at him. She wanted him to crack the seal and see what it was.

"I already have one. I'm reading it right now."

The elder's Bible was worn and had written notes staring from tattered margins, and many loose pages peeked from the edges. To her surprise, the elder asked, "Do you read the Bible?"

"No, sir," she said, seeing an opening to engage the old man further. Her demeanor was tinged with reverence.

"Why not?"

"I'm not a religious person, just a freethinker."

"People who read the Bible aren't free to think? Aren't we all freethinkers?"

Helena was too nervous to answer.

"I'll accept this on one condition."

"Okay, sir."

"Call me Agya. You have lived here long enough to know what Agya is."

"It means *Father*."

"Good. Here's the condition: If you can answer this one question, I'll accept your gift."

Helena looked lost and nervous.

"Tell me one word that appears in the first sentence of the translation of this Bible."

"Hell?" she guessed.

The elder shook his head. Her clasped hands trembled, and her legs fidgeted.

"No."

"No is the answer?" she asked.

"I mean, your answer is incorrect."

She was silent. The elder was quiet, too, for a part of him was drawn to her.

"I'll give you another chance."

"Satan," Helena said. She didn't wait for the elder to shake his head before blurting, "Beginning?"

"Correct."

Helena was delighted but didn't display it.

"I have to revise my condition."

"Too late for that," she joked, hoping to soften his hard, flat emotion.

"I gave you only two chances, and you were wrong on both counts but got it right on the third attempt, which falls outside my condition. Correct?"

"You're right, Agya Kobi."

Helena wasn't taken aback when he told her to keep the Bible. He would assign pericopes for reading and discussion. Helena liked that; she wanted nothing more than to have extended conversations with the elder, even if it involved religion, a subject she didn't care about much. She saw in the old man's proposal an opening for friendship.

Chapter

26

*T*he children of Enkoho flocked to Gyambibi when he emerged from the path leading from Aduman. They held onto him, pestering him with questions about the next story-telling session. After lowering the load he was carrying to the ground, he huddled with them. He repeated the excerpt he'd narrated the previous Saturday, only adding that from this day forward, one needed to score at least eighty percent on both spelling and math quizzes to be part of the listening audience. With that, the children disappeared, some promising to meet and study together that evening. But not before two groups of four hauled off the two sacks that Gyambibi had lowered to the ground. They contained gifts he had brought for the children. These, too, were for those who qualified for the storytelling session. The children had multiple reasons to pass both quizzes, as most now had two meals per day. Days of one meal per day weren't far behind.

Karikari, lured outside by the noise, watched his son. Upon seeing how slowly he walked behind the children, he decided to go over to him. He embraced Gyambibi and signaled to put some distance between them and the children. Karikari told him that Yaw had returned with news that Preprah was back from America. Yaw thought Preprah should be in America, working on Yaw's dream to live there. Preprah's return was an affront, a breach of their pact. It was more than a breach; it was a betrayal.

Gyambibi walked to his brother's bedroom to cheer him up.

"Happy to see you," he said.

"Happy to see me?"

"It's been two weeks."

"Why are you here? Can't find your room?" Yaw complained.

"Stop being hostile!"

"What do you want?"

"Can't we talk like normal siblings?"

"What do you want?"

"I'm happy to see you. And so is Dad, but he isn't happy to see you like this," Gyambibi said, leaning against the closed door.

"And who's responsible for me being like this?"

"You blame Dad?"

"Why not? I followed him everywhere, on business trips...everywhere. When he wanted to start a business in Accra, Kumasi, and wherever, I followed him every few days. I was patient and never complained because I told him my goal was to go to America, and he promised to send me."

"Did he promise that?"

"Not exactly, but he didn't object."

"He lost everything; that wasn't his plan."

"I had long told him to send me to America, and he had more than enough money to send me before the flood. If he had, I wouldn't be here."

"Is America the only place to have a life?"

"What do you know?"

"What do you mean?"

"The ruthless monster Preprah just returned from America, on vacation here. There, you happy?"

"Why use such coarse language to describe him? What did he do to you to deserve that?"

"That was his aspiration—to be a ruthless monster—before he left the village. He would have burned the village to the ground if I hadn't pointed out his stupidity to him. You were too young to have known about it, but he told a father to allow him to date two of his underage girls because their combined age was close to his. The fool survived that day because he knew how to dodge a bullet. He's back, and he doesn't finish a thought without signing off, '*My mouth, your ears!*' The only English he's learned in America, I suppose. He only speaks in capital letters now. It would impress you also to know that *your* man is far too sophisticated for commas and full stops. Like Danfo, he goes on and on and on when talking about anything. He couldn't wait to let me know what he knew about everything. It was as if he was teasing me. Mr. Brain-Dead made it to America and is back...on vacation. He doesn't have half the brain I have, yet..."

Yaw didn't know that when Preprah was transferred as an orderly to the second battalion, he had changed, according to some. However, nothing would quell Yaw's belief that Preprah was a consummate idiot. The man who once thought "to" and "from" meant the same thing couldn't possibly grow out of his idiocy, Yaw recalled for Gyambibi.

"I don't understand why you're placing the blame on Dad. Preprah went on his own. Danfo didn't have a hand in it."

"His father didn't know about his plans. Mine did and does."

Gyambibi said nothing in response to de-escalate the anger that was brewing in his brother. He returned to the front porch. Yaw joined him later and asked if he had brought anything to eat, staring at the two sacks on the porch. He pried open the first, which contained gallons of palm kernel oil and packets of flour. When he found nothing interesting, he turned to the second sack and removed packets of rice, bars of Key Soap, and so on. Finally, he retrieved some Ovaltine biscuits, which prompted Gyambibi to remark, "They're for the children."

"There's more in there," Yaw said and stepped aside.

The bickering ceased when they heard whistles indicating approaching women. Helena balanced a pail of water on her head without the aid of her hands, just like Jeefa and Efia on either side of her. The pail swayed, and Helena paced her steps. She lost some water here and there but was determined not to use her hands. She had managed well from the river to the edge of the village, but now the pail swayed more, perhaps because she was self-conscious and trying to avoid embarrassment. Water came over the edge of the pail and splashed her path. She stepped in it, and her wrapper loosened around her waist. More water splashed when her feet slid away from each other, and she headed for the ground. Her wrapper came off as the pail broke free, exposing her white skin and undergarments. Helena and Efia broke out in laughter. A woman ran to fetch her wrapper and wound it around her. Helena was sorely embarrassed.

Chapter

My Mouth, Your Ears

*P*reprah's large head peeked out from under a Yankees cap. He wore jeans with an Adidas logo showing on his T-shirt. In his peculiar fashion sensibility, he had tied a head-band around the cap with the expression: One Life and Counting, Folks. Each letter was written in red, white, and blue—the colors of the American flag. Preprah shielded his eyes behind sunglasses, sporting a gratuitous yet venomous smile.

For several days, Gyambibi had mulled over why Preprah wanted to meet him alone. It was also apparent that Preprah wanted to help him but not Yaw.

"You look as good as ever. You've always been handsome, Gyambibi."

Preprah rose from his chair and hugged Gyambibi. A waitress passed by, smiling at him. Preprah winked at her and turned to Gyambibi.

"You know where I can find a florist? I mean a place to buy flowers."

Gyambibi was stricken off-balance by the question. He was on the verge of asking if this was why Preprah had invited him here but restrained himself. Besides, who would have the stupid idea of selling flowers when they're everywhere?

"I gather you're shocked because I asked about flowers. You have a lot to learn. America opens your eyes, my friend. *My mouth, your ears!*" he said with a smile. "That's how you appeal to a woman you like."

Gyambibi looked at him curiously as if to say, "Maybe in America, but this is Ghana."

Seeing that Gyambibi was eyeing his T-shirt, Preprah told him that America understood the concept of branding better than any other country. America understood that clothing labels need not be hidden. Though he conceded that not every article of clothing in the US followed such protocol, he predicted that America was on the right track.

"Look at this," he said, flexing his chest to show the imprint. "You don't have to look hard to know that Adidas designed this."

A different waitress passed by, also winking at Preprah. All the employees at the restaurant knew he had come from America. Another waitress walked over, not to take his order but to chat. After introducing Gyambibi, Preprah had forgotten about him, delving into life in America. Gyambibi didn't know what to make of all this, whether it was fabrication or not. He was embarrassed and wished for it to end.

"Flowers appeal to women?" Gyambibi asked.

The waitress winked at Preprah and gave them space.

"Yes, my friend. You don't know about these things because you're still as good a boy as I remember. Let me tell you about women. My father used to say that if women were as intelligent as he is, there would be none for men to marry. He's right! Remember that woman was formed from the rib of man. Yes, that's right, women came from what was already made; thus, by their makeup, they'll go after what's already made. Women like 'made men,' accomplished men. That isn't a surprise if you know where they come from. The strategy for a man in romance is to show women that he's accomplished, and they'll naturally flock to him. *My mouth, your ears!* Look at the waitresses. Every one of them wants me. I look like someone with a house and cars without even having to say so. Give a woman flowers, and she'll think you're full of love, even if that's the furthest thing from your mind," he said, unconsciously imitating Danfo throughout.

Listening to Preprah speak after eight years, Gyambibi had the uncanny feeling of listening to Danfo himself. Preprah was now in the image of his father: he spoke with careless bravado, giving little thought to his words.

"I tell you, women like material accomplishments. No one cares how educated you are, you know, because no one can see what you've studied. However, they can see what you have. See this gold-plated watch? Everyone can see that I'm living the good life. Nobody cares about my suffering—that is, who I *was*—only my success, what I am now. The mouth is burdened with groans and complaints about life when suffering; in success, the mouth rests: success speaks for itself. Get wealth, my friend, and the world couldn't care less about your suffering. Look like a million dollars, and women flock to you. These are the daughters of women we're talking about. On the other hand, daughters of God care about a happy and meaningful life with a man, not what he has; but they're a rare find. In America, as in all over the world, even here, daughters of women are all over the place. We have to make the most of what we have, you know. As for the daughters of God, your mother was one. May her beautiful soul rest in perfect peace. I don't know how good a man has to be for God to send him one of His daughters. Your father's a good man, so it makes sense for God to send a good woman like that to him. Perhaps you have to be good to have a daughter of God. Rosemond Adwoa Brago is a daughter of God, too. That she's married to the most evil man on Earth defeats my premise. How could God send such a good woman Agya Kobi's way?"

Gyambibi was both surprised and piqued by the ease with which Preprah navigated this discussion. The most pitiful of men, when it came to matters of women, was now a master of the subject. The same man who thought Efia's growing belly wasn't a result of pregnancy but of having too much to eat—a hope he clung to until Asamoah's birth. Preprah, once upon a time, thought a woman was someone who hated poverty and loved the good life. To which Yaw had demanded, "Name one man who loves poverty and hates the good life." Yes, that same Preprah had now mastered all things women. America was becoming more impressive than Gyambibi had previously envisioned.

Chapter

28

*P*reprah met Gyambibi again at a different restaurant. This time he was in a Hells Angels jacket with New York embossed on the back. He didn't have to say where he had come from. Just so no one was mistaken, in case another New York existed, his necktie embroidered with the American flag made everyone understand that he had come from the one in America. Also, just like the other day, he was drenched in women's fragrance.

"Why this place?" Gyambibi asked. They were south of Lascala, Teshie, at a restaurant on the beach.

"I didn't like the waitresses at the other place."

"You aren't married?"

Now in his thirties, Preprah, like Yaw, was well of age to be married with a family. However, a wife and family meant nothing to Yaw without going to America first.

"No," stated Preprah.

"You couldn't find a woman in America?" Gyambibi asked.

"There are women there, all right, but they aren't the type for men like us. American women and a man's peace of mind don't see eye to eye."

"I don't understand."

"It all goes back to the beginning, to Eve and Lilith, the mothers of all women. This is where I disagree with my father, if ever. The Garden of Eden couldn't have been in Africa. It wasn't in the Middle East, either. It was in America, for the spirits of Eve and Lilith are present there. You see the spirits of Eve and Lilith dwelling in American women, no doubt. You won't find more refined women anywhere, but you can't live with them. *My mouth, your ears!* Men have tried and woken up with bullets in their throats, their brains on the other side of their pillows. I read of a man whose head almost came off, his throat slit from ear to ear. A knife was found in his mouth. Another woke up dead, his intestines wasted away from years of ingesting ground glass in his food. Six apartment complexes down the road from where I live, a man whispered something to his girlfriend. Nobody knew what he said. He didn't show up for work, and his friends searched all their hangouts. Nowhere to be found. The police broke into his apartment, and there he was: his lower lip had been cut off and stapled to his right earlobe, and his upper lip had been similarly relocated to his left earlobe. He was hanging by his tongue with a posthumous note, actually a question, attached to the roof of his mouth: 'What was it you were saying?'

"I was right about Efia, after all; she's one such woman. She fell for me after I joined the military because, in her mind, I'd become capable of killing with reckless abandon. Now it all makes sense what Yaw read years ago, that some American women are attracted to serial killers, felons, gangsters. His only error was saying 'some of them.' It's all of them. Happily married men in America—excluding the dead ones—are either felons, ruthless monsters, drug peddlers, serial killers, or gangsters. So are the women. Opposites don't attract there.

Romance in America is a death trap, my brother. Some men go to foreign lands for a wife, but that's of no use because once in America, their women are eventually taken over by the spirits of Eve and Lilith. America would be more potent as a superpower if she enlisted more women than men in the army. For the women are war machines, but they've been repurposed into homemakers who do their killing at home. Dying at the hands of these women is the easier part. They want men to cook for them, do their laundry, and clean the house. And when they're done transfusing their estrogen into you, the children are yours for caretaking. Now you've become a mother your mother wouldn't recognize. These women have a strange aversion to opening doors too. Men follow them everywhere, opening doors for them. I shudder when I see testosterone-filled men reduced to docile pets. You see them walking the streets every day, bursting with masculinity. Then they turn the corner, go home, and assume their role as women. And forget about the law intervening on their behalf. Women and married men wrote the laws. No man had a hand in it. *My mouth, your ears*!

"I can't look at these men in the face, my brother. I mean, how revolting is it to look at a face bearing the scratches of fine, manicured claws of a woman? I tell you, American men get slapped every day. They got it worse than us.

"I know a man, my coworker actually—God have mercy on his dying soul!—who had the impaired foresight to marry one of these women with five children. Owing to his undiagnosed stupidity, which he mistook for kindheartedness, he adopted all five children and treated them as his own. Four years into the marriage, the woman filed for divorce on the grounds that they couldn't reconcile their differences. Men are men, women are women. The differences here will never be reconciled, so how could divorce be granted on such grounds? But it is Americans we are talking about. They only think outside the box: they can go to the moon but can't cure baldness ravaging the male species here on Earth. Anyway, after the divorce was finalized, the man was held financially liable for those five children who didn't come from him. I see him at work daily with the terminal look of a man with a bushel of maize around his neck, circling his own coffin. My brother, God gave each person a brain, which should work fine on its own by design, but such occasional explosions of idiocy among us clearly demonstrate that some need to be taught how to use theirs. American men! Remember them in your prayers. Gyambibi, the men look like men as far as the eye can tell. Shake their hands, and it's a different story. Those hands have seen too many dishes to belong to a man. Try shaking their hand; they grip yours like a greasy pan about to slip out of their grasp."

In Enkoho, Yaw had read more widely about America than anyone else, yet Gyambibi had heard nothing resembling these accounts. Nevertheless, Gyambibi gave him the benefit of the doubt, noting that it might be a unique experience based on where Preprah had lived in the United States.

Before Gyambibi could ask for clarification, Preprah added, "These American women don't have that soft touch, that something, that womanly spirit that our mothers exude. They're fierce and temperamental, harboring an inveterate tendency for turning men into unrecoverable idiots. I can't find the words to describe them; the best I could do, linguistically, right here and now, is relate them to a drill sergeant who doesn't want you winning an argument in your sleep. Marriage to them is a life sentence in a warzone. Those words don't even capture the spirit of what these women really are. They're unnecessarily independent and have no respectable use for men.

"In some cases, they've slipped into their own thoughts that they're no different from men, so they don't even have the willingness to have a child. Men don't carry children, so why should women? Their logic goes. In the most unfortunate circumstance that they bear your child, know that single motherhood is a badge of honor to American women. These women, my goodness, are so different from women everywhere else. And, of course, I may be incorrectly assuming that they descended from the same women God created six thousand years ago. A part of me suspects these may be a special breed of women created by Satan himself to disturb the order God has intended for humankind. Absent this theory, the demonic spirits of Eve and Lilith possess these women. Nothing else explains their behavior better."

"What about African American women there?"

"I've told you already, young brother. Sure, America has its racial problems, but Eve and Lilith are no racist spirits. They're equal-opportunity, possessive devils. Besides, you see, the proprietors of racial ignorance have hoisted on the world the belief that God didn't create, and has no associations with, Africans. We're close but not quite human, and our brain is the same color as our skin. Some daughters of Mother Africa, uncomfortable in their own skin, actually believe such nonsense. *My mouth, your ears!*

"Get involved with American women and watch things go wrong. They'll remind you of being the *other* Black: you from Africa. Some are even ashamed to identify with Africa, the land of their ancestors. I've met folks from some parts of Africa who, having succumbed to the shame of the grotesque caricature of Mother Africa drawn on their minds by people who think us lesser humans, originate themselves from the Middle East or the Caribbean or wherever. I never knew Ethiopia was in the Middle East, Ghana was the colonial spelling of Guyana, and Tanzanians were Germans. Can you believe it? I've met men, women, and children from parts of Africa with tongues as undiluted as Mother Africa's who place their heritage anywhere but Africa. The greatest compliment to them is to say they don't look or act African. They have the whitest of names, having bleached away the very soul of Mother Africa. Hear them speak English! It's like they are gargling with bucketfuls of Rs because they've learned that Americans love their Rs. My brother, Africans don't just imitate stupid; we outdo the originators! These people are ashamed of Mother Africa. Can you believe being ashamed of your own birth mother? Believe me, these are folks to die twice; they're already dead to Mother Africa. So, you see, America isn't a place for unmarried people like us. That's why I'm here on vacation."

There was a complete absence of Preprah's former left-handedness. His right hand now dominated his gesticulations. This would explain why he and Danfo had become close and why Danfo now even bragged about him being his son. Gyambibi wondered if this change also explained Preprah's newfound intelligence. He wondered about the other part of the change, too; that is, if it accounted for Preprah's unfiltered thoughts and coarse behavior.

Something about Preprah made Gyambibi feel full, though his stomach was empty. While all the hyperbole could have trimmed the edges of his appetite, it was probably the fact that he was sitting across from a successful man whom everyone had thought would amount to nothing, the sheer surprise of it accounting for his lost appetite. Related to this was the fact that any casually cosmopolitan person would have viewed Preprah's appearance as clownish. The overbearing scent of women's fragrance, the leather fringe running the entire length of the outseams of his pants combined with cowboy boots, exacerbated that perception. Not to mention the silver bracelets on each wrist and gold rings on every other finger of his left hand. There was little doubt he had come from America because he seized every opportunity to establish that, but the excesses were humiliating: Paying for his services in dollar equivalent rather than cedis, showing pictures of himself at the Empire State Building, Times Square, on Ellis Island, and several other landmarks in New York City—this just to remove any doubt that he had come from America.

"I don't mean to change the topic, but you asked me to meet you here," Gyambibi said.

Two bottles of Guinness arrived. Gyambibi reminded Preprah that he didn't drink. A waitress was there before his fingers snapped.

"My young friend here, I forgot he doesn't drink alcohol. Please get him a Fanta."

The Fanta arrived promptly, but Gyambibi wouldn't drink it yet. He waited for a response. Preprah broke away from chatting with the waitress, who commented on his tie of the American flag. He gave her five dollars for the compliment. The sheer ostentation added to Gyambibi's feeling of satiety.

The purpose of the meeting: Preprah wanted to help Gyambibi. Leaving the restaurant, the two walked off to his car so Gyambibi could see what was in store for him. Preprah said he had shipped the car ahead of his vacation. Preprah was an auto-mechanic engineer and worked in Detroit for General Motors. Employees were allowed to purchase two cars a year at cost. He would give four of his coworkers money to buy two cars each for him, creating a surplus of ten cars a year. He wanted Gyambibi out of the military to focus on selling the cars in Accra. For his compensation, Preprah would quadruple his military pay.

Gyambibi needed time to think it over but expressed his gratitude. What bothered him, though he didn't ask, was why him? Why not Yaw, who had endured so much for Preprah? For now, Gyambibi would put that aside, for his father needed his financial support. Yaw and the children of the village needed help too.

"Who's that beautiful girl who always follows you around?" Preprah asked.

Gyambibi couldn't seem to recall since all the village girls followed him.

"Your father's best friend's daughter," Preprah said.

"Jeefa?"

"Yeah, that girl is special. It would be best if you married her. If you entered America and found a certified devil for a wife, nothing would so closely mimic the hell of the Bible. I know of a Christian who became a Christian for that reason. And if you entered the land with a real witch of a woman, you unluckiest of men would be in a war intended for God Himself. American women would seem heavenly by comparison. So think about marrying that good girl. *My mouth, your ears!*" Preprah said with bluntness and confidence Gyambibi would never have associated with him heretofore, before asking, "Will you marry her?"

"I don't see myself marrying anybody else when the time is right," Gyambibi said.

Already, he could read the masked delight on Gyambibi's face. Preprah implied with seriousness and a twisted smile that Gyambibi should contain his excitement because this was just the amuse-bouche. It would get better, he assured. "When the business grows," Preprah said, he "could bring Gyambibi over to the United States to focus on shipping the cars to Ghana and selling them." Preprah discussed plans for adding a boutique dealing in brand-name clothing and women's fragrance for men. All these would be under Gyambibi while Preprah focused on his day-to-day employment with General Motors. He added that it would be good for Gyambibi to marry Jeefa so that life in the United States would be easier for him, for reasons he had explained earlier. Only, Gyambibi had to park Jeefa among the friendly people of Mexico, away from the violent, demonic possessions by Eve and Lilith in the United States. He could visit her as needed.

Preprah advised him not to take too long to get back to him. He preferred they talk elsewhere, outside the barracks, when Gyambibi was ready. Preprah returned to the field engineers' barracks in Teshie, where some of his former platoon mates still were.

Gyambibi returned to Enkoho that weekend, going straight to his mother's gravesite to narrate Preprah's plans for him. For the first time, it appeared Agnes responded because the wind became quiet. Maybe it was her speechlessness from excitement. Perhaps, too, she was saying it was a bad idea. Karikari was too inebriated to advise his son. Gyambibi didn't want to seek Yaw's input for apparent reasons. He couldn't go to Danfo because he was at Healer for reasons unknown. Against his better judgment, he had a hunch to go to Agya Kobi. The elder told him to have nothing to do with Preprah, but he didn't elaborate beyond that. Jeefa told Gyambibi to accept the offer for the same reasons that Moro had given him.

Gyambibi met Preprah at the Lascala restaurant after roll call on Monday to say he had accepted his offer.

"Do you recall Salifu?" Preprah asked.

"Uncle Salifu. He perished in the rainstorm!" Gyambibi said, shaking his head.

"No, not your uncle," Preprah said.

The Salifu he meant had met Helena and Mawuli, so he thought Gyambibi had met him too.

"Did he live in our village?" Gyambibi asked.

"No, no. He's from the North. You'd remember him if you met him. He has a tribal mark you can't forget."

This Salifu had been in the United States at the same time as Preprah but had returned to Ghana for good. Now he sold kebabs at Kwame Nkrumah Circle in Accra. Sometimes Preprah conducted business through him. He wanted to take Gyambibi to meet Salifu, but to meet Salifu was to understand that America or the United States should not be mentioned in his presence. It was a warning worth repeating, and there was a story behind it. Preprah recounted an incident that took place in New York City: One day, Salifu was on the train with Preprah, returning home after a work shift around the port authority. Also on the train was a group of girls, likely high school students, sitting across from them. One girl gestured with a finger, and the rest stared at Salifu and Preprah. One of them, the leader, wasn't particularly impressive to look at as far as beauty went. She was rugged and masculine-looking. Anyway, she walked down the aisle in their direction, stopped across from Salifu, and trained her eyes on his face, traveling every millimeter of his facial peculiarities—or, they might have thought, imperfections.

"Man!" she exclaimed. "How'd you get those scars?"

Salifu looked at her casually. Others in the coach, all quiet, seemed to expect his reply. Everyone was interested in his tribal markings. He said nothing but smiled at her, essentially saying he appreciated her curiosity but wasn't interested in discussing his tradition, which would likely only be treated with incivility. Only the miracle of coincidence could explain what happened next. A piece of lint entered Salifu's eye. Irritated, Salifu's reaction to the particle was a spasm of hostility erupting between it and the student's eye, which, unfortunately, was perceived as an unholy wink. She retorted harshly, especially after her curious inquiry didn't invite her desired response. "Noooo! I don't like men. I wouldn't go for one with a torn-up face if I did." Her frank words elicited laughs from her friends. When Salifu's face lit up, Preprah knew what he was going to say wasn't good. In a crude, extraterrestrial brogue with a vague semblance to the English language, Salifu blasted away.

It went something like this: "Interesting, Miss. I look at you and see a son that your parents wished they'd never had. Pick on a boy your own size. Your friends are decent to look at, and they don't make fun of how I look. On the other hand, you're drawn to me, I guess, because we have something in common: we both aren't pleasant to look at."

The words gushed forth with the clarity of a lizard attempting patois. Nonetheless, everyone miraculously understood him. Nature had him speak the cleanest English his mouth could speak when angry, adding: "If I take a brick to my forehead and wake up tomorrow attracted to women who look like me, I'd still skip you."

Some of the onlookers shifted nervously. The masculine-appearing girl turned red, and her friends joined her in verbally assaulting him.

"You don't say that to a woman in our country, you stupid immigrant!" one said. Salifu replied that the "scars" on his face were sensitive in his culture and should not be laughed at. But they continued to behave as if he had said nothing, ignoring his referencing her insensitive curiosity.

"You ugly idiot, you don't say that to a woman!" said a fast-talking, slim girl with the prettiest face.

"Stupid African, bottom-of-the-heap trash," another girl said.

Salifu stared at her and shook his head, his mouth contemplating a response.

"Stupid African trash, I am. I may be related to your parents, though. It's a secret; keep it between us." Salifu whispered loudly to the student, who unleashed a torrent of cusses and waved goodbye with obscene gestures. A Hispanic friend followed her out of the train at the next stop. After they were gone, the battle appeared racial between an army of White girls and a lone, scarified African man.

"Stupid man!"

"Dumb African!"

"Stupid, ugly immigrant!" the girls continued.

Salifu was too irritated to stay silent. His next attack went like this: "Who was talking to you, you tiny thing? Slim has ruined what passes for beauty. You remind me of a newspaper with missing pages. You don't look all right, just like me. Please don't join them in assaulting me. It would help if you teamed up with me instead. I could say the same for that one...this one... you...and you too. The decent-looking ones haven't insulted me yet."

At this point, it seemed either people's stations for getting off the train lay ahead, or they didn't want to get off when their stop came. Everyone wanted to see this spectacle through to its end. Salifu veered off into a monologue about how Americans see themselves as the center of the world, perpetuating a sense that they matter more than anyone else. A country that's an amalgam of the earth's diversity yet also a place of extreme insensitivity toward others who look different. America—a land of intelligent people but known for some of the most irrational people in the world; America—a country whose natives have become forgotten spectators while the descendants of immigrants consider themselves nativists. America—a country on which the soul of Mother Earth looks daily and cries because the natives' voices are no more relevant than a lizard's; speaking about the preservation of their ancestral lands is drowned out by the cacophonous voices of greedy and insatiable industrialists.

"So it's offensive here to question someone's gender, but it's all right to question the unquestionable from a foreigner?" Salifu concluded.

"You stupid immigrant, you don't say that to a woman. Ugly man!"

"Go back to where you came from, if you don't understand you shouldn't say that to a woman. You people are polluting our country, making life harder for us. Life would be better if people just stayed in their own country. Why can't people stay in their own country? Stupid immigrant, go back!" said one of the girls.

The discomfort of the unfolding sent a middle-aged woman to the girls' corner to calm them. It was of no use. The girls ignored her and another man who said, "Girls, enough!"

"If my ancestors had never met yours, if your forefathers had kept to their ancestral lands, perhaps you wouldn't be seeing my face today to be offended by it!" Salifu pushed on.

Salifu was so angry that his broken English was broken even further. Preprah knew what would happen next, and it did: Salifu began lobbing his mother tongue, Hausa, at them. Salifu's English was decent any other day. But if the target of his anger could no longer understand his English, that person might as well hear him in Hausa. As if to forewarn his target of the inevitable, his broken English would speed up and decay into incomprehensible English, interspersed with Hausa, after which all traces of English would be lost.

The onlookers were frozen, unable to understand him. Preprah, whose mind wanted to de-escalate the conflict, should have left him alone. However, his telling Preprah to avoid saying this or that inadvertently gave insight into what Preprah was saying. This was what Salifu was saying, clearly, a pent-up feeling about America in general boiling before he met the girls: Every time he spoke about unsavory happenings in Ghana or a country in Africa—be it a civil war, corruption, a coup d'état, or an outbreak of famine—his American audience seemed to savor it with amusement. It was almost like some unexpected entertainment, a geopolitical minstrelsy of sorts involving *others*. At the same time, whenever he observed something unsavory about American culture or politics, not to criticize per se but to point out problems connecting humanity, he could see the discontent on the venerable faces of his audience. "Our problems don't lie with people coming to our land," he said, "it's when foreigners try to subvert or usurp our system to strip from us what we inherited from our ancestors when we resist. No foreigner, white, olive, or yellow, going about his or her life in my country is made to feel unwelcome. Not one I know of. I'm here to work, not to steal anybody's country. The natives are living with that pain; I won't pour salt into their wound. America is a place of work for me, not a place to live out my life."

"If you don't like it, why don't you leave?" the masculinized female spat.

Salifu responded: "You should be man enough to go back in time to ask your ancestors if this was how they were treated when they met my ancestors—an encounter that has something to do with what America is today. When my ancestors met yours, they saw strangers to befriend and help. My ancestors saw fellow humans with whom to share God's Earth, not inferior people to exploit and condescend to. And if I had seen you in my country before today, or if I'm ever to see you in my country after today, like most of my countrywomen and men, I would treat you better than my own. Do you know why? Because my ancestors lived a life of kindness and tolerance long before they heard of something called the Bible. I bet you don't know how far your fathers traveled to make what you call America today. I was tempted to tell you to study world history, but that would have been a shameful betrayal of my inability to tell the obvious: that you don't know of the existence of a world outside your fifty States. Outside that are the oceans, farms, and forests from which your food is sourced. Sometimes I forget that your America is the paradise the Bible speaks of, with no wrongs and sins to complain about. The rest of the world falls within the boundaries of hell, whose sins we all should be at liberty to yell about from the rooftops. Why is this not a surprise? If the tolerant natives and heirs of this beautiful land are unwelcome, like annoying pests squatting on a land that has long belonged to your ancestors' overactive imagination, who am I, a mere stranger from a faraway land, to be surprised at you?"

"Trying to sound all intelligent, like you're somebody. I bet you're a security guard. He could be a caretaker for some old man, wiping his behind. That's what you lowlifes are good for here," one of the girls said.

"Enough, girls!" an onlooker yelled.

"Stocking shelves in a grocery store is more like it. Loud-mouth, two-legged monkey; you think you're smart?" the rugged female added.

"Stupid, ugly immigrant. Go back to Africa!"

Insults rained down from all sides, calling Salifu every name they could muster.

"We could leave this place for *you people* and move to Africa. In three short years, *you people* would come to us in Africa looking for work. Hopeless! Return to Africa, you ugly, scarred monkey," one of the girls said and spat at Salifu. The saliva hit the window and slid onto his seat.

"GO BLACK TO SWINGING ON TREES."

"When the rest of the world eats, *you people* wait outside for the leftovers. You dare insult us, YOU TALKING ANIMAL!"

The statement, like bullets, pierced his armor-less soul. It felt as if the words, when they had settled on him, made him heavier than he was. *Go back to Africa*! His skin and scarified face could put him in many places outside Africa, so this meant more than xenophobia. There was something about the statement. It wasn't spoken because he had said much about coming from Ghana. No, it was more than that. It wasn't like being told to "Go back to Hungary," "Return to Yemen" or "Go back to Vietnam" or "Return to Mexico." It was nothing of the sort. *Go back to Africa*—in its superficial simplicity, the statement ordered him back to his continent. Further deconstruction revealed that it mattered not which part of the continent he came from, thus depriving him of a national identity and placing him in the broadest category of his *kind* from *that* continent, which in the language psychology of the girls, amounted to the world's refuse dump whose inhabitants are unworthy of comingling with *their* kind.

Salifu adjusted himself and sat down, oblivious to the spit covering the seat. He felt the words. He had a sudden awareness that it wasn't just the girls taking turns repeating the statement; everyone on the train was. He glanced about, only to see everyone's mouth shut save for the girls yelling at him. *Go back to Africa; go black to swinging on trees!* From his seat, he could hear millions and millions of people shouting the same words at him in a country he had mistaken for paradise. It was as if these daughters of Mother Earth were telling him that the children of Mother Africa didn't belong here. His anger gave way to sadness.

Salifu's next words seemed out of place. Perhaps they were meant for the girls. Maybe they were for the onlookers. Maybe they were for Mother Africa. Maybe they were for all. Perhaps they were for none. "Sorry. I'm sorry," he said and, with deep sadness lingering over him, got off the train at Yankee Stadium, five stops before his station. Preprah returned from work twelve days later to find that his friend had left the United States for good.

On Preprah's visit to Ghana from the United States, locating Salifu would have been a lost cause if he hadn't remembered something Salifu had said at the Wackenhut Detention Center in Queens, where they first met.

"I told him either his father died before he was born or his father died when he was young," Preprah told Gyambibi.

"Why would you—"

"He almost jumped out of his senses with disbelief. He thought I was clairvoyant or psychic!" Preprah laughed.

"What?"

"I'd asked what he did for a living so that we could plot a strategy for asylum. He'd said he sold kebabs. Of course, cooking of any sort is for women. That's true the world over, except in America. His father must have been absent from his life not to have taught him that. My guess was right; his father died when he was two. He barbecued and sold kebabs? I gave him a lesson right there. You see, after birth, the first kitchen a baby's food is prepared in and the table he dines at are the same. It's called the breast. There's a reason breasts belong to women. As you know, breast milk dries out at a point, so cooking for women is a natural progression from that, or the child starves to death. God isn't some one-eyed hermaphrodite who didn't know what he was doing."

It took another guess—that Salifu would return to what he did when he came home—to find him. Days ago, Preprah had toured several night markets around Kwame Nkrumah Circle to locate him. It seemed the same air of sadness that had followed Salifu out of the train still clung to him. It was then that Preprah decided to caution others not to mention America in Salifu's presence. This sentiment hadn't come from Salifu. Preprah felt the encounter on the train had changed his friend for good, so it would serve him well if others didn't remind him of it.

"He's back to selling kebabs. Can you believe that? He forgot everything I told him. Man, what those girls said to him must've erased all the lessons I gave him." Preprah let out a sigh. "I need to repeat that lesson. I thought about doing it when I saw him last Thursday, but how could I, without reminding him of America?"

Preprah was silent as if mulling over a way to reach his friend.

"I need one more chair here," Preprah said to a waitress and asked her to bring another waitress.

"Sure, I can get you another if you expect more people."

"Just one would be fine."

"Moro isn't coming. I forgot to mention—"

"What happened?" Preprah asked.

"His superiors think he's inciting the noncommissioned and junior officers against contributing to the bazaar."

"He'll get himself dismissed one day. Anyway, the extra seat isn't for him. I was hoping this fine lady would join us," he said after the waitress he had asked for came. The confused waitress's expression gave way to a smile when Preprah winked at her. She would join them after servicing another table.

Preprah was on the verge of commenting about how kind of a man Air Vice-Marshal George Yaw Boakye was when a waitress winked.

"Howdy?"

The waitress's initial excitement was suddenly tainted with jealousy. She thought Preprah had her confused with another waitress.

"No, I'm Kukua," she replied.

Preprah laughed one of those ubiquitous laughs that filled the waitress with no purpose other than to laugh with him.

"How do you *do*? In America, we say howdy."

"I see, sir. I'm fine, sir," she said, hiding a burst of laughter.

"*How do you do* is nineteenth-century English. You're stuck in the era of 'thou findeth me irresistible-eth.' Step into the now, beautiful. I hope to get to know you and bring you to America so you can learn twentieth-century English."

The woman blushed and walked away, saying thank you and smiling.

"Is that old devil still alive?" Preprah asked Gyambibi.

"Who?"

"Efia's grandfather."

"Yes."

"Unbelievable. How do evil people get to live so long? Perhaps that's the key to longevity."

"What makes him evil?" Gyambibi asked. He had an interest in this: he wanted a close-up perspective of someone who held a view of Agya Kobi that was different from his. His own suspicion of the old man was now beginning to grow.

"He killed his great-grandson, Asamoah. He killed his son, Papayeasa. He's been killing people in the village since I can remember. Why do you think I've not returned?"

"You destroyed his farm," Gyambibi pointed out.

"Right, but that was why I left. There's a different reason why I've not returned!"

This exchange aroused another important finding from his trip abroad, which Preprah thought was worth bringing up. He wanted the entire village to benefit from his time in America, not by offering alms but by sharing something that could put the whole village at ease and help it focus on working, rather than fearing, to better itself. It was about the location of Satan on Earth when he was cast down from Heaven—the fear of which had descended from elders of generations past to the present through guarded word of mouth. The villagers needed affirmation or disproval of their fear so they would know how to proceed in life. There had been no definitive answer for centuries, but now, Preprah had the answer. Under the right circumstance, he should ask for an audience with the elders to relay his findings, but Gyambibi knew he couldn't. So he had a message for the elders through Gyambibi:

"Satan is in America and always has been. Go and see for yourself. He fell from Heaven and landed there. I have my reasons to believe his exact location could be in the northeastern or the southern states, though a compelling reason could be given that he's on the West Coast. You wouldn't believe the open debauchery, malice, and whatever other activities Satan partakes in with his free time paraded right before you. I heard the nation was founded on the beliefs of the Bible, but the Holy Book isn't applied uniformly across the land: the northeastern and western States keep their Bibles open, so they know to do the opposite of what God commands. They prefer their tobacco rolled with the pages of God's Word before smoking it. The southern States keep their Bibles open so they can practice everything God commands except where He talks about thy neighbor. This excludes us because thy neighbor implies a human being, and Black doesn't meet the criteria. Live among them and be as quiet as a church mouse, as kind as the Good Samaritan, and they will still be suspicious of you. Had the Good Samaritan been a Black man in a southern state of America, he would have spent the rest of his days on the gallows or charged with robbery and the attempted murder of the man he tried to save. These prejudiced minds know one type of Black man. Every step you take will be under their watchful eye. They would go through your mail and trash and harass people who know you, to try to understand your suspicious behavior. Suspicious because you don't fit their mold of a Black man. I'm nowhere near as religious as you, but Satan would have better luck making Christianity unattractive to you through these folks than he could through atheists. The presence of Satan is felt even among the agnostics there, who accept your humanity because you walk on two feet. Don't be quick to breathe a sigh of relief just yet, for these people thank their lucky stars that you stand between them and the apes. My brother, Satan has touched every part of that land. Tell the elders that the centuries-old dilemma for our village should be put to rest. They would be crazy to think Satan lives anywhere else. Satan may go from place to place, but they shouldn't doubt where he calls home. It isn't Enkoho."

Preprah's attention turned to a waitress who seemed to have been taken by what he was saying. Preprah's conversation soon turned braggadocio. Gyambibi couldn't stow away to save his ears, so he had to intervene: "Agya Kobi once told me, as far as the Bible goes, that Satan's location was somewhere in Asia, in Bergama, called Pergamum in the Bible."

The mention of Agya Kobi had an immediate impact. Preprah forgot about the waitress.

"And you believed what the devil told you? In a way, you could because it takes one devil to know the location of another. But assuming he's right, who stays in one place from birth to death? Even the Israelites spent four hundred years in Africa before the journey to the Promised Land. If Creation occurred six thousand years ago, who in his right mind thinks Satan has been staying in one place for all those years and longer? He's in America. In fact, the Bible references Africa, Europe, the Middle East, Asia...yet the Americas are left out. Why? Satan's permanent residence."

Preprah scanned the restaurant for the waitress he had asked to join them. She had her eyes on Preprah wherever she was. They exchanged smiles.

"She deserves a rose, I tell you. Flowers capture women. I understand you don't grasp this flower-and-romance concept. It's wonderful if you know how it works. In America, a woman will accept flowers because she understands she's delicate and beautiful. The irony is that you don't say it, for that could get you into trouble. Tell a woman you like her because she's beautiful; somehow, that's like saying she has no intelligence. To tell a woman you like her because she's delicate like a flower is to say she's weak, and that infringes on gender equality. I like giving flowers to women because it says the beautiful things the mouth can get into trouble for. She accepts the flowers, and you're set. The relationship takes off, and you quickly learn that you're dealing with something that resembles tree bark more than a flower. That's why I fancy giving women a whole tree over a flower. *My mouth, your ears!"*

When the weight of Gyambibi's plans had settled on Moro, he also wanted to leave the military, but only if he would be paid as well. He had an idea for honorable discharge: faking insanity.

Gyambibi knew about the scheme, but his conscience wouldn't go along. Moro went with it, showing up naked one day and wrestling a platoon mate to the ground during roll call. He was committed to the 37 Military Hospital, where nurses and his attending psychiatrist were shocked to see that 2000 mg of Largactil couldn't subdue a man. Naked with saliva running down his beard, Moro chased after mosquitoes in high heels all day.

Through the psychiatrist, the hospital staff learned that Moro was from Air Vice-Marshal Yaw Boakye's village, even though the only connection Moro had to Aduman was to place his residential address there for the age-old reason that Enkoho did not exist. Unknown to him, the Air Vice-Marshal kept a close eye on all residents of Aduman in the military. Moro would later find out that the psychiatrist knew the Air Vice-Marshal; this dictated the kind of treatment Moro would receive. The psychiatrist didn't say why he had to forgo anesthesia during Moro's electroconvulsive therapy sessions. Instead, he had orderlies pin Moro down. Weeks of receiving electric shocks to his head while awake seemed to have re-attached some loose wires in his brain. The psychiatrist was impressed with the changes he saw in Moro, writing to the medical board: "[Moro's] former behavior of run-ins with his superiors, insubordination, emotional outbursts, constant fistfights with platoon mates, and uncontrollable anger were telltale signs of a psychiatric disease that wasn't diagnosed when entering military service. His transformation under my care is, in non-scientific terms, miraculous. I would be at his service should he relapse. Needless to say, the man is better suited to serve our country today than before. I have never seen this therapy work so well."

Moro walked out of the hospital with fear of electricity and wires. The sight of utility poles would send him into a panic attack. Ordered to the office of the Air Vice-Marshal after his discharge from the hospital, Moro protested through tears that a follow-up appointment with the psychiatrist was unnecessary.

Chapter

29

The faceless entities didn't stay behind in Enkoho all the time. They followed Gyambibi into the military and everywhere else, it seemed. The business with Preprah didn't take off. Not even one car was shipped to Gyambibi because Preprah lost his employment with General Motors upon his return to the United States. Preprah's friends also lost their jobs in the same mass layoff. Unemployed, Gyambibi returned to Enkoho. Preprah, perhaps haunted by his role in Gyambibi's situation, arranged for him to meet the man who helped him get a visa to America. The process would be easy because, unlike Preprah's, the intermediary wouldn't have to start from scratch. The intermediary explained the process in simple terms: Preprah would mail his own passport to him, and he would have it stamped for arrival and departure in Ghana. The passport wouldn't be stamped for departure in the United States, an impossibility if Preprah wasn't traveling, so there would be no problem on that front. Gyambibi could then go to the United States with Preprah's passport as if he were Preprah returning from another vacation. He needed a haircut to resemble Preprah. That was all he needed. The intermediary assured Gyambibi that all Black men look alike to the White man. Gyambibi was uncomfortable with the idea: the deception, the lie, the impersonation. However, he wasn't the type to insult Preprah and the intermediary for their time, so he would have to think about it.

A part of Gyambibi now regretted not heeding Air Vice-Marshal George Yaw Boakye, who sought to talk him out of leaving the military, even threatening court-martial. But Preprah's promised pay and Gyambibi's hope of ending the villagers' suffering were just too strong. Gyambibi spent his unemployed days in the village. He taught the children every other day, with lots of homework in between. He got his father to cut down on his drinking. Karikari was on the brink of stopping altogether when, as destiny would have it, Danfo visited. With him was Mawuli, who brought up the idea of digging up the buried treasure. Mawuli acknowledged the dangers before his friend but then tried to persuade him of the merits of the idea. Indeed, the value of the treasure was simply matched by the dangers involved in retrieving it. Mawuli was motivated to minimize the risks because of his own financial situation. Because he worked for Karikari, he was affected by Karikari's fortune reversal. In this time of hardship, however, Karikari helped him now and then. But that only went so far. Karikari objected because the proposal could kill him and everybody in his family. He started drinking again to erase the memory of this meeting.

Gyambibi, privy to this meeting because his father had told him, said nothing to Yaw. They were worried he would succumb to the idea to fund his way to America.

Meanwhile, Gyambibi visited Moro for input on what Preprah had proposed. Moro was now at the MATS (Military Academy and Training School) in Teshie, transferred there from the base workshop in Burma Camp. Jeefa and Helena joined them a few days later with a cooked meal. Outside of the ladies' company, Gyambibi laid out his concerns and intense discomfort with Preprah's proposal. He threw Moro a letter he'd received from Preprah. He had underlined a section: *Indeed, you're a rare man whose conscience is cleansed daily. You're still too young to fully appreciate that we live in a dirty world where doing all you can to survive is the norm (if death isn't in your immediate future). The "Americans" the world knows today didn't enter the USA with a visa. I believe the word* visa *entered the lexicon of international travel after these people had settled everywhere they wanted and needed to keep others at bay. Those people arrived in America uninvited and, worse, without breaching their conscience. The British have a word for it: survival. I'm not asking you to kill anybody; I'm not telling you to steal from anybody; I'm not advising you to hurt or dispose of one's humanity. And I'm not forcing you to prostitute your conscience. You lost your employment because of me, and this is how I intend to remedy it. I'm awaiting your response, and so is Mr. Nkansah. Don't take forever to accept or reject my help.*

"Do you think he wrote this? Can he even spell *conscience*?" Gyambibi began.

Moro said, "'*My mouth, your ears!*' doesn't appear anywhere, but that's beside the point. He's now an engineer in America, so he should be capable of writing this. He isn't the same fool we knew. I tell you, his transformation belongs on the pages of biblical miracles. But that, too, is beside the point. My brother, what issue with conscience do you have? You worry too much. No one would ask so many questions when given a chance to go to America..." Moro paused and searched for words to drive home his point. "Perhaps I'm mistaken. Are we talking about America, America? Look, when it comes to *that* America, the only question worth my time is *when*? Besides, you know the condition of your father. As Preprah would say, your brother Yaw is one '*My mouth, your ears!*' away from the asylum. Anyway, with you in America, that would give Yaw hope that he could make it there. And I don't have to remind you of your own situation. I know Jeefa would agree."

Gyambibi understood but still was bothered by *how* he would get to America. Why should they make it so difficult to enter a country that people must resort to deception?

"Gyambibi, you're overthinking this. Look, Enkoho is the most difficult place to enter on Earth. No one even knows its exact location. Going to the US is easy if you only have to impersonate Preprah."

Gyambibi again got the idea that putting much distance between himself and the village might break its hold on him. It was a theory worth exploring, for Preprah still had no pull in the village. What's more, Gyambibi couldn't overlook his father and brother's conditions. He couldn't ignore the children of Enkoho; he couldn't ignore Enkoho. In the end, he surrendered.

While preparing for the United States, Gyambibi became violently ill. He had chills, intermittent bouts of vomiting, malaise, and high fever. By all indications, he was septic. Helena felt his forehead. This wasn't a medical problem for Healer. She advised Jeefa to talk to her parents about how to handle the situation since Karikari was out of town, visiting Kofi Nsenkyire to borrow Gyambibi's pocket money for his travel abroad. Helena found paracetamol, penicillin, codeine, and ibuprofen in the house, but now she wondered if they were what they claimed to be or if they were merely a malaxation of maize and cassava dough. Nothing explained her newfound doubts about medications she herself had used now and then, except that she was beside herself seeing Gyambibi so sick. Her nervous behavior resembled a new mother seeing her newborn on the brink of death. She wanted to help him but feared she might worsen his condition. Arriving in Enkoho as a skeptic of spirituality and the occult, she had seen enough to know that Gyambibi could die before the day was out. Now she knew to pray and study the Bible with Agya Kobi. She wondered if she should take Gyambibi to Okomfo Anokye Hospital in Kumasi, where she worked, but decided to wait for Jeefa's response. They could find men to carry him through the forest if it came to that. Now Helena knew, through the queen, that Enkoho was a *few* miles from Aduman. She needed to find the *path* marked by teaks. Just seeing the trees wasn't helpful. Only when one had acknowledged that they marked the *path* to and from the village could one gain clarity of the direction to take to and from the village. If one deviated from the *path*, the distance could turn into ten, twenty, fifty, even a hundred thousand miles or more—depending on how many times one circled the village to get back to the *path*. Even with a compass, nothing would change; it would point in the same direction as one circled the village. Rarely some stumbled across Enkoho by chance. But the villagers didn't see it that way—far from it; rather, they believed Enkoho wanted these people there.

Jeefa rejoined Helena, noting her gratitude. Jeefa had a fire started and water boiling as instructed by her mother. Daavi had returned from Healer with freshly plucked leaves of the neem tree, which Jeefa rinsed and put in a pot of boiling water. She entered Gyambibi's room and walked outside with him, gently lowering him into a chair close to the boiling water, which had turned olive green. A cupful of greenish broth was administered. It was bitter. Helena prayed for God to calm her fears.

Helena watched nervously as Gyambibi, seated, hunched over the boiling broth. Jeefa gave him a ladle to stir. Helena flinched, almost protested, when a thick wool blanket was draped over him and the boiling neem leaves, sealing in the heat. Then Daavi got out a packet of camphor balls and dropped three into the boiling water while Gyambibi stirred the potentized herbal broth. Inhaling the vapor was part of his treatment. Jeefa was composed, though she was being eaten up inside. Helena was more fearful. Gyambibi was feverish; he needed something cool, not hot, to relieve his fever. Camphor! Helena wondered what medical utility it held. Aromatherapy, maybe, but Helena struggled to make sense of it. She wondered how hot vapor penetrating the nares and pores of someone feverish could help. There would be an escalation of his fever and a worsening of his condition. Yet the more she thought of it, the more it made sense. While he cooked in the tent of neem vapor, his body would become hot. So when the blanket came off, followed by a bath with the same broth, the temperature differential would lend to a quicker cool-off. Perhaps this was how the concept of evaporation resulting in cooling had entered Healer's materia medica. Healer would visit later for more treatments.

Chapter

Stygian Whirlwinds: A Journey Through Eternity

*A*fternoon came too soon. It seemed an afternoon in the middle of the night, an afternoon not preceded by daylight. Whatever it was, it was not usual, for the entire village was asleep. Crickets were awake, but the rest of the world was quiet, except for distant clashes of stones.

Agya Kobi sat on his mat, unable to sleep, when the clashes of stones grew louder to the point of rattling his bones. His feet found strength, and he stood. He walked to the window and pried open the curtain. Two warring factions were engulfed in a fight. He looked back at Adwoa Brago, who was asleep. He tiptoed around her and left the hut. No one was in sight except behind his hut, where the two factions fought. Hiding behind a tree, Agya Kobi witnessed a spectacle that made no sense. He knew none of the fighters. He wondered if his seclusion had dulled his ability to see new people who had relocated to the village.

The fighting continued. He went indoors and pinched his wife awake. He beckoned her to be quiet as they walked behind the hut, hand in hand. Agya Kobi asked her when these fighters had moved to the village. Then he realized his wife was no longer holding his hand. He turned, but she was gone. Alarmed, he ran back into the hut. She was asleep. He wondered what had happened. She had held his hand, and they had walked out of the hut together and seen the spectacle, hadn't they?

Confused, Agya Kobi went out again. These were people from a different era—ancestors of Enkoho and possibly people from nearby villages who were cutting each other up. He brushed off the spectacle and went back inside to sleep. Then it came to him that his hut was not in Enkoho—although he was asleep in Enkoho. Sweat had carved his outline on the straw mat; Adwoa Brago was beside him, though he could not say if it was really her. The Eternal Lamp was there, alive, just as it had always been. It had turned midnight into afternoon. Agya Kobi couldn't say why or how.

The sounds of clashing stones alerted him again. This time, he wasn't on his soaked mat. He heard a grunt, then the sounds of someone in despair drew him back outside. He turned the corner, then another corner into the forest. A woman in a loin-cloth was holding a boulder over the head of a man whose hands were tied behind him. Before Agya Kobi could tell her to stop, the woman dropped the boulder, crushing the man's head. She couldn't see or hear Agya Kobi. He looked about, noticing that he was not in Enkoho, not even in Ghana or Africa, but a distant land where the man's head was crushed. Nothing made sense.

After a while, he turned to the woman, who was eating pieces of brain matter from the man she had killed. Agya Kobi ran to his hut to shut the door. But he realized that his hut no longer had walls. He turned to look at the door, but it was gone. Along with Adwoa Brago and their belongings. He went out-side to find two boys hunched over a body. He yelled at them, but they didn't seem to notice. He ran toward them, and when they heard his footsteps, they ran away, one with a leg and the other clutching a breast and an arm. The body parts belonged to the woman he had seen earlier.

Agya Kobi followed the boys into the woods. Their run gave way to a walk when they knew he couldn't catch them. They went through the forest with ease, apparently from a faraway land, their skin hue unlike anything Agya Kobi had seen before. His clothes caught on bristles, which took him some time to untangle. After he was free, the boys were gone. But something else urged him to keep going, instructions bellowing from the Eternal Lamp, which he had absentmindedly taken with him, following a path he wouldn't normally have followed.

He walked and walked. His clothes got thinner as the air started to feel icy, though the sun was up; he felt neglected, alone. Then the boys reappeared, and he realized they were heading to his farm. When he arrived, hiding behind a tree, he saw men and women, again of a different shade of human-ity. Goads, plowshares, and mattocks tore into each other. He couldn't say why they fought, but the skirmish was intense.

"How could you do this?" a disembodied voice asked.

"Every human is different. All I have to do is point to another and remind him how different he is," another responded.

While Agya Kobi thought, the Eternal Lamp flickered and al-most went out. Confused, he gave it a swirl to see if it was out of kerosene. When he knelt to examine the wick, a yataghan flew past his head, lodging into the tree behind him and felling it. Prying away the brush into which he had fallen, Agya Kobi was surprised that the Eternal Lamp had landed erect, its wick now intensely aglow. The clash of metallic weapons filled the air, overwhelming his already confused mind.

When he got on his feet, the slaughtering had ended. A pregnant woman was standing over the dead bodies in shock, unaware of what had happened. She froze when she locked onto Agya Kobi, knowing he was from a different era. She said something to him, which he couldn't respond to because the language was unfamiliar. She took a step toward him when the blade of an axe entered her back, emerging from her belly with the head of her fetus at the tip. Agya Kobi watched in horror as the fetus crawled toward him with the axe embedded in it. The head of the axe was larger than the fetus's head, but the fetus survived and crawled on. It grew with each movement toward him. The Eternal Lamp told Agya Kobi the fetus wanted to tell him what its mother couldn't: the reason for the carnage.

A few steps from him, a trebuchet propelled a fiery projectile at the fetus, scorching it to empty blackness. The pile of dead bodies burst aflame as more projectiles landed. Agya Kobi turned and ran, vomiting from the intensifying smell of burning flesh. The stench was now on his skin and breath. He wiped his mouth with the edge of his forehand but couldn't eliminate the smell. He continued to vomit. He could see a finger, an eye, and strings of burnt skin in the vomitus. He couldn't return to the village vomiting human flesh but couldn't stop regurgitating human body parts. Tired, weak, and dehydrated, he turned around and walked toward the river in Enkoho.

When the river came into view, it was wider, deeper, and endless, coursing through a scantily treed landscape. Herdsmen watering their flock didn't notice him as he continued to vomit. The river was thick and glossy as he looked at his reflection, which grew larger and larger until it spanned the breadth of the river. The flame of the Eternal Lamp jolted upward while he watched, confused. It kept going up with him until he was hundreds of feet tall, with his reflection spanning the breadth of the river.

Slowly, one side of his reflection became grayer and grayer as the other side became darker. He faded from one side of the river toward the other. When he looked about, he saw the herdsmen across the river. Somehow, he had crossed as well. Dusting himself off, he saw reflective droplets of water around him. When these disappeared, the air became dusty, then impenetrable. Whispers of wind blew sand particles everywhere. When the wind died down, pyramids rose from the sands, at which time he knew he was along the Nile in Egypt.

He couldn't say how long it had taken him to walk from Anatolia. He couldn't remember how long he had explored the entire Levant, where war had fallen from the heavens and was raging among many countries—a war involving angels and demons, God and Satan, sibyls and witches, the living and the dead, peace and gossip, kindness and greed, and man. Man seemed lost, for man only fought against man rather than join a side of the warring factions. Agya Kobi ran, searching for a band of marauders that had flailed its victims, disappearing into several countries whose names he couldn't remember.

The ornateness of Asia had driven him farther East. He had visited every country in Asia but couldn't stay for long. Vegetation formed his diet because he couldn't go near animals, even the free-roaming ones in the forest. Disembodied human spirits inhabited them; thus, they were human and couldn't be eaten. The human spirits that inhabited animals didn't die of natural causes but war. Though meat was on the menu wherever he went in Asia, what he craved was deemed inedible because it contained the spirits of their enemies.

Agya Kobi faced resistance, trying to force his way into Europe. The resistance had come from disembodied humans and the potent stench of death. Along the Mediterranean Sea, he saw Adolf Hitler, Caligula, Genghis Kahn, Attila the Hun, and Evil Eye drinking blood from chalices of human skulls and chatting macabrely from a promontory overlooking a vista of tortured human corpses. A disembodied voice whisked him away before they saw him.

Agya Kobi believed he had spent thirty-three days gliding past Bergama on his second trip to Asia. He went farther into India, then China and its exurbs. Looking down in the middle of the South China Sea, he saw a fire burning deep. The water couldn't put it out. A whizzing sound broke the water's surface; smoke billowed, propelling him far above the waters, where he could see all of Asia and beyond. Beneath his feet, he could feel what had drawn him back here: hundreds of thousands, perhaps millions, of wooden boxes about a third the size of a person. Each housed a corpse—some were men, some women, and some children. He knew he was up in the air to see how far the buried coffins stretched. He couldn't tell where they ended. The corpses had their bellies slashed open with swords sticking out of their heads and bamboo piercing their tongues. He looked down as the smoke slowly faded, lowering him into the water. He heard sobs from the water, and a hand emerged from a coffin. He reached down and held it. The coffin broke apart, revealing a girl lying in it. He lifted her in his arms and went ashore. She had been in the water for three days. She was neither hungry nor thirsty, although she was weak. After her tears were wiped, she regained strength. Agya Kobi asked what had happened to everyone. These were people from all of Asia, she said. Who had done this, he asked.

When she opened her mouth, an axe found her head, burned through her spine, and split her in two. Her blood flowed into the sea. It didn't dilute out but maintained its dark redness and created an inlet into which the coffins sank. Agya Kobi couldn't see anyone. He froze, wondering what he had just witnessed. His thoughts couldn't settle before he felt the ground trembling, undulating toward him. Sand rose and fell, flakes rising into the air and clouding the seashore. His fear started before the dust cleared; in front of him stood a man.

"What does it mean?" he asked, wiping sand off his knees. He found himself on the other side of the Nile again, though the pyramids weren't visible anymore. There were no humans around, yet disembodied voices came from deep inland. He could see nothing, not even the Eternal Lamp. He couldn't walk south as he had hoped. Every place he had visited overflowed with viciousness and evil. Not one place was without its share of violent death.

The sides of his leg itched from the brush of cacti while he was in the heart of America. Some were stuck in his flesh, so he knelt to pull them out. When he raised his head, he saw a man aiming a gun at another man. A bullet severed one man's arm before he had a chance to fire. "You can't have it, you can't have it," he cried in a strange tongue, which Agya Kobi understood only after the Eternal Lamp told him what he meant. Another bullet tore off the man's other arm. Two more bullets tore off his legs. The wounded man stayed upright on his bleeding knees. The other man knelt before him, embraced and kissed him on the forehead before pushing him off the bluff into the hands of other conquistadors, who were wielding tridents, waiting to feast.

Agya Kobi visited the Americas more than any place, yet it appeared it was his least-visited place. He saw the same things every time he explored the lands: creeks of red blood and brooks of white blood—similar to what he saw in Asia and Europe, respectively. And then there were crying rivers of black blood; actually, these were tributaries of the Atlantic Ocean with vast channels of black blood connecting the African continent.

Thinking about Karikari's family caused a heaviness in Agya Kobi's chest that radiated to his feet and forced him to the ground. He had barely caught his breath when he saw Gyambibi detained in a building with others in Queens, New York. There was a rope around Gyambibi. He wanted to be free, but every time Agya Kobi tried to untangle the rope, his hand went through like it wasn't there. The symbolism of all this came to him when he learned that Gyambibi didn't trust his intentions and that the rope cut across the land, traveled through the Atlantic Ocean, and continued eastward to Enkoho. Strangely, Gyambibi was in America but was also in Enkoho—at the same time. The feeling of Gyambibi rejecting Agya Kobi persisted as he walked the terrain.

Rain started falling. Agya Kobi wasn't thirsty but had a sudden urge for the taste of water. He collected some in the well of his palm, noting that none of the water escaped. He turned to look at the back of his hand, only to find it dry. The water hadn't fallen out when he turned his palm face up. He drank it.

It was salty. He looked up, confused, and had the sensation of the Eternal Lamp telling him that each handful he drank was a reservoir of tears that had come over him in every place he had visited but which he couldn't shed because of a presence about him. After having his fill of tears, he noticed his feet for the first time because they were drifting beneath the water. His hands flapped about, attempting to swim. He strained all efforts, but like a bar of steel, he quickly went under. Deeper and deeper he sank, his hands limp. After several hundred feet, his feet touched something soft. His eyes, red with irritation, looked down. There were corpses everywhere of the dead Asians he had seen. Beneath him was the little girl. She wasn't halved but whole and alive, waving at him as he drifted toward the surface. She was indifferent, her face a strange mixture of hope and hopelessness. He was fixated on her, with a burning intent to bring her to the surface. She didn't speak, but he understood she wanted to be left where she was. In fact, she pointed up to him, indicating to avoid a black mass that appeared above him. The shadow moved aside, and a hand reached out and pulled him into a galleon. Onboard, he saw an old, worn-out man seated across from him. The same man had first appeared to Agya Kobi by the seashore in Europe, then in Asia. He had sat on the beach with his feet pointing outward. His footwear measured over two feet; they were black and laced to his knees. In examining the texture of the material, Agya Kobi found they weren't footwear but the man's actual feet. His left-hand was brown and his right-hand yellow. His hair was off-white, but his ears were of carnelian splendor. His scalp was patched in black, brown, yellow, red, and white skin, extending into his brain, of which Agya Kobi could see every part.

He tried to understand why the man was fully clothed, with the winds of the high seas bearing witness, but at the same time, he didn't appear to be wearing clothes. Moreover, Agya Kobi was the one he pulled from the ocean, yet he was dry while the rescuer's clothes were soaked. Agya Kobi looked at the man's head draped in a cloth. He couldn't figure out how he had gotten on the ship or how the man who brought him aboard made it to where he was sitting. He approached the man and sat across from him. The stranger pointed in a direction.

"That's Ethiopia, I know," Agya Kobi said. But that wasn't the answer the man was looking for.

"Somalia, Kenya, Tanzania," continued Agya Kobi.

The man kept pointing, and Agya Kobi kept guessing, belting out the names of countries along the coast as they traveled southward along East Africa. This went on for months until he realized the man pointed and made an arc, indicating the other side of the continent. Once Agya Kobi understood, the man removed the cloth and wiped away his tears. It told Agya Kobi all he had suspected about the cloth: it only left the man's head to wipe his tears. It was wet with tears, not water, as he had initially thought. The man wasn't from a race he knew, but something told Agya Kobi he was British. They shared a meal of fish, skinned and eaten raw. Agya Kobi was new to this, but it was his only way to survive on the ocean. The man didn't steer the rudder but allowed the ship to drift. Agya Kobi was aware that the ship was moving toward wherever they were going. His rescuer didn't speak, only wiped off his tears now and then. It went on forever; he lived to wet the cloth with his tears. The man was capable of speech but never spoke. He used sign language to describe the carnage he had seen in Europe. The man could read his thoughts and was filling in where Agya Kobi hadn't penetrated inland.

"My daughter takes you to see what she wants you to see. Seeing one is seeing them all. Europe and Antarctica are no different," he said through sign language.

Agya Kobi didn't know what he meant by *his daughter*. Perhaps he was talking about the little girl who turned up everywhere he went.

The flame of the Eternal Lamp flickered wildly. Not understanding why he was suddenly nervous, arrows flew by, then the blast of a mortar shell. He looked about and was greeted by the tropical sea of the Cape of Good Hope. Its sheer ambiance told him that the erstwhile waters of the Sahara had relocated here. He traveled inland through dense forests where the indigenes had been banished. The rest of the land had tall, beautiful buildings built of diamonds with roofs of gold. He could hear the sobs of children, of women, and of men. One pierced through the others. It wasn't because it was louder, but rather it was familiar, as though coming from someone he knew. He moved farther north, then west, south, and east—in circles. The sobs grew louder and more focused when he saw the Eternal Lamp flicker in a direction that was neither east, north, south, nor west. He was descending a knoll when a familiar face showed up. Seated against a tree, her chin on her propped knee, a girl was crying—tears mixed with phlegm dripped down her legs. Her skin was black, with prominent cheeks, jaws, and big, weary eyes. Everything about her bespoke African heritage, yet he felt in her the presence of the little girl he had seen in Asia.

"Why are you sobbing?" Agya Kobi asked.

"Not me, but the ancestral spirits," she said.

He had seen this girl in every place he had been, conforming to the physical features of each.

Crossing into Namibia, Agya Kobi continued northward but was pulled westward. Large footsteps led him to the shore. Feet in wooden greaves pointed out from the sand with the rest of their owner buried deep in the soil. The littoral serenity, save for crashing waves, evoked a strong emotional response of loneliness. So intense was it that he started wondering where Adwoa Brago was. There were ripples of unexpected calmness and peace, sitting alongside an annoying whisper of silence, hopelessness, and dark uncertainty. It was a conflicted feeling, like being in two opposite worlds at the same time. He walked away, only to find himself moving through the ocean, suspended in the water. When he looked back, the feet pointing from the sands had disappeared into the soil. He saw no one at first, but about twenty yards out, he noticed the galleon he had boarded earlier. A man in a burnoose emerged when the hatch swung open. He dragged himself onto the deck and sat in the same corner as before, still not talking. His shins were adorned in the same wooden greaves Agya Kobi had seen on the feet protruding from the soil. The stranger looked away and pointed into the ocean. Agya Kobi saw nothing beyond blackness. He turned to the man as if to say it would be better to tell him what was down there, for he couldn't see into the dark water. The man's hand insisted he should keep looking, saying he preferred not to look at what he was pointing to because he couldn't bring himself to see what was down there. For this reason, he had chosen to bury himself underground when on land. It was best not to see.

The man's burnoose was of one solid color, but Agya Kobi couldn't seem to determine what color it was—one color but also all colors. Averting his gaze from the color of the burnoose, Agya Kobi looked into the water at distinct shapes of humans: corpses of Black children, Black women, and Black men. The stranger knew Agya Kobi had seen what he wanted him to see and pointed far beyond where he could see. The corpses stretched much, much farther than he had thought.

Having traveled all this time, Agya Kobi was famished and weak. He looked everywhere but saw nothing to eat. The stranger handed him a fruit he didn't recognize—a fruit with animal flesh and juices of red blood. It was disgusting and alluring at the same time. Over the next few days, he attempted to eat this fruit. Each day he tried a bite, only to find his stomach convulse and empty the nothingness residing within. These fruits the stranger took back and ate with ease, with blood from the fruit dripping from his fanged teeth. His mouth was red. Every part of him the fruit touched left a bloodstain. Agya Kobi tried another bite. Blood dripped from his nose and turned him nauseous. He vomited, and so much blood entered the ocean that the dead bodies disappeared under dense, macabre redness. Even though he was famished, Agya Kobi didn't go near the fruit again.

The stranger held out his finger while they drifted. Agya Kobi was flung about so many times he became seasick. He held onto the gunwale and, looking down, saw corpses disposed of in the crepuscular ocean, which had turned into a storehouse of all the dead he had seen from all shades of humanity. Agya Kobi had seen so many dead bodies by this time that one would think he had been hardened. That wasn't the case; in fact, this time, he cried.

Traveling up the African continent, he saw much bloodshed from expanding wars among ethnic groups. After spending one hundred eleven days trying to understand, the young girl who showed up everywhere he went explained to him, "The leaders of the People have associations with gods from faraway lands—gods with colorless skin and diamond teeth. These gods are rich but covetous, merciful but ruthless, and live in the TODAY and TOMORROW. These African leaders have been educated to live accordingly but told to restrict the knowledge of the People to TODAY. Moreover, these leaders' family, friends, and association with the gods are more important to them than the People. But the People have recently learned that their leaders don't want them to know about TOMORROW because that would lead them to the knowledge that their resources are being diverted to the gods, who in turn protect the leaders and their stolen wealth."

On the 666th day, Agya Kobi was confronted with the disembodied presence of King Leopold II—one of the gods with colorless skin and diamond teeth. At his feet were men, women, and children, too many to count, on their stomachs with their backs facing the sun. Their hands reached deep into the earth, mining gold and diamond for the god. The aggressive sun had bleached their skin into the earth and stained it black. King Leopold, standing thirteen feet tall, wielded seven ivory stakes, each about a foot long with a shank and an eye the size of an egg, through which emerged a tense rope of iron. Every aspect of these looked like threaded needles, only much bigger. These the god used to clear the field of tired workers. As the leader of the people pointed out those who were too weak to work, the god plunged the stakes, one at a time, into the back of someone lying facedown until it emerged from the belly. Then he plunged the stake into the belly of the next weak person and pulled it up from his or her back. One after the other, he sewed up a million people, with many millions to go.

"Solutions to the world's problems are in the hands of those who have a stake in perpetuating them," the stranger said, leaving Agya Kobi with these words as he reached Enkoho. Agya Kobi didn't know how long he had been gone, but it was probably years.

Evening was dawning when Agya Kobi heard the faint voice of his wife thanking Nyamenkum the Gossip for some spices she had gotten from her earlier.

Returning from the market, Adwoa Brago was excited about certain happenings in the village that she wanted to share with her husband, who was staring at the walls. Agya Kobi saw bloody veins crawl over their walls; burnt human flesh covering them was beginning to slough off. Adwoa Brago was laughing as she talked about Danfo. "Do you not hear?" she asked. Agya Kobi stared blankly at her. Adwoa Brago narrated the lengthy incident involving Danfo and every turn it took, making every effort not to miss a detail. She laughed throughout, not seeing her husband's partially eaten lunch splattered on the floor.

Now the veins on the walls were less defined and bloody, and they were the shade of olive brown, having blended with the mud walls. Adwoa Brago's voice was clearer now to Agya Kobi, but his mind was still elsewhere, roaming the country-side after touring the dark world. Slowly, every scene of the vision faded away, leaving his encounters with Gyambibi at the Wackenhut Detention Center in Queens, New York. Agya Kobi started to sob when it dawned on him that Gyambibi did not want his help anywhere in the world. One quiet moan later, the elder slumped against the wall.

Adwoa Brago was in the grip of rib-cracking laughter as she recounted the incident involving Danfo. She didn't appear to realize there was something wrong with her husband. Helena, however, came by and was alarmed. Alerting the village was pointless because no one would get involved to help Agya Kobi. Helena carried the elder on her back and ran to Healer. Adwoa Brago wailed behind her, fastening her wrapper.

It would appear that the history of Gyambibi's mysterious illness had quietly receded from the memory of Enkoho. However, it was resurfacing in the person of Agya Kobi. Somehow the toxin-tainted food had found Agya Kobi alone in his house-hold. Unknown to the villagers, whoever, or whatever, was after Gyambibi was also after Agya Kobi. The same force was also behind Karikari's hallucination, which had escaped every-one's attention because of his heavy drinking. Unfortunately for Agya Kobi, he had to keep today's hair-raising experience to himself. Nobody would care because he must have been the hidden cause of his own "experience."

Moreover, the timing of his "experience" was suspicious when Gyambibi had recently fallen violently ill. Karikari, Danfo, and Mawuli suspected that the old man must have gotten hold of Gyambibi's plans and wanted to destroy them. Thus Agya Ko-bi's claim of food tainting was intended to divert attention else-where.

Out of the hundreds of people in the village, when only Ad-woa Brago, Helena, Yaa Adubia, and Efia believed him, and hostility pushed all others away from accepting his explanation for the hallucinations, Agya Kobi's descent into life's abyss of scorching loneliness had just begun.

This hallucinatory journey of horrors would one day lead him to who meant him harm, as well as Karikari's family. Agya Kobi would be right in his conclusions while alive but wrong on the same facts after his death. It was Enkoho, after all, where even facts shape-shifted.

Four randomly placed huts sat across from three clustered huts. The former held patients of Healer's while the latter housed Healer and his family. A shrine hut sat at the center of the three clustered huts. Agya Kobi was in the hut for Healer's family because Healer had relegated his patients to his wife while he attended to the elder. This had never happened before. No one saw Healer or Agya Kobi in days.

Rumors spread of Agya Kobi's death. Muted celebrations stood in certain corners of the village: Evil was dead at last, and so were the problems of Enkoho. Danfo wasn't happy about the rumors, however. The elder knew more about the buried treasure than anyone, so he couldn't die and take all the secrets with him.

"They don't have to die. Please. What can I do to save their lives? Please. Please!"

Agya Kobi was heard screaming these words in his hut— words his wife hadn't been there to hear herself, but Nyamen-kum the Gossip, living next door, had.

From this, Danfo gathered a man confessing his sins when Agya Kobi had only been protesting against a massacre in his hallucinations. But to Danfo, the elder's perceived confession wasn't enough if he didn't divulge his knowledge of the buried treasure as well. As far as Agya Kobi's perceived evils, all deaths in the village were somehow connected to him, even those related to attempts at retrieving the buried treasure. Agya Kobi ought to confess to these deaths as well as his knowledge of the treasure for all to be satisfied. Importantly, the village needed the treasure to rebuild, so Agya Kobi's death, if true, would curtail Danfo's hope. His mood wasn't bright today.

With him on good terms with his son, Danfo's bitterness could now be sourced from Agya Kobi and women. So his recent fistfight with Nyamenkum the Gossip was also responsible for his sour mood. Nevertheless, a sliver of happiness came to him by way of his new wife, an excitement he held onto while en route to Karikari's.

Karikari had borrowed money from Nsenkyire and reached out to Danfo to talk about Gyambibi's pending trip to the United States. But when Danfo got there, all he talked about was his new wife. Unable to get a word in about his reason for inviting Danfo, Karikari was forced to listen to Danfo brag. Karikari felt the sooner he got that discussion over with, the sooner they could talk about what mattered. Danfo walked out, angry at his friend's suggestion that his new wife resembled his ex-wife. Certainly, the last two wives were of the same build, age, and mannerisms—like Esi Eluwah. To Danfo, Karikari's input carried the unholy impression that Danfo was still in love with his ex-wife. Nyamenkum the Gossip was blunter about the similarities between the two women, telling everyone that her friend, Oforiwaah, had returned. This third wife, Regina Asiedu, gossiped as much as the first and second and was, therefore, always in the company of Nyamenkum the Gossip. Danfo was content with her because she didn't cook meals saltier to force him to eat less so that her cooking would last the whole week. His headaches were less, and his heart didn't beat as fast as before. There had been times when he couldn't feel parts of his face; food would fall out of his mouth. Not anymore.

Barbara Akosua Oforiwaah had had to go. Not only was her cooking a risk to his health but also to his love for food. By

Danfo's account, she was a terrible cook, and being drunk did nothing to mask it. Moreover, when she cooked, she tasted the food too many times. Not only did she consume a sizable portion of the meal before it was done, but Danfo also contended that when he ate her cooking, he tasted her saliva too. After years of ingesting her saliva, he thought it was no wonder his detractors thought he behaved like his ex-wife. What kind of wife eats half the food before it's done, then shares the leftovers with her husband? What a terrible way for a husband to live! After years of being underfed—with his wife becoming bigger than him and visually daunting—his frustrations grew, especially when words could no longer subdue her. Even more frustrating, she ate what he didn't when he lost his appetite. The ghosts of his parents were angry with him for staying with her for as long as he did. The changes in his body confirmed his suspicion that Oforiwaah was curing his flesh in anticipation of his death. He was her one hundred twenty kilogram retirement fund, enough of him to last her unbridled appetite for many years. And for that, the disdainful witch had started to cure him by oversalting his food so not even an ounce of him would go bad.

Anyone who knew of Danfo's teenage life wouldn't be surprised by his romantic difficulties. His foray into romance started with a girl with crippled feet. Their romantic dalliances involved Danfo carrying her on his back into the forest. Under cover of night, they crisscrossed the village as one with love holding them together. Those were the good old days of romance for Danfo that no woman with two good legs could match. The cripple passed away before they could get married. Psychologically, some villagers held that this explained Danfo's once hatred of Preprah, with Preprah's perceived disability somehow serving as a grotesque reminder of Danfo's once good romantic life.

Not much had changed when it came to Danfo's preference for women. He measured the quality of a woman by the pound. His women were taller and bigger than he was. The "more" of a woman there was, the better. He had to ensure he wasn't shortchanged if he was paying the bride price. Oforiwaah met his criteria well but was hated nonetheless. Rumors said she had just one breast, and her left breast was actually a prosthesis. Should this be true, to Danfo, she was as good as a left-handed witch.

His new wife was better to him, and his mind was in such good health that he was angry in realizing the kind of existence he could have enjoyed all these years. He accosted Healer for all the herbs he had forced on him when all Healer should have done was tell him that his witch of a wife was bad for his health. One problem with his new wife, though, like the others before her, was that he couldn't keep her away from Nyamenkum the Gossip. But that was a small price to pay to eat good food. Besides, days ago, he had beaten Nyamenkum the Gossip severely enough to cost her some teeth. This would teach her to be mindful of talking about him to his wife. He had appeared before the elders before coming to Karikari's house today. Danfo's defense:

"I know not to hit a woman. I wouldn't do it...but common sense tells me that when circumstances call for hitting a woman, at least for me, I'll hit her hard enough to erase her memory. But here we have a clearheaded witch who says she knows who hit her. It wasn't me. Why would she drag me before you for something God knows I didn't do? But I guess children of Satan need no reason to hate the children of God."

"Are you a child of Satan?" One elder quipped, pointing his staff at Danfo. The others restrained him to allow Danfo to make his defense. Danfo looked at this elder suspiciously and thanked the rest before resuming.

"If you gossip as much as she does, your teeth age faster. Premature aging of her teeth because of gossip is responsible for her missing teeth, not me. I confronted her about the gossip she spread about me. She opened her mouth, and her teeth fell out...I mean...I probably should correct the last statement: she opened her mouth, and I saw gaps where teeth should be."

"How does that explain her broken face?" an elder asked.

"I don't know, that's a question for her," Danfo quipped, knowing she couldn't speak. Her mouth had become a den of swollen tongue and gums. Her speech was hoarse, and the elders couldn't discern what she wanted to say. Her eyes were shut, so she identified her assailant by his voice. Luckily, there were witnesses.

"A witch with a broken mouth and speech...the price to pay for gossip. No human could do this to you. Only the gods could," he said after Nyamenkum the Gossip had identified him.

"You're very inappropriate, Danfo," another elder said.

"What's inappropriate is what I leave out, not what I say, because what I say my mouth has already declared appropriate." He looked through the gathering of elders. Witnesses entered the room one at a time, and their stories were compared, and they all said the same thing.

"You can't rely on them; they're liars," Danfo said. The elders, incensed, gave the impression that the hearing was over. They had to confer and decide on a punishment.

"Why the haste to decide when you haven't heard my side yet?" Danfo asked.

"You've said more than the woman you've battered."

"No, I haven't! And I've battered no one. Have you heard from witnesses who support my side of the story?"

"None of the witnesses supported your story."

"Those are *her* witnesses."

"You have witnesses?"

"Elders, if you listened to the accounts closely, there were only four witnesses, if indeed there were any: her missing teeth and my fists!"

"Who has time for this nonsense!" one elder exclaimed in fury.

"Allow him to say what he has to say," another replied, turning to the accused. "We don't have all day, Danfo."

"I need just three points to dispel her lies: One, she has a small mouth for someone who lives for gossip. Two, her teeth aren't located outside her mouth. Three, how could this fist, just look at it...such a behemoth...," he said and raised his right arm, examining it before the elders, holding and extending it for their examination, "...a masculine ruggedness of a weapon... how could this behemoth have invaded her small mouth to extract those missing teeth?" Scouring his mind for something else he might have missed, he added a belated point number four. "And where are those teeth, Elders? She would have brought them with her if her story were true. When was the last time you examined her mouth? The gaps in her teeth could be teeth she lost twenty, thirty years ago."

He was fined three goats and three cartons of Schnapps for his offense.

"You make the case for why procreation should be regulated. I hope The Village sends you and your children down under to save innocent people who come before you from injustices. I hope The Village is listening. Do your thing, kill them, kill them all! Nonsense!" Danfo lashed out, quickly withdrew the insult and made another plea. "My fathers, forgive my tetchy outburst. You don't deserve it. But hear me out one last time. Some of your families sought refuge in my house during the cataclysm. My roof fell off. Did I slap any of you with the charges for the roof?"

"None of us here, or our families, sought refuge in your house. We all know that some of the elders who aren't here, yes, their families did. But your logic is deranged. Those families didn't tear your roof off. The storm did."

"Neither do I accept *your* deranged conclusion. Those families were in my house when the roof blew off, just as I was in this witch's vicinity when her teeth fell out. I mean, when I noticed her missing some teeth. Do I have a right to tell those families to pay for my roof because they were there when it came off? You all know I was sick last month. Healer wanted two hens for his services when I couldn't afford a vulture. I have no money. If you're determined to hold on to your one-sided conclusion, then tell those ingrates to help pay for my roof because, after all these years, I still haven't found money for it. That part of my house is wasting away because it's exposed to the elements. Maybe I could rent it after replacing the roof to generate the funds to buy the goats and Schnapps for this witch!" Danfo argued.

He quickly reminded them that they were presiding over a case involving a witch caught flying on a log of wood in broad daylight.

"The blood on her teeth and gums, have you determined if it isn't menstrual? And don't overlook the scratches on her face when interpreting the collective evidence. Her injuries are consistent with a catfight over the last piece of human flesh and a gourd of blood. You owe it to your conscience to investigate which of our people has been eaten by this woman and her gang of witches. No doubt she lost some teeth gnawing a human bone.

"You all judged me guilty before seeing my face today. For the umpteenth time, the voices in your head aren't mine; I prefer to be in your faces than in your tiny heads," Danfo concluded, knowing he couldn't change the outcome of the proceeding.

This was the fourteenth time he had been fined, but Danfo had never paid anything. The elders knew Chief disliked him, but Chief didn't enforce the fines against Danfo. That some thought him insane underscored Chief's attitude. Like the rest of the village, the elders were divided over Danfo's sanity or insanity. Many disputes had come before them, but none of the parties involved were as eloquent and witty in their defense as Danfo. "Heck, he makes more sense than some of us. How can he be insane?" one elder had asked. Most of the time, the elders decided against him, not on the merit of his accusers but on the testimony of witnesses. Absent witnesses, the charges against him disintegrated. Indeed, some of the elders who held him mentally competent were victims of Danfo themselves. Either that or a friend or relative had been a victim. This informed their hostility. Chief, who watched Danfo in polite silence, acknowledged the strengths of the faction of elders on the side of the divide that Danfo was sane. But Chief observed: How could one who's sane and has the presence of mind to willfully commit a crime provoke the gods by feigning innocence when doing so carries more dangers than the penalty the crime demands?

It had escaped the elders each time, but Chief never sat in on cases involving others. He had a hidden interest in cases involving Danfo. It wasn't coincidental that he decided to sit in on this case when he should have been in the sister village, Braha, for a secret meeting. His presence was particularly worthwhile when Nyamenkum the Gossip was also present. Danfo and Nyamenkum the Gossip were under his watchful eyes in a way that no one in the village knew.

Danfo had left for Karikari's house after the proceeding, haunted by the elders' threat: we will see to it that you pay this fine. The threat could have been why Danfo had left Karikari's house angrier than necessary for what he felt was an inappropriate comment about his new wife.

Karikari saw another day ruined by Danfo's behavior and was left alone in his living room with no one to deliberate Gyambibi's trip. Mawuli was in the Volta Region visiting relatives.

But later in the day, Danfo changed his mind and returned to Karikari—with his new wife. To Karikari's recollection, Danfo's first wife was Esi Eluwah, then Barbara Oforiwaah, and now Regina Asiedu. To tell Danfo that he won't participate in his insanity, Karikari bluntly addressed Danfo's new wife as Esi Eluwah. Danfo took no offense this time because he was dealing with the rumor that his case would be referred to Healer to collect the fines against him—a recourse he dreaded because there was more Healer could do to force him to pay. Danfo suggested they abandon Gyambibi's plans for America and use the money to pay the fines against him. He told Karikari that it made no sense to send Gyambibi abroad when they could focus on the buried treasure, which could solve more than Karikari's money problems. Karikari was speechless; he could not grasp the foolishness he was hearing.

Chapter

A Fugitive of Dystopia

*A*fter several hours of walking through the forest, Gyambibi and Mawuli joined Karikari and Danfo, who had left two days prior so as not to arouse suspicion, in Kodee. Gyambibi's sudden illness gave them a reason to hide his travel plans. Only the trusted were privy to his agenda, which included Jeefa and Moro. As the travel day approached, Gyambibi's excitement about it had waned, replaced by anxiety.

Aunty Tabuah gave up the front-passenger seat to her brother; her husband, Takyi, was at the helm of the Datsun. She and her nephew, Gyambibi, were in the back, alongside Danfo. The rest were in a second car that traveled behind. They drove south on the Kumasi-Accra road at a relaxed speed as trees disappeared behind them.

This trip was at the core of what Gyambibi wanted out of life. He pined for the restoration of the ruined village and its deflated sense of community to its pre-cataclysmic state or better. For this alone, this trip, as far removed as he would be from those he loved and cared for, was paramount. He gazed through the open window and saw in the distance farmers at work. Meadows flanked both sides of the road, beyond which were dense forests. They drove past a bus, loaded and sagging at the rear. It had atop it all sorts of foodstuff, sheaves of plantain, bales of secondhand clothing, and luggage. Some passengers were laughing and chatting; others were sitting quietly.

The thought of making a transit in Great Britain was one cause of his anxiety. Great Britain: another paradise on Earth to the leaders of Ghana! Gyambibi would go through Great Britain on his way to the United States. He had the feeling of going to heaven by way of paradise.

Perhaps to distract from his discomfort with the trip, Karikari talked about Gyambibi when he was five. He narrated an incident that Dr. Maarten had told him during one of their excursions to the greenhouse. Xada had asked Gyambibi about one difference between a child and an adult. Gyambibi had thought for a slow minute and said a child understands God better than adults. Why? He said Jesus implied so. They all laughed.

Hours later, they were on a street in Accra, dimly illuminated at some points by streetlights. They slowed when they approached the densely populated area of Osu. Through heavy pedestrian traffic, Gyambibi's gaze pierced either side of the road as trickles of light from lanterns advertised the sale of *kenkey* and fried fish, *kelewele,* rice and stew, sugarcane, pawpaw, and pineapple. America wouldn't be anything like this, indeed. The pangs of leaving behind his homeland, his people, and his culture for something different resurfaced. Karikari calmed his nerves with yet another story. Esi Eluwah had told Karikari about this, which involved Gyambibi's teacher, Nyamenkum the Gossip, before the school building was destroyed. At the time, Gyambibi had heard from Asamoah that Nyamenkum the Gossip was telling stories about Karikari behaving like he was the most important person in Enkoho. Then came the time when Gyambibi used that as a backdrop for a writing assignment. After grading the report, Nyamenkum the Gossip asked him how he had come up with the characters.

"If the characters look familiar, it's because they're from this planet. If one's particularly familiar, it's because she's from Enkoho," he had told Nyamenkum the Gossip. She knew he had written about her. Karikari had laughed it off.

Jeefa latched onto Gyambibi at the airport, her eyes full of tears. Gyambibi whispered something into her ear, and she nodded like a consoled child and took a handkerchief to her eyes. Suddenly he was nervous again.

His father approached him with two men. Sensing that Gyambibi was troubled by something, his father excused the men and pulled him aside. Gyambibi assured him all was well. They rejoined the two men, who asked for his luggage.

Jeefa, yielding to her emotions over Gyambibi's close departure, left them and stood outside with Aunty Tabuah. After Gyambibi's luggage was tucked inside the plane, they received word that boarding had started. The two men reappeared, and after Karikari slipped them an envelope of money, they disappeared with Gyambibi through a door accessible to employees only. Danfo and Karikari rejoined the others.

It was a medium-sized aircraft, and Gyambibi had an aisle seat. A woman squeezed past him to the window seat. "Abrantie, ete sen—*Gentleman, how are you?*" the woman asked, reminding him of how his mother used to address him. The two struck up a conversation. The pilot greeted the passengers over the intercom and noted that the weather was good in an undiluted British accent. He was informal and spoke with a tinge of cockney. They should expect a smooth flight. Gyambibi put on his seatbelt. Instructions for emergency evacuation and the location of the lavatory were issued, after which the lights were dimmed for takeoff.

There was a jolt as the plane started off the tarmac. Gyambibi's feet searched for the floor, though they were anchored there already. The contents of his stomach were also nervous and sought to escape as the plane turned. Soon they were high up in the air, and he could see the Atlantic Ocean before the plane turned inland. All his problems were now behind him. He was on his way to the United States of America: that celestial kingdom whose citizens are special clones of God Himself; the United States, a country where only those conceived souls who are destined to be rich develop into full-term babies, while the poor are graciously miscarried.

The passenger beside him spoke through the entire flight, keeping him calm and distracting him from his anxieties. Time flew by quicker than Gyambibi would have thought. Suddenly a static noise crackled overhead, and a familiar voice pierced through:

"Promise kept...smooooth flight," the pilot said with a cockney drawl. "Half an hour from Great Britain. Great Britain, you heard that right. What's great about it is there for all to see. The secret of our greatness is a secret. We go from place to place, country to country, like the Gypsies. The Gypsies would be similarly successful if they knew our secret," he said to laughter.

Before final instructions filtered through the intercom, some started in and out of the lavatory. Disembarkation forms were handed out. Descent to Heathrow Airport was announced, and instructions were issued for all to remain strapped in their seats.

Already aware of the good things ahead, Gyambibi made his way off the plane behind the woman who had sat next to him. Entering the airport, not only did the atmosphere look different, but the air even tasted different. After exchanging good-byes with the woman, they parted ways. Gyambibi continued on, following signs to his connecting flight, which would leave for the United States in two hours. It occurred to him that he hadn't secured his luggage off the plane. He stopped and looked for someone to ask where to pick it up. He caught sight of two officers, a male and a female. These, he would later learn, were some customs interdiction officers. They told him his luggage would be loaded onto his connecting flight and let him know where to catch a bus to his terminal and about the check-in process. Going through customs was orderly and not cumbersome. He thought it was part of the process when his passport was withheld and was told to wait. A man and woman came for him. The man was portly, had a stern look, and didn't come across as someone who played with his family if he had one. The woman was innocuous and reserved but also possessed the same look of seriousness. Gyambibi wondered if their disparate dispositions were just a ploy.

He was led into a tiny room and instructed to occupy an empty chair, one of three flanking a table. The woman sat across from him with a dauntless countenance. She skimmed over a few documents she'd pulled from a file. Gyambibi was flooded with perverted probabilities of why he may have been singled out. His mind was cemented on making the connection of his next flight. His eyes darted all over the small room. Gyambibi knew they had him under a microscope for reasons he would soon find out.

"I'm Agent Luckburn. This is my partner, Agent Margaret. Let me get to the point: I have zero tolerance for nonsense and winding explanations," he cautioned, while Gyambibi debated in his mind if his plan had been unraveled. "The only thing shorter than me is my impatience for untruths. Don't worry about your luggage. It'll be loaded onto your flight. What's your name?"

"Preprah...Preprah Antoagyei."

"What's your profession?"

"Auto-mechanic engineer."

"For what company?"

"General Motors."

These were serious-looking folks, not anything like the pilot. They hadn't smiled or even come close to that since he encountered them. Gyambibi knew something was amiss. For one thing, there was no way they could have known that the passport wasn't his. If they did, he would be on the next flight to Ghana, not in a little room being questioned.

"When did you last travel to Ghana?"

Gyambibi began to fidget. "March twenty-first."

"And you left on?"

"April tenth."

"Yes, April tenth. For what reason did you visit Ghana?"

"To bury my mother."

"To bury your mother?"

"Yes."

It was a timely recall. Preprah and the intermediary had prepared him for these questions, just in case. If Gyambibi was Preprah, then he must answer questions about him correctly. No room for mistakes, Preprah had said. To Gyambibi, the passport travel history suggested that Preprah had been frequenting Ghana. As a result, they wrongly suspected that Preprah, in this case, Gyambibi, might be involved in some unsavory endeavors. They'd patted him down and searched his clothes. They'd searched his luggage as well, as Gyambibi found out later. All this was before the questioning, which made Gyambibi realize something else was amiss.

Why had Preprah been against the suggestion of a direct flight to the US, bypassing Britain? Preprah had said that because Ghana was a former colony, Britain would look favorably on Ghanaian citizens. Also, because Britain had good checkpoints to thwart their plan, if he made it through Britain (which Preprah assured he would), the United States would let him in, for Britain would have endorsed his legitimacy.

Now, however, he wasn't so sure of Preprah's explanation. If he had intended a transit in Europe, why choose a country that had colonized Ghana? He couldn't shut his mind off another intruding thought: his father would be reduced to nothing should he be repatriated.

While the agents huddled outside, he knew he had to exude a genuine appearance of a person with nothing to worry about. He looked at the whitewashed ceiling for insects to take his mind off the agents. Besides a fly buzzing around the light bulb, he saw nothing else. He got up from his chair and skirted around the table and chairs with his hands in his pockets. The room was very clean. No other insects existed there. He had to find something else to occupy his nervous mind. He found one in the recollection of the woman who had sat next to him. Undoubtedly, it had also been her first time traveling on a plane. Her marveling at the airplane and uncouth comments about the views below, when everything else was a desert of blackness save for lights on the plane's wings, told the story of someone who, before that time, might have thought of a plane as a crocodile thrown off some planet. Gyambibi had been resting his head on the armrest, but he had still gotten an earful of her unsolicited biography.

She was pulled out of school because her parents couldn't afford her and her two brothers' fees. She sold smoked fish with her mother until she was nineteen, when she earned enough money to sell slippers. When she saved enough, she branched out into secondhand clothing. The business was challenging, but she clung to it. One of the male hawkers, from whom she took advice on her trade, expressed a romantic interest. They merged their businesses and married before he left for Great Britain. He sent her letters monthly, which her brothers would read and translate for her. Even after they were away in school, she went to them to read her letters for her. So there she was; after nine years, her husband had finally sent for her. That spoke to the faithfulness, studiousness, and honesty of this man. The praise-singing for her husband went on long enough to distract Gyambibi from his fear of flying. The woman then asked Gyambibi's ethnicity because he spoke Twi with a tinge of Fanti.

"I have an Ashanti father and a Fanti mother," he answered.

When Gyambibi mentioned that he was from an area near Aduman and Kodee, he learned she was from Tetrem. From then on, he was interested in talking to the woman because he had heard about Tetrem but had never met anybody from there. He disclosed that he had heard his grandfather was from Tetrem. When she got up to use the lavatory, Gyambibi realized all the talking was refreshing, as it took his mind off the jolts the plane experienced when it hit pockets of wind, which otherwise would have sent him into another round of nausea. The pilot's promise of a smooth flight was a disappointment. The woman's first words when she returned were to ask his grandfather's name. When he told her Yaw Donyinah, recognition of the name added another passenger's voice to the discussion. What a small world! She had heard the name many times from her mother. Gyambibi had to tell her to lower her voice.

Moreover, all the stories she had heard associated with that name bordered on a folktale. She looked at Gyambibi closely, and his handsomeness was a replica of the legend associated with that name. She said she would have to call her siblings and relatives to tell them that her mother hadn't suffered from schizophrenia or, worse, witchcraft. She may have been among the many women jilted by Yaw Donyinah. Recalling that conversation was a refreshing respite from the windowless room Gyambibi found himself in.

If Preprah was so sure that the officers in the US couldn't tell them apart, why send him through Britain? Preprah's answer, which seemed reassuring at first, now seemed worrisome. Moreover (it just occurred to him), there might be people of Ghanaian ethnicity working at the airport. Couldn't those people tell him from Preprah? He barely finished that thought when he realized Agent Margaret was standing in front of him.

"You're nervous. Why are your eyes so red?" she asked.

Gyambibi reeled back in the chair, jittery. A sweat broke out under his armpits and trickled down his sides. He wasn't fancifully dressed. His father had bought him a three-piece twill suit for the journey, which he later realized wouldn't be proper. His father had also bought him singlets, seven pairs of pants, and fifteen shirts packed in a Samsonite suitcase. He couldn't take a suitcase full of clothes because it wouldn't support his story of someone who had made an emergency trip to Ghana to bury his mother; instead, it would implicate someone traveling abroad for the first time. He was now wearing a Bonsoir dress shirt and tweed pants—the latter heavily starched, creased, and reminiscent of his military days. He couldn't mimic Preprah's fashion sensibility and refused to wear the clothes that Preprah had suggested. The left-facing fly pants and Lacoste shirt he had recommended were clearly for women. Preprah must have thought they were for the left-handed.

Cold sweat trickling down his sides caused Gyambibi to itch, but he was too anxious to scratch. A blend of nervousness and sadness overcame him—he could be sent back and left unable to help those who needed him. Failing to explain why his eyes were red with nervousness would unravel his scheme. He knew that. The answer came to him before Margaret completed the question, but he held off answering because his conscience stood in the way. Yet on the other side of his conscience, the pressures of poverty stood tall. None of the money Preprah had promised to fund this trip, namely the plane fare and fee for the intermediary, made it to him. His father had to acquire a loan, for Preprah was still unemployed.

"What a hard life she lived! I was a difficult child, but she didn't give up on me. I'm emotionally broken because my mother didn't live long enough to enjoy the fruits of her sacrifice in raising a troubled son who's now an engineer in America. Just sad, and I'm emotionally broken, madam. I just buried her...I've told you already. The memory is raw."

Taking longer to answer the question added the effect of someone in deep emotional pain. Agent Margaret left the room and returned with her partner. They didn't wear that questioning look they had sported in the beginning.

"Is this passport yours?" she demanded.

"Yes!"

Inchoate excitement shot through Gyambibi's bones because the agents couldn't tell him from Preprah, although the dissimilarities were so glaring that his skin began to laugh within the privacy of his shirt.

The first day he got hold of Preprah's passport, he almost gave up because there was no way anyone, White or not, couldn't tell him apart from Preprah. He studied the picture for weeks to mimic himself after it. Then he gave the passport to Danfo for safekeeping until he boarded the plane, as Preprah had directed. Besides the fact that he was Black, male, and had a haircut mimicking Preprah's balding head, there was no way he should be confused with that dolichocephalic countenance. Despite Preprah's hairline receding from a vast, pimpled promontory of a forehead glistening with shea butter, somehow Gyambibi clung to the idea that he wouldn't be found out. Again, the echoes: to Whites, all Black folks look alike. Yet worrisome was the thought that he was considerably taller and had more sculptured features than Preprah, who also had a birthmark on his right cheek. Well, you couldn't determine one's height from a passport picture. He assured himself that the agents couldn't see past his Blackness and the fact that he was male. Their minds had superimposed Preprah onto him without registering the glaring inconsistencies. Being asked if the passport was his reassured him that they weren't dubious if the person sitting in front of them was the same person in the passport; if they knew the two were different, they wouldn't waste their time asking.

Gyambibi was excited after Agent Luckburn whispered something to Margaret and left the room. They might search his luggage again, he thought. Nothing to dread; everything in it belonged to him. He looked about casually. Though Agent Margaret's eyes were trained on him, his sweating had stopped. He wanted to keep it that way and needed another mental distraction. Just then, he remembered something he had overlooked in his preparation: Preprah wore an earring. Which way is the face oriented when taking a passport picture—a bit to the right or the left? The answer couldn't come to him; he had never taken one. Was Preprah's earring in the left or right ear? His brain started to overheat. He had no mirror in front of him, but he knew the anxiety he felt then turned his eyes blood red. Could the agents have seen this discrepancy? He turned slightly left and then right, intending to hide the "ring ear" from Agent Margaret.

Meanwhile, he kept his eyes away from her as she continued to stare. An idea came to him. He planned to say it was a clip-on, but his hyperactive conscience intervened. He was uneasy with yet another lie and nervous at the thought of lying becoming routine. But he wouldn't have to lie, for it suddenly came to him that Preprah wore an earring only after his return from America, not as an idiot in Ghana when he had taken the passport picture.

Slowly his eyes returned to their natural color. Margaret asked him about his work and the trip he claimed to be returning from. Gyambibi knew she was looking for inconsistencies in his story and for signs of guilt as conveyed by his body language.

Why am I being detained? That was too forward and worrisome a question. He had played the part of one who was not worried or in a hurry to get to his destination, even if he didn't want to be late for his connecting flight. He had to maintain that façade. He knew his guilt would be laid bare without asking the question. He would have to rephrase it and attach a context to throw them off.

"This isn't my first transit through Britain, madam. Is there a problem?"

Before Margaret finished saying he had to answer their questions, he asked for a cup of water. It was a pleasant exchange between the two. After the water, Margaret turned her attention to the task at hand, the cause of which Gyambibi didn't have a clue. As Margaret's questions mounted, he had difficulty keeping calm. He was bothered by their suspicion of him. He wanted to continue to appear like someone with nothing to worry about. He would achieve that by splitting his mind in two: half responded to her; the other half recalled a discussion en route to Kotoka International Airport. Danfo's dislike of Nyamenkum the Gossip and his constant troubles with her were discussed during the airport drive. The story of the origin of their animus was as follows: Danfo had taken up taxi driving on his first attempt at "escaping" from Enkoho. This was when he learned that his wife, Esi Eluwah, was too insubordinate to his liking; he had asked her to make meals for him for work, but she had refused because he didn't give her enough money for food. If she were to send him off with food, that would reduce what she had prepared for the week. As a result, on the first day of his job, he prepared his food, ate to his fill, and packaged the rest to go. His first passenger was a young woman, her daughter, and her son. Their destination was Prempeh College. This was when Esi Eluwah and Danfo had moved to Nkenkaasu, not far from where he'd picked up the passengers. They drove south, and along the way, Danfo noted that his belly was rising like leaven-treated dough. Soon, his stomach began to growl. Desiring to make a good impression on his first passengers, he kept driving until a couple of miles within view of the college. He knew the food he had made wanted to exit his body through every orifice. He kept his discomfort to himself, shutting off his thoughts of everything around him, focusing only on getting relief from the violent whirlwind running amok in his gut. He leaned sideways to create an outlet for the overbearing growl of magma bubbling under him, but the rearview mirror reminded him of his passengers. He was forced to pull off the road. With his hand over his mouth to calm his eructation and stomach cramping, he ran to a nearby bush and yielded to the inevitable. When he returned about a half-hour later, his passengers had left. For the next few hours, he drove about looking for them. The incident spread throughout Enkoho when Danfo moved back, through Nyamenkum the Gossip when she recognized him. Danfo had been ashamed by her recount of the incident, including embarrassing details Danfo thought only he knew. And twenty years ago was the first time his fist tasted her rumormongering mouth. He had waited patiently until he met her at the farm. His first of many encounters with the elders, Danfo had said they shouldn't preside over this case unless they themselves were wizards. Nyamenkum the Gossip's injuries were a matter fit for the witch court because she was a witch—a daring one. He explained that he had been in the forest hunting when he saw Nyamenkum the Gossip flying high in the sky.

"I summoned the help of God, then Jesus. Nothing happened. If I hadn't done something fast, she would have killed me. I summoned the Holy Spirit, and thunder cracked across the sky with dense flickers of lightning. I saw her fall from the sky, and then I fell backward. The next thing I heard was a loud crash. She had struck a tree, tumbled down its limbs, and fallen to the ground. It takes a skillful witch to fall over thirty meters and not break her bones."

As evidence, Danfo presented a log of contused wood as Nyamenkum the Gossip's flight vehicle, which some people had seen him carrying hurriedly from the forest. All heard the thunder, and all saw the lightning. Both seemed out of place. The memorable lightning had sent fire down Karikari's palm tree and torched some of its fronds. Everyone remembered it. There was no rain or clouds—just thunder and lightning, coinciding with Danfo's version of events.

The memory and step-by-step recount of the event calmed Gyambibi—the calmest he had been since the interrogation began.

Agent Margaret left the room, unable to tell Gyambibi had been distracted by something the entire time. Gyambibi feigned a sneeze to hide his laughter. He straightened his collar, smoothed the wrinkles in his pants, and paced the claustrophobic room. A third agent who stood mostly outside the door took the place of Luckburn. This agent and Margaret ordered Gyambibi to his seat. In her hand was his passport. Gyambibi glanced at his watch. Several hours had passed. He asked what time it was and learned their times diverged by five hours. In a panic, he asked if his flight had left several hours ago. They reminded him that New York was five hours behind their time zone and added that he had been with them for only eight minutes. Gyambibi realized his error and quickly muttered that he wanted them to be conscious of the time of his connecting flight. They told him it was about two hours away. His time disorientation resolved, he sat up confidently. By all indications, as far as he could tell, he was in the clear. He had ample time to refresh and collect himself before boarding the connecting flight.

"You say this passport is yours," Agent Margaret reiterated.

"That's correct, madam...sir," Gyambibi replied.

"Did you answer truthfully?"

"No reason not to."

"Just tell us if this is truly yours."

"I don't understand."

"Tell me if this is you!"

Agent Margaret tossed the passport at him, which glided across the table. He understood what they were doing, so he would take the passport, pretend to examine it and tell them that it was indeed him as he had claimed. However, what was supposed to be a casual glance turned into something else. As he looked at the picture, his heart fluttered; his palms were covered in sweat. On the passport's picture page was a woman wearing braids, her lips subtly parted by the excitement of a chance to be going to America. It was Efia.

Chapter

32

"**T**here aren't any good men left in the world," Efia told her grandmother after another romantic relationship dissolved.

Adwoa Brago told her granddaughter: "No, it's you who are impressing upon men that no good women are left in the world. Every terrible man or woman wants a good woman or man to marry. It beats common sense why it doesn't come to you, or them, that good men and women aren't looking for terrible women and men like you. You dare say such foolishness in this hut? Hasn't life taught you anything at thirty-eight, that marriage is a lifelong journey to be undertaken with all the seriousness in the world? I'm unaware of a relationship that ends on good terms. It's oxymoronic. Your relationship disintegrates, fine, but after that, shouldn't you stay unattached for as long as it takes until you find a man who embodies your long-term relationship ideals? Not you. One relationship ends, then you hop on the next man who walks by. When another man you think suits you better comes along, you latch on to him until another 'better man' shows up. You park there until yet another better man turns up. Your school days were spent chasing after men and not studying, and you want to make up for what could have been a rewarding life by jumping from one man to another and hoping to strike gold one day? What reputational trail are you leaving for men to see? They're also saying, 'There aren't any good women left in the world.' There surely are more rotten men than there are women, but you, of all women, dare say something about that? After leaving a relationship, shouldn't your goal be not to let history get too excited about repeating itself? This time you got involved with a married man with children; you came into that knowledge at a certain point and still kept pursuing him. What outcome did you foresee trying to get on board a moving train, Efia? You were already involved with Mrs. Sackey's son when this married man entered the picture. You had both feet in a relationship while your hands scoured the world for other men at the same time. And now you're bitter because a man has done to you what you've been doing to other men? Have you forgotten the golden rule? I forget that people like you think doing the right thing belongs only in thought and not in action. I don't feel sorry for you. Look elsewhere for sympathy. The whole forest takes notice the day you turn over a new leaf."

Chapter

33

*P*reprah angrily wrote to Gyambibi after his repatriation:

I didn't think I needed to tell you to keep your travel plans to yourself. That you would be so careless when Enkoho is anything but normal troubles the mind. Your repatriation occurred because your plans got to Agya Kobi. It was expected that you would tell your father. My father knew because he was the conduit for the consummation of the plan details. It was understandable to tell Moro because he's your best friend, but why tell Mawuli? Why tell Jeefa, Daavi? That was how your plans got to the devil. Jeefa must have told the White girl with a craving for death, who, in turn, told Agya Kobi. And here we are! Now my passport is confiscated. I should have heeded my inner voice: having broken free from the hold of Enkoho, any further entanglements with it could reverse my luck. How on God's Earth could a man's picture turn into a woman's? And is this transformation temporary or permanent? I hope it's permanent so it will not be traced to me. I'm not worried about the name being linked to me because they'd think someone was trying to impersonate me. If not, how do I file for a missing passport after it has been linked to illegal entry to the US without implicating myself? I could face prison time and repatriation. Gyambibi, what happened to your intelligence that once enthralled all of us? Luck, help me!

Karikari learned of Gyambibi's repatriation from Danfo. He took the news well, with the help of alcohol. He was resigned to the reality that failure wasn't the anomaly but the norm when it came to his life. Gyambibi hid in the barracks, embarrassed to return to Enkoho. Beyond embarrassment, the magical transformation of Preprah's picture to the likeness of Efia awakened his sleeping fear of the dark forces that inhabited Enkoho.

Chapter

Memories of Blood

*T*he desire to thrive finds refuge in the fertile mind of the hopeful while the hopeless wither away under the crushing yoke of life's tedium. Before day's end, Karikari would have lived on both ends of these words that had kept him motivated in times of having it all—words that now meant little more than nothing as hard times rolled on. His days were fraught with emptiness and uncertainty, and his nights turned into sleepless days. The wiles of materialism ensured that the nights he spent in bed to sleep off the worries of life were instead spent retracing the thorny paths to prosperity. He sometimes envisioned himself climbing a rope ladder frayed three rungs from the top, at the very end of which was tied the fruit of prosperity. Midway into the climb, he would become aware of a yoke strapped to his back that would impede his ascent. He became nervous about the frayed rope, but then wings would appear on both sides of him, stretching to the ends of the horizon. With that, he forgot about the dangers and made it up the frayed rope— only to fall to the bottomless vale below, the wings having disappeared. On other nights he saw his future in the stilled waters of a lake: he would swim great distances but couldn't leave the confines of the lake. One day, he made it out of the lake but was kept at its bank. He wondered why his shadow wouldn't leave the lake too. He stared down into the water until he woke up. Whatever the oneiric symbolisms, waking reality convinced him that his hands couldn't get hold of the paradise that his heart had dreamed up. His dreams dissolved in the stagnant waters of a lake and never manifested in his preferred land of boundless fortune. Most mornings, upon waking, his sore body and the tear- and sweat-stained pillow recounted the trails of his tortuous midnight journeys. His legs ached, unwilling to get out of bed; they had given up for covering so much distance that never got him any closer to his paradise. The challenges of reclaiming his former life had gone from daunting to insurmountable.

A tragedy of life: anxiety now replaced comforts, and convenience took the place of choice for his children, who no longer consumed from bountiful choice but from what convenience brought them. Soon, the quantity of food became an issue, and the brothers no longer ate from two separate bowls. When Yaw's hand fetched food from the bowl, he watched to ensure Gyambibi duplicated the amount he had taken, not more. A familiar memory from Karikari's childhood turned his stomach sour. Times were hard, but the worst hadn't even arrived. Fate knew he was right to think so. He was certain that life would glue his eyes open to the devastation of his misfortune on his children, who hadn't known pain in life, only stories of his childhood that he had told them, including his first suicide attempt. Karikari didn't want to live to see his children suffer. Perhaps his way out was digging up the treasure? Yet this was unthinkable because if he made a mistake or overlooked a detail, the deaths of his sons were also certain.

After years of pursuing that which continued to elude him, he ran his fingers through his beard one day, feeling the pressure to end it all. After Mawuli left for the second of his biannual visits to the Volta Region, Karikari went to the farm alone. Rarely did he ever do this, but no one made much of it. It was the weekend, and Tabuah wouldn't be visiting. She had noticed a change in her brother, but nothing overtly alarming other than the observation that he was unkempt.

Karikari knelt in front of a palm tree. Of all the vegetation on the farm, this palm tree and a few others had survived the cataclysm, pest infestation, and other agronomic adversities. His own hands had planted it at the urging of his maternal grandmother. It was the same palm tree that marked Agnes's burial site.

The palm tree was like his first child. It symbolized where he had been before fortune found him and was a testament to years of happiness and how life was supposed to be after his grandmother's death. It was a part of him. Over the past several weeks, he had mulled his connection to the farm and, significantly, his emotional connection to this palm tree. It made some sense to include it in his final decision. They started life together, so it made sense they would end it together. He had tapped it days before—for wine. Kneeling in front of it, he lifted the gourd into which the wine had dripped. It was all alcohol now. Agnes and his unborn child were buried adjacently, and only two steps took him there. He told them about his decision and determination to join them before the day was over.

Karikari reflected on his life: as far as he could remember, his problems had started at a young age, beginning with the death of his mother. By Agya Kobi's account, Karikari had spent sixteen months in the womb. Such prolonged gestation might have presaged his destiny of struggles. It was as if his destiny was intricately intertwined with poverty: no matter how hard he tried to slip out of its grasp, like a jilted lover who wouldn't let go, somehow, someway, poverty always found him. He was frozen in it. His thoughts jumped from one subject to another, all having to do with his hard life. Nothing had come to him easily. At twelve, he had to drop out of school to fend for himself because his mother had died giving birth to Tabuah. They were then shuffled between relatives whose attention was mostly on their own children. One morning his uncle, with whom he and his sister were staying, woke up to find Karikari gone, leaving his sister behind. His uncle wasn't interested in his whereabouts; he only wondered why he hadn't taken his sister with him. There was a stash of money in Karikari's grandmother's pillow that was supposed to be his and his sister's after the grandmother's death. The pillow and its contents disappeared when she passed. Karikari suspected his uncle. Save for the grandmother and a few others, the buried treasure had claimed the lives of most of Karikari's relatives before he returned to Enkoho.

Karikari had worked as a porter and sometimes as a shoeshine boy on the streets of Accra Central. In the evening, without a place to call home, he slept in vacant kiosks. He recalled going there after work, often crying himself to sleep, wondering what had become of his sister. He was a child, incapable of providing for both of them. The thought of bringing her to live with him was painfully unfeasible. He was too young to be on his own. One day, he carried a load for some shoppers accompanied by their son, who was about the same age as him. The load was a bag of maize, more than half the weight of his emaciated frame. He would periodically steal a glance at the boy and then at the boy's parents, crying in his heart at the kind of family he and his sister would have had if their mother hadn't died. He stole a glance at the boy again. The longer he stared at him, the more familiar he became. Finally, he remembered who he was: Opoku Afriyie. He had certain distinguishable features: well-attired, talkative, and fleshy due to his affluent background. No one had better grades than him in class. He was Chief's nephew.

Additionally, not only did his parents buy him all the required and recommended books, but he also had a private tutor. Even though most of his classmates felt repulsed by his standoffish ways, Karikari liked him. Afriyie was superior to him academically, but he knew that shouldn't be a reason to be envious of him, as was the manner of some of his schoolmates. He had gone to him occasionally for help with schoolwork. Afriyie had helped him once but had declined subsequent lessons because his parents had told him to focus on himself.

Karikari was lanky, wore the same tattered clothes, and scrimped the little that came his way. He had a reason to thank God for his shabby appearance, for it concealed his identity from his former classmate. Interestingly, when he offloaded the bag of maize into the trunk of their van, Afriyie's parents were ready to hand him his pay when Afriyie pulled them aside. After a brief discussion, his father recounted the money and returned the rest to his wallet. Karikari was certain Afriyie had disapproved of his parents picking him to carry their load.

Why would he say something to make his parents rethink Karikari's remuneration? What did he say? Is that what money turns people into?

He retired to a vacant kiosk, characteristically quiet and un-aware of greetings from his friend Salifu, a crippled panhandler, with whom he had formed a familial bond. Salifu hadn't been born crippled. His parents had had difficulty conceiving. They told him he was a miracle baby, but he never knew why. What he did know was that after his birth, his father didn't work on Saturdays anymore. As a cattle herder, his father worked Monday through Saturday. They would go to church on Sundays. His father added Saturday to their days of worship, mainly fasting and praying. This change in his work habit was to show his eternal thankfulness to God for the child. Then came the fateful day: the first and only Saturday after his birth that his father took the cattle to the field. Why this came to be, he didn't know, but he remembered his father proudly telling his mother that he would like his son to learn the ways of cattle herding. In the afternoon, his mother cooked a meal for his father and took it to him. With a glint in her eye, his mother only told Salifu that his father had a surprise for him. The cattle became incensed at the sight of them for reasons his father couldn't say. They ran amok, stampeding. Salifu fell when he ran, and the stampede trampled his spine, immobilizing him instantly. He couldn't have been more than six years old. He didn't remember much about what happened afterward, except being in the hut of a herbalist. When his parents visited, his mother always cried. His father never had a tear in his eye. However, what he saw in his father was the same thing he recognized in Karikari: something was broken. His parents were never the same. Then he saw them no more. Chances were that the stress of his deformity and the struggles he would go through in life might have killed his father. His mother may have taken her life after that. Salifu couldn't say in certain terms what had happened to them, but he knew that if they were alive, they would be in his life. All the cousins he knew, all the aunts and uncles, they couldn't have all died too—but he never saw any of them after that. He didn't remember the hundreds of miles of the journey to Accra. What he remembered was that God chose a day that his father had dedicated to Him to make him a cripple and remove his parents from the earth. This was the story he had told Karikari when they first met.

Karikari's chin rested uncomfortably in the cradle of his open palms, his sad eyes staring at the floor of the kiosk. He cried to see the face of his deceased mother. He meditated on the words of his ex-schoolmate until he fell asleep. Hours later, Salifu heard him sobbing, prompting him to break his silence and talk about what was consuming his friend. After sharing the details of his incident, Salifu said:

"Karikari, don't be too hard on yourself. Don't resent that rich boy in your heart, either. Remember, brother, only you can identify with what you, *we*, are going through. Don't expect others who are well off to understand. Look at me: I don't know if my parents are dead or alive. What I do know is that somebody took me to an orphanage, where people with pain greater than my own surrounded me. I had to leave. Did my parents take me to the orphanage because they were ashamed of me? Are they alive? Has God blessed them with other children whom they're not ashamed of? I can go to Bawku for answers, but I won't. If I find even one 'yes' to my questions, the shock won't allow me to see the next day, so I prefer not to know. Whenever we're late going somewhere, and you're in a hurry, I can tell you wish I could hurry as much as you. I don't get upset with you because I alone can understand that. You have two functional legs. I never get angry with you, even though I hurt inside, because you're my only family. I'm nearly two years older than you, but I find in you my younger and older brother. I say nothing even when you offend me because I don't want you to resent me."

Karikari remained somber, although by now, he was tinged with solace.

"People hear my story, but painfully, some think it a clever lie to win sympathy. I'm a panhandler, after all. No parents who struggled with conception would abandon their child no matter his disability, people whisper in my absence. Many a night, I've cried myself to sleep. Sometimes it's better to hide your story; it causes less pain than to share it and be met with doubt. If I could grow legs, the first use I'd put them to is to walk to my Creator and ask one question: 'God, why?' You're my only family, Karikari. Your relatives have abandoned you, and that's your main issue. I, too, have been abandoned. But know this: our lives won't be this way forever because seasons change."

Karikari took these words to heart and, years later, realized how prophetic his friend's last words were. As was true of his character, he didn't forget about Salifu. When he inherited his grandmother's farm, he went back for Salifu and a couple of others with whom he had toiled on the streets of Accra Central. However, because Salifu was a cripple, Karikari didn't want him to do farmwork. While the others worked the farm, Salifu stayed behind and kept stock of harvested crops and sales. He proved trustworthy and hardworking. Without a wheelchair, he moved about by dragging himself on the ground—relying on his muscular arms.

Their bond wasn't familial, but in a profound way, it was. Their bond was so genuine that Yaw and Gyambibi thought Salifu was their father's actual older brother—hence naming him "Uncle Salifu."

A spirited man full of life and goodness, Salifu was always happy. He didn't allow the unpleasantness of life to derail his happiness nor the strain of his infirmity to inhibit him from putting smiles on the faces of the downtrodden and fortunate alike. But just like sprouting foliage indiscriminately cut down by a disgruntled farmer, Salifu's life was cut short, perishing in the cataclysm with Agnes. Karikari never had closure because Uncle Salifu's body was never found.

Karikari took a sip of the wine and blew off the foam that had formed around the mouth of the gourd. He stared into the river. The ripples caricatured his reflection into a grayed, scraggly man several decades older than his age. He laughed. With his arms outstretched and gaze fixated on the heavens, he muttered under his breath. Again, there was prolonged laughter from him, then another gulp of the wine, which found its way past his epiglottis into his lungs. He coughed so hard that his ribs began to hurt. The laughter still didn't escape him among these mumblings and wild gesticulations. He beat his chest and yelled to expectorate the frustration.

He walked about to strips of dry bagasse from the plantain plant he had felled weeks ago and separated each into strips of elongated fibers. He tied the ends until a rope of about ten meters emerged. Satisfied with the quality of the rope, he made a noose out of one end. Then, as if confused, he leered about, finally locking his eyes on a boulder and walking over to it. He tied the free end of the rope around the boulder and threw the end with the noose over an overhanging tree branch. Birds sputtered off. The noose hung several meters off the ground. He pulled back the rope and slipped the neck of the gourd into its noosed end, tightened it, and slung it over his shoulder. After struggling to climb the tree, he untied the gourd and placed it in a cradle where the branches came out of the trunk. He slipped the noose around his neck in preparation for removing himself from the brunt of poverty's physical and psychological severities.

Are some people destined to be miserable in their short existence on Earth, while others attract the niceties of life no matter their shortcomings? If one is mired in the incongruities of life, is it a surety that one must endure the same until the end? Doesn't Destiny also have surprises, sometimes opening doors of opportunity when one is down? And if Destiny is frugal in providing for a broken man, doesn't the Will allow the Self to strive to overcome Destiny's frugality? And what of Providence! Doesn't Providence break through the unyielding affairs of Destiny on man's behalf to soften its grip on him? Don't Destiny and Providence collude with the Will to make life unpredictable, less monotonous, and more exciting?

Apathy seemed to have displaced Karikari's Will. He thought Providence and Destiny had no other purpose than to destroy him, and he couldn't do anything to stop them. He was on the verge of surrendering. He let out a grunt, feeling queasy as the minutes ticked away, wondering if this would be the day to end all the disappointments of his life. Inasmuch as a part of him loathed what he was about to do, he had depleted his stores of hope that would normally blunt against consideration of blatant self-destruction. Then again, why would one cling to life when detached from any reason to look forward to the next sun-up or sun-down?

Every man creates his own tomorrow by looking forward to living one more day. As such, and merited by his hopeless situation, it seemed right on this day, at this time, for Karikari to stop creating more of his tomorrows. Assuredly, this would rid him of life's challenges and pain in all its varied manifestations, particularly the constant struggle to come out ahead and escape the indignities of failure. Living in doubt and fear of never being able to accumulate enough in life against the swift hand of time was also an inescapable drag.

Living through unpredictable cycles of pain, joy, and stagnation for reasons tied up in the crucible of one's destiny, man has an empty impression of his life's purpose. Yet when circumstances provoke the desire to achieve, he must find his purpose in life, pining for release from the tyrannical hold of poverty and the irritations of life, all while waving a scathed arm at humanity for rescue from drowning in the lake of utter hopelessness. Moreover, the burden of fulfilling the mandates of a perfect God on the one hand, against the expectations of imperfect man on the other, proves an unsettling challenge, as is dealing with the constant yearning of the Conscience to superimpose its dictates against the body to freely pursue the pleasantries of life, whether good or evil. How Karikari wished he could yield his body to all the toxic pleasures on Earth so that after his death, even if his family gave up his body to the elements, not even vultures would have use for it. Except, his conscience and fear of the retribution of God got in the way, always.

"Gyambibi! My son after my heart!" he exclaimed in an onslaught of emotional pain. Having recalled memories of his childhood, he also recalled that Gyambibi had spent fifteen months in the womb—a sign that he might be on the same path of suffering as him. His fears that Gyambibi's uncommon good looks and aura of debonair innocence would send him down the same reckless path as his father, Yaw Donyinah, seemed assured. Gyambibi's life thus far had followed a trail of unexplainable suffering; Karikari couldn't bear to see more of that. When this cycle of misfortune started, Karikari had laughed at one point for not being able to afford a new pair of shoes for Gyambibi, thinking it would soon pass. Unable to afford new shoes, he had to have the toecap of the shoes elongated instead to accommodate his growing feet. In hindsight, the memory was painful.

Was there an ethical encumbrance of what he was about to do? He wondered. Straightaway, he mulled the eventualities of war, looking for ways to rationalize its relationship with suicide, if any. This led him to the thought that both the religious and heathen alike could justify armed warfare. Participants of warfare do so volitionally on account of a marching order: kill or be killed to attain an end. In the vein of that logic, what is suicide then, if not to oblige the marching orders of one's inner voice to attain an end, say, to erase the pain of being thrust to the margin of existential decrepitude? How would his death differ from the heroine Yaa Asantewaa, who died in exile fighting the colonialists in the War of the Golden Stool? Why discriminate between one who dies for one's country in war and another who's a casualty of war within oneself? Who gets to decide if one is an act of valor and the other a self-seeking, cowardly betrayal? Can't both be equally selfish as well as valiant?

The sudden onslaught of ideas to fight off any thoughts that might discourage him from what he was about to do surprised him. It was as if there was a mind superior to his own, outside his body, which he could draw upon in complicated matters like this. What if suicide is a violation of the Creator's designated purpose for life, for humanity's use of free will? Karikari's conscience confronted him with yet more obstacles.

What is the Will? Do babies have a Will? Does every person have a Will? Do the mentally infirm have a Will? Suppose one mentally competent person burned down his neighbor's house in a rage. Suppose another, under a schizophrenic fit, burned down his neighbor's house for believing it harbored an invisible army sent to kill him. Wouldn't society be more forgiving of the latter than the former? Yet if both exercised their Will with the same outcome, why judge them differently? Does man excuse the action of the lunatic because his reality is distorted? If so, does it not mean the action emanating from the Will is subject to man's judgment—according to society's definitional perspective of reality? Does this not render the Will an illusion or a perception subject to man's interpretive license?

And what if all thoughts and deeds are tenants of man's destiny, thus predetermined and unable to be altered? Meaning Karikari's broken life and decisive suicide were preordained? If the Will isn't an illusionary artifact, could one exercise it to alter one's destiny? And if death is man's ultimate destiny, shouldn't suicide, an avenue of death, be something that man could sub-

ject himself to if he so willed it? Again, Karikari sought to subdue his dissenting conscience.

*What about one's tacit obligation to society in its collective
pilgrimage here on Earth? Why deny society the privilege to
learn from you, change your life, or benefit from your existence? Why deny your Creator the opportunity to mend the
mishaps of your broken life? Why not believe you can still win
the fight instead of surrendering midlife? Why don't you live
regardless and let natural circumstances dictate when you go?*

Did I hear you say that? I should determine to live and leave
my death to diseases and accidents, you say? And may I ask,
when do diseases and accidents have more rights over my body
than I do?

Did you go to God for help?

What do you think are my motivations for suicide? First,
I want nothing to do with this existence. Second, I want to
talk to God—face-to-face. I have questions for Him, and those
questions can't wait. I want to roast His logic for man's toilsome existence.

*What if you arrive at a different location other than where
God is and don't get to confront Him?*

I would still have one of two goals accomplished. Better odds
than my luck with moneylenders or anything I've put my hands
to in the past several years.

Perhaps the only person ever to do this, Karikari next counted
the pain in his life—not moments of pain but pain, as if it were
quantifiable—to see if it underwhelmed or overwhelmed his joy
in life. This would make it easier to decide between life and
death. But joy is something we recall on a whim, whereas pain
doesn't need our recall because its memory is always there: that
indelible burn that melts into the soul. The exercise revealed
something else: his pain and joy were intertwined. His pain had

its beginning in the decisions he had made in the time of joy. His joy had led to the path of pain. In the end, pain, which has a longer memory than joy, handed him the verdict of death: because life is nothing but an annoying distraction from the freedom from pain that death offers.

He might have overlooked some aspects of the impropriety of suicide, but before he could think any more about it, into the shade flew a piculet midway into Karikari's next swig of palm wine. The bird's quick reflexes took him in; in its head movements, as it surveyed its environment, he found a new appreciation for beauty. Surely, the bird couldn't have as many problems as he. Well, if anything, it may be escaping from a predator. That's its only worry—perhaps an occasional disturbance of its habitat too. Besides that, it has no problems. A sparrow flew by. Karikari noticed how alive it was. Then two more flew by, avoiding the tree as loquacious winds swayed it. The essence of life emanated from them too. Also, life glowed through a skink that morphed into a creek flowing into the river, which had turned semi-fluidly orange with alternating, glossy waves of red and green streaks. Butterflies were vibrant and colorful, hovering above vegetation with even livelier umbels. The world around him was more alive than he had ever seen it. He had attained oneness with the hidden beauty of the world. Everything was alive, including grains of sand, as he would soon see.

Music was also alive, but not in the florid sense as portrayed by poets; it was alive like humans. He heard music. He saw music. Segments of a song that touched and resonated with his feelings were repeated in a discordant fashion, like a broken record. However, it didn't sound broken. It was seamless like it was composed to be.

How come this seemed a new reality? Perhaps, he thought, the pursuits of life had blinded him to these.

Are you getting away from your friends, the sparrows that flew by?

He mimicked an embrace and hoped the piculet would oblige. The bird, however, had dug its beak into its feathers and was ruffling them. He laughed at the bird for pecking at his overture. Nevertheless, he appreciated its lack of concern. How fortunate this bird is, he thought. How free. It can fly away from its problems and find a new home, new friends, and a new life without having to worry about gossip over its abandoned past life. It didn't have to worry about its chicks, for after they leave the nest, unlike man, they will not return, even after living in the harshest conditions of the real world. How fortunate it would be to be a bird. How fortunate it would be not to know shame! Agitating the tree after the gourd made another trip to his mouth, the alarmed bird sputtered off. He sighed, alone again. His eyes filtered through the porous canopy of leaves, watching as the bird flew into patches of radiating clouds, turning them into a soothing blend of wild colors known and unknown to man.

The bird flew downward into another tree. Karikari was drawn to it and kept staring at it. Staring and staring until it was no longer a piculet but a horned owl. He rubbed his eyes. It was a horned owl. It opened its beak. Karikari couldn't have foreseen what would happen next, the ornithological progression of what the bird had started. It pulled its upper beak backward between its horns until it disappeared into its head. Its lower beak stretched downward into its neck. Then it shrieked from an endless cavern of throat. Karikari could see an essence drifting from his head into the owl's mouth. The beaks reemerged from the owl's head and neck. Then the wind swayed the forest, sending branches that blinded his line of sight. When it cleared, the owl was gone. How helpful could owls be? How was it that he had never noticed owls could be this helpful?

Then the piculet reemerged where the owl had been, this time on a tamarind tree. It frolicked to Haydn's *Agnus Dei*, interrupting the ensuing silence. From another side emerged Mozart's *Lacrimosa*. The tunes dredged up memories of that long-lost craving for a carnival of sweet sounds that had the strength to subdue a troubled human spirit. The mystery of who was playing the songs on the farm occupied him for several minutes until, sandwiched between these two songs, a flute arose carrying Kofi Sammy's *Agyanka Due—Orphan, My Condolence*.

The syncretic melodies merged into a colorful mist and spun upward, breaking a cloud into colors more intense and inviting than anything he had ever seen. Though they had blended into one harmonious melody, he couldn't break from the emotional cadence that the songs evoked separately.

Suddenly he was overwhelmed by memories of his childhood and adulthood, memories of his entire life—nothing pleasant, just repressed memories of the pain of persisting in the droughts of life. He looked all around for the presence of Agya Kobi. He wasn't there. He wasn't even in the country, to be certain, as he had gone to neighboring Togo to visit his granddaughter, Efia, who was married there. It didn't come to him that Agya Kobi's name had passed through his mind without his being incensed.

To Karikari's estimate, the tree on which the bird perched was about fifty yards away. From that distance, the tamarind tree seemed scorched by atmospheric adversities. It moved forward with a droopy gait, its branches covered in alternating stripes of bloody and blackish pus, as well as enchanting mystery, moving in intricate patterns that gave life to the dead tree. It seemed lonely, like him, and that spoke to his soul. Its limbs were like warped memories of death piercing the heavens. He could see gelatinous cakes of black ooze from its twisted bark. He wondered if the tree was indeed fifty yards away; no, it couldn't be more than twenty yards away. Taking a breath and still fixated on the tree, he took several swigs of wine and determined again, with a newfound assurance and mathematical precision, that it couldn't be more than four yards away, a close enough distance to have a conversation with the distinctly visible bird against the backdrop of a fuzzy blur.

When he resumed conversation with the bird, he noted that everywhere he looked, nature itself was frustrated with living and empathized with him. Some of nature's neglected tenants spoke with him in strange tongues, requiring him to summon his linguistic portfolio (imparted by the spirit of nature itself) to help him make sense of what he was being told. At the foot of the tree, a dejected grain of sand looked up at him, saying it couldn't live any longer after being ostracized from the company of xenophobic red clay with whom it shared ancestry.

"God *created* everything, man included. And man is *uncreating* everything, God included," said a rusted washbasin with urgent forthrightness before seeping through the alkaline pores of the dying Earth. A senile leaf had shed all of its moisture for crying incessantly because it was on the verge of being destalked from the community of leaves for its poverty of chlorophyll. Last to contribute to this extemporaneous outpour was an itinerant mirid that left the gathering in a torrent of tears after relating its impending death due to the scorching toxicity of pesticides that had despoiled its relatives of the unmerited gift of existence. It would, therefore, die, its corpse littering the forest floor without the benefit of a burial. "See how man has raped God's virgin Earth!? We see here man's painful design to assert his relevance above all else, to rid the earth of the memory of others on a discretionary whim!"

The ground trembled with weary cries of humanity. A stream of tears swallowed up a litter of decomposed dreams and hopes and dragged them along its path, forming a tributary along the river.

While he dwelt in the tree, he lowered the gourd from his mouth after yet another drink and let go of it. It crashed on the bulged root of the tree and shattered, sputtering its content. Then everything became quiet. He noticed that the dead tree was now a lonely hundred yards away. All movements had slowed so much that his frustration with life passed before him as ripples of confused dreams. A whydah in flight, a foraging doe and her fawn were all silent. Even the anxious winds had acquiesced. The remote sounds of hoes tilling the earth and cutlasses slicing through weeds were filtering through the silence. He could hear a handsaw seething at a bough. The air was no longer air but a trickling sweat of pain and struggle. In these, he heard the stories of how tiresomely man had to prune the Tree of Life for food. Indeed, there is nothing easy about life if one is constrained by honest work. Such is life: happiness is too farfetched, and hardship is too entangled with daily existence. But the unpleasantness of life wouldn't be complete without our fellow man piling pain on top of an already toilsome existence. Alas! If only the heavy hand of God could stay away too.

Karikari heard the footsteps of people returning to the village, although he was several yards removed from the main path to the farms. Before, he didn't think others were on the farm, but he was wrong. Except these weren't people, per se, but light with strong emotional essence. He knew they were humans, although they had no physical forms. Fear was aroused in him but not sufficiently to make him want to run away. Hadn't he seen humans like these before? Then he remembered the only other time he had seen people this way: before the palm tree against his house crushed Asamoah to death. Recalling the sad event, Karikari's conscience held no pain for the boy, not because he died years ago and the pain of his death had washed away but because he now realized that death seemed more worthwhile than life. That poor boy had more to gain from death than continuing on. As he watched the people disappear on the path, he noticed another light, black, moving away from the path as if hiding as another person appeared, this time coming from the village. He knew the human identities of all the lights and what they were doing, save for the intent of the one hiding. Karikari had already submitted to the pull of death to care about the intentions of the living. That is, except for the intention of this man, well known to him, drifting behind the trees.

His attention diverted from the man to the mirid. "We all descended from the Garden of Eden, after all," Karikari said, intending to persuade the departing mirid that, be it today or some other day, willfully or not, everyone will have to part with a world that isn't theirs to seek eternal rest beyond the reach of man's decadence. Before he was finished, the mirid was gone, still aggrieved by its imminent demise.

Karikari turned his attention skyward. Everything was alive. He looked around, and the youthful essence of life glowed through everything. If this was Destiny's way of deterring him...

Death returned with its conniving sophistry: in what sense could Life hold more value than Death when Life, despite all its protests, eventually surrenders to Death? A sincere answer Karikari could find in his heart alone and nothing else. That is to say, an inventory of his life and not somebody else's would yield a truthful answer. For life is what he had lived, not how others believed it to be. This, in a way, undermined his conscience's pleadings for life because at the forefront of him was the running sore of his own reality—searing poverty, pain, and weariness—not the ephemeral, evasive artifice of happiness he had pursued to date. He had fed the entire village at one point but now struggled to feed his own family. The crux of his argumentation was simple: forget everybody, for in death, in dying, or in the pursuit of death, selfishness is a virtue. In death, the living is separated from the nonliving so dying, or the pursuit of death, should be an exercise to keep the living away. When he was in pain, he alone felt his pain. When not afflicted by his pain, the pain of others was with him. So each day, when the sun's forgetfulness made it show its face on Earth once again, and when remembrance sent it away to return to the departed heavens, in that entire expanse of time, he tended to the burden of pain, whether his or not. He awoke in pain and went to bed in pain. His only reprieve came on rare nights when sleep filtered out the worries of life. He craved such nights; if only they were unwakeable. He wouldn't have to accept others' reasoning to live. Sure, others had traveled the same path as him but allowed logic to pull them away from death. Surely logic was able to persuade them with the funereal faces of their daughters, sons, mothers, fathers, sisters, husbands, wives, neighbors, or friends. But if the living cannot be grateful for your lifetime of feeling their pain, thinking your suicide is selfish and are saddened by it, then they never deserved your empathy in the first place because your suicide is that one time you cared more about yourself than them. But why value personal relationships above the value of your own decision to surrender to death when all will eventually surrender to it? Why live in eternal pain while clinging to the hope of a life that may never bear out? When you can't see or hope beyond your present condition and your mind remembers nothing but your own failures, doesn't living turn into humiliation? Why look to another for a reason to live when one doesn't live for another?

Karikari looked up; the departed heavens weren't returning to Earth with answers. Life never has a happy ending when Death always stands at the end. The thought of prolonging life toward the inevitable, sorrowful ending when he was so close right now caused his mind to ache. Through the lofty leaves, he saw that the melodies, alive and frolicking, had cleaved through a string of rolling clouds. With the clouds parted, he had a foretaste of the life beyond when he perceived Uncle Salifu on extant feet and without traces of infirmity or worry, hollering, "Come home, brother. Come home!"

With that, Karikari lunged forward, casting aside all moral scruples, as Death welcomed him with a celebratory guffaw.

Chapter

35

" **T**he mirid, the mirid—tell him he won't die; life won't be this way forever. Life will change; it always does." Karikari wailed for the mirid when he regained consciousness. He yelled confusedly and belligerently; he was irritated because no one believed he could see air, hear insects talk, and even hear washbasins speak lucid language uncommon to humans. The villagers were convinced of Karikari's near insanity as they carried him to Healer for treatment, blood pouring from his severely wounded body.

The villagers had had enough. On the evening of Karikari's suicide attempt, a mob took matters into their impoverished hands. An inferno raged, aided by the nocturnal wind, fire screaming in all directions of Agya Kobi's hut. The thatch was gone in no time, and the trusses smoldered. If the villagers' frustration with evil could melt clay, the proof was here. Leading the mob, Danfo had brought the gallons of kerosene and gasoline he had stored in Karikari's house. The intent was to burn down Agya Kobi's hut and everybody in it.

"Enough is enough!" yelled someone from the mob.

First, the rainstorm had robbed them of their possessions. Then the mirid infestation ruined their harvests. Now Karikari's attempted suicide! All spoke to the evil among them that they had to annihilate. Danfo led the mob in chants as Agya Kobi's hut screamed in flames. The victory was celebrated with gallons of palm wine. They were intoxicated before setting fire to what they thought was Agya Kobi's hut. They were doubly intoxicated during and afterward, except Danfo, who, inexplicably, was sober—perhaps for the first time since exiting the womb.

Early the next morning, the elders summoned the mob participants. After the intoxication had worn off, they realized their error: they had burned down Yaa Adubia's hut. Fortunately, no one was injured because she wasn't home. The incident happened during one of Yaa Adubia's attempts at *escaping* from the village. She had left right after carrying Karikari to Healer in a wheelbarrow. The elders charged Danfo and the mob with the responsibility of rebuilding Yaa Adubia's hut. The entire village lent a hand because Danfo's original intent of burning Agya Kobi and his hut was a good cause.

Uncertainty hung over the village with rumors of Karikari's attempted suicide. The rope had come apart in the middle; his face hit a branch and was propelled against another that cut deep in many places. He couldn't feel his legs when found. If Karikari had begun to crumble under the pressures of hardship, what hope could there be for the village? Healer massaged Karikari's wounds with a medicated poultice to stop his bleeding. He was administered a blood tonic. Healer couldn't say how long it would take Karikari to recover.

It was at Healer's place when it became clear that Karikari had begun to grow weary of God's mysterious ways. He would later shrink from Preacher and church services altogether though Preacher visited, read the Bible, and prayed with him. Karikari couldn't bring himself to throw Preacher out because he had nothing but goodwill in his heart, someone who came by not to beg alms but to give of himself.

Karikari also began to grow suspicious of the global order in which countries like Ghana were shortchanged in international commerce by more powerful nations. He began to distrust the leaders of Ghana, who located paradise outside the borders of the country they were entrusted to lead, the same leadership that didn't grow opportunities for parents like him, their children, and future generations. Karikari was now becoming suspicious of everyone and everything. He began to drift into reclusion. Another significant change in his thoughts was that perhaps Agya Kobi wasn't more evil than everyone else. In fact, life had been better when the elder was near. Since he peeled away from the elder, life had turned worse. And so it came naturally when Agya Kobi visited him at Healer, Karikari asked for his help with Gyambibi, who was still trapped in the barracks. Agya Kobi visited Karikari daily with a Bible clutched under his armpit. He read passages from it and prayed with him.

Gyambibi, however, was now disgusted to talk to Agya Kobi at the barracks. He met him with mangoes in both hands. Though he had lost weight from the stress of his situation, he wasn't hungry; he just wanted to avoid handshakes without appearing disrespectful. He believed what had happened in his life had its source in the elder. Nonetheless, Gyambibi learned of his father's suicide attempt from Agya Kobi and suspected the injuries had affected Karikari's brain. There was no other explanation for his father to have asked the elder to come and talk to him!

"Everyone says you knew of Asamoah's death before it happened," Gyambibi began.

Agya Kobi implored Gyambibi to oblige him with a word of prayer before they talked. Gyambibi kept his eyes open while the elder prayed.

"Don't believe everything you hear. You should know that much, Gyambibi," Agya Kobi said. Gyambibi now believed, like everyone else, that Agya Kobi wielded religiosity to mask who he was. The evidence was too much to ignore: the elder knew of Asamoah's death before it was mentioned to him. A passport Gyambibi had seen many times, with a clear picture of Preprah, suddenly turned into a woman's. These defied logical explanations and pulled him toward the collective belief of the villagers. Certainly, Agya Kobi wasn't what his cantankerous mind had perceived.

"Were you crying before Nyamenkum the Gossip broke the news to you?" Gyambibi demanded.

"I was."

"Why?"

"Asamoah."

"His death?"

"Yes."

"But you just told me not to believe that. So you knew about it before it happened?"

What Agya Kobi had wanted to say: *Before the sun awakens, before we turn on the light, before we strike a match, darkness has already won. Darkness prevails until we bring light to it. So is the human experience and our natural state before we take a step or lift a finger. Gyambibi, I have taught you this. Apply this to my life in a slightly different way: The villagers say I'm the devil. I'm judged guilty before I open my mouth. My mouth and actions are all the light I have to change the darkness of people's thoughts, but is there a need to exert myself when what my mouth says is worthless to the darkness of people's perception of me?* Agya Kobi couldn't bring himself to say these things because Gyambibi was now one of the villagers who thought his words worthless.

In his defense, he could only say, "Yes, but it isn't what you think." Agya Kobi's eyes were watery with pain. It was clear the memory of his great-grandson was aroused, but Gyambibi wouldn't succumb to the pretense.

"I want to understand: you knew of Asamoah's death before it happened."

"Yes," the elder couldn't lie, fearing the consequences of their sworn oath.

Gyambibi was shaking, hearing the icy rumors confirmed. He refrained from asking how Efia's picture magically appeared in Preprah's passport. Karikari and Danfo, even Aunty Tabuah and her husband, all believed Agya Kobi had done this through occultist machination. Though Gyambibi hadn't been back to the village since his repatriation, he was certain the news had spread there. So to ask the elder about the picture, just for the sake of investigational curiosity, would doubtlessly arouse his suspicion that Gyambibi wasn't fully convinced. Gyambibi was too angry to sow any doubt in his conclusion.

When he first got hold of Preprah's passport, not only did he examine it for weeks before handing it to Danfo for safekeeping until his travel, but he had also gotten it four days before his travel. Moro had used the picture as a guide for Gyambibi's haircut. The plan was not to cut his hair the day before to avoid the appearance of a new haircut. And before they left for the airport, they went over every detail, reexamining the picture for comparison. They replicated the process at the airport. Danfo had held on to the passport before boarding began, ensuring it didn't get lost. For over three months since his repatriation, Gyambibi had scoured his mind for possible human avenues that could account for what happened. In the haze of confusion and anger, the theory that initially made sense to him was that perhaps the British wanted to repatriate him and, by extension, Ghanaians as retaliation for the end of colonialism. "If we don't want them ruling us, then they don't want us in their country, even if their country only served as a transit to another destination." As unreasonable as this theory was, it held promise to the waning intellect of Gyambibi until Moro asked: "How could you have such a skewed view of the British, particularly since you've been fond of and complimentary of all things British? They left our shores about two and a half decades ago, and they suddenly decided to turn hostile? How could they have gotten hold of Efia's picture to plant in your passport?" Gyambibi conceded Moro was right. In essence, there was no human explanation for the transformation of the picture. His perceived mistreatment of Agya Kobi by the villagers had been misguided. The villagers were right: Agya Kobi was evil and bent on destroying everything close to him.

Efia was married and lived with her husband in Togo. She hadn't been seen in the village for months, so the elder remained the sole culprit to have somehow adulterated the passport. Gyambibi didn't have to tell Agya Kobi about his plans for the man to know and destroy them. The man knew by divination. What's more, Mawuli and Danfo had had no contact with Agya Kobi, so there was no way either one could have gotten Efia's picture from him to plant in the passport. Even if, somehow, any of them had chanced on a picture of Efia, how could they have planted it so neatly en route to the airport without anyone seeing it? Curiously, why was it a picture of someone from Agya Kobi's household? To Gyambibi, the elder wanted all to know he was responsible.

Agya Kobi wasn't making headway, so he told Gyambibi the purpose of his visit: to beg him to return to the village. Karikari and everyone craved his return. Though he ached to visit his mother's gravesite to tell her what happened on his trip, Gyambibi said he would go anywhere but Enkoho. As if returning to the village was by choice.

For months, Gyambibi hadn't known his peace of mind. He was restless, both when asleep and awake. Karikari tried to keep him away from Agya Kobi when he was a child. Now he had a strong urge to keep his father away from the elder. The signs were all adding up for him: Agya Kobi was destroying them both.

Karikari later told Gyambibi how Yaa Adubia had found him. Karikari said he had seen Danfo hiding out in the bush, moving from tree to tree to hide from others at the farm. He couldn't say if it was a vision or a figment of his imagination. Whatever it was, Danfo responded to Yaa Adubia's screams when she found him. They carried him to the village in a wheelbarrow. Karikari fell out of the wheelbarrow twice, with Danfo handling it. Yaa Adubia took over. The wheelbarrow was hers for transporting her harvest to the village after her husband died. The right-hand grip was misaligned by several inches compared to the left grip. It had never been realigned, so she had acquired a posture that slopped to the right after using it for several years. She was one with the wheelbarrow and handled it like no other. Karikari said her skill saved his life.

There was more bad news from Enkoho: In Gyambibi's brief absence, some of his friends had died from consuming a toxic variant of cassava tuber because of hardship. Gyambibi felt responsible for the deaths, for had he been there, he would have warned them. Besides the observation that none of the ancestors or current elders touched this strain of cassava, it wasn't clear how he would have known it was poisonous.

Despite the pull to return to Enkoho, Gyambibi couldn't go, at least not yet. The village knew of his attempted trip to America and repatriation. So did his brother, Yaw. If what Preprah did to Yaw constituted betrayal, Language would need another word for what his own flesh and blood had done.

Chapter

36

*D*anfo had joined Karikari at Healer's. He was there with his own problem. A discoloration ran from his chin to his cheek, involving a part of his ear. Karikari wondered what had happened to his friend. Danfo told him before he could ask. Every domestic injury he sustained was explained away as a hunting accident without saying how it had actually happened.

"What a dangerous job I have. That's an understatement for a job that employs the tools of the military. My job is war, pretty much, if you think about it, except it's more dangerous. Mysterious beasts I encounter. It's a hazardous job, and I must do it daily!"

Karikari looked at Danfo's cheek, covered with the herby residue of an attempt at self-treatment and a blatant attempt to hide it from all until he was healed. Unsuccessful at treatment, the area was a confluence of green, yellow, and black scorched flesh with intervening cakes of rusty-red pus. White, flaky residue demarcated the margins of his burnt cheek. His face had seen the underside of a red-hot pan, it seemed. The injury was also consistent with his face having seen live coals. Karikari was on the verge of commenting on the utensil Danfo's wife had used this time when it came to him that Danfo would never admit to losing a fight to his wife.

Nearby was another patient, a man whose swollen foot was propped on a stool. Healer was with him minutes after he had been administered *akpeteshie*. The alcohol burned his tongue, forcing a spit out of him. The man stared at the world outside the hut when Healer's wife and an aide immobilized him. Healer took a knife to the man's swollen foot and made incisions to drain it. Screams numbed Danfo and Karikari, who knew their problems were minor compared to the shrieks from the other side of the partition.

Chapter

My Future Ex-wife

With no functional radio box bearing news of the world outside Enkoho, the coup d'état of June 1979 got to the village by word of mouth. A flight lieutenant and his cohorts had banded together with junior military officers and overthrown the government. It wasn't the lieutenant's first attempt. "Every failed coup is just practice" must have been coined for him. The details involved the execution of the sitting president and senior military officials by firing squad at the Teshie shooting range. Among the dead was Air Vice-Marshal George Yaw Boakye, whose ghost and Gyambibi would cross paths one day. Accra erupted in gunfire, the United Nations condemned the executions, and the world watched as the country went from one military rule to another. This wasn't a concern in Enkoho, however. The village had its own problems to bother with the overthrow of a government that cared about itself and nobody else. The villagers were saddened by Gyambibi's repatriation, which had dimmed their hope for a better life. Stepping into that hopelessness were Danfo and his problems with women.

"Marriage should have a shelf-life of six days. A *man* should have the option to renew on the seventh day if he's still alive," Danfo asserted.

"What is it about the seventh day?" Mawuli queried.

"God abandoned creation on the seventh day."

"Creation was finished by day six. God rested on the seventh day," Mawuli corrected.

"It was finished as a rough draft. What was created through day six was only *good*, not the best. In many places of Genesis, we read that God created so and so on such and such a day, and it was good. God didn't set out to create something that was just *good*; He intended perfection. But as we all know, God didn't get the chance to put the finishing touches on the *good* to get the *best* because Eve came on the sixth day, and He was gone on the seventh day. I guess having Eve on top of Satan was too much for Him. Which brings me to this point: for the life of me, I've never understood why marriage has to be a lifetime affair. If God ran away after creating the woman, an ominous sign for all men, why should the *man* be expected to live with her for a lifetime? Men were created in God's image and should follow His lead. God left before He could tie up the loose ends of His own creation: that's why we have diseases when God, in whose image we were created, carries no diseases. Creation wasn't completed, so we have climatic and geologic adversities, pain, and suffering. God, having run to safety from the woman He had unleashed on the man, sent Jesus Christ to promise man a future New Earth, where there would be no diseases, no pain and suffering, and no marriage—a do-over in which God's original intent for the earth, before the woman entered the picture, would be realized. And God, knowing Eve had set in motion Adam's death, also promised man the resurrection. Even Heaven itself must have been contaminated when God went there after creating Eve, so God promised Himself a New Heaven too. A *new heaven* and a *new earth*! It's there in the Bible. Read it. Six days of marriage are enough to gauge the scope of destruction ahead. Men should renegotiate the marriage contract. The terms should be subject to weekly renewal if the man is alive and willing. Beginning every week, we should have the right to decide whether to stay and die or leave to enjoy our God-given life. Married men die before their wives. Those are the statistics. Shouldn't we be concerned?"

"Married men are expected to die before their wives when they marry younger women, sometimes even girls, and when they marry multiple women," said Mawuli.

Disgusted by what he heard, Danfo stared at Mawuli and unleashed a couple of breaths, a sign of the onslaught to come: "Men were created at a disadvantage, so marrying younger women is how we level the playing field. Essentially, a man who marries a woman his age is searching for his mother. And a man who marries an older woman shouldn't be allowed outside, unsupervised. My witch of a wife doesn't even know when she was born, so my misery is beyond everybody else's, dead or alive. But look, you're a disgrace to manhood and the Bible! For such uninformed nonsense to come from a Christian is baffling. Read the Bible: Adam was created before Eve, so he was older than Eve," Danfo retorted.

"By hours, by a day...to say Adam was older is a stretch," Mawuli said.

"I can fairly assume that you had liquefied grass for breast milk as a child, Mawuli. Logic hates you as much as luck hates me. Adam and Eve may have been created hours or a day apart, but that doesn't rule out the possibility that Adam, on the merit of his stage of development when he was created, was older by several years, likely by decades. It's a reasonable assumption that, developmentally, Adam was in the advanced stages of dementia. For how could a man of sound mind who had it all—peace of mind, happiness, health, sinlessness, wealth, power over all God's creation—not ask the obvious when Eve the Subverter was presented to him as a wife? How could he not have known that by the mere curvature of Eve's mouth, she was headed for the forbidden fruit right after she had been instructed against it? There's a much deeper truth to unpack, but that isn't why I'm here."

"Some juvenile rant, that is," Karikari commented, who had been watching silently.

Danfo was incensed. How could these grown-up minds not see this plain truth? He would make them see it another way:

"The first miracle Jesus performed was to turn water into wine at a wedding. The idiots gathered there and lazy minds of to-day miss the greatest point Jesus ever made: that a man signs away his sanity at the point of marriage, so he needs the cover of alcohol to blend in with the crazies. I've never met a sane married man, and neither have you. So let's accept our sorry situation for what it is. Women shouldn't be grouped with humanity because they're so different. Even their understanding of 'in sickness and in health...till death do us part,' a most basic concept, is different. I declare to your hearing today that to married women everywhere, there's no difference between death by natural causes and death at their hands, sickness by natural causes and sickness at their hands. The two are the same. It's no shock Regina spends her days plotting to cut me limb from limb. Every wife on Earth shares that feeling. Look, God and our forefathers got one thing correct: the relationship between a husband and wife is special and necessary. Everything else they got wrong. *Till death do us part*! Where's the fairness when the statistics don't favor us, with married men everywhere dropping dead before their wives?"

"You don't have to stay married if you don't want to," an onlooker said.

"Only if my wife understands that," Danfo responded. "Each of my wives, by strange design, seems not to have divorce in her language. When Esi Eluwah left, her folks brought her back, saying married people shouldn't live apart. When Barbara left, her folks did the same. Now it's Regina. She left, and her people brought her back. You all saw it!"

Mawuli and Karikari hid their laughs behind clenched teeth. They couldn't admit to him the truth that everyone knew: that Esi Eluwah, Barbara, and Regina were the same woman.

"Their folks are right. God hates divorce," an eavesdropper said.

"Don't soil my bitter afternoon, woman. Your god isn't my god," Danfo said.

"God can do what He wants. He's God," Karikari contributed.

"Don't get me started, Karikari," Danfo said. "Be mindful of loosely applying the masculine pronoun to God because I'm starting to believe God isn't one of us. For how could a man do this to his fellow man?"

"What sex do you suppose God is? Doesn't His name give it away?" asked Mawuli.

"Some foolish questions you sometimes ask, Mawuli. God's name is YHWH. When the entire English-speaking world can't agree on whether 'h' is a vowel or not, how the heck am I to know if YHWH is a man's, a woman's, or a hermaphrodite's name?"

Mawuli wasn't offended. They all knew Danfo was angry before he joined them under the baobab tree. He must have gotten out of a fight with his wife, and the feeling that his arguments weren't taken added to his irritation.

Karikari's vapid contribution, or non-rebuttal, got the attention of Agya Kobi, who, taking a detour from his evening walk, intervened and addressed Danfo: "You have interesting ways of relating the Bible to arguments. And...?"

Agya Kobi's uninvited participation drew a surprise. He rarely did farmwork nowadays because of weakness. Adwoa Brago and Helena assumed the duties of the farm. Daily, he walked the breadth of the village, cutting through the center and around Mr. Nsenkyire's family-house complex, stopping at the church building to chat with Preacher if he was there. Other times, as today, he skirted the village. It was a way to get his blood moving. Always with the Eternal Lamp in hand. On these strolls, he never added his voice to anybody's or greeted anyone because his gestures weren't returned. No one could say why he dared participate in something involving Danfo. The references to God may have lured him. Perhaps, too, he had gone without a "normal" conversation for so long. To be in the midst of fellow men talking about anything might have proved tempting. But Christians didn't want him, so why would he think he was wanted here, especially knowing that Karikari had pulled away after recovering from his injuries?

Danfo hesitated. He focused on Karikari and Mawuli.

"It's insulting to think we have to throw away who we are because of the threat of eternal damnation if we don't subscribe to Christianity. Foolish for others to think it necessary to introduce their god to us when Xada and Dr. Maarten lived among us for years without being forced to adhere to the tacit demands of *them*!"

Them! Danfo wanted to trap Agya Kobi into broaching an anathema: using explicit language about the faceless forces of the village.

"Nobody worships *them*, but most here worship God," Agya Kobi replied.

"He had to slip that in there. Old man, we know you're one of *them*. You're flattered by that, aren't you, having the power to decide who lives and who dies?" Danfo accused.

Agya Kobi saw through the dangerous trap and skirted it: "No foreigner introduced God to us. That's like saying the Portuguese or the British introduced food to us. We knew God before they came to our shores. What they did was introduce *how* we worship God. You know the appellations our ancestors applied to God long before the colonialists invaded."

Danfo wasn't interested in engaging the old man, but Agya Kobi continued anyway:

"This isn't any different from Apostle Paul telling the people of Athens, in Acts 17, that they were worshiping the same God he worshipped but whom they designated an 'Unknown God.' Many cultures knew of a divine, monotheistic, albeit a triune, God before the advent of Christianity and pollination of Western culture and religions here as well as in the Near and Far East. This, in and of itself, speaks to the consciousness of souls of a supreme deity. Christianity didn't come about overnight, and it isn't a figment of history; rather, it's the byproduct of the fulfillment of thousands of years of prophecies and the Almighty's grand scheme to standardize and universalize the worship of Him by 'foreign cultures' that didn't *intimately* know him."

As with anything about the elder, Danfo was disgusted. He had to respond, although through an ad-hominem assault:

"People respect the words of the old because they've experienced more in life. That's true, just not in the case of this aged mud. The man is filled with bitterness because of his failures. His life is an obituary. He has nothing for our children except to fill their heads with his god and bitterness, preaching to them about man is evil this, man is evil that. I have never met a man so disgustingly preachy. See how preachy Gyambibi gets at times? That's Agya Kobi influencing our children. He thinks being preachy erases our memory of who he is? Evil monster! I heard he told Gyambibi to rely on God for a wife, but he forgot the only useful lesson worth learning from his Bible about God giving a wife to someone. Who gave Eve to Adam? Of course, it was God. What happened to Adam when God played a matchmaker? The first man created was the first man to become homeless. A happy man minding his own business was turned homeless by his wife. That belongs on Adam's headstone. Eve! I'm no etymologist, but I think the name Eve derives from Evil. Heck! Eve and Devil are the etymologic ingredients of Evil. All women descend from Eve—I mean, Evil—a useful truth every man should hold. Our destruction lies at the core of women's existence. But I digress: Adam lost everything by way of his wife. What's the lesson here? A woman doesn't cease to be a woman, even if God or a god gave her to you. If Agya Kobi's God couldn't prevent the destruction of a man by a wife He Himself made for him, what hope could there be for innocent young men destined for victimhood at the hands of the daughters of women? Our children would be advised to steer clear of this buffoon! Finding a good wife depends on a knack for discerning good character and, most importantly, a lifetime supply of good luck. My sad life as a married man bears out the fact that my ability to discern a woman, like any intelligent man, can't see past the grace period to the true nature of the woman I'm tethered to for life. And, more importantly, good luck opposes my existence. Pray for luck before you pray for a wife. That isn't all; this aged mud is filling our children's heads with that inner-beauty nonsense. Our children don't have the sophistication of mind to understand that inner beauty is the most insidious and destructive of them all. Inner beauty is evil hiding on the inside and waiting for the right moment to come out. What does this aged mud know?"

"Eve shoved nothing down Adam's throat. Adam was his own man who made his own choices, leading to his downfall. Anyway, some of us have wonderful wives. You couldn't say Agnes wasn't a wonderful woman. I'm aware that nobody likes me, but that doesn't take away from the fact that all judge my Rosemond Adwoa Brago to be a good woman and wife. Your experience as a married man doesn't speak for the world at large," Agya Kobi rejoined.

"My experience doesn't speak for all married men, of course. But take all married men and subtract those who walked out of the womb with all of their mother's estrogen. What's left? All unhappily married men, whose voices I represent."

Before Agya Kobi could issue a neutralizing riposte, Danfo had pushed him to the ground, intending to keep him down until he turned into sand. The Eternal Lamp had slipped through the elder's fingers and landed erect. It had a mind of its own.

It was common knowledge that, besides Preacher, the elder was the only intelligent force who could outwit Danfo's apocryphal rants. Danfo knew this, so he ensured the elder's mouth didn't find its way to another rebuttal. Danfo sat back down in a peal of confusion. Passersby walked back and forth, not knowing what had happened. Agya Kobi was unable to lift himself. Nobody wanted to get close to him, let alone help him up. He writhed with every effort to stand. Karikari looked at him; the reference to Agnes had annoyed him. He had no desire to help him, either.

"There was no need to push him down!" an onlooker yelled.

"Your wife's alive because you know we're watching," Danfo yelled at the elder as the crowd thickened. Danfo was admired for his action, for many wished the elder dead. Danfo was the only one who came close to forcing the hand of death on him. What's more, he had survived the encounter without any untoward outcome. But he wasn't finished:

"I've often said that Adam wasn't a smart man. Dementia is the strangest of diseases; it devastated the father of all *men*. How Adam got the disease, I don't know. Eve is my only guess. In any case, the God of the Bible is the God of choices. If not for dementia, how could the obvious have escaped Adam? Why did he not query God as to why He didn't present him with, say, a hundred women—some good, some evil, some in between—so he could make his own choice? It was either dementia or God deliberately created the man much slower than the woman. Why would God present Adam with only one woman, Eve, who was evil through and through? Why? You want to know? Satan gave God grief. God created Adam in His image and Eve in Satan's image so Adam would share in His grief. He is God, right? He is all-knowing, and He knew what Eve would do to Adam. With Adam, God sought a companion in suffering. In God's image *men* were made; in God's unhappiness with Satan *men* will also share. Women!"

Danfo turned to the boys among the gathering: "You won't even know what to do with what women say. Ask your mothers! Ask them! Half of what they say, they don't mean. And half of the half of what they say that they mean, you're not to take seriously. And half of the half of the half... take note, children...half of *that* is meant to distract you from who they are. Can you believe it? Weeks ago, my wife was sick and sent me to the market for a febrifuge. I chose not to go because I knew better. At the marketplace, on that day and at the exact time when I was to be there, a fight broke out between two women, where their merchandise turned into weapons. And then entered a hero—a self-assured man who kept his head in his wife's purse. The wife was dazzling in the finest lace her husband's money could buy, while the husband himself, constipated on stupidity, had on clothes so worn and cheap that one could see through him. The man ventured between the fighting women at his wife's urging. Apparently, he was too stupid to know she was plotting his death. His face was caught between clashes of tomatoes, onions, yams, peppers... Disgust won't let me repeat what their claws did to the rest of him. The fool looked surprised, as if he had awoken to find Satan's claws in his entrails. It could have been worse had he not been wearing second-hand clothing. One of the women grabbed him by the collar, the other grabbed him from behind, and the shirt came apart in a hundred pieces. Used clothing saved his life. That man's suffering was meant for me. But I knew better than to have a hand in healing a sick witch. In my wife's miraculous recovery, I saw that she had wanted me dead that day. She recovered without the febrifuge, a trap all along. Days of coughing, a spiking fever, and covering our floors with bloody vomitus and phlegm led to a miraculous recovery that devastated my hopes to date. I don't wish her dead; I just hate that she's undead and spends her days plotting *my* death! Where was I? Yes! Last of all...asking about the remaining half of the half of the half of the half of what women say...I guess I'm right, yes, asking about that will be the source of all the misery you'll know as married men.

"Esi Eluwah! Make no mistake, boys, when I laid eyes on that woman, I knew I was looking at my future ex-wife. What I didn't count on was that she would have the idea to take my soul with her when her time came. So accept my advice, boys: eat breakfast and leave the house. Return for lunch and leave. She can't kill you in daylight unless she's a daring witch. Evening is a different story, which points me to the fact that dinner is tricky. Skip it if you don't want to die in your sleep. Don't take my word for it; just ask those whose fathers are dead!"

Danfo looked around and continued his monologue: "You see how bald some of us are and wonder why. There's no mystery to it. No man wants to go bald. The hair on my head started disappearing, and I didn't know why. However, the hair on my back, chest, and everywhere else flourished as if hairs from my scalp were redistributed. I knew why, or so I thought. Everywhere on my body where hair flourishes are places that are always covered. I found proof of that in women. There's your answer to why your mothers aren't bald: they wear a headscarf. The sun doesn't bear down and shrivel the hair on their head. That's right. So I, too, started wearing a headscarf; but then, my hair fell out faster than when I didn't wear one. I'd been wrong all along. The answer had been before me all this time: women. You see, hair needs nutrients to grow, but how do you get nutrients when forced to eat nothing or face the alternative of eating grass and weeds? Preprah informed me that it goes by the cryptic name salad in the West. Nothing cryptic about that when one can make out '*some* (men) *are lazy and dumb.*' Men of the West! They have lost their minds, not knowing that they're on a diet of grass and weeds in their entire married life. And scientists the world over wonder why forests are disappearing?

The British! Their women have outwitted them, and they don't know it. See why they have a queen ruling them? Married men are the most miserable of all God's creation because we have restricted choices. We go hungry or eat grass, lose our minds, and wake up one morning to realize that the winds of immense frustration and stress have taken hold of our scalp, ripping out a thousand hairs daily. The devastation launches on two fronts: first, the hairline recedes in a direction that looks away from your wife—a reminder of the danger and cause of your balding. The second line of attack consumes the top of your head. When the two balding patterns collide, a wife smiles more often than when she first married you, not because she's thankful to God for blessing her with a soul mate, but because your end is deliciously near. Now you're bald, like when you exited the womb, but this time you're working your way back to nonexistence. And whatever hairs survive your wife's cruelty, she will turn each one white. White men have got it worse because they already have white skin. It's anyone's guess how to tell apart a bunch of White men whose wives have done to them what Esi Eluwah has done to me. None of you is bald, boys, not because God loves you. Get married and find out!"

Danfo looked around, casting a suspicious eye at Agya Kobi, who was still on the ground. Danfo collected himself and reminded everyone that women are expected to be efficient at evil and outwit men at every turn because they were created *after* men. Because women came after men, God must have avoided in them the mistakes He made in creating men. Thus women are improved versions of men, with the added danger of being created in the image of Satan. Danfo then turned to the boys again and resumed his lecture:

"See how quickly you get to your hairbrushes and combs today? Marry, then take the same brush or comb to your head, and it will return to you with everything atop your head. It isn't the brush or comb responsible for your baldness. Your wife would have uprooted every hair already; the comb or brush would only be raking them off for you to see what she'd been doing if you're too stupid not to know already.

"You may be right to think there must be bald women somewhere in the world. Certainly, but those are women who want to be men. There's a price to pay for everything. Look at all of Creation: every animal has male and female counterparts, yet only man suffers this fate because of his woman."

Danfo expected a challenge but got none; the villagers knew him too well to argue with him when he was this agitated. The crowd's adult makeup was mostly women who knew of his violent interactions with other women. These women were there because Danfo was known to slip secrets into his outbursts absentmindedly, like when he once said that sons and daughters of Enkoho were lured back to the village by Agya Kobi via the occult, even when these sons and daughters were far removed from the land, even abroad. Gyambibi's repatriation from Britain days after this pronouncement proved that Danfo was right and that he knew things others didn't. Not long ago, it was rumored that Danfo had implied that a villager, a man, intended to sacrifice one of the other villagers to enrich himself via the occult. Every woman understood this potential victim would be a child, hence why nervous mothers were there in great numbers to gather if Danfo would reveal more. The timing of the rumor couldn't be discarded: famine raged, and desperation was rampant. Even Professor Tetteh's help was sought to examine some crops that bore a resemblance to cassava to see if they were edible. Professor Tetteh wasn't in the village as much as before, and no one knew why. The reality was his fear of the village stood in his way. After the deaths of two people, he sent word from his office on the campus of the Kwame Nkrumah University of Science and Technology that he *felt* what had killed the two villagers was a variant of bitter cassava tubers with high cyanide content.

Silence of the crowd forced Danfo to go on: "There must be bald animals somewhere in Creation. Of course! The bald eagle, the national bird of America! The modern Founding Fathers of that country must have a reason to associate the whole nation with a bald bird. Of course, that's red coils of smoke, a strong signal to the outside world of what their women are doing to them. When you see a vulture outside, be reminded to pray for every man in America. That means all you boys should pray for them too. That could mean every second you're outside. A mammoth task, indeed, but that's the least you can do for your fellow men. I know, I know, it's too much to pray for millions of people whose names you don't know. Remember this one name, though: President Ronald Reagan. I worship this brave man who singlehandedly stands between the lives of all the men there and their dreadful, fierce, concupiscent witches of wives. Mr. Ronald Reagan can do that because he's a cowboy. One can't be a cowboy without horses and cows. See how animals are working with one man to advance *my cause* when your worthless fathers refuse to join me here? Tell your bald fathers that this proves they're inferior to horses and cows, and I say they deserve all the misery that lies next to them in bed."

Danfo met the crowd with uncontrolled grimaces and misplaced excitement when the villagers couldn't grasp his connection of bald birds, horses, and cows to the emasculation of American men.

Next, Danfo walked the boys through the process of his son's balding, a case study: Preprah's golden years were when no girl liked him. He had full hair. But he still showed signs of balding at sixteen because he lived with his MOTHER. The military opened the floodgates of women to Preprah. His balding began. Then came America and her women. My goodness, those American women! Danfo showed pictures of Preprah with a well-nourished face but bald as a desert. With her advanced medicine that could bring the dead to life, America couldn't stop Preprah's progression into complete baldness.

"That brave son of mine is doing his part by volunteering as a plumber in America. Somebody has to deal with all the pipes clogged by men's hair."

Then another rush of speech followed as if he had forgotten an idea he should have mentioned earlier: Baldness is as much a problem of plants as it is with man and animals. The bald cypress is native to America: an orchard of trees resembles stranded witches in a wig waiting for a hairdresser. Not surprising. My goodness, what savagery Satan has wrought in America! If Danfo's calculations were right, America would have more bald men per square mile than any country.

"Women have more in common with trees than with men. In the West, it's fitting that women and flowers go hand in hand. Salad: diet of the forest! I can't believe I'm mentally intact, conjuring the imagery of this nauseating culinary oddity. Such a diet would naturally belong to the palate of women; for vegetation, trees are like women. Understanding how women think is like trying to understand how trees think—the utter pointlessness of it all. Women don't even understand women. That's why God asked Adam about the breach of the *forbidden fruit* when God's querulous anger should have rather been trained on Eve, who breached it. God knew it would have been pointless talking to her."

Nyamenkum the Gossip had joined the crowd, her demeanor a mixture of elation for seeing the elder in torment and a desire to have Danfo punished for assaulting the elder. Her presence plunged Danfo into confused annoyance.

Agya Kobi was still unable to get up. Though he said nothing beyond writhing in pain, he was still a threat to Danfo, who imagined him arguing a point:

"Why would Adam need a hundred women to make the right choice? With hundreds of millions of women available at the time of your marriage, your odds of picking a woman not Esi Eluwah were much, much better than Adam's. Yet you picked

Esi Eluwah, the Eve of all women on Earth today, you say. With much, much better odds, how could you be so sure that Adam would still not have chosen Eve anyway?"

Danfo forgot about the children and turned to the writhing elder, further intending to teach Nyamenkum the Gossip that he could win a fight with words just as easily as he could with his fist, her missing teeth serving as a clear reminder. Danfo lashed out, "But that would still be his choice, wouldn't it?" By answering a question no one heard asked, he confused the crowd.

"And I thought she'd be ashamed after I unraveled her scheme." Danfo turned to the boys, continuing the narrative of his wife planning to kill him. "I came home for lunch days ago. Surprise, surprise! At first, I thought she'd used her proficiency in witchcraft to miniaturize the forest into my bowl. A mound of carrots, spinach, nuts, and every leaf imaginable, likely including poison ivy, sat in front of me. 'What's this?' I asked. 'It's good for you,' she said. Science tells me I'm sixty percent water, meaning I'm forty percent flesh and bones. How do bones and flesh survive on a diet of the forest? She exposed her intent without my involvement: 'It's healthy and will help you live longer.' How did she know I won't live long without this strange diet if she didn't plan to kill me before my time?"

Danfo was alarmed by what he felt were women's devilish schemes: "My knowledge of science may be outdated, but I think there's a clear connection between diet and a child's development. Women start controlling you in the womb: You eat only what they eat. Don't let any woman tell you that's foolish talk because girls in the womb also eat only what their mothers eat. That's fitting for girls because they take after their mothers anyway. Where was I? Yes, there's a connection between diet and when your bodies start to produce testosterone in large enough quantities to turn you from boys to men. There's a connection between testosterone and when you start to acknowledge women. And there's a connection between women and death. That isn't the end, my young friends. After death, your body's either cremated and your ashes lifted into the air for Mother Earth to sniff, or your body's buried whole or in pieces, depending on your wife's preference, in the womb of Mother Earth. Then comes the afterlife. If you know anything about God, God is everywhere, just like women. Satan isn't everywhere but goes everywhere, like a woman with her husband's money. So there you have it: Heaven or Hell, your life is superintended either by a woman or by a man with a woman complex. As boys, the only education that matters is knowing women. Your life or death, happiness or sadness, is in their hands."

In the continuum of Danfo's outburst, the children were quiet, taking in everything he was saying. They held their breath as Danfo paused and quickly scanned the crowd for an adolescent, feminine voice that said, "Keep talking; your wife isn't here to shut you up. By the way, we know her hands punch harder than your mouth."

A scan of the crowd produced no female to be the next punching bag of his pillory. It must be the shape-shifting voice of Agya Kobi. Danfo looked at him, still grimacing with pain. Danfo leaned to the side, intending to land his entire weight on the elder. That way, he thought, he could blame the elder's death on losing his balance. However, Yaa Adubia's quick reflexes pushed him to the side, with both crashing beside the elder.

"What's wrong with you, Danfo? What's the world coming to!?" she screamed.

Women and children flocked around her and examined her bones to see if they were reduced to powder.

"What's the world coming to? What's it coming to? It isn't ending. You, women, won't bring the world of men to an end." Danfo lashed out and looked curiously at Yaa Adubia's hands, not knowing who she was initially. But the weary, hardened, sixty-year-old sinuous hands had enough sad stories to tell about life than Danfo had the patience for. Danfo concluded that the hands that had pushed him to the ground didn't belong to any of those eight witches from Enkoho whose hands intruded in his fistfights with his wife.

Nevertheless, after ascertaining that it was Yaa Adubia, he contemplated if she deserved to lose some teeth for pushing him down and talking to him that way. He was restrained by the outcome of those "witches" he had decided to beat up. Nyamenkum the Gossip had been the first on the list, but she had escaped by being with Barbara Oforiwaah shortly after her own fight with Danfo. The next two "witches" on Danfo's list, he battered severely. Word got out that Danfo was going from hut to hut beating up every woman in the village that day. Those with their husbands at home stayed put; those without husbands, or those whose husbands weren't home, went into hiding. Some men immobilized Danfo, and the matter of the two battered women came before the elders. The elders were incensed by their inability to curtail Danfo's behavior; they drew up ways to bypass Chief's nonenforcement of fines against Danfo. The two battered women they sent to Healer and told him that Danfo was responsible for his fees. The battery was severe enough that the treatments cost two cows, four goats, and two cartons of Schnapps. Danfo knew better than to do anything short of paying Healer-cum-fetish priest. Ironically, he had paid it all, relying on his wife's help. The elders resorted to the same tactic to have him pay the fines for his recent battering of Nyamenkum the Gossip. Besides, there were too many witnesses here to cripple his self-defense defense, if he were to beat up Yaa Adubia and the matter were to come before the elders. So he left her alone.

Karikari and Mawuli were long gone. Danfo stormed off, swatting away the hand of a woman asking if his wife was home.

Some children went to help Agya Kobi, but their mothers shouted them away. Yaa Adubia helped Agya Kobi to his feet. Helena, drawn to the area by noise, met Yaa Adubia halfway and walked the elder home.

Nyamenkum the Gossip looked for Esi Eluwah in the crowd and, not seeing her, hastened to the marketplace.

Chapter

38

*T*he mood summoned by the Ramblers International Band's medley of *Ama Bonsu* and *Better Ni* was refreshing. It was a rare feeling of bountiful happiness bordering on euphoria that Danfo had rarely experienced. Danfo snapped his fingers, gestured at the wind, and hummed along. He hadn't been in such a good spirit in a long time, not because life circumstances had changed for him or anyone in Enkoho—it was the lush confluence of musical instruments, human voice, rhythm, and lyrics. If God ever took a break to relax, these songs would make him appreciate man's ingenuity over his heavenly orchestra. The moment was carefree, a moment for relaxing and doing nothing else. It came to Danfo that the songs might be about the woman in his life: Esi Eluwah. Only she could ruin the moment without even being there. Just then, the songs attained a certain dryness and senselessness, even insulting. The songs stopped playing on their own.

The only radio in Enkoho still didn't work because the torrential rainfall had dismembered its external antenna. A sole gramophone in the village was housed indoors, at least several hundred yards away from Danfo's residence, making it impossible to hear any song it played from where he was. Somehow, Wulomei's *Meridian* filled the air in Danfo's compound. From the quality of the song, he knew they were coming from a live performance. Seated on his porch, members of the band appeared in his compound with their flutes, percussions, guitars, gongs, etc. The folksy tune awoke his connection to the land, melting away his depression. A flurry of the music turned him dreamy. In his enchanted elation, he counted the band members but couldn't arrive at a number. That troubled him. So he recounted, arriving at a number diverging substantially from his initial count. He counted again, but the number diverged even further. He counted again; the number had decreased even more. Now there were only two women and a goat who weren't part of the band. In these, Danfo recognized Esi Eluwah and Nyamenkum the Gossip.

Tied to a tree, the male goat nibbled on cassava and plantain peels. Esi Eluwah stroked its fur from the top of its head down to its tail. She scooped some of the peels and fed the goat. Danfo had a hunch the goat was eating its last meal. Here animals killed for food deserved their last meal. It works similarly to how man is treated the world over before his execution. Nyamenkum the Gossip spread the goat's hind legs wide. Esi Eluwah grabbed all the flesh hanging between its hind legs—she massaged it at first, then squeezed until blood broke through the skin. The goat bleated with pain as the two women laughed. They stole glances at Danfo, who twitched and flinched in his chair, keeping his trembling knees close together. The performance was for him. Nyamenkum the Gossip repositioned herself and handed Esi Eluwah a large, rusty sickle, which she grabbed, and, with one straight swoop, removed the goat's genitalia. She cut off all the flesh between its hind legs. The goat bleated and thrashed around, blood spurting from a large hole. Danfo's loins went numb.

Esi Eluwah's left leg immobilized the goat's front legs with immense, superhuman strength. She took a knife to its throat and sliced through flesh and bones in one swoop. Danfo watched with apprehension, knowing the women intended this for him. Then the dismembering began after smoking off the fur. Esi Eluwah cut the goat open, dug her hand into its body, and ripped out the heart. She threw a casual glance at Danfo. Nyamenkum the Gossip followed, after which the two erupted in laughter. Much sweat trickled down Danfo's neck, back, and sides. They were practicing what they would do to him one day. He regretted allowing Esi Eluwah back into his life. He had the urge to go indoors to inspect if all his "parts" were there. When he opened the door, on a hunch, he turned back to cast one long look at the women, only to see them frozen in place. Then he knew they wouldn't proceed if he wasn't there to watch. Yes, the performance was meant for him alone. He slammed the door and went inside. A short time later, he came out, clutching a machete. He had to stop this madness before fate donated him to their fantasy one day.

"Get out of my house. Get out. Witches! Esi Eluwah, go back to your folks. I've repeated a mistake I never thought possible: becoming your victim twice. Get out! Out! And don't step foot here again. Out! Nyamenkum, the next time I see you here, I'll remove your remaining teeth, mouth, and head while at it. Get out!" He chased them to the boundary of his house where, in the farthest corner, he saw Karikari heading in his direction. Danfo snapped out of the nightmare, having fallen off his bed and in a pool of sweat. He staggered onto his porch and walked about to ward off sleep.

Then it came to him that he was late for his meeting with the men of the village. He didn't remember much about changing clothes or leaving the house. All he remembered was being at the meeting, where a podium was erected for him. It was in the bush. He scanned the gathering, looking at every person. Karikari and Mawuli weren't there, but that wasn't the subject of his confusion. Men he had known for decades were in wrappers, earrings, makeup, and headscarves or wigs. He had heard that married couples tend to act alike at a point, but this! He shook his head in disgust. So all his male friends harbored a fetish for cross-dressing? He swung his head in all directions to clear his vision, then scanned the gathering again. He saw Esi Eluwah, and that told him everything. It was all women, indeed, and not cross-dressing men. He was at the wrong meeting. He couldn't say why some women in the village had a secret meeting in the bush. Then he looked at Esi Eluwah again and got a sense of the purpose of the gathering. He was alarmed: "Witches! Witches! You devils, a bunch of witches...no wonder I don't recall how I got here. Whichever of you was kind enough to fly me to my meeting brought me to the wrong venue. I'm not one of you. I don't have a taste for human flesh and blood."

Esi Eluwah licked her lips. This rippled across the faces of everyone in the gathering—everyone licked their lips. Danfo knew that Esi Eluwah had transported him there to feast on him. He pushed the podium at a group of women who lunged at him and ran. He stumbled, falling on his face. He woke up. He had fallen asleep again, and his nightmare had resumed.

Danfo buried his face in a bucket of cold water on and off for several minutes. Still, the substance of the nightmares wouldn't leave.

He was en route to Karikari's house to discuss the details of Gyambibi's second attempt at America when he saw he wasn't alone. An army of flies followed and swarmed his person, with some settling on him and some buzzing around him. He wondered what had invited the gregarious armies. It hadn't come to him that he had fallen asleep right after smoking and gutting the deer he had brought home, his only kill in months. Maybe the relentless flies weren't flies, he thought. They were a reminder of Esi Eluwah and her unseen friends. The flies wouldn't leave him alone, now inciting fear to make him want to pray them away. He prayed, but now the flies multiplied. Esi Eluwah and her army didn't respond to his prayers, so this was expected. The insects had doubled because he had double-vision then. That the insects were transmutations of Esi Eluwah and her gang was now real when an insect stung him on the ear six times. It reminded him of how Esi Eluwah could throw multiple punches with no rest between. It was her witching in broad daylight. Hysteria was fomenting. A much-needed ablution would resolve whether witches or the smell of carcass on him was responsible for the flies. He returned home. Hours later, the issue was still unresolved, with the insects and their guests infiltrating the spaces of his pants and shirt. Changing out of his stale clothes hadn't come to him. He left for Karikari's house.

Aunty Tabuah knew somebody in Kodee who knew somebody from Aduman who could work on Gyambibi's path to the United States. The months since Gyambibi's return to Enkoho saw nothing but planning, replanning, and planning to enter America. Preprah wanted no involvement. All understood why.

Karikari had concluded that America was a better option than digging up the buried treasure—the latter idea Danfo had revisited. But if this second attempt failed, Danfo warned, it could be the last time Karikari would see his son. Karikari and Tabuah weren't persuaded. Moreover, witnessing Preprah's success convinced them that the rewards of making it to America were far greater than the demerit of repatriation when weighed against the immense dangers of digging up the treasure.

Months earlier, Karikari, Danfo, Gyambibi, and Tabuah had gone to Aduman to meet Ofori or "Mark of the Beast." He was so nicknamed because he was obsessed with the biblical symbolism of 666. He would work on Gyambibi's trip to America.

Yaw hadn't welcomed the opportunity to go to America when his father, brother, and aunty offered it. He rejected what could have been a surprise realization of a lifelong dream. He declined not because Chief would be suspicious since he had announced another piece of gold jewelry stolen but because Yaw couldn't conceive breathing the same air Preprah breathed. Yaw would resign to village life and help his father on the farm. Karikari and Gyambibi didn't foresee this. In fact, Yaw was responsible for returning Gyambibi to Enkoho. Gyambibi had no explaining to do, Yaw said, for they were both victims of Preprah, a charge he repeated several times, sometimes even in the presence of Danfo.

"We went over everything before we left Kodee. We saw and examined Preprah's passport at the airport, which was in Danfo's keeping. Gyambibi and I were in the car with Danfo, who, again, had possession of the passport. How could he have manipulated the passport without us seeing him? Are you saying that Preprah, somehow, knew the agents who interrogated and repatriated your brother? Preprah isn't unscathed in all this. You should know that his passport was confiscated. Wouldn't he have been here twice already if he had it?" Karikari tried to get Yaw to reconsider his nascent animus toward his once-good friend.

"I don't have answers, but I know Preprah was involved with what happened to my brother."

"You know?"

"I feel it."

Preprah's betrayal had cut Yaw deeper than anyone imagined.

"Preprah and I were born weeks apart. Since we could talk and walk, he'd been by my side more than he'd been with his parents—unlike now, of course," Yaw said.

"We understand your feelings, but let's not blame the innocent," Karikari replied.

"If I don't know what he's capable of, no one does. He's more dangerous than Agya Kobi. I'm his best friend. I *was* his best friend. Am I the only person who thinks it odd that he would return from America to propose starting a business with my brother and not me?"

"I wondered about that too. You were very angry that he was here on vacation instead of staying there to help bring you over. The entire village knows how upset you were. It must have gotten to him. I suppose he changed his mind and instead decided to help your brother. He must have thought you were envious. It was better to help someone from the family than his platoon mates with whom he stays when he's in the country. But if he wanted nothing to do with you, why did he write to you to meet him on his first vacation?" Karikari queried.

"There's something wrong with that. We've been angry with each other over the years, but nothing changed. What's different this time? God help us all. He may be planning to get rid of us. If he could plot to turn me against my brother, he has no good intentions for our family."

"Now stop that! Why would he plan to kill us?"

Yaw had one piece of advice for his brother: "Keep away from him if you make it there."

Since Gyambibi's return to Enkoho, Jeefa's life had attained normalcy. She and Helena cooked for him. When she alone was with him, she sought answers about his repatriation, a subject Gyambibi had stayed away from when she visited him in the barracks. Now Gyambibi felt he owed her the details of the story, which he did. However, he would only go so far and not more because of his conclusion that Agya Kobi was responsible for what happened, and it had happened because Jeefa must have told Helena, who in turn told the old man. Gyambibi, this time, withheld from Jeefa his plans for a second attempt at America.

Chapter

Journey Through a Cul-de-sac

O n October 27, 1979, Gyambibi arrived in Guinea. "Mark of the Beast" Ofori had feared Gyambibi would have another unsuccessful trip to America if he arrived a day earlier. He told Gyambibi that this was his second attempt to the United States, so if two were multiplied by three hundred thirty-three (the number of days since they first met and went over possible reasons for his repatriation), that would be 666, the so-called "Mark of the Beast" in the Bible. That could auger another failure. It was wise of Gyambibi to keep certain details of his failed attempt a secret out of concern that they might frighten Ofori—evangelist and all. In any case, Ofori was pleased that Gyambibi followed his direction. Everything would go as planned, he assured Gyambibi, for others who had followed his instructions had made it to America.

Ofori hadn't stopped talking since he picked up Gyambibi at the airport. Perhaps his vocation as an evangelist was to blame. Gyambibi was divided: a part of him was attentive to the new country he had entered, and another part focused on the incontinent mouth responsible for his trip. Ofori was comfortable talking and did so with the urgency of expecting Armageddon before the day's end.

The Guinean air was thick and scented like Ghana's but with a hint of something French.

Some backstreets were sparsely lit, and the roads were unpaved in some places, like Ghana. As he took in the city of Conakry, he couldn't foresee what could go wrong on this second attempt. His father had financed the travel with yet another loan from Mr. Nsenkyire.

The darkness of the road reminded Gyambibi of the darkness that had befallen his father. With the failed suicide behind him, destiny promised another life, but not necessarily a better one. The deterioration of his finances after the cataclysm seemed to have no end. Subsistence crops didn't bring in money as cocoa did. All his farmhands were gone because he couldn't afford them, so he worked on the farm with Mawuli and Yaw. Now the farm was sprouted with cocoa, which would take another three to five years to yield. Gyambibi thought about their fate if he were turned back.

Gyambibi could tell Ofori was looking at him, aware that Gyambibi wasn't listening. In order not to offend him and to feign interest, Gyambibi asked what Ofori did in Guinea. Ofori caught on to his ruse because that was precisely what he had been expounding on. Ofori eased himself into answering the question to avoid awkwardness. He said he evangelized in both Ghana and Guinea. Ofori didn't mind repeating, "My patrons are nice people; they're doing God's work. Anybody who does God's work has taken on a noble cause. If only my pay was better." Gyambibi knew he added the latter to address the glaring inconsistency in the unsavory means he used to earn extra income.

"Perhaps they think Africa is one big farm, and you can eat your way out of low pay," Gyambibi said, attempting a joke.

Ofori shrank from the statement and said nothing. Gyambibi changed the subject.

"Your family sent you some items in my luggage."

"You're a good man, my young friend!" Ofori was happy that the items he sought from his family had made it.

The last time his family had sent food for him through a friend, the items made it to the airport all right, according to the friend. It was when the airplane was in the air that this friend claimed to notice the items on the tarmac, as if that was believable. "I made nothing of it. Then I heard him tell others that I believe in God, so I'll believe anything. He thinks I believed his story."

They arrived home, where a woman greeted them in a vaguely familiar language. Gyambibi guessed it was French. He couldn't tell if she was Ofori's wife and didn't ask because he felt it was improper. Maybe she merely volunteered to cook and clean his house. Gyambibi would learn shortly that Ofori was well-liked in the community. After the formal welcome, the woman told them there was no water at home. Gyambibi had said he wanted to bathe before dinner, which was prepared and served before they arrived. Ofori only had to tell a girl he needed a bucket of water for boys and girls to arrive with several.

Gyambibi turned to the television, which was blaring in a language he didn't understand.

"Don't worry. I have a friend to teach you the language so quickly that you can do without English if you want...for the second phase of the trip," Ofori assured.

Yes, a second phase. There would be a third phase, also. It involved more phases than the first attempt, meaning there were more possibilities for something to go wrong. Gyambibi needed to learn French for the next phase as a necessary step. The plan was laid out as thus: Phase one, enter Guinea with a Ghanaian passport—accomplished. Phase two involved using a Guinean diplomatic passport to enter America. A complication produced phase three, which wasn't planned but a consequence of Air Afrique making a transit in Senegal. Ofori oversaw every detail of the plan, including securing a diplomatic passport and visa.

Customs officers were unlikely to be suspicious of a foreign diplomat, so the diplomatic passport was the route Ofori reserved for people like Gyambibi, though it cost more money.

Realizing his guest didn't feel at home, Ofori asked Gyambibi to change into something casual to visit some friends in the Ghanaian quarters. After washing up and eating dinner, Gyambibi threw a T-shirt over the same patterned pants he had worn. Something else pulled him away from the house besides the French-speaking television programs. His host couldn't stop talking about how evil the world was. It was depressing. It wasn't that Ofori's talk of evil was overbearing; it was just that it heightened Gyambibi's sense of what could go wrong. He needed to hear something else. Gyambibi stepped out of the house to remind Ofori that they were to go somewhere away from his apocalyptic narration.

He was already seated in the car when Ofori joined him. The weather was chilly. Whether a wild guess or coincidence, Danfo appeared to be right when he said that harmattan would arrive early in Guinea, making it colder and drier than Ghana because, by his recall of geography, Guinea was a tad closer to the Sahara desert. Thus, the balm he gave Gyambibi proved beneficial, as he smeared some of it across his lips. Not wanting to renew his host's discussion about the harshness of the world, Gyambibi kept applying the balm. The only semblance of conversation came when he thought they were speeding because the streetlights flickered so fast, and he yelled for Ofori to slow down. But they had already slowed down because they were in a populated area. Ofori looked at him and asked if he was okay. Gyambibi nodded and licked his lips until the harsh taste of the balm had worn off. Then he started to apply it again. Any conversation would have to wait until after he had left the country. At least Ofori gleaned as much. Ofori had thought of him as respectful when they had met in Ghana, but as the evening unfolded, he saw that Gyambibi appeared to have weird tendencies. When they arrived at the Ghanaian quarters, where a gathering was being held, Gyambibi was already woozy and laughing for no reason.

An elderly woman approached and walked off with Gyambibi. She seemed like someone from a hundred years ago who didn't belong in the gathering. Gyambibi registered no surprise to see this woman. Neither did she. They seemed to know each other, though Gyambibi had no friends or relations in Guinea. Ofori, who must not have seen the woman, felt Gyambibi needed space. He told Gyambibi where to find him before leaving to mingle with some friends. He couldn't get Gyambibi's sudden weird tendency out of his head. The woman and Gyambibi rejoined the gathering, but not for long because they made their way over to a man about Gyambibi's age. It was Asamoah, Agya Kobi's deceased great-grandson. Excited to see him and without memory of his death, Gyambibi kept walking toward him until Asamoah disappeared into the darkness, parting with the words, "I'll come for a visit."

The visit didn't last long, for Gyambibi wasn't himself. He was sick, or something was wrong with him; his mysterious illness had resurfaced far away from Enkoho.

Ofori prayed for him when they returned home because he wasn't well. He wasn't fully himself until days later. Then a telegram came from Kumasi, asking Gyambibi to call home. Ofori left to make the phone call for him while his housekeeper cared for Gyambibi at home. Ofori learned that Karikari was very sick and that Gyambibi was needed at home. When Ofori told him, Gyambibi wanted to return. One thing troubled Ofori: if Gyambibi went home, how could he fix what ailed his father?

Ofori saw how conflicted Gyambibi was and offered advice: "Manna didn't fall into the tents of the Israelites. It fell outside, beyond their camp. To get to manna, the Israelites risked snakebites, a prick by a stone or cacti, an attack by a predator, a sting by insects, a slip on the ground, et cetera. There were risks. Manna still falls today, though it goes by Opportunity.

I don't know of an opportunity without potential risks. Your father isn't well, and adding to that, your conscience hasn't stopped bothering you about how you're to get to America since I met you in Aduman. I know. It's right to abandon this trip because of the wrongness of it, the deception. So, too, it's right to have the means to help your father! Sometimes a wrong stands between two rights, and you can't jump over the wrong but must go through it to the other side, wherein lies your chance at possessing what you need out of life. No one can decide for you. How do you suppose you can help your father by returning home? You know from your Bible that the Jews were promised a land flowing with milk and honey. But they had to learn the hard way that between milk and honey was a road flowing with cow feces and venomous bees. Such is life, Gyambibi."

Ofori was an evangelist—surely one hardened by the realities of life. His dressing was average, he didn't carry himself in a special way, and he didn't carry a preacher's moral deontology. The man existed in an equilibrium of characters: he could pass for light just as easily as darkness. He was nothing like Preacher from Enkoho. His glaring shortcomings notwithstanding, the man was practical and blunt. He was frank about what he did, right or wrong, with no trace of fakery.

Ofori suggested he continue on his journey. "Go on. I will pray for you; I will pray for your father, too."

Gyambibi sent telegrams to his father but didn't get to speak with him before his flight out of Guinea. In the meantime, he and Ofori went over the travel details. Two others would be going with him.

The day to leave for Senegal arrived. The trip to the airport was an opportune time to discuss what was on Ofori's mind. He asked why Gyambibi had walked away when they were at the Ghanaian quarters. Gyambibi said that he didn't recall walking away. He had a vague recollection of seeing his great-grandmother and Asamoah but wasn't sure if it was a dream or his imagination. Ofori's seriousness and unequivocal disposition told Gyambibi that he had acted strangely at the gathering. He didn't want to give Ofori a window into the mysterious happenings in his life, so he stayed away from what Ofori was alleging. That would terrify Ofori, evangelist and all. They talked about other things the rest of the way and arrived at the airport four hours early. Again, Ofori was trying to avoid the number 666 through mathematical convolution that was sure to confound gematria. Gyambibi waited by his luggage when Ofori left to fetch an airport employee he knew. He returned to say the friend wasn't there. They ate an early dinner and talked a little. Ofori left again, returning an alarming one and a half hours later with a worrisome look.

"What kind of luck did you bring with you?" he said. None of the ten people he knew who worked at the airport and were supposed to work that day had shown up. The auguries of the trip had just begun.

Ofori returned to the airport without a word, leaving Gyambibi distraught. Everything he had eaten moments before he emptied behind the restaurant. He was still nauseous when Ofori returned. With him was one of two people with whom Gyambibi would be traveling. Gyambibi recognized him as one of Danfo's nephews.

Danfo's nephews and nieces were the most determined of humans. They came to Enkoho from other villages. When they earned enough, they relocated to metropolitan Kumasi—and from there to any part of the world where the aroma of a better life arose. Success was measured solely by going abroad, to the White man's land, and returning home as burghers. The historical forces responsible for cementing such generational psychology weren't clear. Danfo attributed it to postcolonial effects: These children never knew about economic life under White colonialism. They could only guess what colonial life was when they heard their elders express sentiments like,

"When the White man was here, I could buy a tin of sardines for this, now I can't. A loaf of bread used to cost this much, and now it costs this." The dilemma of two colonialists struck these youngsters. The first was colonialism under White people whose allegiance was to a foreign country, and the second under Black leaders whose only allegiance was to themselves. The British were in Ghana as a way of expanding their empire. However, the Black leaders who took over understood the job description to mean expanding their stomachs. So the national pie was caught between the wallet of jilted White colonialists and the sticky fingers of shortsighted recidivists; thus, the citizens, with disinherited and emaciated lives, were left to look elsewhere for survival. To these youngsters, colonialism of yore seemed a happier time; hence their fealty to their ancestral land was gradually supplanted by a yearning for the foreign land from which the White colonialists came, which, coincidentally, happened to be in the same direction where their leaders' compass of patriotism and stolen wealth pointed.

"The British were a gluttonous bunch who munched on a big chunk of our national pie. And our Dear Leaders of today desire the very bones of mosquitoes falling into the dough of the national pie to pass between their teeth. With our own kind over us, there's no chance for even leftovers after they've generously donated their conscience to neocolonialism at the expense of our children schooling under trees, eating dirt for food, and drinking mud for water," Danfo conceded.

Gyambibi held his breath and kept his abdomen taut, his mouth sealed. Only the beaded sweat on his forehead spoke of his ordeal. Anxiety would unravel him if it wasn't checked, so he pushed his mind away from the trip onto something else. Ofori didn't think Gyambibi was the unconcerned type, so his curiosity was aroused when Gyambibi's expression became nonchalant. Yet Ofori could see the questions in his eyes. Pretending not to be worried about the trip, Gyambibi wanted to know why Ofori was involved in this line of work. Ofori said he did this on the side because of life circumstances. That in no way justified him, he clarified. He would get another line of work if he wasn't convinced of the paramount need to teach others about the gospel of Jesus. He could tell Gyambibi didn't understand, but he wasn't willing to say more.

Gyambibi needed a distraction to hide his anxiety, so he didn't want the conversation to end suddenly. He kept away from the subject but gave Ofori a doubtful look. Ofori continued: after middle school, he worked for his father and became a Christian convert. He was on the verge of delving into the circumstances of his conversion when it came to him that Gyambibi wanted to know why he needed this double life. Ofori said it was all right with him if some thought he wasn't a good Christian because of this work he did; however, he took issue when some thought him bad or immoral. Gyambibi heightened the questionable look that asked: so what kind of life circumstances could justify this double life? Again, Ofori offered that his pay for missionary work wasn't what others thought, and it took him through two weeks at the most. Again, Gyambibi was silent, his face asking yet another question: nobody forced missionary work on you. Why accept a noble cause and taint it with these things?

"Okay, look! My pay was halved, inadvertently, by the same person who converted me, oversaw my training, and offered me work as an evangelist...missionary."

Gyambibi's interest was piqued. "He didn't live up to his end of the agreement?"

"Life circumstances."

"Did he say why?"

"I've hesitated to tell you, but I have to. It's a small world, so I ask that you keep this between us. He got a girl pregnant. Abortion wasn't an option because he didn't want to add murder to his sin of adultery. The problem is that he can't send extra money because he will have to explain the purpose to his wife."

"His wife doesn't know?"

"No. The child has to be cared for. He broke down, not knowing how to support the child without his wife knowing about it. I told him I'd split my pay with the child's mother. He's a good man, Gyambibi. He is, but man is only human. The child I speak of is in Aduman. You saw her. She's half-caste; there's no doubt his father's White, and there's no doubt he's the father. He himself doesn't doubt it. He's a nice man."

While planning for this second trip, when he went to Aduman to see Ofori, Gyambibi met the little girl twice, who had a familial relationship with Ofori. It had been a mystery to Gyambibi how two parents as black as bitumen could have brought forth a half-caste without a genetic predisposition. Mystery solved!

"I see," Gyambibi said.

"We're all sinners, the Bible says."

"Does he ever plan on telling his wife?"

"Many times we've talked about that. He wants to, but the calendar doesn't seem to have an appropriate date for it. I don't condemn people, my friend. That's God's business. Neither do I judge, whether good or evil, though, over the years, I've learned how to tell if one has the potential for good or evil. There's a definite way to tell. Look at the person, study his or her manners for a day or two, look in his or her eyes to see if he or she has a soul, walks on two legs, then study his or her life philosophy and belief structure, and ask if he or she loves God or Satan or doesn't care about such. The collated data should place him or her in one of four categories: rock, human, tree, or animal. If he or she is human, then he or she is capable of every good and every evil under the sun. How do you judge a *good* person capable of all the evil in the world or an *evil* person capable of all the good in the world? Delusion is thinking some are good or evil because they come from this or that corner of the world, because they're this or that shade of humanity, or because they're from this group or that family. We should call out hypocrisy when we see it but should refrain from labeling people evil or good until they're dead and no longer capable of change. When one's alive, one is neither good nor evil; one is merely human, capable of both."

Gyambibi mulled over what he'd just heard, shaking his head. Ofori was imperfect, as Gyambibi had been told, but he was blunt. Gyambibi wished to know other aspects of the story: how it had happened and if Ofori's employer went on missionary trips with his wife. Also, it would be worth his time to know why Ofori had started out in Aduman but was now in Guinea. Gyambibi believed him when he said he would stop doing things that conflicted with his missionary work once he came into money to do a genuine business.

"What if God calls you to account before you find the means for a genuine business?" Gyambibi asked.

Running his fingers through his beard, Ofori said, "The exact question that haunts me in this line of 'work.' My brother, whoever thinks Christianity is easy isn't practicing it correctly."

Gyambibi shared the story of a Canadian military expert, a colonel, who was posted to Ghana and resided in the Teshie barracks. The colonel's wife was with their maid every moment of the day when the maid became pregnant, taking her to the doctor's appointments and everywhere else, right up to the day she gave birth to a mixed-race child. The colonel's wife realized her husband's involvement. On the day of the child's birth, when the colonel got out of his car and was heading home, he made out a double-barrel gun aimed at him from the other side of the screen door. The last time anyone heard of him, his ghost was haunting the residences of pregnant women in Saskatchewan while his wife was in Ghana.

"These things can end violently," Gyambibi said.

"Yes. Satan has succeeded with the husband, and there's no telling what the wife would do if she knew her preacher-husband has a child with another woman," Ofori said, asking, "Are you all right?"

"Yes."

"We have to leave."

"Where's the telegram?" Gyambibi asked as if that was more important than the trip. He needed to keep talking to take his mind away from his anxiety. He had to see the telegram; it had been on his mind since Ofori mentioned it. Ofori searched his wallet, where he was sure he had put it, but couldn't find it.

"You've not left my side since I arrived. When did you get the telegram?"

Ofori explained that a member of one of the churches he ministered at had handed it to him when they were in the Ghanaian quarters. He used the church postal address for his mail, he explained. Gyambibi asked again where the telegram was, incensing Ofori, who said he didn't know what had happened to it. He was certain he had put it in his wallet. If not, it should have been in his pocket since he wore the same clothes to the gathering. They stopped talking about it as they made it to the airport.

There were important things Gyambibi needed to know about his trip instead of arguing about a telegram. He would be going through Senegal, a transit that underscored his anxiety and crisis of confusion. Gyambibi had concluded that it likely had everything to do with Ofori choosing a day that wouldn't violate his quotidian instincts, which revolved around 666.

Ofori introduced the second co-traveler when they convened at the airport. They were all traveling under the same modus operandi, so they went over the details together.

Boarding the plane at Conakry met no obstacles. Gyambibi's boarding pass alone got him inside the plane, not his passport. His luggage made it on board as well. A flight attendant walked toward him and handed him his passport. His co-travelers also got theirs. He put the passport in his carry-on and walked to the lavatory, simply to see how his co-travelers, seated behind him, reacted to theirs. They were examining every page. Returning to his seat, he looked around to see if others had seen what he was doing. The realization that he was changing came upon him: his conscience burned with the unease of having to look around. He couldn't reverse the hand of fate that had led him there. Doing that would take him back to a life of poverty, a wilderness of unpaved paths.

He examined his passport midflight. It had all the correct information, with extensive travel history, except it wasn't stamped for departure from Guinea. Realizing that, the passport slipped from his sweaty palm onto his lap. He stood up and looked for his co-travelers. He couldn't see them but heard them casually chatting. He fell back into his seat, scraping against the armrest. He had no way of correcting this error before landing. If ever there were a road from Senegal to America through which one could travel with a passport not stamped for departure—that road, if it even existed, would have roadblocks that could only be cleared by dishonesty. That wasn't taking into account how he planned to enter Senegal and stay a day before clearing immigration to leave the country. So many ideas entered his mind; his conscience fought against all of them. He felt his conscience was growing dirty around the edges—he was fearful that this would slowly eat its way into every part of his conscience. More worrisome, would he ever be able to rehabilitate his conscience back to its former pureness once he was finished doing what he had to for survival? He thought of what lay ahead, of how hard it would be to get on his connecting flight with a problematic passport. Provoked by the discovery, he remained jittery.

Going to America turned out to be trickier than living in poverty. Going to paradise is always trickier than going to hell. Then he remembered Preprah: those you call Americans today all saw an opportunity to better themselves on land that wasn't theirs and took it. It's called survival.

He didn't remember when the plane touched down in Senegal. He saw himself in one line leading to an immigration officer. His co-travelers were in a different line. He didn't remember getting to the front of the line; suddenly, he was handing his passport to an officer who looked at him as if his face was twisted.

"Welcome to Senegal, sir," he said in French.

Gyambibi's mouth uttered a few garbled French syllables and nothing more. The officer seemed taken aback by Gyambibi's lack of verbal response but kept up his friendliness. The immigration officer pointed to the missing departure stamp, followed by questions in French. Gyambibi was listening but not hearing. The officer repeated word for word what he'd said as if Gyambibi hadn't been listening. Gyambibi was a lip-reader this time, trying to decipher any semblance of English. The officer realized he was talking to someone who spoke no French yet held a diplomatic passport from French-speaking Guinea. He called for his supervisor, who he thought was nearby. He wasn't. He left his post to go find him.

While Gyambibi waited, he thought about how attempting to go to America through Britain hadn't gone well. So why Ofori would think that going through Guinea and Senegal would serve him better, he couldn't grasp. Gyambibi's travel plans had been arranged around avoiding the number 666, a task achieved by Ofori. Gyambibi had a knot of discomfort in his throat for not telling him to keep his gematria nonsense to himself.

Waiting for the officer's return, nervous sweat clung to him as memories of repatriation materialized. What happened next was surreal: the officer's superior was in the amorous grip of a woman. Gyambibi heard him yell something at the officer and slam a door. The officer returned and threw Gyambibi's passport at him without a word. Gyambibi held it and stood there, not knowing what would come next. He knew he was free to go when the officer called for the next person in line.

Outside, Gyambibi waited for his co-travelers, who he saw ushered into a room. He wanted to tell them about the problem with their passports. Perhaps they hadn't studied theirs as closely. The thought left him sweating. Two hours later, his co-travelers were cleared. They'd been searched and interrogated on a suspicion of a different kind.

Gyambibi wasted no time telling them about the problem with the passports, but unlike his, theirs were stamped and proffered no obstacles to boarding the connecting flight at 10:15 p.m. the next day. He alone had much to worry about.

They took a taxi to a hotel at about 11:00 p.m. They had no local currency to pay for their stay, so they arranged to pay after exchanging money the next day. The night was a sleepless one for Gyambibi. For a moment, it made sense for him to turn around and head home. Even if, by some miracle, he made it to America without the departure stamp, repatriation was sure to be the outcome. However, the dire condition of what he would return to if he were to go back home was the impetus for him to forge on, no matter the dreaded outcome.

Morning came sooner than his eyes could shut for sleep. They met a Ghanaian who took them to a Forex Bureau. Gyambibi told him of his situation and asked if people accepted bribes in Senegal. The answer was yes, as in every place on Earth; it depended on the individual. Gyambibi didn't find the answer satisfying. He thought of many options while his co-travelers talked about what they would do when they got to America: the types of employment they desired, even houses they would later build back in their village. Gyambibi couldn't be part of that conversation. Getting aboard his flight tonight was his problem. So absorbed was he that all he remembered was leaving the Forex Bureau with CFA francs bulging in his wallet. On their way back to the hotel, Danfo's nephew asked him why he had changed more currency than he needed. He counted his money. Yes, he didn't need that many CFA francs. He wouldn't return it, for that would cost him more money. He had a more pressing matter to mull; he told his co-travelers that he wanted to know his fate the soonest so he could start his journey back home if life didn't look on him with pity. He wanted to be at the airport early for that reason.

American customs officers were aware of fraudulent means to enter their country, so they might examine every passport closely for its country of origin and travel history. Ofori had advised Gyambibi to carry his wits about him for questions they might not have considered. But how would Gyambibi overcome this impediment without a genuine departure stamp from Guinea? If an officer in Senegal could do so easily, couldn't the wide-eyed customs officers in America detect the missing stamp just by sniffing the passport? Perhaps he was overthinking it. He wouldn't take a risk, though. A departure stamp from Senegal would do, he reasoned.

At the airport, he chose to be first in line for those to be processed for departure. When he was called to the desk, he walked up, resigned to whatever outcome destiny had planned. Ignoring the fact that he still had some CFA francs on him, on a hunch, he dropped a twenty-dollar note on the counter, opened his passport, and pointed to where the departure stamp should be. The officer picked it up and stamped it. It was that easy. Gyambibi couldn't process what had just happened. Shock prevented him from examining the stamp. Off to the departure hall he went to wait for his friends. He wanted to pray but didn't know if he should pray to God for himself or pray to God to remind Ofori to pray for him. Ofori must have been praying for him, for he couldn't believe how things had turned out. One of his co-travelers joined him, and they waited for Danfo's nephew.

Gyambibi examined his passport. The departure stamp was faint, so he wanted to have it re-stamped. He had to think of a way to seek permission to leave and reenter the departure hall. He had twenty-three hundred CFA francs left from the money they had exchanged that morning. He told the two officers at the gate to the departure hall that he had CFA francs on him that he wanted to give to his brother outside because he would have no use for them in America. They permitted him to leave. He returned to the counter and told the officer that the stamp was faint, and it was re-stamped. When he returned to the departure hall, he had to go through the same gate he had exited, which meant he encountered the same officers who permitted him to leave.

"I didn't see my brother. He left. Here, you take half, and you take the other half." One of them refused to take the money, so the other took the twenty-three hundred CFA francs. The impact of this unplanned charity couldn't be overemphasized in later retellings of his story.

Danfo's nephew had still not made it there when Gyambibi got to the departure hall. They were seated in a waiting area when a name came through the overhead intercom.

"Seseku Buari! Seseku Buari!"

The two looked at each other.

"Seseku Buari!"

Four customs officers entered the departure hall with the concentrated resolve to defeat a one-person army that had invaded their country. These were big men. At almost six-foot-two tall, Gyambibi wasn't small, but he would soon see how small he was when these men hauled him out. They branched out and focused on where Gyambibi was seated. There was no escaping. Gyambibi stood up as the officers neared.

"I'm Seseku Buari."

Several questions from all the officers converged on his ears. He couldn't understand one person in French; four was a cacophony. Gyambibi was silent. The lead officer told the others to withhold their questions. Gyambibi deserved to respond to one question at a time. When he repeated his question, Gyambibi finally spoke. In English.

When asked about being a minister who didn't speak the language of the country he represented, Gyambibi told them he was a Guinean but raised and educated in Ghana, hence his limited use and inability to retain the French language.

"Only you could do this," one of the officers said, telling the others that his suspicion had been right.

Was Agya Kobi the source of Gyambibi's problems? Could the evil in the village be following him wherever he went to render his undertakings worthless? Events from years prior, some taking place before he was born and some he had witnessed, had always bothered him. First, he wondered about the bizarre, aurora borealis-like phenomenon in the sky that had preceded the cataclysm. Not everyone saw it, he remembered, but could he have been the only one to have seen it? If so, could this have been a hallucination he experienced, a figment of his imagination? He knew that wasn't it. He reasoned that if that was real, then his touching Atobrah's corpse was also real, though his mind couldn't process the forces behind the disappearance of the corpse. And there was the unsettling spectacle that started it all: seeing Agya Kobi merging in and out of a tree. Was it a spectacle rooted in witchcraft or a mere hallucination? If all these were hallucinations induced by doctored food, then who was behind it, if not Agya Kobi? Terror filled him at the unthinkable possibility if it wasn't Agya Kobi.

Gyambibi ran from such a thought. What he saw was what he saw; it wasn't a hallucination. Besides, such happenings wouldn't be outside the realm of possibility in a village replete with strange happenings, where an argument between a pregnant woman and a barren woman ended in the pregnant woman prematurely giving birth to micro-preemies resembling mudfish, none of whom survived, and the cause traced to fish from the Enkoho river, whose consumption was taboo. The barren woman had offered the fish as a truce without disclosing its source. Adwoa Brago witnessed the incident, and the recall fomented Gyambibi's anxiety.

Unlike Preprah, Gyambibi had as much luck as the first person from Enkoho to attempt to leave for life overseas. This villager saw failure with every attempt made. After his fourth repatriation, he remembered hailing a taxi at the Kotoka International Airport to connect a bus to Kumasi. He got off the bus when it stopped for a bathroom break, only to realize he was floating in the forest on an improvised wooden palanquin with metal poles and screws sticking out of him, enveloped in the bitter aroma of confusion and damp vegetation. Every bone in his body was broken from a motor vehicle accident. His family was transporting him back to Enkoho after modern medicine had done all it could. Drunk on sorrow and resignation, he was deposited at Healer's, his last known address.

Many unexplainable events flashed before Gyambibi as he wondered what had actually followed him out of Enkoho to Guinea and now to Senegal. For a moment, reality and unreality were the same. Only a close circle of people knew of his travel plans: Tabuah, Karikari, Danfo, Yaw, Mark of the Beast, Moro, and, to a lesser extent, Preprah. Yet the telegram to him in Guinea didn't bear any of these names. It was a name "Mark of the Beast" was certain had been none of those. He was struck with the contemplation of whether the dark forces that haunted Enkoho could follow him out of Senegal to America. Or, what if Yaw was right about Preprah? What if Agya Kobi was no more evil than Preprah?

Gyambibi often wondered if, during their tenure in Enkoho, Dr. Maarten and Xada sensed the dark energy of the village but pretended otherwise because their scientific minds conflicted with metaphysical realities. Gyambibi had written several letters to them at their university and home addresses in the Netherlands for their views on the science of rain falling upward and an explanation for how trees could sway without earth tremors or the wind blowing. Quite possibly, Dr. Maarten and Xada did not experience these phenomena. And quite probably, the inquiries reawakened experiences they'd kept to themselves, and their non-response communicated their fear of Enkoho.

These thoughts caused Gyambibi to be worried. As he was hauled out of the departure hall, dangling between two tall officers with his feet off the floor, the officer who had gotten the twenty-three hundred CFA francs muttered something to him in French, which Gyambibi hoped was to assure him that there was nothing they could do to stop him from getting on the flight. Outside the departure hall, where they held him for interrogation, were the belongings of Danfo's nephew. He had run away. Handled by a different officer, Danfo's nephew couldn't respond in French when he was processed, so his travel plans came apart. The officers told Gyambibi that Danfo's nephew's initial excitement abruptly melted, his frightened speech turned lispy, and he fidgeted in a confused and nervous heap. After he unraveled, he told them about Gyambibi.

Gyambibi remembered this nephew very well out of all of Danfo's nephews and nieces who had come to live in Enkoho. Sometimes he would have food at Karikari's house. It appeared out of character to have given up Gyambibi. Gyambibi couldn't shed the thought that perhaps through the agency of humans around him, the evil haunting the village could follow him to the farthest reaches of his life's journey. Danfo's nephew had given him up, but Gyambibi considered that he might not have been aware of doing so.

The other officers had left their superior in charge of Gyambibi.

"You!" the man said in disgust, then also left.

With nobody guarding him, Gyambibi could run away like his co-traveler, but he didn't. They had no plan to arrest him, for they wouldn't leave him unattended if they did. Moreover, they didn't indicate that they were pursuing Danfo's nephew or show any interest in his immediate arrest. They would have to leave their post to do that. That would be a matter for another time; they could arrest and prosecute him later since they had his picture. Gyambibi, on the other hand, would stay and see this to the end. Whatever would be would be. The supervisor returned, saying, "You!" followed by a few frustrated sentences in French.

The officer he had given twenty-three hundred CFA francs to, who had seemed to assure him earlier, returned from guarding the departure hall and engaged his superior, saying that they had no cause to hold Gyambibi when they couldn't prove he wasn't a Guinean minister who had been educated in Ghana. He argued that he believed Gyambibi was forthright because he didn't appear nervous, as would be the case if he were lying. As his flight time neared, one of the officers came to Gyambibi, but this time to ask him for money. He didn't speak English, and Gyambibi didn't speak French, but somehow Gyambibi understood that the thirty dollars he gave him weren't enough. The money wasn't for him alone; he had to share it with another person. It wasn't clear if the other officer with whom this officer would be sharing the money was the lead officer or another. That didn't matter to Gyambibi. In the end, forty dollars solved his problem, and he was on his way to America.

Preoccupied with thoughts of Enkoho, of things he could neither understand nor explain, Gyambibi's mind had room for little else. But that little else was frustration at Ofori complicating his travel plans, which had increased his odds of failure. So preoccupied was his mind that he didn't hear the pilot announce a descent midflight because of turbulent headwinds, an announcement that normally would have fomented enough anxiety to replace his frustration. Nobody could have foreseen how his father's suicide attempts would affect him by making him afraid of ways in which his own death could come. His mind was off the flight until he reached New York.

At the John F. Kennedy International Airport, Gyambibi didn't feel alone, seeing other arrivals from every shade of humanity. There were multiple lines, each leading to a counter with a customs officer behind it. He scanned them and saw a Black woman. She would understand him. He looked at his passport picture to ensure it hadn't morphed into a woman's. He was nervous, knowing many things could go wrong—wrong he didn't yet perceive.

How would he greet her: Good morning, madam; hello, madam; or simply, hi? He was traveling with the passport of a French-speaking diplomat, but he only knew a few French phrases. How could he be a French-speaking diplomat and not know French? That was the question that made him most nervous. He was certain that any French he attempted would come out English. Looking at the woman at the counter and the way she spoke, the curvature of her mouth informed him that her tongue hadn't traveled the road of the French language. She wouldn't try French with him. Yet what if she remembered a few French sentences from school and wanted to show off? The thought unnerved him.

From a distance, Gyambibi examined the female customs officers: Their hairstyle, the presence or absence of earrings, and their fashion proclivities. What if the Black woman didn't call him, but the woman of Asian descent processed him? Or the Caucasians? Or the men?

Ofori, or "Mark of the Beast," had caused him unintended pain. The number 666 had consumed Ofori. He saw it almost everywhere and tried to avoid it. Gyambibi's trip from Ghana to Guinea had been delayed for that reason. On the day of his departure for Senegal, before leaving for the airport, nervous of what lay ahead if he was turned back, Gyambibi told Ofori that he had exhausted all six hundred cedis in his savings account. Ofori opened his Bible and tore a bunch of pages out. The number 666 had come up: six hundred cedis that Gyambibi had exhausted, plus sixty-six books of the Bible. Gyambibi saw that he had torn out the Gospel of Luke. Ofori explained that the book should not have been canonized because Jesus didn't need four Gospels about his ministry, and Luke, in particular, was a Gentile. Even reducing the Bible to sixty-five books wasn't enough. Out of his fee, which Gyambibi paid before parting ways, he returned twenty dollars, which, incidentally, had gotten Gyambibi the departure stamp in Senegal.

Gyambibi came to himself to concentrate on how fast the lines were moving. He was met by the intimidating presence of the Black woman behind the counter across from the queue. Everything turned black: the Blacks were black, Whites were black, and everything in between was black, except for the lights shouting overhead, which had become the hostile sun stealing across equatorial Africa. It was more than that: its brilliance had a seraphic sheen. This must be the light at the end of the tunnel that the nearly dead experienced. It was the light of heaven. It was.

He saw a group to the side for the first time, their feet shackled and hands cuffed. They must be fearless adventurers like him, circumventing life's harshness by using its backdoor. The world had become one—no disunity, no hostility. Those in handcuffs didn't seem to worry. Those in line didn't seem to worry. Just him.

He felt the overhead light on his face. His forehead was hot as if the beaming light was resting directly on it, scorching it. His forehead began to itch. He attempted to pry the light away, only to realize it was several feet above, nowhere near his head. He drew a sleeve over his forehead. His stomach jumped into his throat, with some contents leaping further into his mouth.

Anxiety forced Gyambibi's eyes onto his Casio watch. The time was 00:00. That couldn't be right. He wiped his eyes and shook his wrist to get the watch working again. The time was 06:66. He swallowed hard and stared at his sweaty palms, which he wiped on his pants. He had to calm down and control his breathing, relax every tense muscle, and convince his pores to ease up on perspiring. With all the bad luck of Enkoho trailing him and the fact that he had a fraudulent passport, he had to convince himself that he wasn't traveling back to Enkoho but would make it out of the airport into the United States. He would need a good ten minutes to calm his nerves, and with six people ahead of him, he had enough time. But before he figured out what exercises to use to calm down, it was his turn. Those in front of him had vanished. He wondered if he had imagined them.

He lunged at the counter, uttering, "Hi," which seemed to roll off his tongue unnaturally.

The Black woman looked at him with a stone face and extended her hand for his passport. He looked at the customs officers to her right and left. They had smiles; even those who didn't smile didn't seem unfriendly. His officer, however, had changed upon seeing him. It was as if she was possessed. While nervous, he managed to look at her with a straight face. She noticed, and his angst inched up. She was disgusted with his presence in her country. She hadn't seemed this angry when she processed the Eastern European or Asian. Why him? Perhaps she was ashamed to see him: the *other* Black. That's it! Affirming what Preprah had told him. She took the passport and examined it, signaling to a man in a corner. He came to her. He had a lanyard with keys and his identity card attached. Gyambibi gathered he must be a supervisor of some sort. The man nodded at her after a cursory look at the passport. The next thing Gyambibi saw was his picture being peeled from the passport. The picture came right off. They knew the picture wasn't original to the passport.

A completely foreseeable end to another attempt at escaping from the village awoke the feeling then and there that the last time he remembered being happy was when he was miserable in Enkoho—which had its expectant arms spread wide for his return.

Printed in Great Britain
by Amazon

36967030R00225